The Irish Singer

The Untold Story Of The West's Most Celebrated Outlaw

THE IRISH SINGER

The Untold Story Of The West's Most Celebrated Outlaw

A Novel

Chuck Pinnell

Santa Fe

Sunstone books may be purchased for educational, business, or sales promotional use.
For information please write: Special Markets Department, Sunstone Press,
P.O. Box 2321, Santa Fe, New Mexico 87504-2321.

Book and cover design › R. Ahl
Printed on acid-free paper
∞

Library of Congress Cataloging-in-Publication Data

Names: Pinnell, Chuck, author.
Title: The Irish singer : the untold story of the West's most celebrated outlaw : a novel / by Chuck Pinnell.
Description: Santa Fe, New Mexico : Sunstone Press, [2021] | Summary: "The origin story of an obscure orphan, Henry McCarty--the real person behind the myth of Billy the Kid--and follows his path to fame through the intricacies and violence of the Lincoln County War in New Mexico"--Provided by publisher.
Identifiers: LCCN 2020052434 | ISBN 9781632933140 (paperback) | ISBN 9781611396164 (epub)
Subjects: LCSH: Billy, the Kid--Fiction. | Outlaws--Fiction. | Lincoln County (N.M.)--History--19th century--Fiction. | LCGFT: Biographical fiction.
Classification: LCC PS3616.I5766 I75 2021 | DDC 813/.6--dc23
LC record available at https://lccn.loc.gov/2020052434

WWW.SUNSTONEPRESS.COM
SUNSTONE PRESS / POST OFFICE BOX 2321 / SANTA FE, NM 87504-2321 /USA
(505) 988-4418 / FAX (505) 988-1025

For Eagle Pennell, Nora Henn, and for Henry.

Preface

The Irish Singer is a fresh look at the most famous of outlaws, Billy the Kid—not merely a folk hero and expert pistoleer, but a mythic icon of the highest order. Countless books have been written about him, Hollywood has told his story over fifty times, there's even a magnificent Billy the Kid ballet lifting his name into the fine arts. What possessed me to enter such hallowed and contentious ground? It's a long story—about a lost boy and a lost world and a long-lost cause—one that rallied against the steepest odds. If you'll hear me out, it's a story worth knowing.

It begins with family and a life on the arid West Texas plains of Andrews County. My older brother and I spent much of our boyhood out there, amongst cowboys and cattle. I carry a trove of powerful impressions from those days: the sharp smell of ozone before a big rain, a terrifying encounter with an albino rattlesnake, the heartbeat of the oil fields thumping away out our window at night, a young stock horse who'd flayed himself open from shoulder to knee on a barbed wire fence, the weathered boards and musky scent of a long-gone era. That scent never failed to spark a tracking instinct in me. I pricked up my ears too, whenever the old ones spoke, especially if grandmother Jessie or my great uncle Horace had something to say. Both were tight-lipped, grumpy, tended to frighten us. Still, when they opened up you didn't want to miss it. Jessie told stories my grandfather had brought back from the Spanish American War. Uncle Horace would spit streams of dark tobacco juice and reminisce on his salty youth. I don't remember who spun the yarn, but one day we heard about a mean little cuss from just across the border—the boy bandit, The Kid. He seemed almost part of the family. We certainly knew his stomping grounds well. For three generations family trips to New Mexico had meant blissful reprieves from the heat and the flat. Curative, exhilarating, routine.

But in the summer of 1984, at the age of thirty, I set out from Austin on a New Mexican adventure that would change my life forever.

The previous winter I'd read Maurice Fulton's *History of the Lincoln County War* and had spent the intervening months obsessed with its complex recital of greed, murder, and mayhem. The story contained an exotic blend of races and cultures, that immense and familiar landscape, a host of extraordinary characters. I was particularly drawn to the Puck-like figure of Henry McCarty, better known as Billy the Kid—a minor but persistent player in the conflict. In Fulton's book, he seemed different from the hot-headed myth I'd always encountered; a bold provocateur for sure, with plenty of blood on his hands, but also shrouded in mysteries and unexplored story lines. No movie I'd ever seen had really tried to capture *his* life. I approached my brother, independent film director Eagle Pennell, with the notion that Billy the Kid's life story might be an incredible untold narrative, and I might want to tell it. Eagle was just then riding high from the release of his second feature film, "Last Night at the Alamo," and apt to be in a propulsive, pacing whirl. But something about this conversation stopped him in his tracks. He was used to thinking of me as the little brother and able guitarist who'd scored his first two films, and not as a writer, or a partner. However, he dove into Fulton's book and soon agreed with my assessment—the real story of Billy the Kid would make an incredible movie, one to reset the Western genre. And we were just the lads to do it.

But what was that tale, exactly?

Digging up information was strictly old school in those days. It made sense to go right to the source—Lincoln, New Mexico. I arrived like a detective intent on cracking the case. Much history had occurred there, including the five-day battle and fiery consummation of the War. The little town was unpretentious and well-preserved, as if Lincoln had managed to sleep through a century. The curving Bonita River singing at the bottom of a protective canyon, the ancient adobes, the fertile vale, the descendants—all seemed drowsing and timeless, waiting for me to arrive. When told that I was writing a screenplay about The Kid, locals pointed me to an adobe at the edge of town. And that is how I met the great lady of Lincoln County whispers, Nora Henn, a world-class historian hard at work on a new chronicle of the big struggle. I knocked on her door and found myself smiling down at an intense bespectacled woman who clearly was busy.

Prickly at first, Nora warmed considerably when she realized how serious I was. I'd come to find out the truth about Billy the Kid and the war that made him famous. She invited me in and motioned to a comfortable chair, offered coffee. We talked at length about my brother and about John Tunstall, the young English businessman whose murder had tilted the county into anarchy. I moved on to the main suspect—offering that whoever Henry McCarty was, he seemed to be a different person from Billy the Kid—and his story, his life, seemed to be lost. Nora just smiled slyly and said nothing. She wrote out a short note. I was to drive to nearby Fort Stanton, show the note, and read something important lodged in the archives there, a WPA pamphlet full of old-time Silver City residents reminiscing on the boomtown childhood of Billy the Kid.

In Pat Garrett's lurid effort at biography, *The Authentic Life of Billy the Kid,* The Kid is violently unstable throughout. According to Garrett (and ghost writer Ash Upson) his career began with a bloody knife-wielding murder, at age twelve. Garrett's penny dreadful eventually made him the most famous lawman in the West and helped propel Billy's rise to mythic status, but except for the blue eyes and a bit of the charm, Henry McCarty was left almost entirely out of it. I hoped to find something at the old fort to challenge that narrative.

Fort Stanton, built of stone and set to endure the ages, had been a spectacular participant in the war. It stood in the summer sun like an old campaigner waiting for the regiment's return. Stately officer's quarters, a broad quadrangle, and barracks that once housed Buffalo Soldiers from the vaunted 9th Calvary—were silent and brooding as I walked to the archive building. A receptionist took my note with a perfunctory nod. She returned a few minutes later with a slim cloth-bound folio. I sat down at a long table wondering how anything big could come in such an unassuming package, but then the old-timers began to speak. They recalled Henry McCarty clearly, and he didn't quite square with the legend of Billy the Kid. The teenager they'd known in the early 1870s was intelligent, studious, cheerful, well-liked, well-mannered, and theatrical. He was high-spirited like his Irish mother, and sometimes mischievous, but a good-hearted and normal boy. His schoolmates particularly remembered Henry's dazzling performances in their school drama productions, also mentioning that he even played female roles with a convincing flourish. I was stunned. How was all this information not common knowledge by now? It was as if John Wesley Hardin had been outed long ago as an avid bird watcher who loved to recite poetry and read Shakespeare—and the shocking reveal was still somehow a well-kept secret. I made a pact right then and there to shine a bright light on Henry McCarty, the man. Only I had no idea how long a journey or how big a job that would end up being.

My project began to lurch forward, dragging along a lot of unfortunate baggage. For all his boundless energy, Eagle was starting to move into retrograde. Addiction had taken root in his young life. He was often difficult, if not impossible, to work with. In addition, the Western was all but dead. But hope springs eternal and Eagle was great at inspiring me, making connections, offering solid insights when they were needed most. We always had the story to kick around, even if it involved far more carousing than typing. The two of us were exactly like the diametrically opposed brothers in Sam Shepard's drama, *True West*—alternately fighting and drinking, and desperately trying to hammer out a screenplay. Our shared journey into the past was fraught with obstacles. It was both communion and penance, and the apotheosis of our brotherhood. Mostly I forged ahead on my own. A script evolved in fits and starts, yet I could never quite see how to carve the Thanksgiving feast into a single serving.

There were further pilgrimages to Lincoln, and beyond, as I hunted down key locations and spent time with Nora. She was always brilliant and sometimes cantankerous—a proud bohemian and a good soul well-loved by the community. Nora had striking peculiarities, strange things that she accepted with calm grace. Like the casita happily shared with her artist husband and the ghost of an elderly woman in black lace. Hers was an eccentric household to be sure, but not too unusual, for the place. Past and present tend to meet on sacred ground in New Mexico.

Back in Austin I continued to pursue a career in music, and in my free time continued a rapt study of 19th century America, reading far and wide. I wanted to differentiate the Old West in every way possible from the trope-laden flapdoodle of Hollywood, entertaining though it may be. In the real West it was rollicking fast-paced faro that ruled, not meditative poker; a whiskey punch was as popular as a shot of rye, honest gunfights were rare as hen's teeth, languages and accents and hats were extraordinarily diverse, and opportunists ruled.

Eagle's alcoholism was only growing worse, derailing a handful of golden opportunities. His demons and habits drove an egregious wedge between us. Eagle never simply came to town for a visit, he roared through on a tornadic bender. He usually had some big deal cooking and chaos following in his wake. We connected less and less. All of our plans for Henry McCarty seemed to gradually fade into nothingness. And the lost boy continued to haunt me.

Years became decades. Nora's book remained unpublished. I went through two divorces and helped raise two sons. The guitaring and occasional film scoring continued. My brother was in and out of rehab and became intolerable to be around, even harder to help. Our relationship lapsed into a final awkward estrangement. Just as I was beginning the most important relationship of my life, Eagle tumbled into a last heartbreaking downward spiral. He passed in the summer of 2002, just shy of his fiftieth birthday.

But nothing much ever seemed to change with regard to Henry McCarty. His life was still that well-kept secret. Henry stubbornly refused to come out of the shadows. At best, in some book or documentary or movie, he'd stick his head out, only for a moment, and grin. His history lay in my head like a sprawling ruin, an unfinished jigsaw puzzle, and its very existence seemed to mock me. I kept it in a locked room. At great intervals I'd stumble on pieces of the story writ large, open the room and fit them in, out of habit. Odd little stories about Henry would come along as well: how he was trusted to tend the baby at Dowlin's Mill, taught English to a child on a remote New Mexican sheep ranch, spoke Gaelic with the niece of an Irish rancher, was a champion dancer of fandangoes, an excellent horseman and superb marksman, was literate, generous, funny, and how his soaring tenor voice filled the church in the middle of the war. Henry McCarty's real life was there, elusive and surprising, but there—a shadow story scattered in the desert.

That long-lost cause was far from mind the night I attended South by Southwest's 2016 premiere of the newly restored "Last Night at the Alamo"—Eagle's widely recognized 1983 triumph of regional filmmaking. The movie and my brother were being lauded by longtime friend and festival director, Louis Black, by film critic Leonard Maltin, and by Eagle's blood comrade in Texas independent filmmaking, director Richard Linklater. There was a packed house of industry folk and festival goers, even a few celebrities. Ethan Hawke sat nearby. It was a big night. I had composed the original score, contributed new music for the opening credits, and sat proudly beaming through the opening scenes.

"Last Night at the Alamo" had aged well, the restoration was gorgeous—but halfway through I found myself pulled into a very different place. Some detail in the film released a guilty flood of memories. Eagle's raucous movie was on screen and his raucous life was playing in my head. I began thinking about our project. Maybe if we had stuck with it and made the film, our covenant might not have been broken, and he might still be alive. Perhaps it wasn't too late, even now, to try a resurrection in his honor. Out of nowhere a chaotic epiphany was beginning to unfold, and Henry McCarty was grinning down at me. My life had suddenly, somehow, come full circle with that long-ago moment in the archives at Fort Stanton—like a giant thirty-two-year wheel clanking into apogee. It wasn't particularly coherent, more a wild trip through a carnival fun house. But I came through transformed just the same. Somewhere in the dark corridors and revolving barrels my ancient pact had re-emerged, binding as the day it was made.

I had a new full-time job: to unlock the puzzle room, begin searching out the narrative, and get back into the habit of writing. What would become the novel began as a film treatment outline, a kind of sprawling Huckleberry Finn styled picaresque. I would follow Henry through two years of adventures in Grant, Arizona—the training ground—before interweaving him into the tapestry of the Lincoln County War. My plan was to painstakingly create a close historical likeness to everyone involved and then, within an accurate framework, turn them loose. And there was good reason to imagine more of all concerned, particularly Henry.

The plan worked, ultimately, but in the initial phase my outline was far too episodic and there were still a lot of unanswered riddles across the board. Then, in the midst of my digging and puzzling, another miracle occurred. Nora Henn's long-awaited book, *Lincoln County and its Wars*, was finally published, five years after her death and thirty-two-years after we first met. Her account proved to be an exceedingly well-written and definitive work, brilliantly supported throughout with letters, depositions, court issuances, newspaper articles, and here and there, with whispers. She often let these epistolary interludes speak to controversy. My mysterious old ally had suddenly rejoined the company, offering a last fateful mentorship.

Here I need to give thanks to Nora's long-time friend, councilor, and publisher, Herb Marsh Jr., President of the Henn-Johnson Library and Local

History Archives Foundation in Lincoln, New Mexico. Herb's able assistance was indispensable throughout, and particularly crucial in unraveling the central mystery of the war, the cryptic Fritz Insurance Settlement, a poorly understood yet pivotal trigger point. Buried within that conundrum was an oddly touching romance—a passion that turned one of the most ruthless characters into a human being.

For the first time, I began to have a tentative grasp on the entire story. Still, I was a very long way from getting that story to the world. Each time I reached out in the direction of Hollywood, I got nowhere. Sage advice had come to me from multiple sources: you need to write it as a novel. I began to realize they were right. The answer had been there all along and I'd been too short-sighted and too intimidated by great writing to even consider it.

Just at that time my wife Patricia was recruited to work for Philadelphia's new progressive District Attorney, to run his Conviction Integrity Unit. Within a month we moved from Austin, Texas, where I had lived and worked for nearly forty years. Suddenly, in early February of 2017, we found ourselves in the red brick heart of a most venerable Eastern city. Patricia dove into the crucial work of investigating wrongful convictions while I opened the heavy door of a writer's residency—and walked in.

The work began anew. I made a crucial decision early on to write in present tense. Six months passed before any kind of confidence arrived. A saving grace was that I could see the characters and the settings and the action, in the most vivid detail. Little by little I learned to write what I saw in a terse rush of words. Along the way a background teeming with relevant material began to jut out, for embedded within that history were some of the hottest issues of our day, his day, any day: identity, race, immigration, religion, and the origins of gun culture in America—all of it inextricably intermingled with an intense experience of the wilderness.

Most of *The Irish Singer* was penned in a rambling Philadelphia coffee shop on Pine Street, in a two-hundred-year old building a few blocks from Washington Square and Independence Hall. I walked to my favorite street in every kind of weather, eager to get there and begin. Afterwards I'd keep walking, on through Old City to the river and back. Some days that walk felt hopeless. More often it was a benediction.

The haunting narrative my brother and I found so exhilarating in the 1980s finally arrived as a completed work in the early spring of 2020. I began my quest with Nora to the right and my brother to the left, and by the grace of some unfathomable magic, I finished that way. Here and there, you'll find a bracing shot of Eagle's boisterous revelatory energy wanting to jump off the page, and often a strong measure of Nora's precision guiding it back in. And as for Henry—the lost boy has finally stepped out of the shadows.

Truth is stranger than fiction, but it is because
Fiction is obliged to stick to possibilities; Truth isn't.
—Mark Twain.

1 SOUTHEASTERN NEW MEXICO 1931

An ocean of parched buffalo grass stretches tight over the hard bones of the earth. Solitary scraggles of mesquite stand like lost souls awaiting perdition. Old-time New Mexicans called it *La Ceja de Dios*, the Eyebrow of God. Nothing moves on the great high plain but a Ford pickup, plying the dusty length of Mayhill Road and pulling for the highway.

They'd been up and doing before sunrise, like always, meaning to get a good early start. Trouble with a pregnant heifer had delayed them over an hour. Dan Jones has eyes now on the rutted two-track and his best Stetson yanked to a sharp angle. The hands are busy; steering with the left and grinding the long floor-mount stick with the right. A cigarette hangs and smolders, flaring bright orange with a good drag. His wife and eight-year-old son are squeezed in beside him, enduring the billows of smoke with a practiced air.

"How much farther, Papaw?"

"We're a lot closer'n when we started," his father answers with a weathered grin. "Quit worrying, we'll make it in time."

The day had risen up hot and cloudless and dead still. Not the slightest hint of rain. Yet at mid-morning a dark line forming on the southern horizon sings a different tune. Glancing up through a dirty windshield Dan notices another tell—a cirrostratus haze drifting in high over the prairie.

"I wish you'd hurry that smoke. Dorsie and I might like to breathe some air fer a change," says Jenny, wrinkling her pretty face with an irritated smirk. She'd given him that look a thousand times. The way it curled her lips and raised a little dimple never lost its charm. Dan takes a last pull and winks at her as he flips the butt out the window. Unimpressed, Jenny looks away, out at the endless scrub and the scalloped clouds moving up from the south. "Looks like there might finally come a big rain."

"It ain't gonna rain. Not here."

"I suppose yer weatherman enough to know," Jenny replies, thinking she might like to punch him.

"Those clouds are moving fast. If there's any rain, it'll be to the north." His eyes return to the ruts and the dirt.

"Guess I can always hope."

Dan learned to read the skies from his father, a cowman of the old school and a man of the 19th century. Buck Jones had lived his entire life on the Eyebrow of God and knew it's every divination. If a crisis was brewing somewhere on the ranch and Dan couldn't work it out, he'd go to his father for advice. He knew Buck would needle him first, but it was usually worth the aggravation.

"Hell, I thought all you needed to run cattle these days was a pickup and a pocketknife."

He'd traded his first truck in on the new Model A and hadn't yet heard the end of it. But Dan put up with his father—he'd just grin and go on. Life was a lot damned better with a Ford parked in the barn and no mistake. He loved tinkering with it, getting his hands greasy, listening to the machine hum then putting it back to work.

After the morning's long eastward crawl, Dan finally drives out on the blacktop. Letting her rip on the open highway a delirious kind of joy with the storm closing in behind and the air beginning to cool. They pass a billboard welcoming them to Roswell in bold letters.

The boy smiles.

First stop is the Gulf Station to wait a turn at its one pump. The truck and several five-gallon cans have to be filled before they can be on their way to the drugstore. Grandpa Buck needs more of the gout medicine that sometimes helps and sometimes doesn't. Groceries and a trip to the icehouse can wait.

They'd been promising a Saturday matinee for some time, and the one on the marquis today is special. The boy had thought of nothing else all week. The Ford noses into a parking spot and Dorsie hops out behind his dad, eager to close the last distance as soon as his feet hit the pavement.

"Just hold your horses," says Dan, looking up at the purpling vault bearing down on them. He leans back in to lever the seat forward and pluck out a dusty rain slicker.

"We gotta hurry," Dorsie yells, running around the truck to grab his mother. He took notice of the crowd as they drove by and does his best to hector both parents along. They're about the last ones to get in the slow-moving line. Dorsie keeps craning his head out to count those still left in front.

Nearing the ticket window at last, a heavy detonation seems to strike their exact spot before rumbling off into the distance. Jenny's nose wrinkles at the sudden whetted smell of ozone. Finally, a light shower begins to patter down on the hard-baked streets.

"Of course it'd rain now we're stuck out in it," Jenny complains. Dan gives her a look as he spreads the slicker over his family. They haven't seen rain since the beginning of summer, but Dorsie is riveted to the hypnotic poster in the display case. Today's feature, *Billy The Kid,* has him bedeviled with a boy's call to arms. Billy reaching for his gun and eyes locked with the indomitable Pat Garrett—both of them in swooping Stetsons and dressed for a rodeo.

The rain is coming in sheets by the time they're past the box office and into the lobby.

They pass through velvet curtains into the half-light mysteries of the theater. To the awestruck boy it's like descending into a cave of wonders. Down near the front they skirt across a crowded row—Dorsie holding onto his mom's hand and Dan finally peeling off the big hat. The excited boy looks over at his dad as they sit down. Dan winks back, sliding the wet rain slicker under his seat.

Skeletons cavorting in a graveyard begin the afternoon's sorcery. Wind and rattling bones and music burst from the speakers with stunning force. It all gives way to even greater magic as the Hollywood oater starts to unspool. Dorsie squirms all through the opening minutes, holding his ears at first and trying to get a clear view around the large woman in front of him.

"Mama I can't see."

"Well, switch with me honey," Jenny whispers, crouching up as Dorsie slips under. His big smile returns with an open view of the big screen.

Dressed all in black and framed against a desert mountain range—The Kid rides warily up to another rider—Deputy Bob Olinger. The Kid offers up a drawling, sneering challenge. And though he bears the name of a youth, he's clearly a good-sized *man.*

"What kind a dirty business are you up to, Bob?"

"I got a warrant here for the arrest of John Tunstin. He murdered a man in Grant's Saloon last night."

"Well, you know Mr. Tunstin wouldn't pull the legs off a fly."

Forty-one miles to the southwest, seated beside a blackened stone fireplace—Buck Jones sharpens the long blade of a bone-handled knife. The old whetstone has a pronounced declivity where the blade had dug into the grit and the spit countless times. Gouty feet have slowed him considerably, but his hands are still deft at their work.

His father's Winchester is pegged above the mantel. A sepia-toned photograph of his mother, "Ma'am" Jones, hangs on the wall. A perfect arrowhead gathers dust on a nearby shelf—whispering there for ages—while a constant bustle whirled around it.

Buck's old grange had once been hearth and home to a large clan. The zenith long past now and their proud numbers sadly declined. He'd lost his oldest brother to a murdering freak, way back in '77. A second brother died of yellow fever in the Spanish American War, without ever having left the gunboat. His father passed in his sleep just after Christmas '99. Ma'am Jones lived twelve years into the new century. The youngest brother was taken by a heart attack while mending a fence and three years gone now. His sisters were married and scattered long before the big turn, and his wife of forty-two years had just passed in January.

He was the last of the old ones on the Jones spread.

A cluster of buildings and row of cottonwoods mark the place from a great distance. The proud line of trees in front, a freshly painted barn and rattling windmill just south of the new house, pens and chutes sectioning out behind. The old adobe sits fifty yards to the north. An extravagant sundown begins to settle over the Eyebrow with the Ford running in underneath and almost home again.

"Guess you were right, the old place is still dry as a bone," says Jenny, disgusted. Dorsie squirms again when his father shifts and turns at the gate.

"Hey button, go on over and talk to grandpa. He may bark a little, but he'll set you straight."

A hired hand lifts his head at the approaching Ford. Reams of powdered dust engulf the entrance crossbar and collapse as the truck hits caliche. The engine unravels at the front steps with a final shudder. Dan shakes out his long legs with chickens scattering, stretches his back and cracks his neck—mugs at his wife. Jenny is just grateful to be out of the tiny cab and away from the smoke and the ruts. Her dimple raises up again. This time with a smile when her boy darts out behind and over to Buck's house.

"Come get Buck's medicine in a bit," she calls out after him.

There's unloading to be done but Dan hesitates a moment, looking over at the old place and the screen door swinging shut.

Everything Dorsie had been thinking seems altered, somehow, once he's in the room with his grandfather. The boy starts to chatter on about the long road and the town and the medicine, afraid to say what's really on his mind. He finally spits it out.

"We went to see *Billy the Kid* at the picture show! I thought it was the greatest thing ever, but Papaw says it was all lies." Buck stops working the knife and looks up. "Says you knew him, *that he used to come to the ranch.* What was he *really* like?"

A soft ray of evening light flares across his weathered face. The eyes look away. It's a rare occasion when Buck Jones will talk about the old days, or The Kid, or the "war"—during the worst of it a rift in the family became a chasm that never quite closed again.

After a long silence he decides to open up to his grandson, for the very first time.

"They been telling the story wrong for fifty years. And your pap was right, The Kid wasn't like nothin you ever seen or heard." Dorsie looks at the floor, away from the heat in his grandfather's hard stare. "Don't suppose that fool in the picture show had any kind of Irish accent?"

"I don't know what that sounds like."

"You probably never heard an Irishman. In the old days they were thick out here. The Kid's family came from Ireland—had a damn wagonload of Irish in him."

"He sounded like he was from Texas, in the picture show," Dorsie said, feeling more and more spooked, like he was treading on sacred ground.

"Speak any Spanish?"

"No sir."

"Hell, he was as brown as he was white. Mexican folk up in the valley adopted him as one of their own. To them, he was a prince...a hero...a kind of wandering ghost." Buck concedes these revelations with all the scornful finality of a cranky old judge. Setting the knife and whetstone down, he rakes a hand across the back of his head—heaves a deep sigh.

"He didn't much care for that name, *Billy the Kid*. Preferred to be called *William Bonney*." His voice easing now and the heat gone. "I wasn't much more'n a boy when I first met him. He wandered up on foot one evening, all but played out—just a boy himself. Come all the way from Arizona, *alone*." And after another silence. "Fetch that arrowhead off the nook."

Dorsie goes to the shelf and lifts the artifact, weighing it in his hand.

"*He* gave it to me," Buck confides—the feeling of that day coming back sharp and pure. Dorsie closes fingers around his birthright, eyes shining back up at his grandfather.

"The Kid could be a tricky little fellow and no doubt. But he was a wonder. Smart as a whip and generous as the day is long...and lord, he could *sing*."

2 Southwestern New Mexico 1875

The desert had offered him scant encouragement. Only the limitless blue sky and an empty road, with little solace to be found in either. But finally, there's something of comfort ahead. A little *jacal* nestled in a protective grove of acacia trees; fertile garden nearby, crude pens jutting out into the scrub, a herd of sheep on the low hill beyond—and *water* for sure. As he moves on toward it, a maddening pain fires in his throat and belly. The barrens had already cost him and only two days out.

In another quarter mile a faint path brakes from the two-track. It leads the rider inauspiciously across a field of graying saltbush, with everything left behind tugging at his sixteen-year-old heart. Still, he rides up like a young *valiente* cantering out of legend into the heat of the day; brilliant red scarf tied around his neck, blue eyes sparkling, handsome face sharply cut in the afternoon light.

"*Buenas tardes, Señor.*"

"*Buenas tardes,*" replies the man, looking up from his row of squash in amazement. Nearby, a woman sits grinding dried peppers in the shade.

"*Cómo esta, amigo?*" asks the visitor.

"*Mucho Gusto, Usted?*"

"*Muy Bien*. I've come a long way my friend, and not seen anything so pleasant as your little sheep ranch. I see God has bestowed many blessings and Our Lady watches closely. And not even a cool spring is missing." He pauses then to cross himself. "May your fortunes multiply and your troubles wane. Forgive me for arriving so abruptly. But now that I am here, I'm happy to work in exchange for water and food—and a night or two off the desert."

"I could use some help it's true. Work is plentiful, it never ends. But there *is* a trouble here also." He wipes his brow and looks from the ground back up into the blue eyes. "My youngest son, Emiliano, has been bitten by a rattler. He is very sick. You look to be someone with knowledge in his head or maybe a bit of magic in his pockets," he suggests, politely, and after a thoughtful moment: "God is busy in his heaven and pays little heed to my sufferings. Our Lady of Guadalupe takes more interest, perhaps she has brought you here to help us."

"That could be, I have great reverence for The Mystical Rose."

"She crushes the serpent and blesses the children," the man recounts simply, now making the sign of the cross himself.

"Maybe part of your son's spirit is trapped, out in the desert, with the snake. I know a thing or two that might help, and I am no stranger to hard work—I will be of service to you in any way I can."

"Please get down from your horse. You must be very thirsty and hungry."

The young drifter *was* parched in a way he'd never experienced before. The hunger not quite so bad yet. And in truth, he knew much more about religion than healing. But from what he'd seen on Chihuahua Hill—back in Silver City—that kind of doctoring is as much showmanship and ingenious magical theories as medical expertise. He dismounts and is led first to water. A spring had been ingeniously cradled and diverted. They sat in the shade and introduced themselves between his long gulps. The woman brought a few tortillas and a paste made of beans and fat and green chilies. She produced a piece of jerked mutton next and the boy devours it all with great pleasure. Finally, he is led inside the jacal.

The swollen and discolored leg is an ugly sight. Emiliano, strong and healthy before the bite, had surely been fighting a desperate battle. But the traveler had seen far worse and putting a hand on the fevered brow—smiles into the boy's eyes.

"You only need a little help to overcome this misfortune. You will see some real magic today. I'm going to beat that demon back down into the earth!"

Emiliano's head turns as the visitor stands to doff his hat in a grand bow. The exuberant gringo begins an astonishing, eccentric little dance. The parents look at each other quickly. They weren't expecting any such odd beginning—the wild capering like nothing they've ever seen. But the ailing son is transfixed.

Gaelic runes and ballads soon filled the simple enclosure with an ancient beauty, the Irish falling on their ears a strange but potent invocation. Then the comic nursery rhymes acted out and sung in Spanish brought a smile. The first they'd seen on their son's face since the rattler struck. Emiliano's treatment concluded with a long *corrido,* the famous tale of the magically transported soldier, and finally, a little actual medicine.

He'd read about poisonous snakebites in a journal, when his family first traveled west. He knew to keep the heart above the wound; this had not been done, and to let the bite bleed freely, which had. And lastly, he knew to make a simple poultice of charcoal powder and water. The man and his wife again looked to each other and then back at their son. After only an hour his pallor had lessened somewhat. And the little smile remained.

Emiliano had been reminded of the joy of life, and that God had placed lighthearted beings upon the earth as well as demons. And this medicine was equally important.

The boy had come face to face with a monster and was luckier than he knew to be alive. But he'd also paid forth a cruel bargain. Part of his innocent soul *did* remain out in the brush. A potent grandfather diamondback had lain out there coiled and asleep, slowly dissolving the fur and bones and meat of a fat prairie dog when Emiliano, chasing a kid goat, stumbled over him.

The old dragon had gone hunting down in the burrows the night before, gliding past the chittering sentries in absolute silence. Deep in the warren he found his prize; a nursing mother—barely squeezing back out with her struggling in his great open mouth. He slithered to his throne and swallowed the fine meal. Happy then to drowse in a sibilant curve for an eternity and let the light come and go as it pleased.

The serpent king was far too content and powerful to be bothered by *anything.* When a keen scent touched his black tongue and alerted him to the boy—it was notice only of an insignificant being from a faraway world. Even when stepped upon and the billowing trunks were an easy target, it only half-aroused him. He struck, finally, releasing a lesser amount of his already depleted venom. But the moment before, when Emiliano saw the elliptical death eyes and long curving fangs—was the harder penalty. Afterwards the snake retracted into its languid coil and the boy ran. Emiliano had been trapped in a nightmare of fear and nausea ever since. Until the stranger arrived and performed his grandiose bow.

By the next day the boy's swollen leg began to drain a little. He asked for something to eat and hunger the best sign now of all. The boy's health was turning and after a long ramshackle section of fencing had been made fast, the visitor knew he must continue his journey west. Though it rattled him down to his bones to ponder what lay ahead, a dangerous journey and an unknown and uncertain future. It made his stomach pull into a tight little knot.

"There is a spring by the road, you'll find it about a day and half out. No more water afterwards and the track becomes confusing. It's really not much of a road—unreliable, splits and splits, fades out." The man shrugs his shoulders and the boy spits. "But the mountains are always there. North to South." With one arm he gestured the run of mountains and with the other at a right angle—*his* path. "You are also going into the new moon and night on the desert floor will be like the inside of a jug." The sheep man grins at the boy. "You must keep the north star to your right."

"Doesn't sound so bad." But his stomach tightened again.

"Travel all you can at first light and in the gloaming, find shade and rest during the afternoon. After three or four days there will be a well-used road and then a little river. A day later, another river. And then you will be there."

"I need to leave soon."

"You shouldn't be going alone amigo. The Devil will likely make a meal of you. Stay here where there is water and food, people to listen to your songs and stories."

"There's no choice in the matter."

"Ah...you can do nothing about destiny, it's true. Still, you could make it wait a little."

"Perhaps you are right," he says this with a begrudging nod.

"Emiliano will be very happy if you stay, even a little bit longer," says the father.

"He'll soon be running wild again," the boy insists, laughing suddenly—he *would* get this crossing behind him. He had big hopes for the future and they sure didn't include being dinner for the Devil. It was only a hundred and thirty, maybe a hundred and fifty miles at most. At least as the crow flies.

The songs and stories continue for another day and their visitor gathered himself. At last he stretches out next to Emiliano for one last sleep within four walls. But he slept poorly; dreaming first of the merciless sun, an endless red desert, and then a red brick city, a darkened stage, the naked odeum and he stepping out into the blue fire.

At first light the valiente saddles Dancer and sweeps himself up with a quick vault. Enough food and water tied on for a couple of days at least, maybe more—and a spring ahead. His heart is strong and head clear. He'd find the way and make it through. Now that the trek is on again—he's certain of it.

"Mil gracias amigo, adios...buena suerte."

"Gracias por tu ayuda, cuídate joven. Hasta siempre!"

The man stands watching horse and rider disappear into the early morning haze, and for some time afterwards. Finally, he crosses himself and begins his day.

An hour is given over to the spring, both of them drinking until their stomachs are ready to burst. It was difficult to leave such abundance in the wild. From there the land became drier and lower and more inhospitable, just as the man had warned.

They descend into an arid bowl of gigantic proportions. Scrubby vegetation spreading before them like a vast carpet rent with holes. Here and there an impressive rock butte rises up, and always, blue sierras extend along the horizon. Clear to the eye but impossibly out of reach. In all that unending space he feels as small as a speck of dirt—and the sole representative of his kind.

He rides on and on. The strange mosaic of desert furze transitioning slowly to a plain of cactus and mesquite; fantastical and menacing, a bristling nightmare landscape of agave, yucca, cholla, and withered trees. The mountains move further off and the softer scrub all but disappears, as if forbidden. *Like trying to cross the Devil's skillet at supper time,* he thought.

Day on the frying pan is an interminable, mortal problem, with another kind of challenge waiting in the night. A long pitiless scorch followed by a treacherous dark. And had he known beforehand what roving the badlands truly meant, the calaboose might've have been preferable after all.

His thoughts raced back to the red brick boomtown he'd left just a week before. He turns inward, away from the barrens; to the fandangos on

Chihuahua Hill and his performances at *The Orleans,* to the ghost of his family life, to the enticing fray with his enemies—and to grand exploits with his friends Chauncey and Gideon. All of it, good and bad, like a rich tapestry he longed to touch. His right hand reaches down to feel of the pouch in his right pocket. Always comforting, it holds keepsakes and coin of the realm. Most of it from his triumph at the Dangler's Derby only a month before—excitement and glory swelling his chest as he begins to recount the great day once more.

It always began with the hanging of the purse—from a pole at race's end. Waiting there for the first rider across the finish to grab it. Four Sundays ago, he was that man. An *Irish*man—a tough little mick and a fine horseman. The crowning moment ran through him again like a kind of fire, and then back to the beginning and every moment in between. The memories kaleidoscoping in his vivid imagination like a magic lantern show.

The Derby was just a makeshift entertainment on the outskirts of town—but as magnificent an adventure as a boy could hope for. The steeplechase wound through and around a long-decaying hacienda and every inch of it a challenge. The variety of horseflesh and saddlery and rag-tag crowd of young spectators an amusing show in itself. Some of them placing little side bets while ten riders jostle forward, then back into a ragged line, then busting forward then back again. The best chance of winning belonged to his nemesis; a street-tough bully named Oliver Maitland—son of a mining engineer and well-mounted on a big Roan. Maitland had won almost every race in the past year. His blunt face turns toward the little mick to spit out a nasty taunt.

"I hear you've been playing a female at the Opry House. Make a real pretty girl, they say. Best let down your drawers and let us see if you're a real man or not."

"I'd wonder about your intentions either way," the Irish boy offers as if he hadn't a care, smiling his crooked smile and easing Dancer back into line.

"Well, all right then, Miss Nancy," Maitland grates, irritated that he hadn't rattled the little prick in the least.

At length, Maitland nods to the flag boy. The waif gives out a blood-curdling rebel yell and lifts his hat high. He holds it there briefly before swinging it down like a hammer—launching the contest into a thundering one hundred-yard straightaway.

The bully jumps in front right from the hat drop, while the Mexican and Irish boy next to him get tangled in a blind switch and nearly go down. The rest in a tight bunch and the air starting to fog into a cloud of fine dust.

"Give'em hell for the sons of Erin!" His best friends, Chauncey and Gideon Truesdell, yell out to him as he roars by, already caught back up with the field.

The call veers to the right and over a series of low walls. Hooves thundering and Maitland just ahead and red dirt blurring underneath. Then suddenly up to the wall and Dancer lifting off the ground and down again to the red dirt on the other side. The others falling behind more and more. Henry looks around quickly to check the field—and there's Hevel Brock—the foul-mouthed grandson of a rabbi soaring over the last rampart without his mount. His Morgan had stumbled and balked at the jump.

"Nicely done, half-dick," yells Moses while soaring past.

"Lick my hole, you darky shitheel," answers Hevel.

"Best keep yo head down, Shylock!" Moses calls back as he flies over the next wall. The two are allied against common enemies and normally pals, but not today. Today it's every man for himself and winner take all.

"*Meshugana klapteh*," Hevel barks at his mule on the other side of the wall, flinging his hat down and giving it a hard kick for good measure.

The field continues to widen as they clear the jumps and plunge one by one down an embankment. The sand coming up fast at the bottom, but Dancer and the little mick managing a graceful landing and on after the big Roan. Choked down now to single file through a long and curving bend of an arroyo, the eroded clay walls just inches away as they lean into the turn. Then up a steep ramp with their rumps on the cantle and hurtling out again into a patch of berms and mesquite trees—the mick lifting his hand to Chauncey and Gideon and flying on across the obstacle field like a maddened barrel racer.

"Look at him go," Chauncey shouts, while pounding his brother with the crown of his hat as they chase after the race.

"He's right on Maitland's tail!"

A chute along a high wall opens to the backstretch flat. The Irish boy and his spotted mare and Moses on his white filly pound along at a dead run, five lengths behind Maitland.

"He's almost on it," Gideon cries out.

The adobe wall is unassailable. But there *is* a notch where an expert jump might clear the wall, though it lands you in a forest of cacti. If you somehow survive the landing it's only a short distance to the terminus, and the flagged post and the hanging purse. No one had ever tried it before.

That notch had deepened overnight—it had also widened—but not so much that you'd notice if you weren't looking for it. A narrow opening in the nopales had also appeared. Maitland passes the notch without a glance and on to the corner and the final straightaway.

Suddenly the little mick bears out to the right and then straight back at the wall, the ground blurring underneath, the opening closing in fast.

The jump arrives with hooves dead on the mark.

Dancer takes to the air, hanging there a long breathless moment, barely clearing the notch and landing down in the opening through the nopales—smashing through and banging on to the finish.

The little mick grabs the purse with Maitland closing in at a right angle, followed tightly by a consuming burst of red dust. The brothers catch up just in time to witness the great jump and final spurt.

"He won! He's got it!" they shout out at the top of their lungs.

Gideon leaps onto his brother's back and the two begin a delirious celebration. A reenactment of the great race; with Gideon tumbling over a small cactus and bowing low while Chauncey races by and onto the finish by way of a mighty leap over a creosote bush.

The victor dismounts and slowly runs his hands over Dancer's powerful flanks, pulling out a few spines and laughing over at the brother's little comedy. Maitland rides up on the sweating Roan ready to spit nails. The Irishman shines his crooked grin, blood trickling down from where he'd smacked into the Nopales.

"You cheatin son of a bitch," Maitland spits out with his broad face in an angry pinch.

"Well Oliver, out here there's only winning and losing. You *lost*...and watch what you call my mother you festerin piece 'a gobshite!" Shouting back while tying the purse to his belt and shoving it down into his trousers.

"I'm gonna take the money and shove the bag up yer ass."

"No sir, I don't think you will."

The bully is down now and squaring himself, the Irishman pulling off his shirt and handing it to Chauncey with a wink. Maitland comes on with a smug little sneer, his first punch misses and the little scrapper busts him a good one with his left.

"Show'em who's boss."

"Hit'em in that fat belly."

The scrapper isn't easy to tag, and a fair amount of dancing occurs circling Maitland's cocky sneer.

"This ain't no fandango, you little faggot. Stand and fight."

The dance continues however, with the bully taking a counterpunch nearly every time he throws a hard right. But Maitland finally answers with a body shot that connects and an uppercut that buckles the knees—and the Irish boy staggers back—the sky reeling above and ground flying up hard.

Maitland pauses to wipe a bloodied nose then moves to get the purse and deliver a kick. But Chauncey and Gideon step forward.

"The fight's over for fuck's sake," says Chauncey.

"The hell you say. I'm taking the purse," declares Maitland.

"Like they said, the fight is over," a tall stranger adds. He steps forward and stands next to Chauncey and Gideon.

"And who the hell are you?"

"The name's Sombrero Jack." When he leans over to spit, a nasty-looking blackjack comes out of his pocket. He starts to swing it in a tight arc. Moses and Hevel had been watching it all and decide now to close ranks as well, the two of them standing abreast.

The little mick sits up rubbing his jaw, amazed at the show of support around him.

"That was one hell of a jump, never seen the like. I believe it won the damn purse," says Moses.

"Looks like you're gonna have to fight all of us," says Sombrero Jack.

Maitland climbs back on the big horse and whips the Roan around with a vicious jerk.

"You sons-a-bitches can all go to hell."

"*Kessen mine tuckas*!"

"I'll settle with your sorry ass later," Maitland promises and Hevel grins back, lifting both hands in a pungent salute.

The Danglers Derby had unfurled again, with new embellishments added here and there—right on to the glorious end and beyond. On to Sombrero Jack, the older kid in the ridiculous headgear that no one had seen around before, and to the heady days and the big mistake that followed.

A choir of coyotes echoes abruptly from the desert, bringing him back to the moment with a jerk. The sun had set while he'd dreamed his victory back to life. Now he needs his wits about him to make the twilight run. And then to face the darkness.

Somewhere along the way boy and horse crossed the border into the Territory of Arizona. There had been no signs and only a diminishing trace of road. It had forked and he guessed wrong. Eventually the way played out altogether, and no choice but to keep moving on into the wild.

Cardinal points and features of the landscape had been an obsession since leaving Silver City, and he hung on them now like a life raft. The Sun unfailingly led to the west, the North Star to his right, and the mountains he memorized and named one by one. The hour of night determined by the position of the Big Dipper. When a threatening intrusion would sound in the dark, he'd listen intently with eyes on Ursa Major—then calculate the time and try to remain indifferent to his unseen companion.

The desert spoke its secrets in a language he was just beginning to understand. An immense borderless field of arcane knowledge, at once intimate and remote, solid and immaterial, beautiful and terrifying—available to the uninvited for a price. The familiarity soaked into his head a burdensome thing, with no regard for human frailty. And every day it cost more and seeps deeper in.

He'd been traveling on from the sheepherder's little kingdom for three days. And *lost* from all marked paths for what seemed an eternity. Not truly lost, for he knew his direction. But the panic of being outside the map is no small thing. Danger closes in, takes on a life of its own. The silence of day sometimes as unnerving as the uncanny bedlam at night. Still, he has courage and faith and looked for a miracle.

It's out there for me, somewhere.

Over and down an uplift—the main track finally reveals itself. He lets out a whoop, jumps down to dance the jig and whoop some more. A frolic of redemption on the ragged edge of the world. And fine enough for the desert god to choke on. Unreliable two-tracks had bedeviled him for days, steadfastly refusing to deliver him up to the promised land—but the hard-used ruts he'd just discovered *would*—and for certain.

The wide road reached north to south, running along a scapular mountain range. Straightaway he guessed wrong, again, and wasted almost an entire day humping toward Mexico. In the afternoon a military wagon headed South revealed the hard truth. Its surly teamster gave over some jerky, let him fill his water bag from the barrel and slapped the reins.

"The track heads west prolly not more'n a mile or two *north* from where you struck it," the muleskinner barks. He shook his head at such poor luck and yelled out to his mules to step lively.

The boy turns Dancer and they head back to the north.

Even with the muleskinner road under him—the night is another tough one. The river still a myth and water bag empty. Its frayed bottom had developed a leak during the day and the bag forsaken before he noticed. He felt cursed and slept poorly. A sound out in the dark, louder and stranger than anything he'd yet heard, had shaken him further. And the Dipper obscured by clouds.

Dawn rose up overcast and sullen, as if it meant to storm. But the demon sun back at full power by mid-day and the same desperate pain in his throat and gut in the afternoon. A crazed dizzy sickness had infected his mind now as well and he travelled on into what seemed a feverish dream.

He reins up to peer at billowing cloud on the horizon, eyes burning and head swimming, a vast field of creosote sweeping down behind him, *that scud might've been stirred up by a dust devil, or it might be salvation.* Dancer is nudged forward at a quickened pace. They drop into another breathless plain with a demon trolling along behind eating his dust and grinning, as if a tastier meal lay ahead. The boy turns to stare. Maybe it was there and maybe it wasn't, chuckling in the grit of the earth. His answer a simple cluck of the tongue and a faster gait.

At the top of the next hill he pulls up sharply, heaving out a sigh like the drop of anchor in safe harbor. Down below a large wagon and long team of mules are at a standstill and finally, the little river shinning back the setting sun. He gallops forward waving his hat at the two muleskinners, determined to hide his sorry condition.

"How do you friends, can I help out?"

"Hell yes, you can shoot Chucho in the foot, serve him right for all his rotten jokes," the teamster yells down from the wagon box.

"*Chinga tu madre, cabrón,* that won't stop me," Chucho answers back, a smile playing on his dark features. Both men are happy to be at the river and the long day about over. The kid jumps down trying to laugh but his throat closes up. He gets right in on the work of leading paired animals out of harness.

"*Hay mucho calor, que no,*" the boy says, taking an active hand in unhitching the next pair.

"*Sí, tanto calor, siempre.*"

"*Claro.*"

"*Que su nombre joven?*"

"Henry McCarty."

"Irish? *Qué Bueno.*"

"*Y tú?*"

"Chucho Padilla. Two worthless niggers, eh, amigo?" says the Mexican. His dark eyes full of a hard-earned irony.

"I'm Irish, it's true, but born in America at least," Henry answers with his own ironic grin. His accent carries a light brogue, with a touch of midwestern twang.

"Me too chico. And that big American son-of-a-bitch over there is Barrett Campbell."

"I'm glad as hell to meet both of you," says Henry.

"You may change your mind. Be careful around this son of a dog, a *brujo* put him under a spell—turns into a goat when the sun goes down... starts humping anything that moves," Chucho confides. He winks at the kid as he walks a pair of mules the last few feet to water, getting down between them for his own long drink.

"Don't listen to that crazy Mex, he's half goat himself," Barrett growls back from behind another pair of thirsty animals.

"I know something about the night, and goats. You two fellows strike me as bulls," Henry answers, after dumping a hatful of water on his head and pouring a long drink down his parched throat. He'd practically collapsed at the river's edge. Dancer had run to water as soon as Henry dismounted.

"There, you see, little feller's smart as a steel trap. What the hell you're doing out here alone I could not say. Lost maybe...or on the run."

"I'm looking for Fort Grant, Camp Grant, or Hopville, whatever the hell it's called."

"It's that way, chico, you're almost there!" says Chucho, pointing to the west and reaching out to shake hands. "The road starts to lift from here, soon there'll be *farms and ranches*, another river, a big rock of a mountain, and the place you're looking for."

"Guess you ain't lost. Welcome to camp mule shit," Barrett concludes. He extends his large hand as well and Henry's palm all but disappears into it.

"Camp Grant and Fort Grant are two different places, but they ain't far apart," says Chucho, laughing.

"Like the Devil and the deep blue sea," Barrett declares.

"I wish it *was* the sea," says Henry.

"That's a mean stretch of hell behind you son," the big man continues, looking the little saddle tramp over. "You're about played out."

"Yes sir, I'd agree with you."

"When d'ya eat last?"

"Yesterday."

"Hungry enough to eat your saddle then, or yer arm. Well, let's get some supper made. Bet you got some stories, kid."

Two hours later the mules have been hobbled, dinner cooked and eaten around a small campfire. Chucho had done the honors; a fine meal of beans and peppers and a big jackrabbit he'd shot earlier in the day. Barrett rolls a jug back to his lips, offering it to Henry afterwards.

"I'll pass on that Taos lightning, or whatever's in the jug. But I'll sure take another round of *guisado*," says Henry, sitting cross-legged and watching sparks fly up into eternity. There was something profoundly reassuring about these two men. He felt safe for the first time since his pilgrimage began. The fire-lit company yielded a small circle of comfort and no mistake—but pitch black waited at the quivering edge ready to swallow it whole.

"You fellows want to hear a joke?"

"That depends," Barrett grumbles while rolling a cigarette.

"Tell it amigo," says Chucho, grinning through his beard.

Just a short one to start with, then a long jape that holds the muleskinner's spellbound. Both men sat stoic at first. But then the performance begins to sparkle. Henry recounts the tale of a drunken cowboy attending a grand performance at the gilded Denver Opera House. Sprawled across three chairs and immovable, the stewed and hulking drover is politely informed that he is allowed only *one* seat and the other two must be released—eliciting a low moan from the would-be theatergoer. All manner of punctilious encouragement fails to dislodge the man. When finally, the sheriff arrives and learns the cowboy's name, he affably inquires, *where are ya' from Sam*? A reply is groaned back forthwith, *the balcony*!

In the end he'd won them over completely—their laughter rolling out into the black like a triumphant cannonade.

"You're a funny little scrub and no mistake," chuckles Barrett. "Say, why don't you and Chucho trade places. He can go back to his sweetheart and you can ride with me for the next load!"

"I need to get off this two-track soon as I can."

"That's a smart answer, amigo," says Chucho, pulling hard on the smoke Barrett had handed him and leaning back to better enjoy it.

"Where's all that freight come from anyway?" Henry asks.

"Fort Leavenworth, Kansas. Feeds every outpost south of the Union Pacific line. It all gets hauled down to a string a'depots all over the goddamned southwest. We get our load at Fort Defiance. 'Bout a hundred miles from here."

"I bet coming back is hell."

"As hard a day's work as you'll ever do in your life. Damn roads ain't worth a shit, mostly," says Barrett. "But there's a freedom in it."

"Well I'm ready to get where all that freight goes," Henry announces, pointing West.

"I assume you don't mean the Fort?" Barrett asks.

"Hopville," says Henry, grinning generously. "I've been hearing about it for two years, time I had a look."

"Okay. Hope ya ain't disappointed. She's nothing much to look at."

"Looks can be deceiving," Chucho replies. "Take you for example."

Barret spits into the fire and shakes his unkempt head, begrudging Chucho a half-smile. "Hopville has two saloons, Tiger Town is the one to visit, all the faro you could want. There's the Chop House, decent chippie cribs. A well-stocked sutler. Excellent blacksmith, mean as hell, but damn good at the anvil."

"Best stay clear of him, he'd eat you for breakfast."

"That Cahill gives man and boy a proper beatin, it's true," says Barrett. "Though he's sure never messed with me." The big man looks up with a flare of pride.

"Don't forget the tequileria and vendador de chiles, la curandera and la adivina," Chucho says. "Over in *La Zona Hermosa*."

"I'll be visiting there for certain, I'm already half-Mexican," says Henry, eyes perked. "And I'll pop that bully right in the nose."

"I'd watch that, like I say it ain't a town exactly. Sure ain't no sheriff or law."

"That suits me fine."

"Coming off this hardassed road—it's a damned happy sight. And there's *hop* if you care to get truly loco."

"You stay clear of that shit too chico."

"And Apaches?"

"They're around but there's been no trouble for two years now. Not since the massacre."

Henry looks down at the word *massacre*, wondering what the story was but not wanting necessarily to hear it just now. "Well I've had my fill of the barrens. There's nothing out here, nothing at all."

"Sí, joven, nada—nada excepto culebras, escorpiones—las fantasmas."

"And the Devil," Henry adds.

"Where's your family?" asks Barrett, his weathered eyes looking up after a silence.

"Mostly dead, except my brother Joe. And he lit out for the Colorady gold fields a year ago—after mother passed. There's my stepfather too, but he doesn't count. He left quicker'n Joe."

"That's hard luck," Barrett says, not knowing what else to say. The kid seems even smaller of a sudden.

"Introduce yourself to Abuelita Hernandez, over in La Zona. Tell her your story," says Chucho. He breathes a deep sigh and shakes his head, his own family a large one and spread from Sonora to Puerta de Luna, New Mexico.

"And Verna, she runs the chophouse. She'll help you out."

"Good to know but I can take care of myself."

"That's right—how else would you've gotten here?" Barrett answers nodding his head and smiling. It was a genuine smile with plenty of heart behind it.

The boy wasn't sure exactly how he'd gotten there—just kept the North star on his right and kept moving—and he didn't know it yet, but he'd just been adopted.

Henry stopped at the meager San Pedro River to bathe and change into his green suit. He'd purchased it for his performances at The Orleans. Best foot forward, always. A faint bugle sounds to the west and he looks up from the river; wet hair tossed back and a crooked grin. *Evening Mess call at the Fort*—it called to him as well.

He rides on to the glorious straggle of buildings under a sky fading from orange to purple to gray. First stop is the Chop House, where lamp light and pungent odors are equally dazzling. He'd soon wolfed down a hearty supper at a cost of ten cents. God knows what all was in the stew, exactly, in all its particulars. There were stringers of meat, lumps of potatoes, chili peppers, maybe cactus as well. It all floated in a thick salty broth that sopped up nicely with a hunk of course bread. He didn't question it beyond the first look and the first taste.

"You were lucky to run into Chucho and Barrett, and not some of these othern's," says Verna Langdon.

"Yes ma'am, I thought so too," Henry answers back.

"Here all on your lonesome then?" Verna asks, arms akimbo.

"Just Dancer and me."

"Well, this ain't the worst place you could be, but it's plenty rough. Got any money?"

"Yes ma'am, but I'll need to find some work pretty quick."

"There's work to be had and plenty of decent folk about. Just keep yer nose clean and let me know if you need help." Verna's grey eyes look right into him. Absolutely fearless. And she stands taller than any man currently in the Chop House.

A celebration on his mind now as he steps outside. The well-lit tavern down the way looks to be the place for some refinements, perhaps some music and gaming, maybe even a single malt or a whiskey punch if they had it. He mounts Dancer for one last short ride. The moon had finally shown herself and hung low above the outpost like a light house, revealing a pile of refuse in great detail. Henry shakes his head, remembering the long dark nights on the barrens and smiling at the two scuffling men who'd just been shoved out of the saloon.

Barrett had called the place *Tiger Town*, but the gilded rubric above the door reads *Elysium Bar*. Under any name an impressive sight to the boy, eyes glimmering in the lamplight and his horse nickering softly.

"Well my beauty, we've finished the race."

Henry swings his right leg up and over the saddle horn and slides down onto the hard-packed dirt with a flourish. After tying up Dancer with a tight bowline he steps up onto the porch. The crooked thoroughfare is given a proprietary up and down—the brawl still raging a few yards away. Their curses and grunts an ugly welcome and no denying the shabbiness of it all. Some of the shanties faced one way and some faced another and a good amount of prairie between most of them. The air smelled like rank garbage; slaughtered animals, shit, piss, and sour beer. A raw medley well known to him from his youngest days in the slums of New York. He wonders for a moment at the impossible distance he now stood from the city of his birth.

Checking his pouch, again, he puts one finger on the last of the Silver City dollars and looks in through a cracked window. The crowded room goes back two candelabrums deep. Men jostle around faro tables on one side of the Elysium. A long, crowded bar graces the other wall, lambent glow softening the strife with a kind of apricot tinged magic. Henry feels clean and well-fed and fully primed now to enter the fray—war bag over his shoulder and *best* foot forward.

A poster of a Bengal Tiger catches his eye just inside the door. Next to it a far more intriguing broadside stands him in place. The image of Lotta Crabtree, the most famous singer and dancer in all of America, stares back at him with stunning frankness.

Something about the defiant eyes, the bold set of her jaw, the thin cigar dangling serenely in her raised left hand—seems absolutely uncompromising and new. Lotta Crabtree is no demure ingenue but a sovereign Queen. To discover her waiting at the Elysium sends a wild twinge of joy coursing through him. If ever there was an omen of estate, here she is.

A happy jangling banjo tune suddenly cuts through the mayhem. He smiles. *By all rights I should be in jail, or lying dead somewhere out on the barrens, not standing here tapping my foot and mooning over Lotta Crabtree,* Henry thinks. He touches two fingers from his lips to her rosebud mouth and saunters to the bar.

"I'll take a whiskey punch if you've got it."

"Just as you say," the bartender replies as he begins to work the soda, sugar, ginger, and whiskey together. "A fine drink for a proper young fella."

"To your health, sir," Henry says and the barkeep nods. The bald crown before him had a peculiar ridge that balanced an ugly rosacea scar on the opposite side of a deeply lined face.

Henry sips the mixed drink with a showy bend of elbow and a grimace. The punch tasted fine but elegant fire leaps back up his throat before it reaches the stomach. Only his third taste of whiskey and this one well-earned.

He sets the glass down and nods to the long row of tipplers. A few men gesture back as Henry catches his reflection in the mirror. He's certainly looked better. Not bad, considering, but a bit shaggy and gaunt for Sunday church. The coat helped.

Definitely outclassed by the elegance of the bar's engraved transept and the elaborate chancel standing behind, Henry drops his head wishing he cut a better figure. The red-scarred bartender in his white shirt and black vest seems almost clerical, the bar, almost holy, and the boy—put in mind of the Eucharist—is *almost* humbled.

He had prayed hard out in the desert, and knew he owed God a sacrament. It would come in good time, and in his own way.

There were no guns or knives out. Forbidden, says the sign out front. Still, that only means weapons are concealed. His own was behind his back. Looking back up again and taking another, slower sip, he notes the blend of soldiers and civilians. An uneasy alliance, he thinks, and commonplace in the shadow of a fort. Not much compared to Silver City overall, but no alternative existed and as such—the place is a kind of miracle.

Drawn into the corner where the lone banjoist shouts out a minstrel song, 'Turkey in The Straw', the celebration gets under sail. With one of his favorites sparking the air and the whiskey punch working down to his feet like dark magic—Henry starts to dance, as if back at the *Orleans* and all had gone his way.

Turkey in the straw, turkey in the hay
With a rump and a riddle and
a doodle de day
Roll 'em up and twist 'em up a
high tuc-ka-haw
Roll 'em up a tune called
Turkey in the Straw.

One fellow is impressed enough to toss a coin at song's end. Henry catches it with a grin and bows low, doffing his eccentric little hat. The coin goes in the mug for the banjoist, able Jake, who smiles and leans straight into another lively tune of the grand Minstrelsy. Henry can't help but join in this time, taking on a verse of his own. His clear tenor cuts through the murk like a sudden shine of moonlight. More than one head turns.

Old dan Tucker was a ripe ole man
He used to ride our darby ram
Sent him a whizzin down the hill
If he hadn't got up, he'd lay there still.

The music and verses jangle on and on, the kid's boots sliding into the beat and scraping the sagging floor, knees whacking together and legs soaring into the Minstrel *jhembe* he'd learned as a button on the streets of New York.

"Give'em room boys, give'em room," Able Jake yells out.

A couple of soldiers who'd stumbled away from the faro game threaten to crowd the show, but the kid slides in between and back to the corner, starting up a last chorus go-round.

Get out da way ole Dan Tucker
Your too late to eat your supper

Supper's done and breakfast's cookin
Ole Dan Tucker just stand there lookin.

Full tilt and fine fettle, Henry could have gone at a cracking pace all night long. But the barrens had taken quite a hungry bite out of him. He grabs the glass up from the floor and sits down heavily.

A longer third drink is smoother and doesn't fire up his throat near the same as the first two. With an odd, blissful expression, the room aglow, his attention shifts to the faro game running hot and noisy across the floor. It seems to jounce right along with the music. And like some new marvel of a song, the rhythmic patter of the dealer catches his ear. He closes his eyes to listen better and when they open again—Henry begins to *see* the game for the first time. It was almost like a stage show, a burlesque, a set piece in a comic opera.

The intricate rounds of assorted bets, the fevered settling after every two-card draw from the box, the frenzied vociferations before and after, the fast-moving play of chips and coppers on the thirteen card field, the money made or lost on every pull—drawing and bewitching him now like a shiver of sirens.

Up and drifting forward in a rapturous haze, the boy wades in amongst the men. Now the long table before him, its oval of green felt presided over by the banker and his barking card-counting sideman, the *casekeep*. All of it emerging together from the mist as the righteous center of a new faith.

An hour later Henry drifts back out exhausted and wondering where to bed down. Campfires out in a broad field suggest the place. He finds a spot amongst wagons and tents and snoring men. Stretching out with Dancer hobbled close by, a sound sleep drops down on him immediately. In the middle of the night he's startled awake and discovers someone going through his poke. Thumbing back the hammer on the old colt he speaks up, "You best get the hell out of my bag."

"Well now I am sorry, I reckoned this was *mine*...in the dark," the man hisses. The trigger goes back one more click, and the shadow withdraws. It could be heard scrabbling off into the night. *Sounds like a damn wharf rat.* Henry turns over wondering if he would've pulled the trigger.

Morning rises up on the high plain cool and clear. Henry props himself up for a better view of the new world around him. Again, a bugle wafts in from the distance. Fort Grant off to his right about half a mile or so. There are large impressive buildings of stone and wood and dust already lifting from the sprawling stockyards. A blunt mountain with massive shoulders of bare rock stands behind the Fort like a warrior of old.

Camp Grant scattered out down to his left, pointing this way and that and not making much sense. It reeks of the same delicacies as last night—the slaughterhouse and pens not far off and that smell rises above the others. The haphazard row of adobes and shotgun shacks are flanked on the opposite side with rows of yellowing tents. No doubt the chippie cribs were there and he looked forward to paying them a visit soon. Further down a warren of *casitas* with rows of corn and beans growing in fields by the river. That must be what Chucho called La Zona Hermosa. The only trees anywhere in sight grew in clumps on either bank of the San Pedro.

And the great desert staring back from beyond the river. Thank god he was clear of it. It still seemed to have its eye on him.

"Hey sonny, can you handle a wagon and an ornery team of mules?" a man with a gray beard and a big belly shouts down to him.

"Sure, you bet. Drove one all the way from Kansas to New Mexico." Henry exaggerates, but the claim partly true.

"Well you can continue admiring the dawn, or you can make some money."

"I'll choose the money."

"Good, I got two wagons and can't skin both, my son Griffin went sportin last night didn't make it back—reckon I'll settle with him later. Got to get these two loads a grain up to the fort. Grain's the best crop in the world—wheat, millet, and rye—grows fast and cuts easy and these blue boys buy up all I can deliver. Yessir life is good—name's Jim Moon."

"Henry McCarty," the boy returns, shaking hands and thinking what a friendly fellow to meet first thing, and what damned hole did that wharf rat crawl off to.

Within two minutes Henry is ready with Dancer tied on the back and himself in the box giving the team a slap and a holler. By nightfall they'd unloaded the wagons, found the strapping son passed out in back of a shithole saloon, and rolled back to the farm. Jim Moon talked a blue streak all the way and often answered his own questions and statements, as if afraid he'd be misunderstood.

"I wish Griffin was as smart and hard workin as you. He's a good'n, just wild and full of oats and cain't hold his liquor worth a damn. Got a hell of a pair a arms on him, could swing a nine-pound hammer through an iron door and not even get out bed," Jim offered, after his son had gone into the house.

"I sure thank you for the work Mr. Moon."

"You'll stay to supper, sleep in the barn, and we'll see what other work I can find for you. I have a notion you'd be a good hand at sheep herding. You're a bit scrawny for cow work, can you cook?"

"Yes, I can," Henry admits reluctantly.

"Well then you'd make a hell of a doughbelly."

He tried to grin back in answer, but it comes out more of a grimace.

Henry is soon making regular visits to the cribs to satisfy another kind of hunger. His first and subsequent tastes of hopmagundy, the magic art by which the earth is populated—are a powerful and continuing revelation.

"Easy lad, you will wear me out," Kate admonishes with a giggle. "Try any more positions on me and I'll charge you triple. Bite your root off too."

She had no intention of doing either. Cat Eyed Kate is fond of the boy, a funny little fellow for sure and always clean.

"You are a most delicious red berry Cat Eyed Kate," Henry murmurs. She on her stomach and he plying the waves from behind. His eyes trace down the lovely curving roll of her backbone, slowly down to its terminus and the cleft with fine hair spreading out over her ample bottom like down. An ambrosia lifts up sharp and maddening and he plies on.

"Kate, I love you most truly."

"Oh shut up."

When he'd finished, she rolls over.

"You are a strange one," Kate offers and Henry leaning in for a kiss. She isn't beautiful of face by any man's standards, but the fine details of her body are mesmerizing and the good heart within her a charm as well. And the kiss a liberty she seldom allowed. "Now get off me you little wolf."

Kate began to clean herself and the boy continues to watch as she dips a towel in the bowl of water. Her breasts move with a baffling grace while she wipes and scrubs, their dolloped curvatures ending abruptly in the sweetest of uplifted red points. Singular creations, they remind him of nothing else on this earth.

"Do you want to clean yourself up?" Kate asks, her voice almost sweet.

"No, I'll leave you on me for a time."

"Well put your britches on and quit mooning. I got other customers."

"Yes ma'am...I sure look forward to seeing you," Henry confides while stretching into his pants. He makes a great show of dressing the top of his wiry frame, lastly donning the hat and taping it into place—all the while whistling and she watching *him* now as he moves toward the tent flap, lifting it with a final embellishment. "Fare thee well Kate."

"Go on you little shit."

Working the range, making ends meet, and learning the game of Faro back at the Elysium—was a tough hustle. And he stooped to some thievery to keep himself and Dancer fed, at first, falling in with some roughs who weren't much better than the wharf rat. When they all were caught stealing mules from the fort, Henry got off light because of his age. And because he obviously had education, displayed a measure of remorse, and showed only the finest manners to the officers.

From then on, he decided to follow Verna's advice and keep his nose clean. The unsavory combination of petty gains, high risk, and low company did not suit him. The same kind of low company and risky grab had led to his arrest and incarceration in Silver City. Sheriff Whitehill trusted him enough to leave him the run of the jail corridor, and a chimney flu became his portal to freedom. He'd crawled and shinnied up and run his fate out into the desert. Avoiding shackles and stockades a number one priority now, above all else. Being confined was just plain intolerable.

Henry even took a job cooking for a big round-up in the fall, though he didn't like the work. Good honest wage at least. His real ambitions arrived at the close of whatever sheep or cattle or farm job that came along—when he'd head straight for Cat Eyed Kate and then the oval of green. After three months in Camp Grant he goes right up to the head dealer, Billy King, out in the street. Billy thought he was being hustled for coin, but the boy was after something more valuable.

"Yes, I've noticed you hanging around, kid. I see you're interested in the game, now tell me why I'd be sharing any secrets with a scrawny little dangler like you."

"Because I'm smarter than both of your casekeeps put together. I don't drink, I don't take hop, and I'll only cheat when you give the sign."

"Well, ain't you the saucebox," says Billy, beginning to wonder just what cut of sharper this boy might be. "Where's your family?"

"I have none to speak of."

"Well that's a shame. And just where did you come from?"

"New York. I was raised in the Five Points, then on to Dodge City in sixty-eight, Santa Fe two years later, lived in Silver City four more years.

Saw red brick palaces rise up from the ground, you'd almost think you were back east," says Henry, with a degree of pride.

Billy King continues to pause in his constitutional. The boy is a suspicious but interesting proposition, a long shot that might pay off. "Let's perambulate. What's your name, kid?"

"Henry McCarty."

"Tell me Henry, how much is, say, seven times fifty-three?"

"Three hundred seventy-one," Henry fires back quickly. Billy King nods, acknowledging the correct answer.

"Well that's an easy one. I'm going to keep asking questions, and you keep answering and we'll see where we get to. So, I suppose you were in trouble back there. And you got clean away from it?"

The kid nods and flashes the signature crooked grin with an extra bit of salt and pepper.

"Out of my way, you fockin little cunt," Windy Cahill barks at the smart-ass kid that had been keeping everyone in stitches behind his back.

"Certainly Mr. Cahill," says Henry as he steps to one side, doffing his hat in a grandiose sweep. The stocky blacksmith had just finished a long turn at the faro table, Henry looking on behind and occasionally mimicking his oafish maneuvers. When Cahill turned to stalk off for another drink he'd practically stumbled over the boy, and now stood dumbfounded at the boy's brazen sass.

"Don't be cuttin shines with me, I'll be glad to put a fist through that fockin grin."

"This little cunt will grin all the more then, whenever I see Windy Cahill," says the boy, undaunted.

Cahill stands there a moment, his blood rising, then suddenly reaching out to collar the boy. He gives him a smithy's slap, hard enough to bust his lip and send him to the floor.

"Forgive me for pointing it out, but me mum hit harder than that," Henry allows, after leaning over to spit the blood out of his mouth.

"Come on, Windy, he's just a boy, let's get another drink," says his friend, throwing an arm out and guiding him toward the bar. Henry sits back against the wall and watches the man's broad backside lumbering away, fingers probing teeth to make sure one had not been loosened.

"You best steer clear of Windy," a fellow Elysian confides, extending a hand and pulling Henry to his feet. "That Irishman's not happy at the end of a day, lessen he's beat someone half to death. Ain't yet seen anyone get the better of 'em."

"Cut from the old cloth, eh?" the boy answers back. "Well so am I."

Henry started a practice of going up to Mt. Graham for an hour of reflection, on Sundays. He thought of it as church and did it for his mother's sake. She would want him to take time for religion, time to remember her guidance and instruction, and his family.

He always began with a proper Catholic hymn, usually *For All the Saints* or *Hail, O Star of the Ocean*. Then a prayer and some bread and something to pass for wine, for the Holy Eucharist. The church would not approve of the unconsecrated promontory as a suitable location, or of himself as the administrator, but Henry had made an entire life of improvising and there was naught left of his old life but himself.

Sometimes the church and his mother's religion all lay in his head in a big tangle. Particularly after his sojourn from Silver City to Camp Grant, Henry wasn't at all sure that Catholic scripture and desert reality were compatible. Truth to tell he'd grown more aligned with the earthy mixture of Christian and pagan beliefs to be found amongst the Mexicans. The hispanicos worshiped God, fervently, but paid homage to a host of other beings as well; demigods, angels, magical saints, local guardians, brujas, spirits, ghosts—devils. The vivid pantheon of characters fascinated and inspired him, and more and more, those beings made a brilliant kind of sense.

His mother had said, many times, the Mexican church wasn't all that different from religion back in Ireland, but he reckoned once you added in the language and the landscape, the people and the saints and the spirits, it *was* different. *Very* different, the warmth and the spice of it already in his blood like a sacrament.

He'd begun his ascent into that world on Chihuahua Hill. He and his mother had been to many a baile on that storied hill. They could dance the fandango as well as anyone there and stood out like flowers in a desert garden—he of the turquoise eyes and she with her honey blonde hair.

But on Sunday mornings he puts demons and local saints and fandangos to the side. He honors his *mother's* beliefs, as if she were still alive.

She didn't always come to him. Nor speak of sweet memories when she did.

"So, my fine young prince, you've been whoring and gambling. A fine attempt you've made to break my heart." He could *hear* her certainly, and sometimes see her plainly as well. She appeared most when she was angry. And she always seemed to be angry with him.

"I'm just trying to earn a decent living in a hard place. And to *live*."

"And as I've pointed out before, you'd not be here if it weren't for the Devil pissing in yer ear, and you a let'n him."

"I can't deny it."

"And your grand plans for the future? I see you carry a gun now."

"I'm only protecting myself, and I will be the *best*, the very best."

"Ha, sounds like yer trying to pull a rose out of yer arse."

And on it would go, the communion and the sacrifice, confession and atonement, and finally, the mercy of God's love—but it seemed to him it was really only his mother's love he felt. In the end she would drift away, leaving him alone again, solemn as a broken heart. The grinning jokester so cavalier and unflappable, brought low by a voice in his head and the memory of a great woman.

But he always felt better riding back.

By late autumn the Irish singer is already well-known to the good folk of La Zona Hermosa. It started with a bad case of dysentery that would not subside, and a visit to the *curandera* and *adivina*—Abulelita Hernandez. He stayed overnight with her and she cured his flux.

Thereafter, he went often to visit with her and other friends. And when fortunate enough, to eat the savory food and to hear stories and songs. He performed magic tricks in return, helped the children with their English—made everyone laugh.

The curandera sometimes told him long winded fables; stories of humble Mestizos dealt a cruel lot and saved by fate, or magic, wild tales of animals and saints, gods and men—and he would sing her a song or tell a tale of his own to repay her.

"Well Irish, if you want to hear a story you must pay." Her broad smile raises an intricate web of lines.

"I will pay according to the quality of the story," Henry barters with a twinkle in his eye.

"Then I must tell a story to change your life. A tale of Mexico, one to challenge your beliefs."

"I listen with an open heart," says Henry, settling himself onto the earthen floor.

'There was once a man, very poor and very hungry. He had not eaten a morsel in days and was desperate beyond measure. He knew of a chicken yard in a nearby village—it belonged to the richest man there—and all he could think of was one of those fat birds simmering in an oven.'

'But he was an honorable man, basically, and loathe to break a commandment, although he had done so many times in his difficult life. Finally, he came to a hard decision; to steal and live or be virtuous and die. It was a simple choice really and the theft was accomplished without much trouble or guilt, after all. He'd wrung the bird's neck as soon as he had it in his bony hands and slipped away already watering at the mouth.'

'Other than the chicken there was no food about the jacal, but a few spices and culinary skills he did possess. Salt and wild herbs and ground chile he rubbed onto the skin as soon as it was cleanly plucked and, stuffing it with a lemon that he'd also stolen, wrapped the bird in a cloth and fired the oven not used in recent memory. He sat back against an *ahuehuete* tree and closed his eyes, already tasting the savory meat. In no time he drifted off to sleep.'

"*Buenos días* amigo, I'm sorry to awaken you from your nap but that is a real fine meal you're cooking. I saw the smoke and then I began to sniff the air and praise the heavens, and all the saints. I've not eaten in days. Might I share in your meal?" asked the man. He removed his sombrero respectfully, exposing a bald head. Despite his clean white clothes—he had the look of a sinful old jackal.

"*Perdóname extraños*, but I cannot share my food with you. I need it all for myself."

"Are you certain? I am very hungry and had heard this village was famous for its hospitality."

"I'm a poor and desperate man and do not trust you. Leave me in peace old man."

"Then you are a fool. And a stingy closefisted sinner...cursed as well."

"It's the truth," the man replied matter-of-factly.

"You have just turned *God* from your table," the Almighty informed and there appeared a glowing crown of light all around his bald pate.

"Then I have chosen well and stand by my decision. You shower the wealthy with love and favor yet turn a blind eye to the suffering penniless folk of the earth. Be off, you skinny old cheat, and good riddance."

"You'll regret this insolence," God fumed as he turned into a great writhing orange flame and ascended into the sky.

'The man rolled his eyes, unimpressed with the threats or the showy exit. He'd known true misery long enough hadn't he, the old swindler could pike off and peddle his lies elsewhere. Moreover, he was proud of how he handled himself. Meanwhile, a rich aroma of roasting foul was thick in the air and he found himself drifting off to sleep again, happily anticipating the feast and the pleasures of the day.'

'The afternoon shadows began to lengthen, and a thrasher emerged from a thick bush to sing through its long, curved bill. A sweet tune filled the air and a light breeze softened the afternoon heat. The song and the breeze seemed to enter the man's sleep, flowing along with his contented dreams.'

"*Buenos tardes, Señor amable,* I'm sorry to disturb your rest, but I couldn't help but smell your delightful cooking on the wind, as I walked nearby. *Muy sabroso*. I am a starving traveler and have come a long way under Father Sun and Mother Moon. But I don't think I can go another step without food," declared a man in dark gray with a bundle thrown over his shoulder.

"You'll forgive me *Señor*, if I appear inhospitable, but it seems to be a day for strange visitors...just who might you be and why should I share my meal with you?"

"I am *Death*, and as always, a busy eremite," the gray cloak billowed and revealed the dark skeletal figure within, yet, a large belly also, and hairy skin stretched tight over it. Long sinewy arms concluded in hands that were like the claws of a beast. But his eyes were honest and tranquil.

'The poor man with his half-cooked bird looked at Death, for some time. Finally, he made his answer in a steady tone of voice.'

"*Señor Muertos,* you are impartial and fair. I see that everyday both the sickly and the well, the beautiful and the ugly, the high and the low, the young and old are all taken by you with an impartiality that is truly admirable. After the hypocrisy of my last visitor, I find your honesty and lack of arrogance...uplifting." The gentle expression on Death's face seemed to soften further. "I will gladly share this bird with you. If you would please to take a seat our dinner will be ready soon, but we must wait a while yet." The man sighed and gestured to a shady spot in the yard.

'And so, Death sat down with the man and they talked of many things while waiting for the chicken to finish cooking. The ward of shades scratched his belly with sharp talons and laughed often, for he told more than one funny story and found the world to be full of silly contradictions and half-truths.'

'Finally, their supper was ready. The man cut the bird evenly with his machete and placed Death's portion on a roof shake, which made a fine plate. The Reaper's eyes glowed as he forked the first bite in. It was amazing to watch how adept he was at feeding himself with those claws. In the end, not a tiny stringer of meat or sliver of skin or splinter of bone was left on Death's plate.'

'The meal *was* perfect and satisfying as no meal had ever been in the pauper's life, despite having shared half of his bird with death. He leaned back and felt a deep contentment. Whatever happened in the future, nothing could spoil the sublime consummation of the moment. And when time came for the angel of darkness to take his leave, he opened his bundle. Out came chickens and goats and the man stood completely astonished.'

'He had expected the strong arms and sharp talons to grab him and stuff his worthless soul into the bag of perdition. He was prepared to except that fate, for what can a man do in the face of destiny? At least he had a full stomach.'

"I will forestall the deaths of these animals, and yours, in gratitude for that simple but superior meal. And to honor your fearless generosity. Farewell, my friend." Then Death turned and seemed to slowly melt into a cloud of mist. Leaving the man with chickens pecking at his feet, goats bleating, and tears forming in his eyes.

'The animals thrived under his care and thereafter milk and eggs and meat were plentiful. He planted corn and squash and a new day was born. Any hungry person could always be sure of a meal at his little jacal. The sun shone, nurturing rain fell, the moon played her tricks but gave a benevolent tug to the fruits of his garden. For the man's *choza* was no longer a cursed place. It had been gifted with some of the earth's greatest magic.'

Henry sat for a moment considering the tale, it had gotten under his skin in a way that other fables hadn't. "An old yarn I suppose?"

"Very old."

"I don't understand it, completely...yet." He wasn't going to admit that it would change his life but that's exactly how it felt.

Abuelita Hernandez sat quietly a long time. The silence began to make him uncomfortable. He uncrossed his legs to stretch and rub, finally gazing back at the abuelita. Her eyes hint at a deeper and more unsettling truth than could ever be put into words.

"You *see* much that others do not. But one cannot come to a complete understanding of the world, as it truly is, in an afternoon. It will take time," she warns.

"Time and tide wait for no man...and you promised to tell my fortune, weeks ago."

The curandera looks at him sharply. She knew it would come to this and reluctant to speak, uncertain how to proceed, shakes her head.

"I have already done it, but the reading confuses me. I've never seen one like it and my poor understanding will not help you."

"Let me be the judge of that," says Henry.

Again, she hesitates. Another silence ensues. Henry begins to hum an old Irish tune and gets up to dance a light jig, aiming his crooked grin at the seer from time to time. He places a generous fold of bills in the little jar on the table next to her chair, before settling back into a cross-legged perch. He looks up with his blue eyes prayerful, imploring. Finally, she nods and begins to speak.

"Many things contradict...big things lie ahead for you and some of it will happen very fast. Against great odds, you will pass through the eye of a needle. But I also see the Fool marching toward a cliff...and leaping into the dark. Strangest of all, I see you will forget who you are."

"Ha! That will never happen."

"I see the possibility of other great destinies. Impossible destinies. But they to, are clouded, and for them you must wait and wait, then wait some more. And when an eternity has passed, you must wait further still."

"When I'm an old man then?" Henry asks.

"*No se.*"

3

Windy Cahill takes a good long break at midday. He would quickly eat his lunch then walk to the Variety Saloon with a pail, have it filled and walk back. The beer helped cool him down and settle whatever hard meal was in his stomach. Then a short nap on the cot in his little room in back. The walk and the beer and the nap his favorite time of day and no man better disturb him in that time of repose.

But of course, this was just the time Henry liked to pester Cahill best. He would fall in behind as Windy lumbered to the Variety and mimic his awkward stride like a circus clown. The peculiar hitch resulted from being kicked in the knee by a filly, and the kid has it down perfect. It's a damn funny thing to see, and always the laughter of those nearby that got Windy's attention.

"God damn ya little hoor's melt, a fuckin crows curse on you."

"Good day Windy, just looking in on you."

And the boy would dance away merry as a cricket. But sometimes he would tarry and Windy would get his revenge. Once he swung his pail quick enough to clock the boy dead on, dropping him to the street. Windy spat on him and went on his way. Henry was out for several minutes just lying in the dirt with the blacksmith's spittle drying on his face.

Another time Windy's new helper, Braden McGillin, snuck up and collared the boy as he shuffled and hobbled along. Windy laid him out and would have done more but Verna Langdon came running out and stopped him.

"Hit that boy one more time and you won't eat at the Chop House ever again." She stands over Henry and between the two Irishmen with a heavy frying pan in her right hand.

"T'aint none of yer business, Verna."

"When it's happening in front of my business it *is* my business. Now you two back away or I'll go to putting a dent in your goddamned skull," Verna clarifies. Her grey eyes had suddenly caught fire and she points and pokes with the fry pan like it was no more than a wooden spoon. "And if'n that don't get it, I'll call for Joseph—and the big dark son-of-a-bitch will kick your lily-white ass all the way back to *Sleego*."

"All right Verna, we were just paying the little dangler our respects. We'll be on our way then."

The incident followed close upon the heels of a prank involving the cot in the little room and a dead rat snake placed thereon.

Down the row from Tiger Town a tented boarding house called the Lion's Den is home to a lucky few. The rickety wooden cots are expensive and hard to come by. If you're lucky enough to gain a birth, one woolen blanket and sheet provided and bed linens are cleaned once a month, whether they need it or not. Under the floorboards a hungry population of vermin and insects reside for free. Worst amongst them are the scorpions, particularly the Arizona Bark and the Black Devil, whose bite is sometimes fatal.

It's stifling in the summer and breezy in winter, but the Lion's Den represents comfort and class in Camp Grant. Also, a degree of security, for your belongings are watched after around the clock. The Elysium work force has long been in residence at this useful establishment and woe be it to any man who set his cap for one of their six cots.

Billy King had brought his young marvel along in a steady fashion and four months after being approached in the street—he installed Henry at the faro table and into the coveted back corner of the Lion's Den. The cot's previous occupant, Freddie Noonan, had lost his way in the world of amber fluid and white narcotics, and had died out on the prairie one cold night. An unfortunate overindulgence had overtaken his weakened body and stolen away with his life.

Henry McCarty reclines on his narrow bed, hard won, with a pile of tattered newspapers at his feet and a thick book in his hand on the twenty-fifth of December 1875.

"Merry Christmas Henry," Jude Ballard says with a gap-toothed smile. Jude traded for the book a few weeks before, thinking of Henry and Christmas coming. Since his arrival, the Elysium had been a much cheerier place to be. He doesn't quite understand the Irish wunderkind, but he knew his love of books.

"Happy Christmas Jude, thank you...you've no idea," Henry wished back, almost speechless, so taken is he with the gift. A new book to read in Camp Grant is like stumbling on a double eagle in the middle of the street.

"Thank *you* for the comb and the hair oil, a right smart gift," Jude insists. Outside the mild winter weather had dropped with a late December cold front, and their voices eject columns of frosted air.

"Well maybe you can keep that golden head tamed now," says Henry, eyes turning to his obscure and much appreciated new book, *Moby Dick,* as fine a holiday bounty as ever received on any Christmas in his life. "You know you can tell a lot about a book just from its heft, nearly six hundred pages here. Mr. Melville certainly has a lot of story to tell."

"I thought you might like it...the man I got it from said he'd stolen it from a library back east. He liked the title. Planned to read it on the journey West but turns out he didn't like it one bit."

"It's about the sea," Henry says, as if that could put the matter to rest all by itself.

"The bonney blue," Jude replies with enthusiasm, the gap in his teeth prominent again.

"The best Christmas present ever I've been given. Even my own dear sweet mother never topped this," Henry confides. He sits up again and his eyes seem lit by a subtle incandescence, looking out somewhere well past the musty tent walls.

"I'm sure glad *my* mother's not *here,* me working Christmas day at the Elysium would give her a fit," Jude answers back.

"Amen to that," Henry says, agreeing. After a few moments he recites a poem he'd just invented for the occasion.

"...On to the Elysium, where the lamp light glows
For Billy King and the blonde-haired beau,
Forward to the Elysium, though it bring but a frown
Oh, the Queen is lost in bloody Tiger Town!"

"You're a damn soft-headed Billy Noodle, if ever there was one. You don't know if you're a gambler, a pistoleer, or a damned *poet*," says Jude with a laugh.

"Ha, why not all three?"

"For now, you're just a casekeep with a big fat book no one likes."

"And I wish I could spend the rest of the day reading it."

"Well, don't start drifting off on the deep now, we got just enough time to eat and get to work."

Something shifted dramatically again in late spring, when Henry traded for a rare Cooper "pocket" double-action pistol. Unlike the Colt, it cocked and fired in one quick pull of the trigger and hid nicely on his slim frame. An unusual gun and an even stranger person who sold it to him. The effusive peddler arrived one day like a sun-crazed diviner. Skin black as pitch, nappy hair grown long enough to pull back in a kind of braid—and gestures wildly eccentric, fitting somehow the deep baritone of his singular patter.

He immediately spread out a number of odd and ends for sale on a piece of black felt—a mirrored case, a folding straight razor with a burled maple handle, a fancy brush with pearl inlay, kitchen items made of tin and copper, a pair of sharp scissors and garnet ring with a deep red stone, some kind of odd dental tool, and the .38 caliber pistol. Henry walks up to have a look. It is all of interest, but the gun leaps out at him.

"The Cooper Double's a rare little item, Irish boy, and I'll be needing at least forty dollars for it," the hawker sings out. His large Stetson had once been white and sported a dark green band with a long feather. He'd shaped and folded an impossibly wide brim into a unique elliptic. The hat a good match somehow for the breadth of his large curving mouth and the strong white teeth.

"I don't have forty dollars, but I need that gun sir," Henry replies, with heat.

"I can feel that. So what *have* you've got Irish boy?" the peddler inquires, looking hard at the kid and folding his arms. The boy's pale blue eyes are a mystery to the diviner, not readable exactly. The man's own eyes have a strange and mysterious sparkle.

"What's your name?" Henry asks, stalling.

"Oscar...Oscar Kitch. On the plantation I was called Othello, which I also like. You can call me any one of them by itself or by the first two in order, or by all three," the peddler answers with a spreading of his arms and a slight bow.

"Well, Kitch, my name is Henry and I will give you everything I have for that gun," he replies, pious as a deacon.

"Ha! Well then what do you have boy, let's see it."

Henry pulls the old Colt he'd bought in Silver City and lays it down. Next he begins to empty his pockets of money, making a show as if it was some magic trick. First, a pile of one-dollar bills pulled from various locations, laid and counted out ceremoniously, two silver dollars from thin air, then four bits. Next a gold-capped tooth. Finally, a chain from around his neck with a locket. He'd won tooth and locket on a wager, but claims to the eccentric wanderer, with a catch in his voice, that it belonged to his mother and the tooth—his uncle—both departed.

"That's a good story my fine little bog-trotter and I don't believe a word of it. Still...we have a deal," says Oscar Kitch, the big mouth stretching open into an enormous grin and a large open hand extending out over the felt. Henry smiles and grips back, hard.

He walks away with the gun and a handful of bullets. And the Ethiopian peddler stares after him still grinning the white teeth bare, arms crossed again between a pair of broad shoulders.

"I forgot to tell you something about the Cooper. Had to dig it out of someone's arse." Henry turns around and Kitch winks at him. "But I cleaned it up right smart."

"Gold is where you find it," Henry replies. The Cooper goes into his belt and his leg kicks out, first his left then the right, feet cutting the dust in the ragged street. It was a dance he'd first seen and learned on Orange Street in the Five Points—the crossing of the djembe and the jig, the shuffle and the reel.

"Masta Jubba and Johnny Diamond could dance no better. The gunsmith will have plenty of ammunition for the Cooper my young lion," Oscar Kitch Othello yells out, looking on with a curious light in his dark eyes.

The gun did have quite a story already and he could see the boy would be adding to it.

"That's a sweet little prize," says Chucho, eyeing the unusual weapon. The Sonoran had returned two days before with Barrett and the mules. They both played faro at Henry's table and were mightily impressed. The kid was doing well in Camp Grant. They'd been back many times on their endless circuit, and each time Henry had come further along.

"You fellows know about guns, I've learned a bit, but how about you schooling me a little more?"

Chucho, being the more advanced practitioner, volunteered to relate what he knew. And not to be outdone, Barrett allowed he had some things to impart as well.

"You know how to take it apart?" Barrett asks the next morning, taking the gun in his big hands.

"No, not exactly."

"Chico, only when you can take the gun apart and keep it clear of slag, put it back together and load it blindfolded, will it return the favor and do something for you, like provide dinner. Or perhaps save your life. *Es el primer orden*!"

"Si, Claro," Henry answers back. Keeping something vitally important clean made perfect sense to him. Chucho's quick hands had the gun in pieces in a matter of seconds. In another quarter hour Henry'd learned the trick as well.

"Pulling the weapon smoothly, firing instantly, hitting your target dead center—*es muy importante*, but second to the first order," Chucho continues patiently. "My tio Francisco taught me many things about the gun, I'm happy to share but you must be more generous at the faro table."

"I'll do what I can," Henry replies with a sly grin.

"Birds on the wing are the best targets. Your trigger finger will be very hungry and very hard to please, and to *please* the trigger finger you must learn to *see* with it," Chucho adds mysteriously, in time Henry came to understand what he meant.

"I might add that pointing the gun *at a man* is a different beast all together," says Barrett.

"I was getting to that. Barrett, this slow-thinking son of a turtle likes to have the last word."

"I've had my gun on a man, and trigger cocked, but he was only a rat in the middle of the night, trying to steal my poke, so I suppose that doesn't really count."

"No chico, that don't count."

Observing the refinements of gun skill, in practice, seemed a hopeless quest—real gun sharks in Hopville being an unlikely occurrence. There were no range wars or barons or high rollers or fancy sporting halls to draw them in.

Moreover, guns are not allowed in Hopville's two saloons, being strictly forbidden by the martinets at the fort and bad for business. Anyone carrying firearms must check them at the door. But it's a lively and venomous crowd on any given night and you best watch your back, for many are still armed.

He'd seen only two displays of temper that had resulted in a square off with firearms. But he learned much from both. In the first incident, one man pulled his hideout, but the other not being armed, was granted a stay until healed with a weapon. The two met in the street to continue their argument. Once reconvened, the newly armed belligerent began to complain loudly about his being so much bigger and so much more of a target than his diminutive opponent.

"I'd say yer at least twice as likely to hit meat," argues the big man.

"Well then, lets chalk out an outline my size on your dumb carcass and anything outside that don't count," the little fellow snapped back impulsively. He hadn't intended to be jocular or any such thing. But it struck both him and the big man, and a few others standing around, as wildly funny. Drunk as they all were—the gunfight devolved into guffaws and was called off.

Henry had darted outside to see the fights conclusion. It could have been a sketch in a variety show but it happened right before him in a kind of drunken glory. Henry took from the failed duel that a deflecting comment, and a joke especially, could be a useful play and a jape should always be in the chamber just as surely as a bullet.

The second gunfight was deadly serious, and Henry observed it as he worked the abacus for Billy King. Something about an argument in the far corner of the Elysium, away from the gaming tables, suddenly caught his attention. Perhaps the way the two men abruptly set their hips and shoulders, as they stood abreast. Next thing they were both pulling.

The man with his back to Henry dropped his right arm, and at the same time yanked at his coat tails with the left as he reached back and lifted the gun out smoothly. And while this was happening the other man fumbled a pull from under his coat—*in front*. Two seconds later he lay on the sagging floors with his blood seeping through the cracks.

The show seemed to slow down while it unfolded, allowing Henry to see the little details with clarity. Wherever your hideout, there must be perfect grace between hands and garment, and an extremely well-rehearsed motion following. No hitch whatsoever, or you'd likely be dead on the floor. The cowboy with the smooth grip from behind was no pistoleer, but he'd sure practiced and perfected that pull.

In early March, a real gun shark arrived in the theatrical personage of William "Russian Bill" Tattenbaum. All heads turned when he strolled into the Elysium. He paused in the doorway, admiring Lotta Crabtree, and giving everyone a chance to admire *him*.

Mr. Tattenbaum stood resplendent in a black single-breasted coat of fine cloth lined with glace silk, a black poplin waistcoat underneath, fancy cuffed sleeves and tightly fit trousers of black pin-striped wool. Matched colts peeking out from under the fancy coat completed the costume impressively.

All of it hanging on his large and vigorous frame with peerless grace. He surrenders the colts at the bar, along with a coin, and turns to the room with a beaming smile glass raised. The performance brought even the tumultuous faro table to a complete halt.

"Good evening to all, my name is William Tattenbaum...friends call me Russian Bill. For I am originally from mother Russia, but henceforth the free-spirited hinterlands of America are my Elysian fields—and I've come a long way to walk the boards of the Elysium Bar—now, good health to all!" The drink tossed back he begins to work the hall, savoring his moment.

"Proud to shake hands with you sir, I was a military man myself," says Russian Bill while pumping a sergeant's arm. "A member of the Czar's Imperial White Hussars, until I struck a superior officer for insulting the honor of my mother, Countess Telfrin."

The accent is suspect, as is the story. But he cuts such a striking and affable figure and plays his part with such energy—that everyone gives him the benefit of the doubt. Even grumpy old Windy Cahill is taken in. He'd been grinding away at Billy King's table and glaring at Henry, but seems awestruck as Russian Bill approaches with outstretched hand.

"It is for that reason I was forced to flee my homelands, good to meet you sir. I like a man with a strong grip, you and I will have a drink and an arm wrestle," Russian Bill says as he releases Cahill's hand.

"Pleased to meet ya, Russian Bill," Windy replies, almost against his will, his brogue thick. The well-dressed stranger before him stands three inches taller and exerts a palpable mesmeric power over one and all.

"Like yourself I'm a long way from home. And naturally, I've come *West*—the greatest landscape on the face of the Earth. It reminds me fondly of the steppe country back home." Next he places a coin in Able Jake's mug. "Love the banjo sir, the minstrel harp."

Russian Bill drinks like a fish and wagers on anything and everything, and as Henry duly notes, rarely lost his stake. He'd draw someone into a bet for whether a man standing across the room, risking at the faro table and obviously on the chaw, would lean to his left or his right to spit. Or whether the next man through the door would be clean-shaven or bearded. Eventually betting, for a heftier sum, that he could defeat any man in the room at arm wrestling. He later announces a display of marksmanship for the morrow behind the Elysium, and of course, with odds and hazards accepted.

His turns at faro were for the sheer wild fun of it, and Russian Bill seems not to mind if the pull box and casekeep went his way, or no. He is particularly fond of reversing a bet at the last moment with a penny on the face card.

"Gentleman copper's the bet. A risky move and for a stout heart only," Henry calls out and the fancy-suited man coppers again.

"Rein it in now gents, time for the pull and to reap!" Henry declares and Billy King pulls. "The pull is a Jack and a three of diamonds and the foreign noble must forfeit, stand aside men and give him room to express himself. You're in the house where faro is king, and Billy King...is the *King* of Faro!"

"Merde!" roars the fancy newcomer, then smiling broadly as he downs another draft of whiskey punch.

It was obvious Mr. Tattenbaum had received a fine education somewhere, for he spoke several languages—unleashing a torrent of French at one point, then German at another, and grandiloquent Spanish to a vaquero later still.

He could also discuss art and literature, even science, with anyone capable of the task. Henry watched it all with the greatest interest and admiration. The man possessed both the common touch *and* sophistication, at the drop of hat.

Several mornings after the grand entrance Henry corners Russian Bill at the Chop House.

"Ah the casekeep, sit down please. Billy King has quite the table! And you, you have great patter and quick hands. Most impressive."

"Thank you, Mr. Tattenbaum, you are an impressive fellow yourself," Henry says with a curious smile. Russian Bill closes the book he was reading.

"I can only be what I am, and my good humor—a product of outrageous health," declares Russian Bill.

"I see you're a reader, have you encountered a novel called *Moby Dick*, by Herman Melville?" Henry decides to sound the depths.

"I'm a well-read man and I've heard of neither book nor author. You have a copy?" Russian Bill asks, after a large bite of bacon and biscuit, and a long sip of coffee to wash it down.

"I do."

"Care to wager on it?"

"No sir I wouldn't, with all due respect. I've grown too fond of it."

"Then you must tell the story."

"It's a nautical adventure. The story of Captain Ahab and his voyage of revenge on a great white whale named Moby Dick."

"Revenge?"

"Moby Dick took the captain's leg, bit it off at the knee, on a previous voyage."

"Ah, I begin to see the pull of it. And this Captain Ahab, what was the cut of his jib?"

"A madman, an ungodly man, but, like a god...Captain Ahab was the king of the sea," Henry adds, eyes searching the handsome face.

"Will you not reconsider a wager on the book?"

Henry shakes his head. The light blue eyes seem to answer Bill's question as much as the shaking of his head, and to pose a number of other questions at the same time. Henry had thought much over the past two days about a new partnership and a way out of Camp Grant.

"How long will you stay Russian Bill?"

"You're a strange lad, but I like you. I'm not entirely sure how long I'll be here. I've come at the invitation of my good friend Captain Owen Smith. We knew each other, in society—back East. We'll have a good long visit and a hunt up-mountain. I'll gamble 'till lady luck turns and then head back down the long road—maybe to Silver City," Russian Bill answers, somewhat cryptically.

"I could tell you a lot about Silver City," Henry states and Russian Bill holds the blue eyes a bit longer. "I lived there nearly four years. Towards the end I started to perform at the Orleans, you'll not want to leave the West without visiting there. A red brick sporting man's palace and second to none."

"And what did your performances consist of?" Russian Bill asks, with growing interest.

"I sang mostly, told some jokes, pranced about in a few melodramas. Even performed *in drag*," confides Henry with a raising of his eyebrows.

"Most impressive, you must give me a song," Russian Bill smiles and *Mollie Darling* comes back forthwith, in a clarion tenor.

The breakfasting crowd, and even the ever-busy Verna Langdon, all stop to listen. A rousing clamor fills the room at songs end and Russian Bill, with folded arms, beams approvingly.

"Well done lad, well done. Have you ever heard an aria or an art song?"

"No sir."

"Owen and I are attending a concert at the fort next Sunday. One of the officer's wives is giving a recital. It's certain to be the epitome of elegance...I insist that you join us."

Henry had never been exposed to art songs, or to a stately military gathering for that matter, other than his brief and ignoble encounter after the incident with the mules and the wharf rats. The concert was to be held in the mess hall, which had been cleared and transformed. Rows of chairs and benches taking the place of the long tables. An upright piano, reasonably in tune, had been placed on a raised platform with a vase of prairie flowers perched upon an elegant little table.

Captain Owen Smith led them into the cavernous building. He seemed a congenial fellow, Henry thought, definitely from the East. He notices a remarkable deference shown by the captain to his eccentric friend.

Three o'clock strikes and the polite murmuring clusters of the officer's elite, begin to break up. Captain Smith motions his guests into the fourth row, Bill seating himself between his two friends.

The young wife of Colonel Peters, a well-trained soprano, no doubt languishing at such a great remove from society—rises on the platform. She smiles at her accompanist, the just-competent Lieutenant Hastings, then a prim curtsy to the audience. She announces her first song as *The Wild Rose*. The beginning strains from the piano flow out, like a simple German folk song, seemingly, and her voice—a dream of romance in high summer.

"Schubert and a poem by Goethe," Russian Bill whispers to Henry with a knowing gleam. Henry can only nod and let the rapturous sounds wash over him, applauding like a madman at the song's conclusion. "Utter nonsense," Bill whispers again, ecstatically. "A boy, a rose in the heather, a prick, a pluck, and death—what does it all mean? Who knows, that's Goethe, and Schubert...*gorgeous*."

Few in the hall understood the language or the story, but the music powerful and whole all by itself. The applause continues and Henry catches a peculiar glance from Captain Smith—as if he wondered why his friend was paying him attentions. Russian Bill seems to notice the look as well and leans toward the captain for a few whispered comments. At the same time, Henry's eyes are drawn to Russian Bill's large hand tapping Captain Smith's knee ever so lightly. The fingertips rested there a moment before withdrawing.

Charlotte Peters concludes her performance an hour later, not fully aware of how powerfully she has moved her audience. She, unused to performing and high entertainment being a rare thing in the wilderness. As they file toward the door Henry is still recovering.

"Your young friend seems overwhelmed," Captain Smith notes politely.

"This was his first concert, of art songs," Bill replies, smiling at the diminutive novitiate at his side.

"Ah, sacred ground," agrees Captain Smith.

A week later Henry received a lesson in the fine art of gun sharking from one who knew it inside out. Russian Bill had been less interested in helping the boy gain a foothold in *this* world, but persistence paid off. The dandy had many insightful tips; about how and where on your body to carry, how to tell whether someone has the courage and experience to fight with his weapon, when to avoid confrontation at all costs, when to talk and when to pull.

"You've definitely got a fine way with your hands, no doubt about that," says Russian Bill after watching Henry draw his pistol from behind his back. He'd perfected the pull, adding some touches of his own.

"Never underestimate a man's inability to feel pain, he may be hopped up or drunk or just plain loco—and if he can't feel pain like a normal person he may well keep coming on despite the bullet you just put in his shoulder or his leg," states Russian Bill, his voice suddenly more serious than Henry had ever heard it.

"Make your first shot count then."

"Yes. You may not get another. Aim at a specific target, the second or third button of his shirt will do nicely. Nail one of those two, or any place in between, and your opponent will drop like a stone."

"Not the head?"

"A head shot is the showiest kind of a mark, most devastating certainly, but riskier to target and hit. If you miss, you'll look like a fool and the consequences could be dire."

"And the belly?"

"It's a slow death but will incapacitate a charging bull." Russian Bill looks down at his young friend and shakes his head. "I do hate to think of you getting in to any such jackpot, to my mind you're more suited for music and refinement."

"Well I hope you're right, but I'll not take any chances—the world is a dangerous place, and it's a long way to the nearest theater," Henry replies. The crooked grin beaming out at his friend like a bright lamp on a dark night.

Sometime later Russian Bill left Fort Grant and Hopville, with a detachment of soldiers and a wallet full of greenbacks. The retreat as abrupt and mysterious as his grand arrival. Henry learns of the departure during his shift and is glum the rest of the night, wishing immediately that he'd worked harder to bring his plan to fruition.

It would have been nice to say goodbye at least, and to thank him again. His lessons in culture and gunplay were worth a great deal. But more than that—he exemplified what resourcefulness, energy, and pluck could accomplish. For seven weeks Russian Bill Tattenbaum strutted through the shit and garbage of Hopville like some outrageous Shakespearean blade. He'd mystified and tricked everyone and yet walked away a hero; proving to Henry, beyond any doubt—that life *is* but a stage—so you might as well write the scenario *and* play the lead.

The blacksmith continues to stir his feud with the sharp-tongued kid, whenever it suits him. The bitter vendetta had carried forth from the summer when it first began into the fall and winter, touching spring and summer again and then fall and winter once more.

Henry grew adept at avoiding Windy, facing him when he chose to, running when necessary. There were quiet periods when Cahill, distracted by other quarrels, would seem to forget him. Weeks and months sometimes pass with the David and Goliath struggle lying fallow. But then a transgression would flame it to life hotter than ever.

Sober he wasn't so bad, at least not quite as violent, and no man would speak ill of Cahill as a tradesman; an excellent blacksmith to be sure. He even sends an occasional heartfelt letter home to his mother.

Encountering the blacksmith drunk can be a chancy thing, however. He bullies any and all, but small fry always the choicest delicacy on the menu. Billy King had become alarmed enough by the near constant warring and harassment, on and off the premises, to have his pit boss intervene. But that had only made matters worse.

Barrett had also made it plain one day, after rolling in to Hopville and discovering Henry with a black eye.

"Windy I'm going to give it to you straight. You're a fine a blacksmith... but an *evil bastard* when it comes to it. Big son-of-a-bitch like you ought to leave scrawny kids like Henry alone, at the very least. The next time you hurt that boy it'll be you and me, and I won't quit until I've put you down hard."

"You better tell him to leave me alone then," Cahill replies. He'd been working the bellows and turned now to stare with contempt. He spat on the floor just missing Barrett's right boot.

"I'll mention it to him. You mind what I said," Barrett answers back, weighing whether he can tolerate Cahill's disrespect.

"I heard you," Cahill replies, as if to say—*go fuck yourself*. The blacksmith knew Barrett was no one to cross. Among other impressive feats, the muleskinner was the only man in Hopville to best Russian Bill at arm wrestling. Still, Cahill knew he wouldn't quit, and no one could make him, not Campbell nor anyone else.

Barrett shook his head and walked away.

On a scorching summer noon, Henry rides back into Hopville from a shooting expedition with a light heart, despite the heat. But when he reigns up sharp to avoid running down a Mexican boy, the mood of the day shifts. The boy had just careened wildly across the street, heedless of traffic.

"*Miguel, que paso*?" Henry shouts and the boy turns his head, revealing a bloody mouth, two missing teeth, a terrified expression. Henry swivels to the right and discovers Windy Cahill and his helper, Braden McGillin, bearing down on him.

"Out of the way ya little cuny," Windy barks.

"Always on the churn," Henry yells back. He rears Dancer and slows the two by cutting back and forth in front of them. Miguel runs on, disappearing into a warren of pens.

"One of these days you're going to have a burning apoplectic fit and fall over dead from the strain," says Henry. He looks at the Blacksmith and at Braden McGillin, a tall, stout Kilkenny man—and clucks his tongue.

"That stupid Mex knocked over me beer, was gonna take it out on his little brown arse. Now I'll take it out of yours," Cahill says.

"Windy I'll 'lope over and get you another bucket of beer, right now, hardly worth depriving that kid of a tooth or me of a little blood. Now just simmer down—I'll fetch two, one for each of you," Henry reasons. He backs his horse away and the two stop advancing. "And a nice piece of jerky besides." This time he'd decided to bargain his way out of trouble and make sure the boy made it home safely. Miguel had been his accomplice in a number of adventures—including the incident with Windy's cot and the rat snake.

As soon as Cahill and McGillin are appeased with pails of beer and a hunk of jerky, Henry went to little Mexico and found Miguel with the curandera. The bruja applying a compress to the hole where two incisors had once been, and the boy's mother standing quietly with a tear running down her cheek.

Henry rests a hand on Miguel's shoulder.

"*Lo siento, amigo.*"

"*Cahill este hombre muy malo,*" Abuelita Hernandez announces. Miguel tries to smile but managing only a grimace.

"Destiny will repay Cahill one day," Henry states.

"Yes, and a good thing," says Abuelita Hernandez. "Thanks for helping Miguel."

"It's nothing. Will you help me?"

"Of course."

Henry rubs his gut and pats his backside grimacing, pretending to be constipated and in need of the strongest kind of incentive to clear his bowels. The comical pantomime succeeds in raising a cackling laugh.

In truth, a vicious little prank had evolved and roiled his brain while he dealt with the Blacksmith and the pails of beer. Windy would be paid back with interest for all the times Henry, and others, had been slapped around and beaten and bloodied. And the curandera would provide the weapon.

She gave him a knowing look.

"Hey handsome, where you been all my life?" Kate always greeted the boy with a cheery come on, for in truth, she cares about him. More than he knew. "What's the long face for? I don't know that I ever seen anything but a smile out of you."

"Sorry Kate, guess I'm getting tired of this damn place."

"We're all tired of it honey."

"Yeah, at least there's your tent. A little slice of heaven it is," Henry offers, the big smile returning.

"Sweetheart, you don't belong here that's for damn sure."

"Oh, I'll leave soon enough. Next fall when it cools off. Been waiting for Jude, we'll go together."

"Good, you don't want to go alone."

"No ma'am I do not want to go alone. It's a lonely place, the barrens, and dangerous as hell. Not a moment's ease out there."

While they talk, Henry is working out of his clothes. He'd been for a bath down in the San Pedro. The soap left a strong alkali scent on his skin and it made him uncomfortable. It was not the most alluring of smells. But the hard spice meant *clean* to Cat Eyed Kate and she loves him for it.

"I smell like a bar of soap, hope you don't mind."

"Smells like home," says Kate when he nuzzles into her arms.

"Where's home, pretty lady?"

"Pine Bluff, Arkansas, little house a stone's throw from the big river. When I was a girl, mother used to say I could go adventuring with my friend's as far as I wanted, but never go further than I could get back on my own. When I got older, all I wanted was to get away and just keep going. Now I'd give anything to see Pine Bluff again."

Henry could see his mood had infected Kate now as well. Melancholy is like that in the wilds, jumping from one person to the next like a fever. Everyone had left something precious back in the world, something they'd likely never see again. A good thing not to dwell on it.

A typical hell-roarin Friday night is unfolding for Jude and Henry, akin to all the wild Friday nights that went before it in Tiger Town. Billy King wears a silver vest under a frock coat and a bowler cocked steeply. He stands presiding over the left table, and his partner, Sam Strickland, works the table to the right, sporting a plaid suit of yellow and brown. Jude in black and Henry wearing the dark green suit from his days at the Orleans—stand each by their banker. A busy night unfolds, loud and lewd.

Two scuffles have broken out already, one a soldier's fight and the other a civilian dispute with knives that got shoved out into the street. Nothing yet had occurred between soldier and civilian, all being at pains to avoid such a risky affair.

Midway through Henry's shift, the blacksmith appears—stewed as a boiled owl.

"Back away cunt and let a man step to table," Windy yelled out as he lumbered toward the oval. The man he shouted at was a thick-set private, though his parade dress coat had been stripped off earlier in the stifling heat.

"Wait yer time Windy, I have this spot and I'm staying exactly right here."

"We'll see about that," Windy answers, grabbing the man by his shoulder and shoving him out of the way. Cahill's friend and business partner, Brady MaGillin, looms menacingly at his side. They could have stood off every man there, drunk or no, and the displaced private decides to investigate the bar, leaving his little bet on the table along with his pride. It was by far the better idea.

Cahill's forge had grown white hot since the night the casekeep slipped a laxative into his whiskey—and everyone knew it. The curandera had promised its effectiveness and she spoke the truth. Later Windy ran from the saloon letting go in spectacular fashion and the casekeep trying hard to contain his laughter.

Shitting his pants for all to see marked a turning point for Windy. Their nasty little war was on again and this time he was after more than just a little blood.

"Calling the turn, gentleman, what's it gonna be. Loser, winner, or the *hock*? If you don't risk a King, can't bed the *Queen*. Lay'em down, gents. Last two cards and four to one odds both ways. You're in Tiger Town now, where faro is king and *Billy King*...is the King of Faro," Henry sings out the familiar phrase with the panache of a first-rate huckster.

"Shut yer hole McCarty you big-eared cunt," shouts the soaked blacksmith.

He kept cursing and drinking on into the night amongst the jostling crowd—watching the boy and the keep and the thirteen cards, and finally the dealer box. His eyes have the red glow of a devil. Braden maintains a position to one side, waiting for the moment he knows is coming.

Finally, at the end of another hand, Cahill places a bet-reversing copper on the King of Clubs. Henry lifts his eyes. Both casekeep and banker have been at pains to keep the game straight, and Billy makes a slight gesture with his chin—but it's a losing bet. Windy slams his fist on the table:

"I don't know how you two are pulling the cheat, shaved cards or a crooked dealer box or sticky fingers, but goddammit, McCarty, you've been fockin me all night."

"The fickle goddess always returns with a teaser, Mr. Cahill, if you but give her the *chance*! A touch of the ardent will put things to right. Have a drink on the house, Mr. Cahill. You're just bucking the tiger, not me."

"And you're a motherless, lyin little cunt!"

"Nicely put," says Henry.

"You're off the board for now, Cahill," Billy King shouts.

"You shut yer gob, Billy fockin King, you slick bastard—stood there and watched him do it."

Henry starts to back away, but too late, Cahill slaps him hard. The blow knocks Henry between the two faro tables.

"You've mouthed off and cheated me for the last time you fockin little ponce."

The banker's eyes go to the pit boss, Eldon, who steps toward Cahill lifting a blackjack out of his pocket. McGillin intervenes, coming up from behind just as the bouncer begins to raise his arm—laying a bowie knife to his ear.

"Let 'em fight."

"Won't be much of a fight. And if you take an ear, I take an eye," the pit boss hisses.

A big right-cross misses as Cahill moves in and the two faro tables are wrested out of harm's way, just in time.

Cahill misses again and Henry counterpunches and dances. Cahill's next blow does connect, breaking Henry's nose and knocking him to the floor. There is a murmured reaction and a sinking sensation in the room. Cahill drops down on top of the boy and with a cock of the head, starts to rowel punches right and left.

Billy King is caught in an agonizing quandary; whether or not to pull his derringer.

"You've had your way, Cahill, now get the hell off him."

But no letting up, and Henry takes it—managing to avoid some of the damage, but one clout away from a lasting darkness.

"You're going to kill the boy, for god's sake," Billy King shouts. His hand starts to reach to his pocket.

Dizzied from the exertion, Cahill suddenly quits swinging and slouches to one side, loosening Henry's left arm. The drunken oaf wheezes in a breath and grins. His arm swings back.

There is a sudden concussive roar, a deep groan—an explosion of smoke as the big man sags over onto the floor. Henry gets to his feet amidst curls of hot vapor, keeping the Cooper pointed at McGillin. Blood streaming down his face and right eye swollen shut—he backs out of the room.

Eldon pivots, swinging the blackjack. He whips it around with enough force to drop McGillin to the floor. Having the knife laid up to his ear was a great irritation *and* a professional embarrassment—but they were square now.

"You boys take Windy over to the fort. Dr. Morris might be able to do something for him," says Billy King to a group of soldiers. "Eldon, see that Mr. McGillin finds his way out."

Braden begins to crawl over to Cahill, blood oozing from behind his ear. He looks at the hole in his friend's gut, knowing there's no hope. "Can't move my legs," groans Cahill. He'd been reamed through from belly to backbone with a lightning bolt.

Four soldiers gather around, and it takes them all to lift the blacksmith off the floor. One man slips in the dark blood pooled there. The pit boss shoves Braden McGillin out into the street, just behind the soldiers with his gut shot friend.

"Sam, Jude, help me get the tables back in place," Billy commands, steady like, though he's as stunned as anyone else. "Eldon get the mop." When casekeep and banker share a glance, they both look as if the bullet might've hit them.

"That's the last we'll see of Henry," says Jude. He could easily have thrown up, thinking of what just happened and what would come next for his friend.

Running on instinct and adrenaline, Henry races down the side of the Lion's Den. Blood flowing heavy, blurring the one open eye. Lifting up the tent next to his cot and sliding in far enough to grab his bag, he decides to lift the sombrero underneath the next bed before sliding out again. He squinted at a fellow rising up in his bed—gave him a hell of a start.

Henry stumbles on through the crooked streets, keeping to the shadows. He trips over a pile of garbage, spittin blood but up quickly amidst a scurry of rats and on to the stable. It all seems to be happening to someone at the far end of a dark corridor. Somehow Henry gets Dancer saddled, pulls himself up and heads to the gate.

But the tall Kilkeeny man is standing there in his way.

"You killed Windy, you sorry little shit. I'll be returning the favor now," says Braden, gun pointed but the man swaying slightly and the boy already on the move.

In the middle of the declaration, Henry disappears over the side of Dancer; his right foot in the stirrup and right hand turning the horse, left slapping Dancer's flank and grabbing for a handhold. McGillin fires, managing to take off a chunk of the cantle but missing the boy and horse entirely, and blinding himself for a second with the muzzle flash.

"Son-of-a-bitch."

That second is all they need. Dancer and her side rider hurtle back into the corral to mix with the agitated, rearing horses. Henry remounts firing his pistol into the air—the herd spooks to either side and closes behind.

Braden stumbles into the pen firing but the casekeep is gone. In a heartbeat they're over the back fence and thundering away into the outer dark. McGillin slumps against the railing and fires twice more.

The gun flashes behind him and Henry hangs on, taking inventory. There's a box of cartridges and some grain, a sharp pocketknife, the bota is empty but he can fill it at the river. He has some food but not much. Wrapped up at the bottom of his poke is a ball of queso blanco, some jerky bought the day before, and some hard candy; two pieces of peppermint, three pieces of horehound, and five lemon drops—his favorite. Just some victuals and treats he's kept on hand but not nearly enough for the journey ahead. It's something at least, and at the last moment he'd grabbed the two books—one a penny dreadful, the other his obscure novel. The inventory fell before his eyes and continued to fall, then felt himself falling too and no stopping—straight down into an abyss.

They crossed the San Pedro and he came awake, leaning the bota down to fill. He thought to tie himself to the saddle and leave it to Dancer. As he dropped back down into the dark, he put his hand on Dancer's mane, gripping the hair with the last of his strength. He knew if any creature alive could carry him safely back across the barrens—she could.

4

Under his stolen sombrero the purpled right eye is still closed; a cut above the scalp line had bled profusely, the broken nose he'd reset is a puffed mess, upper lip split in two places and scabbing something fierce. And the sun bearing down on him like the eye of an angry god.

"We're on the dodge now, and no mistake, my beauty. We'll get clean away and take no chances and henceforth, you shall know me by an alias... Kid Antrim." Dancer snorts, as if in response and Henry tries to smile. He only gets about half-way there and gives it up.

The kid had earned himself a badge of courage and the festering scar of a killer. Another kind of merit was accruing for wayfaring in the desert alone, again, this time with a busted head. He'd hated leaving the muleskinner road—but it had come time to roll the bones and head out into absolute wilderness.

A new discipline begins. One centered around water and grass, staying on an easterly course, using the markers in the landscape and in the sky. The North Star and the Big Dipper greeting him at night, handle to the West and dipper toward the east. His mother had called it King David's Chariot and in late summer it rides low in the sky, on and on toward the morning sun. He looked for it in the dark night to read the hour and settle his nerves.

The sun has another story to tell, but like an oracle of old—the cost of knowledge is always high.

Out on the barrens, away from the river—finding water and keeping your direction is a pathfinder's challenge and a gambler's choice. Dancer can survive on the rough forage available here and there and go a day without water, a second if required, but on the third water must be found.

It is the third day.

What looks to be a deep cut slashes across the lowering plain ahead of him. Soon they'll drop down into it and maybe find a seep spring or a creek. He wishes he could sing or whistle, but his split lip is still too sore to allow it. His tongue stuck on the roof of his mouth—feels like two pieces of sandpaper rubbing together. Just no spit, only dry heat and dust and grit.

His mind is never short of dreams though, or questions. The farther he goes into the unimaginable isolation, with the harsh demands of the sun plaguing every step—the harder he works to keep it all at bay.

There are long conversations in Spanish, and prurient explorations with an imaginary querida, through layers of diaphanous lace down to a final glory of flesh. He sings songs in his head, embellishing them with first one instrument and then another. He recalls stories in the greatest detail, sometimes inventing new plot lines and adventures.

A talk with God in the morning, and one with his mother just now. They both were angry.

"Well dancer, shall we see what fate has in store? We may yet tell God to pike off," Henry croaks out in a harsh whisper, his eyes searching the bottom of the canyon.

They work down fifty feet and at least find cooler air in the deep shadows. Another half an hour and further down—they find a clear spring. He looks about warily, other animals will covet this treasure. Shocked at his appearance, he pauses only a moment before plunging his head down into the cool water.

The next day both eyes are open, and the lips are healed up enough to sing. That alone changes everything. *All the purest things seem to come together when I sing,* he thinks. The smartest men probably think too much and don't sing enough, is the next thought. The day begins to pass, more easily than the ones before it.

Oh, had she but told me before she disordered me,
Had she but told me of her malady in time,
I might have got pills and salts of white mercury,

But now I'm cut down in the height of my prime.
Get six young soldiers to carry my coffin,
Six young gir...

Dancer has already caught the unnerving scent. She rears straight up and drops Henry on his feet, stopping the chorus mid-phrase. He has the pistol out in an instant and aimed at the big rattlesnake directly in their path, killing it with a second shot.

Henry walks over to admire the animal, grabbing the big snake and letting out a whoop. He lifts up the enormous specimen, longer than he is tall, with exuberant pride.

"Hopmagundy!"

Soon a fire is blazing at the foot of a magnificent outcropping of red rock. He'd been angling toward it when they came on the rattler. The sandstone bluff stands aloof and stoic like an ancient centurion. It stands on higher ground, and the encircling dirt porch offers a view of all approaches for miles around. An excellent place to bed down for the night.

He notices strange markings up under a ledge; concentric circles and curious animals, round human faces with almond eyes. Ancestors of the current natives, he supposes. The striking artistry of their rock carvings is not lost on him, but it's been a long haul since the last hot meal.

He removes his shirt and gets right to the grisly work.

Henry opens his pocketknife, slits the rattler down the middle of its belly and begins to neatly peel the skin away. It comes off in one long piece, his boot on the stump of its head and the dead snake fighting and writhing all the way.

Extending his arm, the big gray muscle wraps around tight, in a last fury. The guts are pulled next and the meat cut into chunks and laid out on a rock. After a short walk into the chaparral, Henry is back with sage and saltbush to rub onto his dinner.

The mesquite stump fire banked now and the snake spitted out over gleaming coals. Roasted well-done and tasting like chicken, *la serpiente de cascabel* is eaten with the greatest relish in the paling dusk. He rings a good portion of the meat on a short loop of hide. Next day it will be hung on the saddle horn to cure.

An immense vault of sparkling stars above and with a full stomach, the darkness feels almost benevolent. Henry takes note of the familiar constellations with a contented smile. They seem like old friends now:

Cassiopeia, Cygnus, the Big Dipper, the Seven Sisters, Orion, and best of all—the mighty Polaris.

Out in the desert somewhere a pack of coyotes, likely coming in off a hunt, start to sing him to his bed. There was little good sleep to be had the first few nights and he begins to drift hard away into dreams.

Henry finds himself racing along a ridge atop the fastest horse he's ever ridden. The night sky envelopes his entire point of view up and down, as if he'd ridden out into thin air and the immeasurable had opened for him alone.

Suddenly a thudding blast of wind knocks him from the saddle.

He awakens wide-eyed, unsure if the sound was a dream or reality. But dust seems to have been stirred and Dancer is reacting to something out in the dark.

Horse and boy stare into a night gone utterly still. But then another peculiar airy sound breaks the unearthly quiet—a steady tapping begins, as if someone were testing the resonant quality of rock—but the sound somehow completely unreal.

The tapping stops and in the silence are sounds even more uncanny and frightening. Something akin to the fluttering of leathery wings, a crackling and rippling of joints, a low thud—like something huge and unknown prowling out in the dark.

The hair on the back of his neck stands straight up and his guts are aquiver. Nothing in his life had prepared him for this moment. Yet, intuition and fear prompt him to fight back. He fights with a sound of his own—the first song that enters his mind—another verse of "The Unfortunate Rake."

Incredibly, it works. As long as he sings, the night visitor is held at bay. As soon as he stops, it returns. And somewhere along in the ordeal he begins to understand the event for what it is, a profoundly awkward conversation. Far easier to talk than listen.

Chucho had said the desert was full of ghosts.

He was right.

Much deeper into the night, boy and horse finally hear something they can place accurately; the low gurgling growl of a cat, a jaguarondi maybe, or a mountain lion. Dancer lifts his head and snorts and Henry grips his pistol a bit tighter. He reaches again to fuel the fire, this time with a bit of a smile.

"I guess we can sleep when we get old."

At first light the boy is packed and riding away from the centurion stone at a fast trot, a ring of snake meat jostling from the saddle horn. From a distance he reins up to look back a last time.

The red butte transforms, only for a moment, into a misshapen face glowering over the desert. After an almost imperceptible nod he turns back to the east and clucks his tongue.

"Where was God in all of that, eh Dancer?"

The day is a harsh and glaring reality. Exhausted, Henry soldiers on without his usual high spirits. All around him the enigmatic desert bares a new and terrible aspect, as if it had finally revealed its darkest secret—and watched now to see if he would be undone by it.

In the afternoon, water is once again a problem. Nothing so heartrending as a dry waterhole in the barrens, and they'd ridden by one already. Between catnaps he scans the horizon. There's not much to see except an endless stretch of ephedra and skunk bush and cactus. Passing a rare flowering agave provides some relief to the eye at least. With a machete he could hack out the base and suck sweet nectar from the root, only there is no machete. The magnificent stalk of the flower meant death for the agave; death is everywhere he thought—only it's alive. Henry soon falls asleep again and the mare keeps moving forward. It's more than a catnap this time, and a good chunk of the day passes.

He falls into another tortured dream.

Awakening with a throat so dry he can't even swallow, Henry discovers they've also stopped moving. There's a sharp odor and a sucking and snuffling sound. He opens his eyes to squint out from under the sombrero at an amazing sight.

Dancer has her mouth down in a small seep spring. It's just a tiny puddle of water spreading out no more than a couple of feet from the base of a rock cleft. They'd either stumbled on it or her equine nose led her there while he slept. He slides down next to Dancer and is immediately dismayed to see a bluish green film overlaying the surface. Cupping his hands, he sniffs at it before taking a drink. After one swallow he spits the rest of the chalky liquid out.

"Well shite. Drink much of this'n we'll be in worse shape than we are now. Hope to God you haven't already. Come away, girl, you've had all you can have."

Dancer keeps jerking her head around as he leads on. He ties her to a bush and goes back to fill the bota. No more than a few mouthfuls a day. Some of it can be used to wet a bandana. He doesn't know what the spring carried, copper maybe.

"We'll be at the Rio Grande tomorrow, with any luck. Just have to keep moving." Back into the saddle with a shrug and a look of genuine misery. *God is testing me, or punishing me, or maybe teaching me,* he thinks. Maybe all three. The schooling had interlaced itself with the heat and the darkness and the more he tried to ignore it—the louder it spoke.

Somehow, he'd known the exact moment when Cahill died. A strange sensation in his gut and heart nearly lifted him out of the saddle the first morning out. An uneasy, tickling pull, as if the blacksmith had some claim on his soul and had reached out to take a portion of it.

The curandera's parable of God and Death continued to needle him as well—as it had since the day he first heard it. That story set his old notion of religion on its ear and everything about his sojourn turned it further still. Perhaps God *was* a bit of a trickster, and other dark beings existed with power over life and destiny. And perhaps the darker beings were not all bad, just as God was perhaps not all good.

And the garbled prophecy, he had ignored it for a year. But out here it haunted him like a ghost from another world. Like the night visitor with its impenetrable story, its passionate yearning to communicate some dark secret—and suddenly listening to the unknown language as if it was all part of a great and incomprehensible plan—but he with only his intuition to guide him.

Whatever it meant, however it all fit together, he knew who he was in the story; the poor man with the stolen chicken telling God to pike off.

The reddish waters of the northern Rio Grande flow broad and shallow around a wide bend, cutting south to Texas through dead-flat bottomland lush with river life. Henry and Dancer approach from the west at a fast canter, a smile breaking in on his mottled face and the horse whinnying.

At river's edge Henry is quickly removing boots and gun and jumping down to plunge headlong in, drinking as he swims. He rolls over onto his back and yells out with the sheer joy of being wet and cool from head to toe. Dancer drops her head to water to drink and drink.

An untroubled day begins to pass into afternoon. While the sun burns and the river spreads wide as a lake, Henry lies reading in the shade of a cottonwood with a lemon drop in his mouth. Dancer grazes in the abundant wheatgrass with equal contentment, now and then lifting her majestic head to roll out a soft nicker.

The Sacramento Mountains reach up from the desert floor like a colossal rampart, separating the high desert from the plains with blunt efficiency. Looking up at the crest, he wonders how much farther to the settlements and ranches on the other side. Tales of Mescalero Apaches had reached his ears; they are only partly subdued, less so than the Chiricahua around Camp Grant—is what he'd heard. But trying to skirt the range to avoid them is out of the question. The only trail for him is over the mountain and the boy has to admit, the rocky and misshapen clefts seem forbidden as the red butte in the desert.

"Well shit," Henry whispers. He'd come a long way to seek his fortune in the land just to the north and east of where he now stood. With a cluck of the tongue and a grin, the former entertainer and casekeep rides forward—and up.

There's a maze of trails at first, but the steepest path seems to beckon. It winds higher and higher above the basin, and more than once he pauses to take in the extraordinary view. A stretch of white sand dunes shimmer along a thin line to the north. Jagged sawtooth mountains lie just beyond, blue and sharp on the western horizon. Overhanging all of it—a massive corridor of cumulus clouds sailing down to Mexico.

Once Dancer tops the last ridge and carries him into a green valley, it feels almost as if the son of Erin has found his way home. The green trail winds through a chain of lovely cool meadows. A degree or two lower and it would be chilly, but instead, the temperature is at a twain of indescribable comfort. After the long ride through unrelenting oven-like heat, and the frigid nights full of mysteries better left alone—to be so extraordinarily comfortable is an indescribable magic.

The steep sides of the valley are covered with Fir, Pine, and shimmering Aspens. The vale itself festooned with blossoms of every hue, and a little creek singing out to him as they pass.

His own hat back on his head now, at its cocky tilt, and a happy fellow underneath. Somehow, he'd not forgotten the little skimmer in the chaos of his departure. He must have grabbed it instinctively getting up from the floor of the Elysium. There it was the next day—stuffed in his bag.

The conqueror of deserts reins up by the creek for a swim. He can't resist the water and its effect on body and soul, not to mention clothes. The last piece of dried snake meat for a repast, and again, as he sits admiring the glorious green country all around him—a bit of heaven in his mouth with the last lemon drop.

Lunch over, he pulls out the bulky novel and begins to read. He tries to keep one eye on his surroundings but is quickly subsumed into the narrative and faraway, out on the ocean—where a towering succession of booms and billowing sheets rise above the quarterdeck and old Ahab has eyes on the horizon.

The afternoon begins to unfold as a rousing literary excursion, with intervals of admiring the flowers all about and trout in the brook, then back to the story. It was his second journey through *Moby Dick*. The book is an education in itself; full of intriguing classical allusions that baffled him, but also brimming with sea knowledge, humanity, and raw adventure. He drank it all in like cool water in the desert.

The strange voyage might well have gone on all day—but his schooling is abruptly, rudely, interrupted.

Henry's eyes jerk up from the page at the sound of hooves, eyes immediately drawn to a small band of Apaches thundering down out of the pines. They come at him from two sides, surrounding him against the unscalable cliff to his back. A hunting party of six fierce looking men wheel around the boy and an angry cacophony of nasal and guttural sounds hit him like a fist.

"What are you doing here, stupid white boy. You are trespassing."

"It looks like someone has tried to kill you already. We will finish you off."

"I can hear your mother wailing already."

Henry recognizes danger with the first taunt. He does know some Apache, a few words at least.

"*Ya-ah-tay*," Henry begins, doing his best to sound respectful and undaunted. "*Ya-ah-tay.*" He meets each man's eye. Then pointing to the west and then to the east, he connects the two points with an arcing gesture of his arm to indicate a long journey and a destination well beyond where they stand now.

"*Haadi'a*," says Henry, pointing to himself he sings a scrap of an Irish air.

"*Soy un jugador*." Henry substitutes Spanish and smiles while pretending to roll dice. "*Ash.*" Looking them in the eyes again. "*Ash.*"

The youngest and wildest brave argues for taking the horse and killing the foolish white boy outright.

"Chisum and his devils are always stealing our horses. I would kill this little fool, leave his meat for the coyotes, and take the horse. It is a fine animal and owed to us."

There are nods and grunts of approval amongst the hunting party. But the eldest, a streak of gray in his braided hair—counsels against such rash behavior.

"This little gambler carries big medicine, if you can't feel that...you've been drinking too much popskull and eating too much agency beef. I think he is just a lost boy. He says he is a singer and a gambler, so am I. Killing him feels bad to me and not worth the trouble it might cause.

"I feel something, old man, but I don't know what it is. I think he is some kind of trickster."

Henry knows he must make his play now. Dismounting, he slowly walks Dancer toward the angry Mescalero arguing loudest for his death, holding out the reins with a solemn, deferential nod.

After an eternity, the young brave finally takes Dancer. There is no doubt it is a meaningful gift—there are tears in Henry's eyes as he gives her a final caress.

"She is a good horse...*un buen caballo.*"

The boy begins to sing, startling the Mescaleros. A showy Gaelic air with leaps and trills—just two verses and a chorus, and an unflinching gaze.

A hard silence follows. Stoic unreadable faces stare back at him. They certainly weren't clapping, but neither had they tried to stop him. The had sat their mounts and listened. Finally, the angry one grunts and nods.

They pause one by one to shout out a final insult, or compliment. Dancer is nearly out of sight, still complaining and calling out to him. His wet eyes follow her up mountain until they're gone and the valley still again.

Nothing for it but to keep moving. With a shrug and another cluck of the tongue, he slings the bag over his shoulder and takes the first step.

So much for a pleasant excursion in an Irish vale. Definitely Indian land and he'd paid the toll. But perhaps he'd made a bigger gesture than he knew, to a stranger and more mysterious god than an Irish priest could ever imagine. Or so he wished, walking on through a field of waist-high thistle. More than ever he felt like the pauper with his stolen chicken, wondering if

Death waited up ahead to stuff him in his bag or set a magnificent treasure before him.

Being set afoot is about the worst inconvenience that can befall a man in the West. To suffer that fate is to be severely disadvantaged and humiliated in the same breath. Both strength and pride are beginning to wane, but Henry straggles on. The snake meat and the bota are gone. There had been water all along the valley, but he'd not seen any all afternoon as he continued east.

On and on, his feet badly used up and blistered—they feel as if they're on fire. The past mile of the narrow trail had gone by with eyes half-closed. His head feels as if he'd been beaten anew. Henry tries to think of good things, sweet memories, but other visions keep crowding in.

He seems to hear gulls crying in the wind. The taste of salt and brilliant light glittering on the sound—the surf lapping at their feet, his little hand in hers. A grand schooner rips across the bay. Catherine turns. Her sunny laugh and blond hair lift on the wind, fine and pure, fading away into the blue.

Blue turns to gray and the sky fills with a choking mist. An enormous mass of people, a terrible roaring and a giant carrying him forward into the dark.

He clasps his mother's hand tightly with both of his, and the blond hair mixed now with streaks of gray, her chest heaving and the death rattle beginning.

He forces his eyes to open, aware of an abrupt change in his surroundings. His legs have carried him to the edge of a promontory, an immense supple plain rippling below like a great ocean. It seems to roll away forever.

Henry looks out at the yellow sea with eyes suddenly clear. The sky above is a deep cerulean blue and enormous white clouds tower straight up into the heavens. Down below a line of trees and a ranch house far out on the waves.

5

Sunday afternoon is often a restive time at the Jones ranch, no church within riding distance but the big noon meal eaten with a certain reverence, the blessing a bit longer, and the family allowed to be at ease afterwards.

But this Sunday is different. Ma'am Jones is uneasy and hoping her husband will return soon. His trip to see a quarrelsome neighbor about their cattle getting mixed together has her worried. The man is known to be violent. She'd begged him to wait and go in the morning, but when something needed doing Heiskell could no more wait on it than stop the sun from setting.

She keeps a weather eye on the horizon, and on the brood of children at play in the dirt yard. Two teenage boys sit nearby, one of them cleaning a shotgun. The smiling crow's-feet around her eyes run in two deep furrows, one curving fold of skin trying to overlap the other.

Noticing an unusual movement about a hundred yards out, she stands up and the careworn eyes sharpen. Not sure what kind of trouble it might be, she hurries the kids up onto the porch.

"Load that shotgun, Buck."

Buck with the twelve-bore and his mother with arms akimbo wait out a few tense moments. But a ragged boy comes staggering out of the scrub piñon, waving and hallowing, and not any kind of danger at all.

"Hello to the house, my name's Henry McCarty and I'm surely glad to see you. Apaches took my horse and I'm in a bad way."

"Good lord. Buck, run out there and help the boy."

"I saw your place from up in the foothills, thought I'd never get here," says Henry. Putting weight on either foot a big problem now, he gladly throws his arm over Buck's shoulder and the strong-armed teenager practically carries him to the house.

"Well, son, you are a sight. Let's get you inside. Boys fetch us water. Plenty," Ma'am Jones commands, shaking her head but smiling broadly.

The lamps are lit, and a gallery of curious young eyes surrounds the grinning boy as his boots are slowly and painfully removed.

"You'll be going barefoot a while."

The youngest children start to giggle at the comic faces Henry is somehow managing, despite his desperate condition.

"Did you get in a fight?" Petey cries out, with a four-year old's innocent curiosity about the bruises still decorating Henry's face.

"I want all of you to find something to do besides bother our guest."

"They're not bothering me," Henry replies. To be amongst a large wholesome clan again like old times and almost overwhelming, like he'd died somewhere up there on the mountain and had now arrived in heaven.

After about a gallon of fresh spring water and some hearty food, an extraordinary peace begins to settle over him. The salve Ma'am Jones rubbed into his blistered feet doing some good as well.

"How'd ya get away from the 'Paches?" Gracie asks.

"Did you shoot'em?" Petey interjects, his eyes like saucers.

The man of the house, Heiskell Jones, walks through the door before he can answer.

"Papaw's home."

"Come see the lost boy Papaw! His name's Henry."

Ma'am looks at her husband, home at last. Her face expresses plainly what she's thinking—you near ruined my Sunday with worry and I hope you're satisfied now.

"I believe this young man's been to hell and back, but he's safe now, and so are you," says Ma'am.

"Tell me some of the story son, not every day a full-grown boy drops out of the sky," Heiskell asks, anxious to avoid his wife's displeasure.

Henry begins to regale the family with a few details of his sojourn, omitting certain unfortunate particulars and creatively embroidering others, and finally, settling into a real story—the *ghost* story.

"...the spook had kept me up till dawn, howling and tapping and make all sorts of strange noises and me singing to beat the band, to keep the spirit world at bay." He winks at the smallest children. "I was never so happy to see the sun rise in all my life. But the bota was empty, had been since the afternoon before and Dancer going on her third day without. So, what do I do? We hit the trail and soon enough I drift off under my sombrero and I take me a long nap and have all sorts of crazy dreams. But when I wake up, there's Dancer having a good long drink from a little seep. She'd found it all on her own and saved both our hides. And that's the story of two days on the barrens. And my first, last, and only encounter with ole Scratch...I hope!"

The children applaud for all their worth, the smallest ones hopping up and dancing around their guest as if he were a conquering hero.

Heiskell Jones sat through the performance smoking his pipe, and grinning hard at the end—figuring it to be a tall tale, but maybe not all of it. He knows there are strange things out there, in the desert and the mountains, and challenges that could defeat a grown man ten times over before noon. And this boy had definitely seen the elephant.

"Tell us about your big fight."

"There was a man back in Arizona, we had a dispute, worked me over pretty good. But I got away."

"And your family?"

"My parents have both passed. Mother had the consumption and I lost my father in the big war. I have a stepfather, but he went to the gold fields as soon as mother passed. My older brother Joe moved on, too."

Ma'am Jones listens to it all with an ache in her big heart, knowing there is more to it and wondering how this ragged blue-eyed boy could have survived everything he'd been through.

"Well, Henry, you're among friends now. And you're welcome to stay here as long as you like," Ma'am Jones offers, her eyes full of compassion.

Heiskell continues to smoke his pipe. He looks at the boy and then his wife, and nods.

"I'm pretty well educated. I can give the children lessons while I heal up—in grammar, and mathematics, and history."

"I don't wanna be schooled," Petey sings out with a big frown.

"I know games, too, and some magic." Henry winks and shines the big grin on the whole family.

A week passes before he can put his boots on again. Henry spends much of that time with the children, singing them songs and playing and, more importantly, making a wholehearted effort at improving their minds. Each morning he sits before the hearth with a makeshift blackboard and gives the promised lessons, holding forth like his teacher back in Silver City—Dr J. Webster himself.

"Who can tell me the name of our new president?"

"Rutherford B. Hayes. Yankee Republican stole his way into office, is what Pap said," says Buck, the oldest and smartest of the bunch.

"Yes, a close election, a disputed election, only won because he agreed to give the Democrats what they most wanted—federal troops out of the South. I read that in the *Santa Fe New Mexican*. *Never* pass on a chance to read a newspaper and read every bit of it. These noggins of ours are big for a reason." He raps the side of his head. "They're meant to hold a treasure trove. Just have to find the trap door and pour it in." Searching for a latch with both hands and then pressing a spot on the top of his head, Henry opens the doors and pretends to tip a jug full of knowledge into his brain.

"Can we play games now? Let's play Squeak, Piggy, Squeak or Throwing the Smile," Gracie squeals. She is seven and full of ginger and ready to bust after sitting still for an hour.

"All right, Gracie. Throwing the Smile."

The class has grown restless, but Henry also managed to give them a few kernels of knowledge that might stick. He also knows when it's time to play.

The object of the game being *not* to smile, a tremendous dare and a delicious provocation is laid bare and irresistible for any child—doomed to failure, of course, but there's delicious fun to be had in the trying.

Henry has the kids, including the two oldest, Buck and Jim, all gathered in a circle. One by one they titter into giggles and are "out" of the circle. Each must pay a small forfeit, a button or a marble or a pretty rock. Buck is the last one to go in the middle, and the oldest and most serious of the children has a few extraordinary faces of his own to pull. The cross-eyed puckered persimmon face manages to crack up his teacher, finally, and Henry's forfeit is a perfect arrowhead.

"That's all I've got to forfeit Buck, found it out on the barrens." Henry has grown close to all the kids, but Buck is his prize student.

"That's a heck of an arrowhead, I've never seen one like it. It's not Apache."

"No, some other people lived out there a long time ago. Comes from them."

"It's so pretty," says Gracie.

"I want one, too!" Petey demands, his face pouting up.

"Well, we'll see about that. In the meantime, how about I show you a magic trick? I'll do the trick and then I'll show you all how it's done!" An excited chorus of approval erupts from the children.

Henry and Buck walk out past the barn after dinner, on out to a low ridge overlooking the southern half of the Jones range. Buck goes there often, just to sit and smoke and be on his own. A few stars are popping out over head and a giant orange moon rising up like a goddess of old. A giant harvest moon, the singing moon—the moon of war.

They look up at it while Buck rolls a smoke, and the talk moves onto a subject of great interest to them both.

"There aren't many white girls in this country, but there's Mexican girls aplenty. At the village dances...you see the prettiest little things, hard to meet though. You have to know how to dance, and *habla español*."

"I'm guessing you don't know how to do either one?"

"I can speak a little Spanish, but I sure as hell can't strut a fandango," Buck answers back with a defeated shrug.

"I can help with that, it's just a quick fancy waltz. Mother and I used to go to the bailes in Silver City. We learned the fandangos together. Spanish, too," says Henry. A prideful memory, those Saturday nights, himself hardly more than a button but already a fine dancer.

"They say a moon like that means something's about to change." Buck's face, earnest and straightforward, is ablaze in a red flare as he lights a cigarette.

"Something's always about to change," Henry replies.

The talk drifts to the country around them—Lincoln County, the largest county in America. More than one New England state would fit inside its borders.

"I knew a fellow in Arizona, used to talk about Lincoln County, all the time. I've pretty much made a beeline straight for it. I hear there's big doin's and dangerous men. Lawrence Murphy and John Chisum." Henry pronounces these two names with energy and respect.

"Well, they say Chisum stays out of it now. Hunkers down with his eighty thousand cows out at South Spring Ranch. Has a hand in the game just the same. There's a young Englishman that's cut himself in, aligned with Chisum against Murphy and the 'House'—he's wealthy and high and mighty they say and smart."

"And what about Murphy?"

"He's sick, got some wastin disease. Another tough young feller, Jimmy Dolan, is taking over. Bunch of hard-nosed Irishmen, the whole lot."

"Like me," says Henry.

"You don't seem hard to me," Buck replies, rather shamefaced.

"I can be, if required. I wasn't born in Ireland but I'm Irish to the bone. Mother saw to that."

"I mean, you ain't cruel or greedy, or nothin—meaning no disrespect."

Henry smirks at Buck's prejudiced view of Irishmen, pretty much the view of all America.

"That's not being Irish, that's just being an arsehole."

"Well, there's a lot of assholes in Lincoln then," Buck answers back and they both laugh.

"You're a smart fellow, Buck. I think you'll be running this spread someday. I can see it."

'How can you see that?"

"I see things...sometimes."

"I don't doubt that. What else do you see?"

"I think something's going to happen to me in Lincoln County."

"All right. What?"

Henry looks at the big moon for some time before answering.

"Romance, maybe I'll find a sweet *querida* at the baile and fall in love, maybe play the blanket hornpipe, you know, hopmagundy." Henry shines the big grin and starts to wiggle obscenely on the ground.

Abashed at the shameless spectacle, which is both embarrassing and terribly funny, Buck looks over at his new friend and teacher with a sheepish smile.

"Cain't help you there."

"I've heard about the villages in the Hondo valley, a little river winding through, each pueblo more like little Mexico than the last, only it ain't Mexico. And each one with a patron saint and a Saturday night baile. A land of milk and honey and peppers and lace, I'm told."

"You'd like San Patricio, then. My brother Bob and his family live just upriver. He'd know who to talk to about work, maybe give you some social introductions in San Patricio. They're old families, go back generations. Lot of manners and a lot of lace."

"*Qué rico*. Sounds like the place for me."

The orange goddess rises higher in the sky, transmuting into a plain white moon between the short space of one look, and the next.

A crystal-clear, spring-fed pool just deep and wide enough for a person to submerge himself and stretch out—lies in a gulch a few hundred yards from the ranch house. A hidden jewel that had never stopped running, not even during the worst part of a long drought. Henry has made many a visit there to bathe.

Whenever possible, and contrary to the habits of most men, Henry McCarty prefers both himself and his clothes to be clean.

After a long soak, he emerges from the water, shivering and letting out a spirited whoop as the water runs over his naked skin. He's thin but finely muscled and moves with an easy grace toward a bench to dry in the sun. Today he's leaving the Jones ranch and going deeper into Lincoln County, meaning to set his best foot forward.

Later that morning the Jones family sends him off wearing a set of patched hand-me-downs and riding a broke-down sorrel. The smallest children start to tear up, especially Petey, his little mouth quivering as Henry says his goodbyes.

"Thanks for the math, and the Spanish," says Buck, gripping Henry's hand and meeting his eye.

"And Squeak, Piggy, Squeak," adds Gracie, rubbing a tear away.

"And the tricks," yells Petey, grabbing onto his leg.

"I'll be back around soon you can count on it. There's a lot more to learn, and a lot more games to play."

He shakes hands with Heiskell last.

"You watch yourself now. There's some rough'ns where yer headed. And you come on back son. There's work for you to do here," says Heiskell with a rare smile.

"You got a home here if you want it. You remember that, Henry

McCarty," says Ma'am, sad to see the boy striking out so soon. But Henry knew the time had come. The right time. He gives Ma'am a kiss on the cheek and a hug, and lifts little Pete up, who'd come running after him.

"That's good to know, Ma'am, very good to know. Thank you for everything you've done for me." He sets the toddler down, gives the other three kids a hug, and mounts up. "May the road be downhill, all the way to your door."

There is a final smile and a wave of the hat before he turns to ride on, taking up the unpredictable journey once again.

A herd of pronghorn antelope graze on tufts of needle grass covering the spine of a bald rim. Except for the grinding of their jaws, they hold perfectly still, like living statues. Suddenly one head pops up, startled by a train of riders passing in the narrow canyon below.

Jesse Evans and his unorthodox gang of rogues wend south along a curving stretch of trail, the boss in the lead, and eight men following along behind. They've come off the main road from Lincoln on the Parajito trail, cutting over into the Rio Feliz valley. A long ride still lies ahead.

Aloof, well-barbered and crisply dressed—those observations register strongly, but you notice the dark eyes first. They see straight through you. Jesse Evans had not been written about much in the newspapers, nor had he been lionized in a dime novel, but his reputation in the Southwest is widespread and unequivocal. A graduate of Lee College in Virginia and a brooding man capable of fine discernments, along with lightning speed and sudden violence.

"Pecos" Bob Olinger trots along behind, bearing odd accoutrements and a malevolent smirk. Tall, broad-shouldered, and savage as a meat axe, Pecos Bob stands out oddly even in this strange bunch; with his long, greasy hair blunt cut to shoulder length, the elegantly tasseled felt sombrero sitting atop, the wicked Bowie knife belted at his waist, the dead flat eyes. He also finds it amusing to wear a badge on his elaborately beaded coat. Pecos was a sworn deputy in Lincoln County at one time—but now bound by no law whatever.

Next in the line an old buffalo hunter and former ranger leans over to adjust his sixteen shot Henry in its long scabbard, then a Missouri bushwhacker, a West Virginia mountain man, an Alabamian hillbilly, and two rogues from Louisiana enjoying a private joke, and finally, a disfigured New Mexican bandolero—silent as the grave.

The company is a shocking sight, moving along the trail like an aberrant band of cutthroat pirates. The whole fierce lot of them forced to a jangling halt by a youth heading straight up the slender path. Somehow the boy neglects to immediately move aside, but instead holds his ground and opens up a conversation.

"How do you, gentlemen? May I trouble you for directions?"

"You best get the hell out of our way shitheel, 'fore someone steps on you," Olinger barks out. Evans turns around and stares at the blustering giant before turning back to consider the boy. He decides to take a moment, if only to spite Olinger—who should have kept his big mouth shut.

Evans sits his horse, irritated.

"What's your name?"

"Kid Antrim."

"I'm Jesse Evans, and these impatient charmers behind me...are the Boys."

"Well hell, I'm honored. My hat's off *to you*, sir. They talk about you clear over in Arizona."

Olinger frowns and there's grumbling from down the line as Kid Antrim doffs his hat. This might take a while if Jesse is in one of his moods.

"What's your story, Kid? Something tells me you've got a good one."

"I had some trouble back in Arizona. At Fort Grant. It was necessary that I leave in haste, had to stay off the road. Of course, beyond a certain point there ain't no road. Made it across the barrens to the Rio Grande and beyond, only to get robbed of my horse by Apaches. After a long walk, the Jones family took me in and saved my sorry hide. Now I'm looking for work around here. I hear there's big doin's."

Evans leans over and spits and looks back at the boy.

"You crossed that desert alone?" Jesse asks, his dark eyes steady and unyielding.

"Yes sir, I did. Twice."

"Can you handle a gun?"

"I'm sure not in your class Mr. Evans, but I carry a Cooper double-action and I'm a good marksman."

The gun shark is silent a moment before creasing a faint smile.

"Well, Kid, you might as well come along with us, if you'd like"—turning to stare at Olinger before looking back at the rest—"might need a ballsy little fellow like you to show these ladies how it's done." The tone of his last statement occasions some eye rolling all the way down the line. Olinger spits.

"You never plow a field by turning it over in your mind. I'd be glad to join in anything you've got planned, Mr. Evans."

Jesse nods and spurs his mount forward without further ceremony. The Kid quickly moves off the trail.

"We'll be riding the rest of the day and all night, but we'll have a sliver of the moon. We're relocating some horses...presently belonging to an Englishman."

"His Lordship, John Tunstall," the Alabama hillbilly says in a gleeful high-pitched crow, as if mocking this particular Englishmen were his life's calling. Judging from the chuckling to be heard up and down the line, it's become a running joke.

Kid Antrim is excited beyond measure to suddenly be on an adventure with Jesse Evans, but the circus surrounding the great man does give him pause. The others seem, to varying degrees, unhinged. When he locks eyes with Bob Olinger, the feeling gets deeper.

But he's made his play, and after Olinger passes by, he grins and shakes hands amiably with the rest, falling in as the last one goes by.

The antelope are unimpressed with the posturing down below and continue grazing in silence. Behind the herd, the braided landscape sweeps impressively up to twin peaks sitting high above the world like enthroned royals.

There's no one to challenge them as they glide down off the hill and begin their raid. A waxing moon provides just enough light for the endeavor.

"No one's minding the till boss," says Tom Hill, Jesse's trusted lieutenant.

"Well, they can't be far off, so let's get this herd and be on our way," Jesse demands in a low voice.

Working the herd out of the enclosure is the easy opening move, but the job snarls once the horses are run out into the night. Few of them are fully broken and while the bulk of the herd is driven uphill, a number of the Boys scatter in a tangled pursuit of the wildest fillies and stallions.

Within a mile, Evans has the herd under control and the scrambled elements of his gang back together—except one.

"Where's the boy?" Jesse asks, craning around in the saddle.

"Looks like the little son-of-a-bitch got lost...or took off. Never can tell how good a man is until he gets thumped," Olinger throws out over his shoulder.

Just as they're considering his desertion, Kid Antrim comes flying out of the dark leading a tall bay mare. He has a filly on a hackamore and his sorrel in a heavy sweat.

"She's a wild one," Kid Antrim yells out.

Evans looks back at Olinger briefly, saying nothing but gesturing his chin with a slight upward jerk before heading forward into the night.

The hardest and most exciting work over, a long and, for many, an increasingly drunken ride back to the gang's mountain encampment ensues. A jug gets passed around and generously tipped. When it comes to his turn, the new recruit hands it on.

They arrive back in the high elevation of their camp the next morning. After falling out for a short nap, Kid Antrim is up again intending to fully gentle his new mount. He begins while the rest of the Boys are sleeping off the big drunk and the long ride.

The supernatural art of horse breaking commences in a crude paddock near the camp. It begins with stroking and humming, then a soft murmur of words—letting her get to know his touch, his voice, and his spirit.

He begins to work her in circles with a length of braided rope, intoning the sounds that will become a vocabulary; clucks of the tongue, whoops, and spirited calls, all unique. The eyes and head and hoofs begin to answer, her mane bouncing with a proud flick.

Their heads come together and a hand reaching out to gently stroke her powerful neck. The humming and whispering continues.

One of the first up from the camp—Frank Baker, the Alabamian hillbilly and camp comedian—relieves himself nearby and accidentally bears witness. He's not sure what to make of it.

Jesse Evans is also up relieving himself when he hears the whine of Frank Baker's voice.

"Hey, Jesse. That Kid Antrim is a precious one all right. He's over there about to propose to the filly. Some damn fancy dressing he's doing first goddamned thing."

"You sound like a fucking rusty hinge, Frank."

"Well, shit, sorry to bother you, Jesse," Baker replies in a false pleading tone.

"Go finish sleeping it off," says the general, patting him on the shoulder and moving on.

The pistoleer is curious about Kid Antrim and walks the short distance to the corral. He hears it first, walking through the trees, and then, at the fence, he sees it.

"Where'd you learn all that?" Jesse asks.

"I've watched many a caballero at work, learned a lot from them and figured out the rest on my own...I love horses, been through a lot with them, saved my life more than once. This one might make the best I've ever had."

"I read a book on the subject once. Can't say it improved my horsemanship much," says Jesse.

"Some things you just can't learn from a book."

Jesse Evans looks at him a minute before nodding.

"Have you named her yet?"

"Just did. Slippers."

"That's a soft name for a hard catch."

"She glides."

"Well, I don't believe you've fully earned this filly yet. But you will."

Olinger had peeled himself off two weeks before, and headed on to Lincoln and his master—Jimmy Dolan.

The two men are regarded differently: Dolan with a certain respect due the *jefe*; and Olinger, as an unhinged loudmouth—but the jefe's hatchet man. There was no doubt about it, Olinger is Dolan's eyes and ears, a spy, and an assassin. Over six feet tall, muscled like an athlete and a wicked brawler, none of the Boys would call Olinger out.

But they needled him just the same.

Jimmy Dolan was not yet thirty years old. His close-cropped bullet head a perfect match for the cruel face and feral eyes. Only five feet two but tough as boot leather and smart. Jimmy'd had a hard life and worked his way up from nothing. Gone into the Army of the Potomac fresh off the boat from Ireland and a mere boy—but he survived two years and the worst battles of the big war.

That was a lifetime ago. Thirteen years on, the little Irish drummer boy had grown into a hard-drinking soldier of the frontier and a ruthless captain of commerce.

Dolan and Olinger were a strange hard-nosed pair and the Boys created their own cockeyed mythology about them—led by the hillbilly from

Alabama, Frank Baker, and the West Virginia mountain man, Billy Morton.

They could all be counted on for whatever mayhem the little jefe called for, but Frank and Billy would also have their fun with it.

"The drummer boy and his lordship are at odds over whose got the biggest trouser snake in the kingdom."

"And more's the pity for *his lordship*. We're going to ride in like fuckin knights of old with our dicks out and settle the matter once and fer all," Frank and Billy had clowned to Kid Antrim one drunken night, wagging the whole affair into a burlesque as they capered drunkenly around the fire.

"We prod to the death for the little drummer boy."

"Hold, Sir Billy, but what of his paramour, the snoop Olinger?"

"May he shit and fall back in it. Ride on, Sir Frank."

"Leave him to me, good sirs. I'll see to it that he sits on that mighty blade when next he squats," Kid Antrim says while hunkering down and pantomiming a sudden prick.

As the days passed and they waited for the next order from Dolan there were many such improvised Shakespearean travesties in thick hollered accents. Kid Antrim would entertain the camp of Southerners with songs like "The Bonnie Blue Flag" and "Rose of Alabamy"—favorites of Frank Baker, who'd decided the boy was a fine addition, and funny as a drunk chicken.

Kid Antrim had also donned his blood-stained green coat and ridden out with the rest, helping deliver a blunt message to Dolan's remaining suppliers—stay with the House or face the consequences. Evans would speak to the Anglo farmers and ranchers, and the *bandolero*, Manuel "The Indian" Segovia, would talk to the *ganaderos*.

Henry had inquired during the long ride, innocently enough, why he was called "The Indian". The bandelero looked at the boy with coal black eyes and said nothing and Henry didn't ask again.

During the parleys Jesse's Boys would spread out menacingly, sometimes dismounting for a closer look at things which might be good to appropriate, or destroy. Frank and Billy usually took the lead in these swaggering intimidations.

Such adventures did not sit well with Kid Antrim.

At a quarter past nine an excited bolt of anticipation runs through the fires and games of the outlaw camp. Dolan and Olinger canter into the light with a loaded packhorse trailing behind. They rein up before the table where

Jesse sits quietly playing a game of patience. A jug sits next to the cards. Jesse nods to Dolan and gets to his feet. He pours out a generous libation and hands it to the boss with a jut of the chin.

The Boys gather around, happy to be resupplied and an impromptu horseback performance welcomes Dolan's arrival. Just a few comic tricks and a well-rehearsed mock fight—a mummers' battle.

It begins with Frank and Billy charging at their mounts from behind and leaping over the hindquarters into the saddle. Both appear to injure their manhood and slide to the ground in pain. Even the sour-faced Olinger cracks up.

Next, Frank and Billy shake it off, remount, and stand up while their horses circle the main campfire. Frank holds a tent pole and Billy grasps a shovel. They swing around the flames standing balanced with one foot on the horse's rump and the other tucked under the cantle.

"Sir Billy, I challenge you to a joust."

"Stand aside Boys while I teach this fool a lesson."

Their lances go up and the charge is on, only Frank swings his pole like a scythe and Billy manages to jump over it. On the next pass Billy swings his pole down like a hammer, clouting Sir Frank who clumps down on his horse and flips over backwards to the ground. Billy's horse rears up and he goes to the ground in a comic tumble as well.

The lance back up—he charges at Sir Frank.

Kid Antrim jumps in now to trip Billy and alter the story. Sir Billy leaps back to his feet and swings wildly. The boy ducks under, Frank receives the punch and over he goes.

While the last two standing try their best to stage-choke each other, Frank sneaks up wearing a wig made of an old shredded blanket. He runs both Kid Antrim and Billy through with the tent pole and they fall in a heap. Frank bows grandly to close the farce, tossing his "hair" with a shake—a signature move of one Pecos Bob Olinger.

The Boys give forth a rowdy stamp of approval, their wild laughter and whoops echoing up into the pines. But Olinger looks away, disgusted by the spectacle.

"I see you've hired another comedian," says Dolan in a thin brogue.

"Underestimate those three at your peril," Jesse replies.

"No doubt," Dolan agrees as he downs the shot of whiskey in his hand.

"I'm sure you didn't ride up here just to see my men act the fool. Let's step over here and talk."

"Ease up, Jesse. We'll council in the morning. Let me enjoy being amongst you sharks for a while."

A hand of five-card stud gets under way, with the little tyrant in a drinking mood and Olinger still red-assed about being impersonated in the mummer's parody. The hatchet man's right hand keeps straying to the bone haft of his knife.

"Wish we had a fucking faro table going. Poker is too goddamned slow," says Olinger, eyeing the table and Evans with equal disdain.

"Then you'd need a banker and casekeep and a pullbox, and a musician to keep everyone hopped up. There are many intelligent men who actually prefer poker," Evans explains.

"The odds are better in faro. A lot better."

"The game we're playing tonight is called stud."

The hulking Olinger, and the diminutive Dolan make a bitter pair for certain, and hard to say which of the two makes the worse impression.

Jesse looks away. After a long drag on a cigarette he inspects his cards. "Murphy is poorly, I hear."

"Poorly? The fockin ship is sinking, right beside the harbor," Dolan replies.

The old man had brought Jimmy along, patiently, for more than a decade. But the younger man shows no trace of remorse about Murphy's impending death.

"It's a cancer?" Jesse inquires, the dark eyes steady as the night.

"He's a tough old Fenian. The bastard will take his time dying."

"Hit me, dammit. I wish you sharpers would pick up the pace," Olinger complains as he grasps the bone handle again.

When one player is cleaned out at the end of the hand, Kid Antrim steps forward out of the shadows and offers to take his place.

"Your deal then," says Jesse.

As if to warn the new dealer, Olinger starts to brag about killing a local rancher and one he knows to be of special interest to Antrim.

"I just killed a man who cheated me in a deal. A man named Bob *Jones*—weren't no trouble a'tall, and I surely enjoyed it."

"Shot bravely in the back over twenty dollars, whilst his family watched," Billy Morton quips from out in the dark and a chorus of snickers follows.

"He had it comin, the stupid sonofabitch, his brood sure fussed over his sorry ass."

"Does it ever occur to you to just shut your mouth? Takes a special kind of shitheel to brag about a bushwackin," says Evans.

Olinger is supremely arrogant but no fool. He won't confront Evans directly with knife or gun, yet while Kid Antrim deals out the hand, Pecos Bob will run his mouth.

"Gun sharkin ain't about nothing but killing your man, Sir Galahad. I haven't seen you pull since you've been amongst us. I begin to wonder how you got your reputation," Olinger says, a challenge in his voice.

Dolan looks up from his cards.

Evans is bored with the rough company, and the thrill of gunplay is not what it once was. Still, he can tell Dolan wants some display here, and Olinger has him spun up just enough.

"Kid, take these shot glasses over by the fire, toss them up, one a little before the other." The Kid picks up two glasses and walks to the fire. He looks at Evans before tossing one and a second later, the other, and then taking a quick step back.

At the last moment Evans erupts into a stunning display of both the quick draw and accuracy, nailing both glasses before they reach the ground. The effect throughout the camp is like magic.

"By god, that's some fuckin shootistry there."

"Damn right."

"A gunshark like no fuckin other, they ain't many's could do that in broad daylight."

"What ya think, Pecos Bob? Care to take up the gauntlet?" squeals Frank Baker.

Olinger pulls out his knife and brandishing it wild-eyed for all to see, first giving his head and long hair a sneering toss. He then flips the big knife from haft to blade and tosses with a vicious muscular thrust. It impales deep into the trunk of a pine tree, smashing first through the glass of an oil lamp hanging there, and spreading fire down the tree and onto the ground.

"Damn, Pecos, you're a knife-throwin back-shootin fire-startin wonder." There's another chorus of snickers from the Boys as Baker pulls the knife out of the tree and hands it back to Olinger, with a flourish.

"One of these days I'm gonna cut yer dingis off with it. You whinin shitheel," Olinger barks and Billy Morton stamps out the spreading flames.

"So, we've managed to destroy two perfectly good shot glasses and a lamp. If you're done jerking off I'd like to continue this game of stud," Jesse states in a voice dry as dust.

The display with gun and knife, impressive as it was, settles nothing between Evans and Olinger. The two men continue to eye each other with professional contempt. Evans picks up his hand of cards, and Olinger drains another shot of busthead.

But Dolan is well-pleased. He sits next to Olinger with the slightest of grins and nods to Evans. Keeping this formidable host of barely controllable men in the field is a challenge and egregiously expensive; the rank and file receive sixty dollars a month, twice as much for Jessie, and separate pay for purloined stock. An extravagance and no doubt draining the House coffers—but he loves, and needs, the power it gives him.

Kid Antrim takes it all in, including the news of Bob Jones's cowardly murder, with his best poker face. He deals out the next hand with a sharper's pace and ease. Evans is far more impressed and interested in that than any of Olinger's horse shit.

"You're a professional."

"I worked as a casekeep under Billy King for over a year, in Hopville, also dealt and played many a hand of every kind of poker game there is. Beat working the chuck wagon. Don't care much for cowboying," Henry replies, with a crooked grin.

"You know, they say Davy Crockett could grin the knot off a log...I believe you could come along and grin that same knot into splinters," Jesse concedes, at length, the eyes at full bore.

"Never knew a drover who wasn't poor as Job's turkey," says Dolan, reaching to pour out another drink, ignoring Jesse's comment.

"A faro sharper eh, you need to set up a game you little shit," Olinger replies.

The Kid looks at Olinger for the first time, giving him a cold stare and holding it, only looking away to deal.

The drinking and the game of stud goes on. They each win a few hands and the talk trails off as the jug empties.

Kid Antrim continues to deal and patter and eye his employers. The man who intends to run the county sits opposite with a smug proprietary air, drunk as a lord. And a killer broods into his cards like some devil straight out of hell.

Henry would proudly ride with Jesse Evans, anywhere; but he's realized he can't work for Jimmy Dolan or be anywhere near Bob Olinger.

The dark night is even darker after the new moon sets. When the Boys finally bed down Kid Antrim slips off into the surrounding forest on a fine mare with the sorrel on a lead rope. They are in and quickly gone, shadows merging into deeper shadow.

The same three men are sitting at the same table with the crack running down the middle, drinking coffee strong enough to stand a spoon in. Morning light does little to improve the appearance of the Irish boss and his hatchet man. If anything they are less appealing in daylight.

Olinger pours out another cup for Dolan, and himself, and leans back to take a drink. He looks over at Evans with his sombrero pulled low, wondering how soon in the progression of events he might be able to kill him.

Dolan brought newspapers along with the dry goods, and Evans has his head gratefully buried in one of them. There's a whole stack to go through: *The Las Vegas Gazette, The Santa Fe New Mexican, The Cimarron News*. Jesse was eager to get to it as soon as they'd eaten, and had already devoured half of them.

Frank Baker's strident voice suddenly breaks the thick silence.

"I know you don't like the sound of my voice in the morning Jesse. But I thought you ought to know—that boy's taken off."

"He's just off working the filly."

"His war bag's gone, and that ole sorrel the Jones's give him."

Olinger's dead eyes lever up, and a fire seems to catch somewhere down in there, back behind the flat brown iris and devil's hole of the pupil.

"Goddamned cunt. I knew he was a treacherous little fuck the moment I laid eyes on him."

"Maybe he took offense at you killing the Jones boy. That family saved his life," Jesse states.

"And maybe I don't give two shits."

"I liked having that boy around. He was smart. Smart as a Philadelphia lawyer. We could've used some more intelligence around here...only you're too stupid and arrogant to see it."

"Well, maybe I'll just trot down the mountain and collar the little chucklehead, and we'll see how smart he is," Olinger spits out, the acid in his voice rising.

Evans fixes the dark stare across the table and stands up.

"I'm tired of this endless goddamned row! I'm paying you two to work together, not pull at the goddamned breakfast table. We've got bigger matters to worry about...that English cunt Tunstall is taking my business, fockin councillor McSween has robbed me blind, and so has Chisum. And you two want a fight over a saddle tramp," Dolan barks, his head pounding and patience exhausted.

Evans sits back down and picks up the paper, giving it a hard opening pop.

"We'll take care of them three," Olinger snorts, gripping the bone handle again and tossing back a lump of hair.

Jessie's eyes return to a column in *The Cimarron News*.

6

The grated iron lid yanks open with a loud screech. Henry looks down the ladder into the dark, takes a whiff and stares back at Deputy Peppin with a grimace.

"Down you go lad."

Another initiate descends steeply into the gloom of Lincoln's subterranean jail. Once his head is below ground the heavy egress slams shut, a large hasp thrown and padlock bolted. Curses and laughter escape somewhere in the crepuscular murk.

"*Come Mierda.*"

"*Puta de madre.*"

Moonlight slices down through the grate, dimly suffusing a room that is little more than a hole in the ground. Locals call it the "pit"—an earthen floor with crude pine logs walls and no air or light save what comes through the bars of the lid. And even in the chilly October night—the stench is suffocating.

"*Ola Señor, que tal?*"

"*Ola, nada mucho.*"

"*Bienvenido a casa.*"

The new prisoner turns into the faint shaft of light, grinning.

"*Gracias. Amigo. Cómo te llama?*"

"*Ygenio, Ygenio Salazar.*"

A conversation begins, halting at first, then flowing in a rapid, singing patter. They talk of the weather at first, and eventually, *sus propias historias*—their own stories, beginning with how they came to be in the pit.

Henry had been caught on a stolen horse belonging to the Englishman, taken peacefully on the road to Lincoln by Tunstall's foreman, Dick Brewer.

"*El Leon*!"

"*Ah, claro*. He does remind me of a lion, I liked him a lot," Henry replies.

"We all respect him. He's a good man."

"And your story?"

"I'm a vandal and a troublemaker—according to Sheriff Brady. Others would say I'm simply protective of my father's land and holdings, and of my young sister, Ariana. My family has been cheated by the House for years, first by Murphy and now by Dolan."

"Credit bound up in the harvest yield, and terms that leave your family in ever worsening debt. I'd be bitter to."

"I threw a rock through a window of the Murphy store when I was twelve, then one at Sheriff Brady himself. More recently, a Dolan man attacked my sister...but I stopped him."

"And now you're in the hole."

Their eyes meet.

"We do business with Mr. Tunstall now, he's a fine man, but Dolan, a real son-of-a-bitch!"

"I've seen that for myself."

Next morning the lid opens again, and Henry McCarty is recalled to the daylight. He emerges squinting up at a tall, extraordinary looking man. A twenty-three-year-old Londoner stands before him, ramrod straight, with a dark shock of hair flowing back off a high forehead.

"Hello Mr. McCarty, my name is John Tunstall," the Englishman begins, with a sonorous voice and the look of a poet.

"I regret the circumstances, but very pleased to meet you Mr. Tunstall."

An air of superiority hangs gracefully on the Englishman's thin frame, and a well-bred civility masks the arrogance and iron hard resolve at his core. Two years on the untidy frontier has not dampened his entrepreneurial spirit or deterred him in the least from his goal—to build an empire from scratch.

The pistol slung underneath his tweed coat is not for looks, and despite being nearly blind in one eye, the Englishman is an excellent shot. He'd also learned to temper his aristocratic bearing with well-placed bits of frontier vernacular.

It was effective.

"I apologize for the inconvenience of leaving you overnight in this unfortunate place. Mr. Brewer has told me an extraordinary story about you. I believe we can come to some agreeable arrangement, concerning the stolen horse, providing the story is true."

The Englishman's broad-shouldered foreman exchanges a friendly nod with the boy. Henry and the filly had been collared on the road to Lincoln. El Leon had quickly drawn his weapon and gave Henry to understand his shenanigans were at an end—but it was a long ride yet and the boy's story had won him over by nightfall.

The bargain was a night in Sheriff Brady's jail, and let the boss have his say.

"I'll not deny I fell in with bad company and came sorely to regret it. Jimmy Dolan and his man Olinger are not to my liking, and I'd be pleased to square my debt to you, Mr. Tunstall. You'll find me a hard worker and a quick study," Henry answers truthfully on all counts.

His first impression of Tunstall is a strong one—he might well run the county one day, maybe the entire territory.

"Mr. McCarty, you shall have your chance to prove both points. Now, let us get away from this shit hole," the Englishman says with a half-smile and a wink.

The Irish deputy standing nearby, George Peppin, slams the lid on the hole again with a disapproving scowl. Giving his jailer a grin, Henry runs over to the grate and yells down to his friend.

"Adios Ygenio, hablamos más tarde."

"Adios amigo, afortunado."

Lincoln in daylight proves far better than his impressions of the previous night. Henry looks up at the steep escarpments winding around La Placita like protective arms. Sturdy adobe and wooden buildings run along either side of the one curving street. A little river cuts along the eastern edge of town, flowing under sheltering cottonwoods—lush planted fields beyond.

The valley seems peaceful and prosperous, and far more Mexicano than Anglo.

At the stable, the red bay nickers to Henry as soon as they enter the barn. That horse had been known to be quite wild. As they saddle up, Henry and the bay keep up a steady conversation and Tunstall's impassive eyes soften a little.

"After such a touching reunion, I suppose we'll have to keep you two together."

Henry also reclaims the sorrel and has her on a lead rope as they disembark from the stable and into the street.

"The Jones family loaned me this little chestnut. I was going to leave her with their eldest son, Bob, over on the Ruidoso, but Olinger killed him over a twenty-dollar debt. Hate to think what that families going through now."

"A time for sorrow," the Englishman admits.

Dick Brewer stares ahead, but Henry catches something troubling, and painful, in his eyes.

When first constructed the big store was immediately christened the "House"; because it was the only building in Lincoln with a pitched roof, and as the unrivaled seat of power—it seemed fitting.

Jimmy Dolan walks through the front door of the House and onto its porch, his eyes resting a moment on the well-appointed casa grande sitting a half block to south—the elegant home of counselor McSween. A newly built fence entirely surrounds the fortress-like compound.

Dolan spits and looks away. He hadn't put in twelve years of hard work and ruthless endeavor in Lincoln County just to let it all go to the devil. He turns and struts toward a late breakfast at the Wortley Hotel like a banty rooster, with Olinger following close behind.

Jimmy Dolan had already been in America for more than half his life. Far enough away from Ireland to near forget his mother's face and the sound of her voice. Lincoln being a very long way indeed from Loughrea, County Galway. He was born and reared in that distant town on the gray lake, immigrating to America at twelve.

At fifteen he was drummer boy in the Union Army and had drummed the lines into many a terrible fray. Dolan learned an important maxim in the great war—keep your head down and pray the Commanding Officer is fearless and unscrupulous. He'd seen for himself how battles were won, and how they were lost.

"Look up ahead, Jimmy" says Olinger, pointing at John Tunstall mounting up. "It's his lordship and that little nibbler. Believe they're headed this way."

The Englishman notices them as well and should keep going, in the opposite direction. But instead, he rides up to Dolan and halts, looking down at the Irishman as if from a great distance.

"Good morning, Mr. Dolan. I've found another one of my *stolen* horses. And one of your men in possession of it, though he does seem remorseful. I believe the man will work for me now."

Olinger swings his greasy locks and glares at Kid Antrim. Brewer sits straight in the saddle, staring at the hatchet man with the butt of his pistol exposed.

"That's a fine run of luck mind ya, but you watch your back Mr. Tunstall. You never know when your luck will turn. Someday the House will get that money you and McSween owe us—one way or another," Dolan answers back, his Irish brogue harsh against the King's English.

"I gather you're referring to the Fritz Insurance claim. That's strictly a matter of legal debate, and the issue is far from settled. In any case I've nothing to do with it."

"Well, your lordship, we'll see about that."

"I'm a Londoner, and an Oxford man. My parents reside in Hackney but I am no *lord*, just a determined businessman. But you may call me your lordship if it suits you. Good day, Mr. Dolan."

The Englishman rides on and Dolan glares after him a moment before resuming his march.

"Damned high-horsed English cunt."

Henry looks back. He pulls his hat from its normally cocky tilt down into a fighting cut, with an exaggerated flourish. Taking in the gesture with a malevolent smirk, Olinger's hand begins to move suggestively on the haft of his Bowie knife.

Twenty-five miles to the east, as the crow flies, amid naked hills and poplar trees and along the little river—Henry begins to learn the charms and secrets of the lush Hondo valley. He'd been to Tunstall's ranch the first time in darkness, as a raider.

Days begin to pass with a charming benevolence. And not just a benevolence he created for himself out of rough circumstances, but that seemed to be everywhere abundant.

He also sensed trouble lurking down the trail, but the feeling was easy to ignore in such fine company.

Dick Brewer reminds him of a hero in one of his books—stalwart, handsome, reserved; with a tousled mane of hair and a natural ability to lead. He stands a head taller than everyone on the ranch, except Mr. Tunstall. There *is* something grave and off-putting about him, for he rarely speaks. But his experience and skill as a stockman are exceptional and to a man, the Tunstall cowboys except his word without question.

The fantastically mustached southerner Charlie Bowdre—a fellow charmer and admirer of Mexican beauties—is first to befriend Henry. A good ten years older, Charlie is always ready to slip from his Georgia drawl into Spanish. He also happens to be a skilled cheese maker, and a fine pistoleer.

Early in the first day of work the two trail up into the hills, first chasing down, and now bringing home a stray heifer:

"That Dick Brewer is a hell of a top man. Sure is a quiet one though. Don't believe I've heard him say more than two words at a time," says Henry, easing down the hill with the heifer trotting along in front.

"Dick is working his way through a misery. Some woman back in Wisconsin done broke his heart completely in two. She broke off the engagement and married another man. That's why he come out here. Only mentioned her once to me, but the pain in his eyes liked to knock me over."

"Time heals all wounds...they say."

"He's got a ways to go."

When they get back the drovers are working the herd, cutting them out one at a time, and heading them into a branding pen. The foreman works the iron and those not in on the job are watching. Tom O'Folliard, another recent hire, yells out to them as they trot the heifer through the gate.

"Hey fellows, y'all are just in time."

"Well Red, I see you need some help holding the fence up," Charlie snorts.

"I like your name, O'Folliard, has a great ring to it—come down from a fine and proper Irish family no doubt," Henry confides to the freckled carrot top from Texas.

"Well maybe. Truth is I don't know. That name is all I got left. My Ma and Pa died of the pox when I was a button, over in Uvalde. Neighbors raised me."

"Well you're a wonder then, Tom, if the pox got your family it damn sure should've got you to, but here you are." The two grin at each other, making light of the situation as only orphans can.

The bull is cornered last and headed into the pen. Suddenly it turns it's bulk on an unfortunate cowboy, George Coe, crushing him against the angle of the chute. Brewer jumps in and, with a prodigious display of physical strength, forces the animal off. The trapped cowboy is banged up but manages to limp away with a grin.

"Damn bull ain't no match for you Dick," George barks out, the rest of the men join in with a whoop.

The high spirits carry over into the night and around a bonfire. Gaus, the German cook, squeezes out a lively schottische on a button accordion. Henry begins to loosen up his feet, first the one then both.

"Look at him go," Charlie calls out.

Tunstall's lean figure emerges from the shadows, a jug in one hand. He draws close to the flames and smiles out at his men, lifting high the libations when the music and the dance achieve a rousing finish.

"Another fine day in the valley...watching you men work, and play, is a sight to behold. Huzzah! (They answer back in kind). Have a drink and pass this jug around...I won't bore you for long, but I have a speech to make."

"You fellows settle down and listen up," says Dick Brewer. He joins Tunstall by the fire and once again the two of them stand abreast like lords of the manor.

"As you all know, we are increasingly on a war footing with the House. There is a storm brewing, with Mr. Dolan and his man Olinger, Jessie Evans, and the Boys—all stirring the pot against me. And there are powerful forces behind *them*, in Messilla and Santa Fe. Dolan will certainly not give up...and I suppose there will be an attack of some kind."

"Let'em try."

"Olinger can suck an egg, the big greasy-haired bastard."

"Jimmy Dolan looks out on the diverse peoples of this county and only sees grist for the mill, his only interest—usury and power. Well...I am also interested in power, and perhaps I'm no better. But with power I would seek to promote the general welfare for all races, establish justice, secure the blessings of liberty—like it says in your constitution. To make of this place a stronghold of prosperity...not English, or Irish, Mexicano or German, but *American.*"

"Hooray!" The men are genuinely moved, almost stunned.

"Mr. McSween and I, with help from John Chisum, will outwit and outlast Dolan and the House. But henceforth, I'll need you men to be soldiers as well as drovers, with an increase in pay of course. We won't start trouble, but we go forth well-armed, in force, and ready for trouble...are you with me?"

"Damn right we are."

"Hell yes!" They all join in another big chorus of huzzahs. Tunstall looks out across the fire at his men, genuinely heartened.

"To your health then." He takes a good pull from the jug himself.

"You boys want to hear a joke?" Henry McCarty is up quickly, ready to extemporize an encore. "I'll tell you the story of Handsome Dan and Whorehouse Johnny, but tonight, Jimmy Dolan will be playing the part of Dan and Pecos Bob...will be Whorehouse Johnny," he says with a bow, raising back up in *character.*

The Londoner must attend to his burgeoning affairs in Lincoln at weeks end. He chooses Brewer, Charlie Bowdre, and Henry to ride along for protection. After a display that erupted one morning with a sudden flight of birds—Henry's skill with a gun became apparent to all.

A bevy of quail burst out fluttering and running from under a sage bush. Henry pulled and shot enough for a meal before anyone could even make a remark.

It's a long ride into town, even over the much-used shortcut—the Parajito trail. Henry and Charlie lead the way, keeping up a running conversation. As they approach Lincoln though, Henry circles back to Mr. Tunstall with a burning question.

"I'm told you have quite a library Mr. Tunstall. It's been a long while since I've had a new book to read. Would you consider loaning one?"

The request takes Tunstall aback at first, but he decides the request is a reasonable one, just unusual.

"What category do you prefer?"

"Anything, everything...but nautical books are my favorite. Ship lore and sailors and captains and the open sea, no place I'd rather be," says Henry, smiling and dipping his head as if trundled on a wave. Tunstall puzzles back at him.

The streets of Lincoln are quiet as they trot past Mosano's saloon and tienda, where Charlie and Dick stop off for a drink and some dinner.

"You boys can roll out on the floor in the front room. I'll join you there later tonight."

Tunstall continues on to his rambling adobe headquarters. He unlocks the door and they enter the first large room. Henry is overwhelmed by a flood of magnificent smells: Arbuckles coffee, soap, coils of hemp rope, new cotton clothes.

"Opening day is Monday," Tunstall states, looking proud.

At the far right end another door opens to the inner sanctum—Tunstall's capacious living quarters. It would hold all of the rooms Henry had ever lived in.

There is a comfortable looking bed and a large armoire. Tunstall leads Henry through without comment and opens another door to an even larger room. This one contains a rustic library of over a thousand volumes stacked on long pine boards. Henry can only stare in amazement.

"And what did you last read?"

"*Moby Dick.*"

"I've not heard of it."

"Kind of bogs in the middle. Great beginning, hell of an ending," Henry replies, his eyes glowing. This boy has an unusual kind of intelligence, Tunstall notes.

"Where are you from, Henry, and where's your family?" Tunstall's dark brown eyes seem to blanch ever so slightly, as Henry looks away from the books and squarely into them.

The Englishman's private rooms are a sanctuary, and he'd not had an intimate conversation with anyone, within them.

"I was born in New York City, raised around the corner from the Five Points. My mother came over from Ireland during the famine, got married in the big city...we had a good life there before the war. Moved to Kansas in sixty-eight, then onto New Mexico. She had the gallopin consumption and we hoped coming West would improve her health...but she passed three years ago. I lost my father in the big war."

Tunstall's face remains stoic, but his eyes flinch once more.

"And what about *your* family Mr. Tunstall?"

"My mother, father, and dear sisters all reside in a great house in London. (He'd paused before beginning.) All my efforts here are for them. These books have made the long journey from our library. Let's see, there is a nautical treasure here, somewhere. Ah, here it is, *The Story of Jack Halyard, the Sailor Boy.*" He hands the book to Henry with the half-smile Henry has grown accustomed to seeing, from time to time. "I'm afraid it's no great work, just entertaining."

"I'll read a great tome, if there ain't nothing else, this will do wonderfully in the meantime. Thank you." Henry smiles as he takes the book.

"The McSweens are giving a dinner tonight, Henry. Will you join us?"

"They may not have enough, and I'd sure hate to put Mrs. McSween out, she's a spitfire I hear."

"Susan's sister and her family are living in the McSween home, whatever they've made for dinner, I suspect there will be plenty of it. And besides, we'd all love a proper concert afterwards."

"Well then, to the manor born."

Tunstall eyes the boy's coat and with the half-smile still playing on his face, strides over to the wardrobe and produces a heavy rib-knitted jacket.

"It's called a cardigan. Wouldn't do for a dinner engagement in London, but we're a long distance from Hampstead. Try it on."

A stranger item of clothing he'd never seen. But Henry takes to it straight away.

"It's a new fashion. Yes, I believe you'll turn out smartly in it. Too tight fitting on me. The book you must return, but the cardigan, is yours."

Henry still has a large smile on his face, a far different expression than the sly nuances of his grin. He's still sporting it when they are admitted into the McSweens next door, clutching his book and looking like a college student.

Susan McSween and the families domestic, Zebrion Bates, are busy in the kitchen. Henry joins them with the usual élan, somehow managing to be of help in a tightly run ship. Alex McSween's young wife is a woman of refinement and style, and proud as a peacock. She is also high-spirited and outspoken, and not to be taken lightly on any matter.

In keeping with the vertical emphasis of current hair fashions, the high knot of pleats and rolls perch atop her well-shaped head like a fancy hat, and the narrow silhouette of her equally elaborate dress makes Susan McSween a singular adornment in Lincoln—much envied and hated by the local *mujeres.*

Her luxurious adobe home is an oasis of culture, with carpets from

Brussels, elegant furniture, fine engravings, an ornate parlor piano, and a violin-playing, liveried black manservant—who is butler, housekeeper, cook, and musician, all in one.

Her home was now filled with family as well. After many years apart, Susan recently welcomed her sister Elizabeth to join them. They'd grown up in Pennsylvania, a large family in a large brick house that stood less than ten miles from Gettysburgh.

That great high-tide battle changed everything in their lives.

"Ah Elizabeth, this is Mr. McCarty. He'll be joining us for dinner, and singing afterwards," Susan enthuses, laying a graceful hand on his arm.

"Ma'am," says Henry. "And who might these little buttons be?"

"This is Minnie, eight years of age, and Joe, who is a proper gentleman already at five. My husband will be joining us later. He should be back soon from Mesilla." Mother and children curtsey and bow. "And what will you sing for us Mr. McCarty?"

"'Lorena ... great favorite of your sisters I believe," Henry states with solicitous charm and Susan smiles.

Music is the way into Susan McSween's rather prickly world, and after a slow start, Henry is beginning to do better in that regard. He also keeps one ear on the spirited conversation drifting in from the parlor.

The discussion, fueled by brandy and machine-rolled cigarettes, began to roil as soon as the two men sat down. Alex was keen to demonstrate the device he'd brought back from New York and began his arguments as he rolled a pile of elegant looking cubebs.

Tunstall watched the brash Scotsman and sipped his brandy, fetching up here and there on McSween's burr, which he found grating.

"I quite agree on the urgency of the matter. But there is more than one way to corner the almighty beef and grain markets at Fort Stanton," Tunstall says.

"But Dolan is more dangerous than his predecessor. Murphy was... predictable. With Dolan nearly bankrupt, and most of his suppliers gone over to you, he's like a wounded animal," McSween offers before emptying his glass and lighting a cigarette for his guest.

"We must put him out of his misery then." Tunstall exhales a large plume of bluish smoke. "I'm sure our pugnacious little Irishman bitterly regrets having hired you to go to New York and sue for the Fritz settlement... even though you were successful."

"He regrets giving me power of attorney, and not having the ten thousand dollar pay out, that's a certainty."

"Convenient of his former House partner to die in Europe and leave a large policy for you to untangle. Holding out for all possible heirs and claimants will keep him at bay long enough I should think. I suppose you have the money escrowed somewhere?" Tunstall asks, watching his partner carefully.

"Yes of course. It's all strictly within legal bounds and all will go where it should—eventually. Meanwhile it's not just Dolan and his thugs we need to concern ourselves with."

"Sheriff Brady and his charming deputy?"

"To begin with yes. Brady will sign a warrant on anyone Dolan names, District Attorney Rynerson will throw out any criminal charges against the House, and boss Catron in Santa Fe will back their play."

"All of them masons and scoundrels," Tunstall adds with disgust.

"And all in cahoots. But if we can bankrupt Dolan, counter his thugs, present Chisum as the head of our bank...I believe the rest may well be persuaded to do business with us," the Scotsman concludes.

Susan enters the room, rather grandly, to announce dinner and to admonish the menfolk. "If you two are going to smoke like chimneys before dinner, I'm going to raise the windows." She also finds it necessary to puncture their grand baronial scheming while pulling the sash and lifting the window. "And if you go much further into this store business you'll both be murdered."

"I appreciate your candor, Mrs. McSween, but I believe you underestimate us," Tunstall replies bravely.

"Luck favors the bold," says Alex, as if raising a toast. Husband and wife share a glance that is distasteful to the lady of the house—the statement and look had called to mind something better left alone.

The evening soon shifts from smoky politics to a congenial and highly palatable meal—and finally to art. The children arrange themselves on the floor of the parlor, excited to have a show to watch. Councilor McSween pours out another round anticipating a fine diversion.

Susan perches herself on the ornate piano bench and adjusts the folds of her silk dress with obvious pleasure. Back erect and head held high, accompanied by the resourceful Zebrion—they begin a pair of simple Mozart miniatures.

Her playing is rather stiff perhaps, and the hardest passages have been rephrased, but the warmth of Zebrion's tone transforms all. Russian Bill came to mind and the Irish singer is in a fine state of transport.

"Bravo," Henry declares and bows low before both Zebrion and Susan.

"Henry will sing, 'Lorena,'" announces Susan. She opens the music and nods to Zebrion and Henry.

"Ah...a favorite of Susan's, and mine," Alex says with a special glow.

The introduction begins, sonorous and plaintive. Henry's voice begins to soar, and a grand moment unfolds.

The years creep slowly by, Lorena
Snow is on the grass again,
The sun's low down the sky, Lorena
The frost gleams where flowers have been;

The lilting voice, a little scratchy at first, soon warms and fills the room, lifting through the open windows.

He'd heard the faint and rarefied sound of piano and violin, and stepped outside onto the porch of the house. Jesse Evans continues to stand and listen, eyes closed. Voice and melody and emotion drift like phantoms from the past in the still night air.

"I believe the little nibbler has returned," Olinger growls. He'd also stepped onto the landing in time to hear the last verse.

Evans brushes past him and goes inside without a word. Back into the corner office and the whiskey-fueled meeting between Dolan and Lincoln County District Attorney William Rynerson. Nearly seven feet tall, the district attorney seems to fill the little room all by himself.

"We're operating in a void out here. I say we fill that void with precise, effective action. If McSween won't pay up, you can go after Tunstall's property. That's a justifiable pretense, let things develop, slowly. You'll know when to move," the District Attorney pronounces with a harsh little chuckle.

Jesse takes a drink and watches the long, heavily bearded face of District Attorney Rynerson, recalling the story he'd heard about him. A tale of cold-blooded murder in the streets of Santa Fe. He'd shot and killed the Chief Justice of the New Mexico Territory ten years before, over a woman. The real power in the territory, Attorney General Thomas Catron—acquitted him with a swift verdict of self-defense.

And now those two jackals watch over Dolan's affairs like a pair of

Olympians. *Their power is nearly absolute*, Jesse thinks. But that didn't free them from hubris, and from being blinded by that power.

Dolan pours another round.

"What say you, Jesse?"

"I'd say to think hard on how much attention you want brought on Lincoln County."

"I believe I'll be turning in, I've a long ride back to Messilla in the morning," Rynerson says. He rises to his great height and looks at Jesse as if he were an insect. Leaving the room he ducks his head to get through the door.

"I'll leave you two gentlemen to smoke and work on your plans. Mrs. McSween, Zebrion—it was a pleasure to make music with you...good night Mr. and Mrs. Shields, Minnie and Joe you two behave yourselves," Henry says, winking at the kids.

At the door he shakes Zebrion's hand and says something quietly, raising a smile on the violinist's sturdy face.

"You be careful Mr. McCarty," Zebrion says, a warning in his voice.

Warmed by the cardigan and still holding tight to the book, Henry is off in search of his friends. Moving along the empty street, whistling, business details he'd overheard begin to stack up. It was all very interesting, very bold, and some of it very curious—particularly a couple of looks he'd caught between Alex and his wife.

"Well, if it isn't the *little nibbler*. That was some fine singin earlier. Maybe you'll want to sing some more...for me?" the voice emanating from a tall shadow who'd stepped out into the street.

"Hello Bob, I guess you're sore because I left the employ of your boss, like I did. But you left me no choice in the matter," Henry offers, quickly considering several alternative plans of action.

"It's a free land they say."

Olinger suddenly closes on him, swinging with his right—Henry ducks under the arc and backs away, but is caught by a chopping left hook. Olinger pins his shoulders against an adobe wall with a powerful wrenching thrust.

"I heard about how you sharked that blacksmith. You won't be sharkin me."

"I'll not be shooting you in the back for certain," Kid Antrim replies, his hand reaching for the hideout as Olinger leans in. The long hair brushes his face and rank breath poisoning the night air. Olinger abruptly head-butts the boy, dropping him to the ground.

The knife is pulled from its scabbard but hearing footsteps, Olinger spins around.

"Why don't you just step out here in the street," says Dick Brewer. The moon provides enough light for their eyes to meet and lock.

"Well goddamn, everyone's out for a stroll tonight." Enjoying himself, Olinger steps forward with a little bend of the knee and a taunting gesture with one hand.

This fight had been brewing for some time and a pity no one is there to see it. Both men are formidable gladiators in the same weight class; Brewer more the bare-knuckled heavyweight boxer, and Olinger, an eye-gouging brawler.

The Foreman takes off his hat and gun belt, dropping them to the ground, along with a knife. Olinger does the same, spiking his Bowie knife into a hitching post at the last.

The two men circle each other and Pecos Bob spews a steady stream of insults—just part of the show and an effective opening tactic against the easily distracted.

"Hey shitheel I'm gonna bust your ass good. Gonna be shittin blood for a month."

But Brewer isn't listening. As they close on each other, Olinger jumps into a clinch and lands a rabbit punch as the Lion pushes him away. Inside, a boxer's strengths can be negated.

Olinger lurches into another press straightaway, as if an embrace was all he really sought, then delivers a flurry of elbows before he's thrown back again. The next time it's a head butt.

Brewer says nothing during the fight, glad to be out of his head and heart and looking hard for his moment. Three explosive punches are thrown in rapid succession as Olinger circles, and one of them connects solid.

Blood running from his sneering mouth and eyes wild, Olinger manages yet another clinch. This time the ex-deputy goes for Brewer's ear, but just misses, nipping the edge and getting a mouthful of hair instead. He hangs on anyway and works one hand to Brewers face, a thumb in one nostril and fingers going for the eyes.

Brewer lands a heavy body blow and strong enough still to throw him back, and this time a crushing right hand connects squarely with Pecos Bob's jaw, at the perfect moment. The punch wobbles Olinger to his core. He instinctively moves back and away, falls to the ground.

He lies there gathering himself, stumbles to his feet. From a belt clip he pulls out a viciously loaded blackjack and, swinging hard and fast as Brewer moves in, catches him square with a vicious blow.

Brewer goes down like a felled oak.

Olinger staggers over to the hitching post, grinning and pulling the Bowie knife and staggering back. He drops down on top of Brewer. With the big knife he pops the buttons off his shirt and starts to shave the hair on Brewer's chest, just for fun, blood trickling and running in places—then reaching back with his other hand for the crotch, groping first before giving it a heavy wrench.

"How do you like that, El Leon?" Olinger roars and Brewer's eyes blaze open. The knife moves to his neck.

The muscles in Olinger's hand and arm are beginning to tighten on the haft when a two-fisted wallop from his own heavy pistol sags him over face first.

Henry McCarty is standing over him sporting an enormous grin.

"How do *you* like it, shitheel." Henry lets out a whoop and executes a sprightly dance step. Dick Brewer sits up and then slowly gets back to his feet. Unsteady, he gives Olinger a long angry perusal.

"This man is a devilin son-of-a-bitch," Brewer declares.

"I think he would've killed you, and me to."

"Maybe...I'm not going to pass judgement on him just yet, this was just a street scrap," Brewer answers.

"I'd say Pecos lost."

"I guess we better haul his sorry ass out of the road. You gave him a hell of a whack."

"He sure had it coming."

They leave Pecos slumped with head lolled to the side and beginning to come to. A livid opening of skin on the crown of his pate bleeds down into lank hair and down into the dirt.

7

"Mother and Father are so proud of you, John." Emily keeps looking back at him and reaching out with a smile. He follows her into the darkening interior. Down long hallways, through the gaslit drawing room and library, on past books towering up into the shadows. She leads the chase, always just beyond his grasp. Dark chestnut hair down and flowing as she turns back to her beloved younger brother.

"They do so worry about you. We all do."

Into the dining room, where a table fully set with candles burning, sits empty. John searches the large room but his sister is gone. He moves to the window, looks out on a park shrouded in fog. An open carriage rolls out of the mist, a grave footman in the dickey box and lamps burning.

The diligence passes close enough to reveal his mother, Ramie, and father, John, sitting in the imperial. They both seem bowed down by a great concern. He calls out, runs after them as they disappear into a darkening forest. The outstretched boughs of misshapen fir trees block his way. But he keeps pushing forward.

Turning, a broad-shouldered figure steps out of the brume and mist, instantly filling his soul with cold dread. The gray huntsman takes another step forward, eyes burning red. But an incongruous clanging echoes out across the dreamscape, freezing the shadow in place.

Tunstall's eyes open, flutter a few times, take in the first rosy light of morning. He and his men are rolled out on the floor, beginning to stir from the night's last dreams.

His had taken him to England, again, and to all his deepest worries.

The German cook bangs the triangle and roars from the yard, where the meals are cooked, "Coffee's ready. Time to rise and shine, ladies."

Sleepily looking over the crew, John smiles as they begin to stumble into pants and boots. This part is a pleasure to him; the camaraderie, the leading of good men, the closeness, and the wheel starting up again with breakfast waiting, biscuits and bacon and easy chatter about the day ahead.

"Only a half-day's work, lads, then off to a Saturday night baile with us," Henry announces as he leaps down off the stoop. He slaps Fred Waite, the olive-skinned Chickasaw cowboy, on the shoulder as he lands.

"Someone tell this stage monkey the show's over," Fred quips and rolls his eyes, but smiling also.

"It's just the beginning sir," Henry replies.

"Oh for Christ sake, grab a biscuit and shut up," Charlie says while tupping out a cup of coffee.

Tunstall, still lost somewhere between Hyde Park and New Mexico, steps out amongst the good-natured carping of his men.

"Sleep well Mr. Tunstall?" Henry asks.

"Yes...I suppose I did. I was pretty badly used up. The road between here and Mesilla is a long one, and full of woe." Tunstall's hair is mussed and falling forward into his eyes, the shoulders slumped.

The young Englishman's life has been overwhelmed by a legal chess match. The three hundred miles ridden in the past week alone—responding to and maneuvering around various warrants, writs, and liens motioned forward by Dolan and Rynerson—is wearing him down to the bone.

"I say huzzah for our boss, the Englishman who will be an American king," Henry yells out.

"To the manor born," Fred roars.

Tunstall can't help but smile again, bigger this time, taking in a long hot drink of strong coffee and starting to come fully awake. The news isn't all bad by any means.

"The legal battles have been a challenge for certain—to say nothing of our stock troubles," Tunstall says, giving Dick Brewer a significant look.

"I say bully for Dick Brewer and the Tunstall cowboys! Bob Olinger bested in fisticuffs. Our cattle stolen *and* recovered. Jesse Evans in the Lincoln pit, and you fellows have put'em there."

"Huzzah!" The same chorus yells out even louder.

Dick nods and Henry pounds him on the back. "Slipping up on them in the dead of night was the trick. Probably saved some lives," Dick says.

"I believe that was your idea, Mr. McCarty," replies John, still smiling.

"Discretion is the better part of valor, especially when hunting Jesse Evans," Henry says with a crooked grin.

"He seems an extraordinary fellow. I quite liked him—not what I expected at all. It was just a brief meeting, with us in the advantage. But he's nothing like Dolan, or Olinger, or anyone else I've met for that matter."

"Jesse's nobody's fool, and that's for certain. I like him too, of course he'd kill us both in a heartbeat if he needed to. And he won't be in that shithole for long."

"I've offered to visit Mr. Evans and to bring him some whiskey. I believe I will, maybe I can turn him. It'll rile Dolan when he gets back from Santa Fe and hears about it—and it's worth it for that alone."

"Mr. Tunstall, you should come to the baile with us first. A little dancing would lighten your soul, considerably. Take your mind off all the business and politics, for a little while at least."

"I'll have to pass, Henry. I've too many letters to write, besides, Dick and I intend to go on a hunt tomorrow. And bloody hell...I need a good rest first."

Tunstall, thinking of the simple pleasures of a field expedition to the high country, is as excited as Henry—in his own way.

"Next time then *El Jefe*."

There are fifteen rocky miles between the Rio Feliz ranch and San Patricio, and the last of it down a steep escarpment switchback. Just a short, light-hearted excursion in the grand scheme of things.

The three are only too happy to have a Saturday night fandango to attend and would have traveled twice as far.

Horacio Ortiz, a San Patricio native with a little sheep camp adjoining Tunstall's land, had invited Charlie and his friends earlier in the week. During all of their long sojourning and cattle work since—Henry had thought of little else.

"How'd you boys learn Spanish and all the fancy fandangos, and when the hell are you gonna teach me?" Tom asks, his freckled cheeks wrinkling with a little smile.

"Where there's a will there's a way, even for a heavy-footed sore-toed clogger like you," says Charlie.

"I got started as soon as we moved to New Mexico, just have a knack for it. Also came to understand this. If you're going to get past all the lace and ruffles," Henry offers conspiratorially, flashing the grin. "You better speak like a gentleman and dance like the devil."

"Tom, when we're through with ya, you'll be a dancing fool," Charlie adds.

"A bigger problem is that grease stain on your dress shirt," Henry says. He'd been considering the matter and had firmly decided on a course of action. "Let's switch shirts and my vest will hide the stain."

"Why don't I just borry the vest?"

"No, you wear the shirt and I'll keep the vest," Henry answers. The vest is finely cut and handsomely fitted, with a touch of gold embroidery around the pockets. A prized possession and it went perfectly with the red scarf.

"You're a handsome devil Tom. You might not be a dancer, yet, but you'll make out okay." For a final touch Henry pulls a green scarf from his saddlebag, tying it handsomely around Tom's neck and grinning at his handiwork. "A little color is a fine thing!"

From the moment they arrive at the baile—Henry is transformed. His language skills are excellent, and manners impeccable. He has the patience and sparkling elegance of a Spanish gentleman, the daring and charm of an Irish rogue.

A feast of color and sound awaits with lamp light a dusky orange and the adobe walls festooned with red, yellow, and blue paper ornaments. Many of the dresses are a deep green. The room swirls with a hypnotic jangle of music. Henry smiles and nods to the guitarist, the mandolinist, and the two fiddlers.

Without a moment's hesitation he introduces himself to a mujer twice his age, and with a gallant gesture, partners up and takes to the dance floor. His friends can only shake their heads at his boldness.

The complicated footwork involved is mind-boggling to Tom. The intricate weave of couples, the fast-paced bowing and strumming of instruments, the spinning ruffled dresses—seem calculated to make his head spin.

Charlie, not to be outdone, soon joins in, with decidedly less foot skill but equal enthusiasm. On his third dance the Southerner sparks an attractive young woman with a crooked front tooth. Something about her gives Charlie a ticklish spinning in his chest.

Poor Tom reduced to standing in the corner and smiling awkwardly at the host, and at his friends when they whirl by.

"*Buenos noches, señor,*" says a plump guerra, fascinated with his red hair and suddenly standing next to him. "What your name?"

"Tom," he replies, noticing the beguiling curve of her full lips straight off, and his head spinning wildly again.

Henry makes sure to visit politely with the elders, knowing full well to take the calf you must sugar the cow. This baile has been a long time coming and he's not forgotten the politics and manners, or the steps. And as the night evolves—his passion for it all only increases.

Eventually, the miraculous enchantment he'd foreseen *does* occur, under the festooned vigas and beginning with the most innocent of gestures.

"*Buenos noches señorita, cómo se llama?*"

"*Adelita.*"

"*Puedo tener este baile, Adelita?*" Henry inquires, his blue eyes sparkling into the lovely oval of her face, lingering a moment on the delicate nose and the parted lips, before returning to her dark gaze—finishing with a graceful bow.

"*Si, Señor,*" she replies, smiling back with a curtsy.

Henry extends his hand and leads her onto the floor, an actual spark jumping between them when they touch. His right hand reaches protectively around her slim waist, brushing over and receiving an intimacy of the rib cage and the pounding heart within. His left taking her right and immediately thrilling to the touch of skin and the fine delicate bones just beneath the surface.

As they spin and step—the scent of her hair, of her body, comes to him like a secret emissary. A messenger with the most private and elemental of clues. His nostrils flare slightly, her lips part again and the dance continues.

In the midst of the waltz, Adelita looks up into his eyes, only for a moment, and a sudden fateful magic fills the little space between them. When his head moves to the side with the next step and turn, Henry follows the arc of her beautifully lifted hair down to the light silk tracing the nape of her neck.

No one had seen anything the least bit scandalous in the way they were dancing, just an attractive young couple and the best pairing of dancers at the baile.

But these two were already making love.

"Are you sure about this hunt? It'll take all day, but I guess we *will* be closer to Lincoln at the end of it—if you still want to visit with Evans," says Dick, eyeing the coffee.

"Have a cup Mr. Brewer, the day can wait another few minutes. And yes to the hunt. And yes, I promised the redoubtable Mr. Evans I'd bring him a jug, it will do no harm to be friendly. Maybe we can drive a wedge."

Brewer gets his coffee and nods, pulling up the only other chair. The stove is throwing off a good bit of heat, if you sit close enough. It'll be a cold ride, but they'll have the sun in the afternoon, once they're out of the canyon.

The two men regard each other with a tacit understanding. Both are naturally quiet and habitually circumspect; Tunstall always plotting ahead, and his foreman tending to look back.

"I believe this new year will see a dramatic change in our fortunes," Tunstall declares, breaking the silence with an uncharacteristic optimism.

"I hope so, John, you deserve it. We've got a tight spot to navigate first," Brewer replies, intent on his coffee then glancing up with a guarded look. Tunstall had come to understand, and to hate this look.

"I suppose you've been renewing your vows again this morning. One day you will forget this woman," John suggests. Brewer inspects his coffee cup with renewed interest. "Of course, that's easy for me to say...I've never been smitten. Haven't had the time I suppose," John admits and their eyes meet again.

"Well you're not missing anything but a living hell. The first year was like waking up every morning to discover your arms been torn off, nothing left but a bloody stump, and you wonder if you can survive it," Dick clarifies, but he immediately wished he hadn't. Speaking about it didn't help. Putting words to it just gave it more power.

"How long now?" Tunstall asks, shaking his head.

"Two years next April."

"That seems long enough Dick. You should concentrate on your future, here in Lincoln County with me. We are going to accomplish great things. Things that I cannot do alone."

"Well, that's a ride I'll take, past be damned," Brewer confides. His face brightens as his friend and employer stands and places a hand on his shoulder.

"Let's be off then."

Afternoon sun pours down on the backs of two Sunday hunters, trailing up into the pines and enjoying the November warmth. Horses hobbled below and Brewer in the lead. Tunstall following along with his one good eye trained on the ground searching for scat. The Londoner is surprisingly at home in the woods.

Arriving at a broad ridge they begin to think of lunch. Brewer offers to scour the thickly wooded knob they've arrived at, before they eat. Tunstall sets his pack down and selects a sheltering tree to rest against. Once he's comfortably situated though, the long hard week begins to tell on him. Despite his intentions to bring down a trophy kill before resting, he begins to nod off contentedly.

Brewer works his way through the crowded piñons, eventually coming up on a vantage point to a neighboring ridge. There a huge elk lifts his head from grazing. He slowly shoulders his rifle and takes aim, but something spooks the animal and it quickly moves into thicker cover.

The day is fine and still and Tunstall continues to drowse. He dreams of Hampstead Heath and the green hills of his youth. He could've slept so for hours, warm in the sun, contented memories drifting like leaves on the surface of a stream.

Back in the shadowy woods a sound emerges, as of some large creature moving through the brush. The leaves of a scrub oak rustle and a large black bear pokes his head into the clearing where Tunstall sleeps. Cautiously sniffing the air, he ignores the man and goes straight for the pack and the food tucked away inside. The contents are soon scattered and the commotion brings Tunstall to his feet.

Bear and man size each other up, ten feet apart, half a loaf of bread hanging from the great animal's jaws. On his hind legs, the bear towers over the man and swallows a hunk of bread and meat. Rather nonchalant, Tunstall thinks, with rifle pointed at the bear's heart.

"Cheeky bugger."

Tunstall fires, not at the animal but into the air. The sudden explosive concussion making a terrible roar, and the bear executing a hasty retreat.

John Tunstall, the Oxford Man and traveler of the American West, came near to pissing himself thinking of the kill and whether a .44-40 slug would put the bear down—but had decided to scare the animal off.

The bear was very manlike, standing there with a mouth full of his lunch.

"What were you shooting at?" Brewer asks, a few minutes later.

"A bear...he was quite far away. I missed."

Jesse Evans, along with Frank Baker, Billy Morton, and Tom Hill, the least talkative and most dependable shark of the gang, find themselves confined in the hole. Surprised, disgusted, and discomfited to say the least. It was all thanks to a warrant signed by Justice of the peace Wilson, and successful execution of it by Dick Brewer.

The Boys are walking about in the dirt yard directly abutting Sheriff Brady's office, and the infamous pit—taking their evening "exercise" in the crisp air and grousing about the turn of their fortunes.

"Come on Brady, you know this ain't right."

"Well now Mr. Baker, maybe I'm just lonely and require your company to make it through the long night,"

"Save your whining for when I can't hear it, Frank," Jesse commands.

"Whoa boss, look what's coming," Tom Hill interjects suddenly.

After covering much ground since their morning coffee, Tunstall and Brewer appear down the street. Brewer with two wild turkeys hanging from the apple and Tunstall holding a fat jug just filled at his store.

They rein up in front of Jesse and the boys.

"Well, here you are Englishman—did you bring enough whiskey to soak us as you promised?" Jesse inquires.

"Yes indeed. I only had a dram when I met you on the trail, but today I have a jug filled to the cork. More than enough I should think," says Tunstall. He dismounts jug in hand.

"I don't care what they say about your Lordship, you're all right," Frank squeals, and, altering his normal mocking tone, dramatically—he reaches out to be the first to shake hands with Tunstall, and to pull the cork. They greet Brewer as an old friend as well, with handshakes and head nods going around the circle.

"Well Dick I don't know if you've got us...or we have you. But let's drink this whiskey and talk things over," Jesse suggests, taking the jug from Frank and tilting it back for a long tipple.

"We have you Jesse, and no doubt about it," Brewer answers.

"For now, and it does amuse me to see you two come around. But you'll get no satisfaction," Jesse replies.

"Satisfaction, the Devil! I never went begging for a woman, and the mules ain't foaled that I would pay twice for. You've got my horses and my prize mules, but you can go to hell before I beg for them," Tunstall declares. "I *will* drink to your good health though," he concludes, grabbing the jug for his own tilt.

"That's salty talk for an Oxford man. I like it," Frank says.

Sheriff Brady, sitting on the porch of his office with a shotgun in his lap, gets up in disgust and goes inside. Deputy Peppin is left to keep an eye on the prisoners and their guests. No telling what Dolan will make of it all when he returns, *the little bulldog's blood will be up and no doubt*—the sheriff thinks to himself as he reaches under a desk for his own turn at the ardent.

"Good for you, Englishman," says Jesse, seeing into the young Londoner at close range, as only he can.

"Tell us some stories about merry old England," Frank continues in the same vein.

Tunstall regards the Alabamian jokester with a wry smile, wondering to himself how this odd person came to be associated with the baronial Jesse Evans.

"Well Mr. Baker, it's not particularly merry, but it *is* very old. There's a fountain not far from my family's house in Hackney, that is no doubt older than the oldest brick building in America. It is civilization at its highest—the oldest traditions and the most efficient innovations."

Jesse continues to watch Tunstall closely and carefully, as if the sudden appearance meant a change in the cards, and he determined to guess the suit.

"The women are prim, the men forthright, and trains punctual. For a nominal fee, you can ride to anywhere in the realm in comfort. None of this bone-jarring, endless back-breaking riding from pillar to post."

"Sounds like a fairy tale."

"Of course, there's Whitechapel, a giant London shit hole. A treacherous pit of sin and vice that has no equal on earth. It's overrun with the thieves and cutthroats and gutter rats."

"Go on," Jessie says.

"Murderous gangs on the prowl the equal of any on this side of the great pond. By comparison, the Boys would shine forth there like paragons of virtue," Tunstall informs as he prepares to take another sociable pull.

"Well kiss my grannie's lily-white ass and hang me for a hog thief," says Billy Morton with a smile, reaching now for another turn at the jug.

"It's all the sunshine and space you have out here—has a very healthy effect on the mind," Tunstall informs the odd company of outlaws and deranged mummers.

Jesse has a rare smile, his taste for the unusual getting the better of his *usual* grim skepticism. And this Englishman *is* remarkable and amusing, all at once.

"Where's Kid Antrim?" Jesse asks, suddenly.

"He and some of my other cowboys went to a baile last night, no doubt some of them are married by now. Henry is quite the dancer...quite the singer too."

"I'm glad he's with you, good place for him."

"And why don't you come to work for me as well?" Tunstall offers. The pistoleer looks away and then back at the Englishman.

The office door swings open and Brady stomps out into the yard.

"Time for you fellows to get back in the hole," the sheriff interjects with shotgun cradled.

"Care to join us below, we can talk over matters at length," Jesse replies.

"What say you Sheriff, mind if Mr. Brewer and I stay a while longer?"

"This little joke is over, you be about your business Tunstall, before I tear up Squire Wilson's goddamned warrant let the Boys go and put you in the hole instead," Brady growls.

The sheriff is a man of fiery passions and impressive displays of temper. Once the fuse is lit, it's only a matter of time before an explosion erupts. Tunstall walks over to Jesse and hands him the jug.

"You and the boys finish this off...remember our good faith here tonight. I think we might find common ground if we chose to. Consider my offer," Tunstall adds as he shakes Jesse's hand.

"There's too many sharks I'd have to kill straight off—were I to accept. Meanwhile I'll do battle with this jug. Englishman you and Mr. Brewer should be making preparations. Jimmy and the hatchet man are fatally short-tempered, more'n our fine Sheriff Brady even," Jesse answers in a low voice.

Tunstall nods and his eyes follow after the pistoleer. Jesse wasn't a tall or particularly big man, but there was immense strength in his presence and an absence of the malignant delirium so many in the West suffered from.

And you somehow knew he could defeat any threat sent against him. A deadly person certainly but having seen him up close and spent a little time basking in Evan's sovereignty, the Englishman wished more than ever he could be turned.

Santa Fe
The Governors Palace
Office of Attorney General Thomas Catron

Thomas B. Catron sits heavily at a large desk, committing his signature to a deed—a mortgage for the House and all its holdings. In size, manner, and motive, he is a courtly Southern version of New York's infamous Boss Tweed.

Catron pushes a stack of bills across the desk with a large plump hand. A much smaller hand reaches out to take possession, and the money goes into the breast pocket of its new owner, Jimmy Dolan.

"So, Jimmy, you're the head man in Lincoln now. You've outlasted Murphy. Well done. Still...first rattle out of the box and you come here with hat in hand, one step away from bankruptcy, giving it all over to me, and small beer at that. That Englishman has just about done for you."

Catron speaks with a heavy southern accent, curling off his tongue like thick cigar smoke—but his thinking is crisp and precise. A graduate of the University of Missouri, and a Confederate battery sergeant in 'Ole' Pap' Price's brigade during the rebellion.

He'd been territorial Attorney General and top dog in New Mexico for many years. His ascendancy began soon after arriving in the spring of 1866. He'd been used to firing the big guns and proceeded to fire off the biggest guns he could find in the ripe young territory.

"I'm only one or two moves away from taking it all back and then some. You can be damn sure of that," Dolan assures, with the blood rising in his voice. He is not cowed, and his composure before the big man is impressive. Boss Catron regards the Irish bulldog for a moment before speaking.

"I created Lincoln County and it will stay in my pocket one way or the other, but I prefer you to be the one I deal with of course, and not the Englishman. Now step carefully and don't start a fire you can't put out. Tunstall probably comes from a prominent family. And make sure brother Rynerson and Brady are doing their part," Catron clarifies and Dolan nods.

"I haven't come this far to just drop it all down the privy. I'll be the last man standing, you can bet your buttons on that."

Catron maneuvers his bulk around the desk with a practiced air, and the two men exchange a strangely involved handshake. On the mantel behind them, hiding in plain sight, is an emblem of the square and compass—the symbols of Freemasonry.

John Tunstall had ridden many a hard mile since coming to New Mexico. He was trying to come up with a number as he trotted along the two-track. The present road was another long one. It led to John Chisum's Southfork ranch. The impressive adobe hacienda with its many rooms lay in the grasslands some fifty miles away.

Bare yellowed stubble curves to the horizon like some vast and gently roiled sheet. But he took the emptiness of it as a heartening palliative against the mountains, where it seemed every tree and boulder hid some grievous trouble and grinning enemy.

The open country was called the Eyebrow of God, *La Ceja de Dios*—by locals. A good name for it he thinks, it *is* like a massive eyebrow, and it *is* high country. But if it is the Eyebrow of God—where the devil is the old charlatan?

If I ever reach the point of death, I shall be called upon to make some disagreeable trip before I'm allowed to go to the next world, Tunstall confides to himself, shivering and hacking in the chill air. The ragged coughing produces a chunk of phlegm, which he spits out with a sigh. He clears his nose with a snort and a thumb alongside the opposite nostril. *Glad mother and sister Emily were not here to see that.*

John Tunstall wished more than anything he were in bed, covered with warm blankets.

For all his endless scheming and effort, and success—he now felt nearly defeated. A final showdown of some sort was coming, he felt certain.

Dolan had appeared out of nowhere one week before, riffle in hand, demanding that they settle their differences right there. Fortunately, Brewer stepped in and put a stop to the frightening and chaotic situation.

He feared an ambush now at every turn.

He hated the very thought of it but it seemed Dolan's majestic boast—that he was backed by Tom Catron and the Santa Fe Ring, and that the Ring controlled everything in New Mexico, including the courts—was true.

He, Chisum, and McSween; were all ensnared in legal quagmires.

Their property and even their lives put at constant threat, and all of that arranged with such breathtaking disregard for legality and fairness, that it could only have been contorted and finagled from the top down.

A writ of attachment had been trumped up and placed on McSween's house and its contents, and because they were partners, Tunstall's store and his livestock at the ranch were part of the same writ—all to answer for the nonpayment of the Fritz insurance settlement.

The policy had become a weapon of war.

And Chisum, presented with a lien against supposed unpaid debts, and being tighter than the bark on a tree, had chosen to spend time in a Las Cruces jail rather than answer that lien. Everything, directly the work of the all-powerful fat man—Tom Catron.

The Englishman hoped to get Chisum's brothers, in the elder brother's absence, to agree to risk some of their men for protection. It seemed a forlorn hope—but he had to try.

Chisum had described the Ring quite well one night, with the kind of poetic clarity that would have pleased Tunstall's old philosophy professor at Oxford. John recalled that bit of eloquence and the affirmation that followed, often, particularly on these long and so often, fruitless rides. It gave him a prideful burst of energy.

Alex was there and Chisum's two brothers, all seated around the fire in the great hall at the Southfork, smoking and listening to the great man hold forth.

"The governor, goddamned hog thief that he is, has said there is no Ring. I am of this opinion as well. If there was a Ring, there would be some show to get through it, or to get on the outside or inside of it. But the thing they got up there is perfectly hard and solid; it cannot be penetrated from either side or end. And when this substance strikes an ordinary citizen, it goes right through him and leaves him in such a condition that he never recovers," the cowman offers with a wink.

"A fine thing then that we are not ordinary citizens," Alex says.

"Indeed," Tunstall agrees, exhaling a cloud of smoke and joining in the chortling round from the well-soaked room.

"With a little backbone, and a lot of money. We will succeed. I'm certain of it," the weathered cowman replies, meeting the young Englishman's gaze with a confident nod.

The night was a revelation of powerful elder friends and the boldness of their combined enterprise. It had come on him as he sat smoking a cigar and listening—the fire blazing, these formidable players seated close around—he was suddenly *sure* he would make a name for himself in the American West.

He continues thinking about that night with hopeful eyes on the horizon. That they could outwit and outmaneuver the Ring had become their own majestic boast. Though it felt hollow now as the long ride tramped on and on.

Things went very well in the beginning for certain, but that had gradually changed. It had all begun to turn against him, somehow, and the puffed-up letters he sent home revealed enough truth to alarm his parents into a state of constant worry.

But John Tunstall was not played out yet, not by a long shot. Chisum was a man of great stature and renown, and *he* was a British citizen from a proud and prosperous family, and McSween had connections in the nation's capital. The American government would definitely be hearing from them. Pressure from Washington might well be the forge to break the Ring's stranglehold. McSween had fired off the first round a week before.

The Englishman stops his musing and dismounts. He unfastens his trousers to make water, then refastening the buttons, he pauses before remounting. His buttocks are cramping again. He tries to massage the pain out of his ass and another sharp wheeze confirms his chest cold is only growing worse.

Tunstall is slow to get back up in the saddle. There's a darkening line moving in on the horizon. Although the combination of blue sky to the south, amber gold all around, and purpling furrows to the north, is extraordinary—he can only hope that there's a chance of making the Southfork before the weather turns truly miserable.

Late afternoon is softly bleeding through closed curtains in a room filled with the sour stench of a fatally sick man. Jimmy Dolan sits at his former bosses' side, an angry smirk playing on pinched features.

Lawrence Gustave Murphy has just heard a recount of the day's news in stoic silence. Though cancer has robbed him of his strength, and whiskey and laudanum are the only medicines he concerns himself with now, a clear-headed Irish sense of humor is still in evidence.

"Don't be so gloomy." Murphy leans over to spit a thick gob into a pan.

"How'd you like to be lying here puking and shitting yourself, feeling the knife in your chest every time you draw breath. Lad, you're a sight better off than me." He begins to sink again, taking a shot of laudanum.

"Never should've signed over the power of attorney," Dolan admits.

"It's a powerful card, and in the hands of a slick shyster like McSween, it's deadly. He did collect a lot of money for us before he decided to rob us blind." Murphy wheezes out a good hearty laugh.

"Come on now Captain, it's no laughing matter."

"Tis' to me...you'll kill the Englishman and the Scotsman too, most likely. Jimmy boy, you are a genuine son-of-a-bitch Irish bulldog cut from the old cloth, and god love you for it. But I'm telling you, sure as the sun shines, you won't be the hero of this story."

"I don't give a damn what this little world thinks of me, and the big world can kiss me arse too."

"Ahh...Jimmy Dolan, always so cocksure. Served you well enough I suppose, and you're lucky to boot. My luck has run out, I'm sick and dying and broke. I've just put up my ranch for sale."

"I saw that, that's why I came. If I had the money, I'd set you up, you know that...until you pass. But I'll need everything I have to finish the dance."

"Don't worry yourself Jimmy, Fair Oaks will sell, and Maria will stay with me no matter what."

A long silence ensues as Murphy starts to choke again, ultimately spitting out some precious part of his lungs, then sinking further, but not before another generous dose of his medicine—this time straight whiskey. Dolan watches this sickening performance with a degree of commiseration, despite the hard layer of iron covering his heart.

"That's one thing 'bout dying, I just don't give a good goddamn anymore. I renounce my former wicked life. I'm leaving the war behind." Murphy starts to laugh again but it only leads to more coughing. "I'll leave that up to you Jimmy boy."

"It's in lieu of a large sum of money owed to the House by his partner McSween. Insurance money," explains Jimmy Dolan, with a condescending air.

Sheriff Brady glances over the document; a writ for livestock in possession of John Tunstall. He signs and hands it across the desk to Dolan, plainly irritated. The sheriff knows this is more than a livestock warrant, that its likely just an excuse to confront and murder Tunstall.

The hard-nosed sheriff doesn't give a damn about the Englishman—but he resents being talked down to, by anyone, especially the brash little upstart before him. Dolan was still a pup back in the old country when Brady had first set foot on American soil.

He'd gone immediately to the West. Ultimately joining the New Mexico Volunteers and becoming a mounted soldier. In fifteen years on the frontier he saw the elephant aplenty. While the Civil War raged back east he fought alongside Captain Murphy and the wily Kit Carson—against the Navajo, and the Apache—even the mighty Comanche.

The arrogance and proprietary sense he has about everything in Lincoln County sprang from those fateful days. After the big war he became a useful cog in the House machinery and Captain Murphy, his brother Mason, regarded him as indispensable. The sheriff had always been the biggest swinging dick of the bunch.

Brady hated now to see his old friend Murphy sick and dying before his time. And he hated seeing the cocky little shitheel Dolan take his business even more. On top of all that, the insolence of Dolan's bodyguard, *his* former deputy—Pecos Bob Olinger—was insufferable.

"The trouble with you Jimmy, you got no sense of style."

"Oh I've got style, it just too new for an old-timer like you." Dolan turns to leave with writ in hand, heading out the door without another word. Olinger, who'd been slouching against the door frame during the whole testy encounter, stares back at the sheriff with a brazen smirk.

"Mind someone doesn't sneak up on your hatchet man, especially that goddamned little runt Kid Antrim. Hatchet Bob won't be worth much with his head stove in," says Brady, winking at his former deputy.

Walking away, Bob raises the middle finger of his left hand.

John had driven himself from his blankets with much to do on a bitter February morning—the first day of the week and the forty ninth day of the new year, 1878.

He sits drinking coffee by the stove and considering the miserable task ahead. A sense of profound dread permeating his thoughts like the freezing air. Into the weary saddle again with his fever and his cough, to move the horses into town. He could ride in a wagon and go the long way around with Fred and Jim, a bit more comfortable, but twice as long.

He intended to move both herd and men into town, where they all might be safe. There was little doubt about Dolan's intentions now and he intended to stay one step ahead of them.

The trip to the Chisum's ranch was a boondoggle and he'd made it back the day before, exhausted and dispirited. The cattle baron was still incarcerated, and his brothers would not act without his say so. It was all on Tunstall's shoulders now and he would not let his father's investment be squandered. He was an Oxford man and would triumph over his opponent, there was no other acceptable alternative.

In Lincoln they'd have some degree of safety at least, he would not be gunned down in the middle of the street, and he would take precautions whenever he left the store or the McSween compound. They would bide their time and wait for outside help.

"Horses are saddled, are you sure about this?" Dick asks, eyeing his boss and wondering if he has enough sand left to make the long cold ride into Lincoln. "You look about played out John. Maybe we ought to stay put for a day or two and let you rest up."

"You're pale as the moon boss, and I can see the fever in your eyes," Henry adds, watching with concern as Tunstall walks to his horse, a bit unsteady.

"We must move now. I can have a good long rest when we get to Lincoln."

"Well hell, God is good, but never dance in a small boat," Henry answers, trying to sound merry.

Jesse Evans and the Boys grimly cut along the bottom of a wide valley. Dolan and the hatchet man are at the head of the column pushing their mounts at a fast trot, Jesse nearly at the rear.

All of the men stiffened by heavy woolen coats and the cold wind blasting down off the big mountain. Conversation dried up a long ways back and everyone had pulled their collars up.

"Frank and Billy, ride up alongside," Jimmy yells back down the line.

"Yes sir Mr. Jimmy, what can we do ya for," Frank sings out in his high-pitched rasp.

"Were you boys in the War?" Dolan asks.

"I tried to jine up but pap kept me on the farm, beat my ass good'n proper for trying to run off to the fight, weren't near old enough he said. Billy was even younger, just a button."

"Didn't stop me," Dolan says.

"We heered you was a drummer boy, under McClernand. The Blue couldn't a won without you and no doubt," Frank crows out, delighted with his quick summation.

"I got plans for you today," says Jimmy, grinning at the mummers and shaking his head at the same time.

"Hell yes, always ready fer a spree," says Frank.

"Bob and I and the rest will take the main road, you boys will be riding the Parajito Trail and we'll meet up at his ranch. If Tunstall is coming in today, he'll be on one or the other. If he should be on the Parajito I want you and Billy to make sure he stays up there," Dolan orders, lowering his voice a notch. "There's fifty dollars waiting if you can manage that."

"His lordship is as good as dead right now," Billy assures while grinning at Frank.

"I figured I could count on you two, Jesse may have different ideas about Tunstall. One way or another I want that cunt dead before we ride out of this wind."

Frank and Billy rein out and return to their place in line. Jesse's head is down, but he looks up as they pass.

They ride up out of the canyon, following the two-track up onto a sun-drenched mesa. Henry and Tom keep an eye on their boss and their rear and flank, while Dick and Charlie take the point and scour the ground ahead.

The air feels a good ten degrees warmer up top. The herd had been skittish and frisky in the cold of the canyon. There'd been a stiff wind all morning, but it died down in the afternoon. Horses and men are happy to feel the sun and stillness, and to take the view. High mountains to the left and flatlands stretching all the way to Texas on their right.

"No wind and the shinning sun sure makes a hell of a difference," Tom says.

"Up here in the winter for certain, down in the desert, in the summer, that's another matter entirely," Henry replies in conclusion.

"Hate to see Mr. Tunstall so sickly, and losing to that sonofabitch Dolan."

"He's not going to lose, and with all the good luck you carry—he can't help but win."

"And if wishes were horses, beggars would ride. We're gonna have to fight our way out of this."

"Bring it on says I."

The broad white double peak of the big mountain gleams down on them in the late afternoon sun. Good company and a perk to the spirit. But ultimately the trail leads down off the ridge and into the shadowed timber-lined canyon that descends to the Hondo valley. It's a long, chilly drop, and quite steep after the first leg.

John Tunstall is barely aware of his surroundings—fever and exhaustion telling on him more and more. The frigid beauty of the day is lost on the fagged-out Englishman, wrapped in a heavy blanket and practically tied to the saddle.

They move into the open mouth of the gorge. Tunstall's head lifts for a moment then droops again.

The train of horses and men begin the switchback descent resigned to another tough piece of trail. Nothing much to relieve the monotony or the deepening chill and Lincoln still a long ride.

But fifty yards ahead a flock of turkeys gabble across the cut with a sudden burst of energy.

"Mr. Tunstall...John! We're going to have turkey for dinner. We'll make you some fresh soup," Henry calls back over his shoulder. Brewer and Charlie are working their way up into the brush and pines as well.

The Englishman barely takes note, burrowing deeper into the wrapped blanket. He slides into a fevered dream of Hamstead Heath in London, a favored place of escape in his youth. A vision of the lush grass on Parliment Hill, as clouds roll by and London smokes in the distance—gives him a flushed and delirious kind of comfort. Something to hold onto.

Jesse had deployed casually near the end of the Parajito Trail, where it comes down off the mesa. He and most of the Boys retired to a grove of piñons to make coffee and warm up, leaving the mummers to wait along the rim—the turkeys had been their lucky break.

Henry tops out on the ridge and is startled to hear a thundering of hooves coming from the left. Wheeling his mount, he sees Frank and Billy bearing down on him with their riffles up. The rest of the Boys pounding along the rim a hundred yards behind—they'd chosen to return at just the right moment.

"Ah shite," Henry shouts as a high caliber bullet rips the air and Slippers rears back.

The old buffalo hunter Buckshot Roberts is dismounted with rifle braced for another long distance try. A second shot cuts through a nearby piñon, taking off the end of a branch not half a foot from his head. The next shots are aimed further down the rim at Charlie and Dick. Henry wheels back around and races along the edge of the canyon, thinking they're at least drawing the Boys away from Tunstall. He continues up into a boulder-strewn knob with a fusillade dusting the ground—all the way to the crest where the others have taken cover.

Tom had stopped to cinch up a notch before leaving Tunstall and was still clawing up the escarpment when the guns start to roar. His head jerks to the rim and back to the trail. Before he's clear on what is happening and what to do next, two riders are crashing down through the brush—straight toward John. Alone and only half-awake, Tunstall begins to look around wondering what had gone wrong with the turkey shoot.

The number of shots fired and the indecipherable shouts seem out of kilter. A sudden commotion hurtling down the escarpment confuses him further. He lifts his head to see Frank Baker and Billy Morton ride out of the trees, gesturing, as if they want a friendly parley.

"Good afternoon yer lordship! T'was wondering if you'd like a cup of tea before we serve this warrant?" asks Sir Frank with a cockeyed giggle, as he lifts his riffle.

Tom dismounts behind a tall pine, heart about to hammer out of his chest.

"Mr. Tunstall, get out of there!" Tom tries to shout, the words almost locking in his throat.

"What warrant are you speaking of?" Tunstall mumbles.

The canyon seems as narrow and confining as the pressure in his head. Baker and Morton, dismounting and cackling and brandishing their weapons, remind him of gargoyles gamboling in a nightmare. John realizes with sudden clarity what their real intentions are.

"Bloody hell."

A sudden flare roars out at point blank range. Tunstall flies off his horse and onto the hard ground with a heartless thud. Frank jumps down and sees that a head and chest shot has for certain earned the fifty dollars.

Tom O'Folliard, shaking from head to foot, stomach wrenched and ass puckered tight—is unable to move. He'd seen some hard things in his life but nothing to match the deviling sadism unfolding below.

Evans bears down the slope with eyes on his two assassins. The mummers circle the cruel scene in a high-stepping riotous dance, as if now a demonic ritual is required to complete the job. Billy Morton decides Tunstall's horse is also to die and shoots the rearing mare in the head, hoping that will add to Dolan's pot. The animal falls heavily, crashing into a gnarled deadfall and throwing up a great cloud of dust.

Finally, laying Tunstall's head on a folded blanket, as if his lordship were simply taking a nap—Frank looks up at his boss grinning like a baked possum.

Jesse ignores the grin and rides over to Tunstall's body for a closer view. Laid out with a bullet hole in his right temple and his head on a pillow, the Englishman does seem to be almost at peace.

"Take his pistol and fire off a round," Jesse orders.

"That's right, son-of-a-bitch fired on me, when I read him the attachment."

"What about the rest of them boss?" asks Tom Hill, having worked his way down from the firing redoubt.

"How are things on the rim?"

"They're dug in."

"Tunstall was the job, and he fell right into our lap." Jesse takes one last look at the Englishman and makes the familiar gesture with his chin. "Keep an eye on those fellows, but let'em go."

O'Folliard crept along just below the ridge line intent on getting away from the mouth of hell and up to the knoll. At last gaining the safety of the massive boulders, he sits, still trembling.

"They've killed Tunstall—it was those two hillbillies. Ain't never seen the like, shot'em head and belly then danced around like it was some kind a shiveree," Tom spits out, almost wailing.

"May well come after us next and finish the job. They got the numbers and the sharks to get the job done properly," Charlie says.

"Peeled us off neat as a pin," Brewer answers back. "Nothing for it but to sneak off, goddamnit, and right now."

"Hell, that buffalo hunter with the Henry could kill us all, just by himself," says Charlie.

"We've got to get to town, and to McSween, and Squire Wilson. We're going to get every one of those bastards' names on a warrant," Dick Brewer hisses this out with a hard surety, his eyes searching out a game trail they could follow down to the valley.

The Tunstall cowboys withdraw, outgunned and outplayed. Creeping down the backside of the knoll like stricken penitents—death hanging over them all. But it stares the hardest into Henry McCarty's soul. His former friends, Frank and Billy, were the triggermen. Their efficiency and depravity as killers and hunters, only hinted at before and laid bare now with sickening finality.

He'd met Jesse and the Boys on this very trail just four months before.

"We'll get 'em. We'll get 'em all." There is a heat in Henry's voice, unfamiliar even to him.

"Goddamn turkeys," Brewer mutters.

There had been a flash and an explosion of pain, but that quickly passed. John Tunstall was safe from the huntsman in the woods now, and headed home. But just as foreseen, he'd been required to make one last disagreeable journey.

Dick Brewer strides toward the Dolan store, a warrant in his pocket and Henry and Charlie at his side. Each man has a rifle and sidearm. But a coursing, zealous rage is their main weapon. Inside are several men they intend to arrest.

A milling squad of buffalo soldiers gives way as the three stubborn volunteers step onto the porch and enter the building.

"You fellows got some stones marching in here with your guns out," Sheriff Brady growls as he gets to his feet.

"I've got a duly signed warrant here for the men responsible for Tunstall's murder. Three of them are standing right over there and I *will* make their arrest," Brewer delivers with enough juice to knock over a glass of whiskey. Brady glances at the signature at the bottom of the warrant and then takes a hard look at Brewer.

"Tunstall was shot in self-defense," Brady replies.

"We had eyes on the shooting, and that's not how it happened. It was an ambush plain and simple. John Tunstall was so sick he could scarcely hold up his head let alone draw his weapon. You men all know me, you know what side of the law I come down on and by god, I will see justice done here."

"Well now you might want to come down off your high horse a bit. I'm surprised you brought this little chancer along," Brady suggests, ignoring Brewer's declaration.

"The name is William Bonney."

Henry's characteristic grin is gone. Charlie looks askance at his friend, more for the use of a new moniker than the insulting tone in his voice.

"A little high fallutin don't you think?" Brady grunts, eyes narrowed.

"Well Mr. Bonney, I'll see you get the same careful treatment as these two. This warrant from Squire Wilson is worthless"—tossing it into a waste bin—"and don't mean a goddamn thing, and I'll have your guns on the table here right now. You'll not be charging in here like god almighty serving warrants and insulting my good nature."

The soldiers positioned outside, on loan from Fort Stanton, have moved into the store and, along with the men whose names are on the warrant, surround the three with weapons drawn.

With no other choice Dick and Charlie begin to comply. They have served notice at least. Bonney, who is loath to give up his prized Winchester, is last. The sheriff steps closer.

"You know, son, we Irishmen should always stand together against the English."

"I'm an American, and you're an arrogant bastard, Sheriff Brady, and just as guilty as the men on this warrant."

Brady takes the rifle with one hand and whips a backhanded blow with the other, knocking the chancer sideways.

"You boys are going down to the pit, for trying to serve an illegal warrant and for raising my temper, and for being lying cunts. Tunstall wasn't murdered. He was shot in self-defense."

As they're marched down the street, William Bonney keeps up a stream of abuse regarding the sheriff's deviant ancestry. He's still talking going down the ladder. "The big son-of-a-bitch hits like a girl,"—and the grated lid slams shut.

Snow drifts down in big flakes, collecting on the pine casket and beginning to cover the ground. The largest gathering of Hispanics and Anglos in the history of Lincoln crowds into the yard behind the Tunstall store. Noticeably absent from the congregation is Jimmy Dolan. But the hard-drinking Irishman watches a growing muster of citizens, and enemies, from the second floor of the House.

"Your lordship," says Jimmy. He nods and shoots back a bracing two fingers worth.

Susan McSween sits down at her pump organ, carried from parlor to graveside, and begins to pedal. Dick and Charlie bellow out a Cokesbury hymn with the other cowboys and anglos, Spanish folk bowing their heads in silence, and the flurries falling quiet like a powerful grace.

Dr. Ealy, the newly arrived Presbyterian minister and first clergyman of any denomination to take up residence in Lincoln, looks out over the gathering with a stunned solemnity. In his first two days in Lincoln he'd been required to perform an autopsy on a murdered man and now preside over his funeral.

Lincoln's most prominent New Mexican resident, Juan Patron, stands ready to translate the service into Spanish. The twenty-five-year-old is a speaker of great eloquence and a rising star in the state legislature. He too is wondering about destiny. By chance, he and councilor McSween had met John Tunstall only one year before on a trip to Santa Fe. It seemed a fateful and calamitous meeting now.

They'd convinced Tunstall that Lincoln County held the answer to his grand quest. The next day McSween continued East to New York City—to sue for collection of the Fritz Insurance policy—and Tunstall accompanied Patron back to Lincoln. The sales pitch continued as the two wagoned South. John's first sight of the Sacramento Mountains closed the deal.

"That is the backdoor of Lincoln County Mr. Tunstall,"

"My God, what magnificent country," Tunstall had replied in awe. An immense backbone of blue mountains rose up from the yellowed high plains in their front, and something stirred that could not be stopped.

The blame for what had come to pass since that day could not possibly rest on Patron's shoulders. Though it seemed to as he stood in the freezing air. Looking out at the lowered faces, brown and white—their hope of deliverance from tyranny and peonage going under the hard ground—Patron longed for a bracing sip of ardent.

The new reverend meets his eye, and begins.

"The majesty of God, whose essence is truth, will and purpose, is at work in all our days on earth...even this terrible day. We are gathered to honor and consecrate a fallen son. An honorable citizen, regrettably young, of faraway England who must now remain here, in our American soil."

Dr. Ealy pauses and Patron translates sonorously, and the patchwork of English and Spanish goes back and forth, knitting together the mixed peoples of Lincoln. But the leaden skies give no sense of hope as they lower the casket. The broad shoulders of the Tunstall foreman are slumped. A smoldering fire burns in his eyes and the snow continues silent and pure.

"I will seek an indictment against Dolan from Squire Wilson, he is independent and will not be turned by the Ring. And I will offer you wages to serve these warrants and to protect Susan and myself. Those are some bare facts to get started with, but I fear there is stony ground ahead. They have only achieved part of their plan."

"No end to their scheming, tricky fuckin bastards!" Fred Waite suddenly interjects, catching McSween off guard, unused to leading a group of rowdy outdoorsmen, and particularly—this group of cowboys staring up at him.

"Killing a British subject, particularly a prominent one, is a grave matter. It may take time, but undoubtably the British Government will demand an investigation, an undoubtably, Congress will respond," McSween declares in his best courtroom burr.

"They better, the damn carpetbagin grifters," George Coe suddenly spits out.

"Maybe in a few years," Charlie warns.

"Well, yes, in the interim we may be required to take the law into our own hands. Dolan won't be satisfied until he's removed every obstacle in his path," McSween prevaricates.

"Put Dolan in the ground, and all the rest of those murderin bastards," Fred Waite insists, getting himself, and the others, thoroughly roostered up.

"Dick Brewer, whom you all know for the stalwart man he is—will lead you in all punitive efforts, which we must be at pains to keep within legal bounds. And I believe he will now stand and speak for himself," the lawyer concludes, sitting down and immediately lighting one of his machine-rolled cigarettes.

Richard Brewer, twenty-nine years old, six foot two inches and 220 pounds, rises from his chair. The long hair and fierce gaze, the powerful shoulders and booming voice more like that of some half-crazed Viking than a cowboy from Wisconsin.

"John Tunstall was a good man, a brave man."

"More goddamned guts than you could hang on a fence," shouts Fred Waite, squaring his shoulders and standing suddenly. "Stood up to those murdering bastards like it was nothin."

"John might have become a great man, if he'd been granted the time," Brewer continues.

"Goddamned right."

"He would have changed Lincoln County for the better, and that's for certain. He damn sure earned the chance to try, and I am to blame for his death, I am to blame. And there will be a reckoning by god, and an atonement for those who took his life. I promise I *will* bring these murdering shitheels to justice. I swear it." Brewer announces.

His baritone voice had never been heard in Lincoln County with anything like the force it possesses tonight—the rowdy gathering had suddenly grown quiet under its spell. "We are not an army, but we are a fierce company—and we will have justice for John Tunstall, and protection for Councilor McSween."

"Say it out Dick, you're the man to lead us."

"Henry thought it up—I second it—I say we call ourselves the Regulators," Dick concludes, putting a solid emphasis on the name.

"Hell yes, the Regulators!"

"The Regulators!"

"Huzzah! Huzzah!"

Susan McSween grinds her jaw and stews over the terrible course of events. Listening from the kitchen to the men and all their passion and bravado is a painful thing to her. Nothing good will come of any of this. Just more bloodshed.

Down in the pit William Bonney paces, staring up into the light when he reaches the ladder, then marching back to the other wall. He'd not been released with the others. Hearing the hymns being sung down the street, he joined in, softly.

He'd also grieved and seethed and begins to think along new lines entirely.

Being confined in the pit is intolerable. Never again, no matter what, and Sheriff Brady will be made to pay along with many another who took part in the murder. A blacker thought keeps tormenting him—everyone he most reveres ends up dead—the painful, unacceptable, monstrous thought keeps darting around his brain like some slippery demon.

His father, mother, and now John. Is he not allowed to have living fealty and admiration, to say nothing of love? He pauses at the ladder, and paces back into the dark.

A mournful quiet reigns at thirty-nine Hackney, drifting down on everything of comfort and beauty like a thick dust. It wasn't the first time such a thing had happened. The black sorrow had invaded their home when their first born, Clara, died suddenly of a fever. She was thirteen. The dust fell heavily then as well, and remained an eternity.

But young Emily and John survived the epidemic and began to carry the family's hearts to brighter times. Brother and sister grew up as close as two siblings might be. Emily had brains and beauty and John likewise excelled in school and life.

Two more girls, Lilian and Mabel, were born in the Tunstall house and the halls rang again with the laughter of children, and now finally the dust cleared completely away.

All the Tunstall children were loved and showed great promise, but young master John was the light of the family.

The Spencerian Sonnet he'd written, and read aloud for his father's fortieth birthday, was a triumph. He'd managed the grammar and the metaphors with an able hand, and the sentiment with a guileless heart. It brought forth tears from his mother and older sister, and a beaming prideful smile from his father.

And the time he rescued Emily from a vulgar encounter in Charing Cross, thumping the rascal a good one in the process—was a legendary event in the Tunstall household.

Lillian and Mabel adored their brother. For though he was far older and towered over them, John would get down and play at whatever game they fancied. And then there was his exemplary term at Oxford, and the glowing accolades of his professors.

But his single-minded devotion to family was the thing they cherished most about him.

It was unspeakable, what had befallen their Johnny—and indeed the horrible reality of it could scarcely be mentioned. No one had the heart.

"I've received a letter from the lawyer, Alexander McSween," John Tunstall begins, his troubled eyes lifting to those of his wife and eldest daughter Emily. She looks down immediately, feeling as if her heart were tied to an anchor and had just been dropped to some unimaginable depth. "He speaks at great length...on how it happened."

"I can't father. I don't wish to hear it."

"Of course Em, I'm sorry darling. There are things in the letter we should all know, however, and consider," the father continues.

"About John's estate, and how much money our fine Mr. McSween is owed no doubt. I don't care about any of it, let them all go to the devil. Why should we have anything further to do with that wretched place."

"For John, dear Ramie, for John. He gave his life trying to build something up there, and I will not let those scoundrels make a feast of what's left. (He closes the letter and looks down, taking his gaze from the misery of his wife's eyes.) I meet with the home secretary Thursday next. I've been assured there will be a federal investigation in America. We can at least hope for some justice, for our boy," Mr. Tunstall concludes, his voice breaking on the last words.

"Of course Papa, John would want us to fight for him...it's just so hard." Emily's large dark eyes, so like her brothers, fill with tears. "Please. I can hear no more tonight."

The dust had returned and all within the brick walls and fine rooms of Tunstall Hall wondered if it could ever be lifted.

8 The Five Points New York July 12, 1863

Four crumbling, potholed streets, deep in trash and excrement of all descriptions, meet at a crudely fenced no man's land. Behind packing crates and rotting fence posts and rusting half-driven nails lies a festering bog known as Paradise Square—a grand placed to get knifed.

Once a bit of clean air and open ground in the burgeoning lower-class life of a young New York, Paradise Square is now a place to hurry by with head down. Into the intermingled Irish and Black slums radiating outward; disease-ridden, lawless, and sagging—but also somehow alluring and prosperous. It is both a dangerous sluice and a warren of protective neighborhoods and corner grocers. For good people live here also. Among the great numbers are plenty of folk who work hard and raise proud families amidst the squalor.

But squalor loves its proper meat.

A slippery soul with a little money in his pocket and a willingness to brace the threat of mayhem, and the stench—might well find an extraordinary night waiting in the lurid alleyways of the Five Points, where the best and most interesting saloons, gambling dens, and brothels abound.

Tensions between African and Irish are many and constant, but in the Five points they live side by side in an equality of poverty and discrimination, and genius.

Here from the very start, Blacks are as numerous as the Irish. Young blades from both worlds contest the streets. But not always violently, they often try to *outdance* each other.

The shuffle and the jig, the djembe and the stepdance, the walkabout and the reel—go back and forth on the sidewalks like a battle of black magic and white sorcery. The great contest on stage between Masta Juba and Johnny Diamond, but a reflection of everyday reality.

So powerful is the fusion of African and Irish that it can be found in all the many black-owned bars and dance halls of the Five Points. Pete William's bar on Orange Street, The Almack, is the alcazar of such places. High and low meet there to have a drink and a *segar.* To toast the Ethiopian proprietor in his blue velvet coat and gold chains; to see voluptuous mulatto beauties and witness the wild new *American* dance—and to take part, either as willing initiate or disdainful voyeur—in the dark carnival of fun.

In another much-frequented establishment, cheaply adorned with nautical broadsheets and a prominent, graffitied portrait of the Queen—another unholy mob crowds in from Water Street. Here race mixing is no open question but a blunt fist of repudiation.

Hustlers eye their marks, a bowlered dancer capers to the rasp of the squeezebox, a fearsome lady bouncer towers over the clientele with a blackjack and pistol at the ready, and an impressive number of bitten-off ears pickle on a high shelf for all to see.

The streets are choked with danglers and pick pockets of all colors, bedraggled prostitutes and starving hordes and hot corn girls, their husbands trailing along just behind. And the infamous gangs strut like lords; battling for turf and nationality, for political bosses, and for the sheer hellish fun of it. They are a force unto themselves and regular folk give them wide berth.

In a narrow byway, members of two enemy gangs suddenly come face to face. The Kerryonian's of the Five Points, and the nativist Bowery Boys—are in a sudden standoff. Obscenities heave back and forth as they edge closer. An Irish giant stands out among the brawlers, Jimmy the Bracer, six foot seven and heavily muscled.

"What a load of foreign shit stands before us boys. You goddamned mick cunts are gonna step aside now and let us real Americans through."

"I'll shove that stovepipe down your fuckin throat before I step aside."

"Everyone of ya Bowery bastards can kiss me dirty arse hole," Jimmy the Bracer roars out.

A Bowery thug throws his hefty chunk of brick and the donnybrook begins. The three stoutest Bowery Boys go straight at Jimmy, one pulling a switchblade and the other two swinging clubs. The Bracer ducks under one blow but takes a heavy blood-letting whack that brings the man in close. Close enough to head butt as he grabs the knife wielder's hand and taking a slashing cut in the process.

In a powerful blur of motion, he has the final bat wielder in a headlock and the other man's wrist in an iron grip, wrenching it back until the bone snaps and the knife falls. All the while the contest thunders on around him.

One Bowery thug slammed head first into the brick wall and another dropped with a left hook. Another swing and a kick and Jimmy has two more down in the street. He braves the rest back against a wall and no Bowery boy left standing will step forward and challenge him.

The fight is abruptly over. The only real hope had been to put Jimmy down with their three best, and that failed.

"Jimmy the Bracer! Jimmy the Bracer! Oooh, Oooh, Oooh," the Ferryonians, Ferry County men all, chant in a deep guttural and the Bowery Boys concede the way.

Six blocks from the mayhem, Catherine McCarty puts her two young sons to bed with a story. Joe has reached his eighth year and Henry his fifth. They sit wide-eyed on the bed in their snug little apartment in a street far quieter, and safer, than the brawling district of the Five Points.

The boy's father, Michael, gone to the great War a year now and sorely missed, the signing bonus to his pretty wife and two handsome boys, and he to the battlefields of Virginia. Catherine is both mother and father in his absence, and the money a poor substitute for the head of the family.

Bedtime is embellished each night with stories of her own design, either completely invented or fables retold. For every time she'd read *Cock Sparrow* and *The Animal's Picnic*, the oral tradition would spring to life tenfold.

"You promised us a New York story tonight," Joe pleads.

"Mose the giant," Henry yells.

"Oh very well, just hold your horses. Let your mother gather herself," Catherine answers.

She'd built a little fire in the stove and made herself a cup of tea. Taking a sip and settling into her rocker, the storyteller is ready now to begin.

"Mose was eight feet tall in his stocking feet, he stood above his fellow men like an olden God of War. His long-tasseled mane was the color of barley before the harvest. He possessed a noble mind and an enormous heart, but his true strength came forth when it was time to *fight*. Old Mose was the greatest brawler that ever struck a blow for the sons of Erin in the New World."

"Mose is the strongest man ever," Henry says, and his mother smiles back at him. Joe stayed quiet like always.

"Other proud men went into battle carrying a club and brickbat, but Mose, when readied for the fray, bore in one hand a huge paving stone, and in the other an oak wagon tongue...and with it he swept away all before him."

"Ten men couldn't lick him!"

"Henry be quiet and let mum tell the story."

"But Mose did have one weakness, and her name was Brianna. She was beautiful and spirited, and she loved to sing. Her voice could charm the very devil and Moses would sit below her window at night and listen."

Henry leaps up when it's finished, far from sleepy and ready for more. He always went through his days ready to bust, finally collapsing as if he'd suddenly been turned into a rag doll.

"No more stories tonight, time for sleep and remember, big day tomorrow lads. We're taking the ferry to Coney Island first thing in the morning," Catherine says. The holiday is a major expenditure of money, and time spent, time that she could be working and earning. But she has her reasons.

"Are there really rabbits there?" Henry asks and Catherine notes the drooping eyelids of her youngest boy.

"Of course, scores of them. And the great wide ocean with wave after wave...wave after wave...wave after wave, crashing on a lovely beach. The sea gulls crying, tremendous ships sailing...sailing...sailing away." Henry had fallen fast asleep, carried out to sea.

On the North Point Ferry, and later on the coach ride to the beach, Catherine instructs her sons on a number of subjects. Despite the excitement of the day, there's plenty of time for math, English, and Gaelic. Joe has little aptitude or interest, but Henry has a natural gift for both language and knowledge. His light blue eyes sparkle when his mother smiles.

"Henry, you've got your father's eyes," says Catherine. She puts her arms around her sons and begins to sing.

Sa mo laoch, mo Ghile Mea
Sa mo Chaesar Gile Mear
Suan na se an ni bhfuairas fe in
O chuaigh i gce in mo Ghile Mear

The coach crunches along the Shell Road with the ancient tune ringing out into the countryside. Fields of grass run to the horizon and occasionally, darting about from bush to hole, are the coneys for which the island is named.

Coming to a halt, both Henry and Joe leap from the coach and head straight to the surf.

"Last coach at four ma'am."

Catherine nods with a smile as she lifts out two bundles. One containing towels and clothes, and the other a picnic and cloth to spread on the sand. Beach combing and frolicking with the surf is the first order of their day at the beach. She sets it all down in a good spot, wishing they had a big umbrella, and runs toward the water.

Henry looks back when she calls to him, drawing his attention to a magnificent clipper out in the sound. Framed against the ocean and sky, his mother's long blond hair let down and rippling, the white sheets of the ship billowing in full sail out on the blue—it seems to him like a scene from one of their storybooks. Henry grabs her hand and together they watch the slim boat run with the wind.

"Ah she's a beauty Henry. A Baltimore Clipper."

"There be pirates aboard."

"Perhaps we best be striking our colors, Captain."

"Never!" Henry shouts from the sand, pretending to draw and brandish his cutlass. He'd never been happier in his life. "We got to catch up to Joe, the pirates will get him."

Back in the city, a gargantuan riot is brewing. An aggressive draft ordinance has gone out from Washington—the first one of the War. Hundreds of young men are milling in the street in front of the Draft office and shouting out their anger.

"A rich man's war and a poor man's fight."

"The well-off can buy their way out, but we Irishmen must fight and die!"

Dark sentiments have been brewing for three years. In the bitter stew is mingled a hatred of the wealthy, profound distrust of the government both local and national, and a racist anger at blacks—their competitors for dock work and the cause of the big War.

It is a terrible day in lower Manhattan.

"Heathen darkies the root of it all."

"Take our jobs and we got a fight for'em too."

"I've lost two brothers already."

"Let the fucking rich fight their own goddamned war!"

The angry crowd presses forward and when someone tosses a paving stone through the window of the Draft Office, the vociferations of five hundred men become one continuous roar.

"It's an ugly fockin day lads, and ugly fockin day."

Except for the absence of their father, the summer day at the beach was perfect. After lunch the boys discard their clothes and go into the water. Joe holding onto to his little brother and the both of them knocked flat by a big wave. After a terrifying moment both spring up gasping for air. Catherine brings them out of the surf to rest on the picnic cloth.

All of them looking up at the clouds, she tells another story—her first visit to the Galway coast, and the little cove where she went for her first ocean swim. Her mother and grandfather had been with her that day. After the swim he'd spooked her with tales of the leviathan's roaming in the deep, and a prophet named Jonah who was swallowed by one. Her mother scolded the old man for always bringing up the shivers, but Catherine delighted in him and he winked back at her merrily.

The McCarty's day on Coney Island passed like a dream. Even the trip back was a jolly adventure filled with laughter and song. But as the North Point Ferry approaches the dock their mood slowly dampens. The ferrymen are all crowding up to the bow and looking at the city. There is a strange sound and an acrid smell drifting out into the bay. Something has them concerned and talking hurriedly amongst themselves and pointing at the docks.

"Watch yourself ma'am, getting those youngsters back home may be a hard job today," one of them says as they disembark.

Three blocks in from the waterfront they are stopped dead in their tracks—an endless stream of humanity is surging up Market Street like a great angry beast. The roar of it is stunning.

"What in the world is happening?" Catherine yells to an old man quickly trundling a cart in the opposite direction.

"Anarchy and ruin, because of the new draft. And now that it's begun there'll be no stopping it."

"No stopping what, what is it?"

"Just hell opening up. It's a riot, a crazy bloodthirsty mob," the old man replies, starting on his way again. "If I were you I'd get off the streets."

While Catherine converses with the tradesman, Joe runs off for a closer look. Seeing his older brother slip away, Henry tugs at his mother's arm but it's too late. A frantic pursuit begins. They catch up with Joe in time to see him swallowed like a tiny morsel to feed the beast.

She screams, grabs Henry and pushes in after. There ahead she spots his blond hair for a moment and drives forward, shoving and being shoved, finally managing to catch Joe by the scruff. But all three are trapped now and borne along in the flood of berserk humanity.

The wave crashes around the East Side Armory, defended by a frantic and outnumbered police force. The tide is momentarily stemmed at the stout doors, and the smashing of windows and a frenzy of looting begins up and down the block.

The doors are soon wrenched from their hinges and the crowd lunges forward, those in front determined to get to the guns locked inside. Henry and Joe cling to their mother out in the surging chaos, terrified—the grand day at the beach obliterated.

A tall man, standing out above the mob like a lighthouse, suddenly notices Catherine as the police begin firing into the crowd. A leering and miscreant rioter has also noticed the tousled blond hair and attractive face of Catherine McCarty—just a few feet away.

He pushes toward her, ready to carry her into an alleyway for a nice diversion. Reaching out he has one hand on a shoulder and drawing the other up for a blow. But before he can strike, Jimmy the Bracer snatches the man back, clouting him with an iron fist and the man crumples to the ground.

"Jeysus, Mrs. McCarty. What in bloody hell are you doin here?" Catherine is wild-eyed but quickly recognizes her husband's friend, Jimmy.

"Just trying to get home, Jimmy Kerrigan. Please help us."

"Well, shite—there's nothin for it but to get you out 'o here," Kerrigan allows, not pleased at all, but seeing what must be done. He had dark plans of his own for the guns in the armory, but decides to set them aside.

The giant lifts Henry up with a wink.

"Hold on tight, laddie. Mrs. McCarty, you and Joe stay right behind me." Jimmy the Bracer begins to plow and beat his way through the sea of rioters. They are hemmed in by buildings on both sides of the streets and the narrow alleys are not an option, but within a few blocks Jimmy has ferried them to a large cross street that *is* open.

Further down they see a black man hanging from a light pole. A mob of distorted white faces yelling out their anger, and one man climbing up to douse kerosene on the lifeless body. Another scrabbling up to set it afire, little Henry in the giant's arms and his mother clinging to Joe—all of them staring.

"Don't look at it," Jimmy yells as he pushes forward.

"I know that poor man," Catherine wails.

Rabid drunken packs of thieves follow along in the wake of marauding rioters, one great evil followed by another. The rioters intent on destroying the police and the symbols of republican power, and woe be it to any blacks in their deadly path; and looters intent only on gobbling up the leavings.

Twice Jimmy had to set Henry down to clear the way, first with fists, and then lifting a huge timber and swinging it like a scythe, Catherine cowering in the doorjamb behind. Desperate to keep the McCarty family safe, Jimmy the Bracer clears the way like a man possessed.

Night has fallen on the beleaguered city by the time his wards are delivered through the inferno and to their home.

The Five Points had not joined in the rioting. Proudly or not, she was a more egalitarian and self-interested borough than the longshoreman district where the beast had sprung to life.

"Thank god the Five Points is staying out of it," Catherine declares.

Henry had fallen asleep but wakes as Jimmy sets him down. He looks up at the giant.

"You're Mose."

"No, little man. I'm not a patch to old Mose. I'm Jimmy the Bracer. Your father and me we grew up together in County Kerry, and I should be lookin after ya, while your father's away," Jimmy admits and Henry hugs the giant's neck, before his mother sends him inside.

"You saved us today." Catherine's voice catches, a sudden emotion overwhelming her, finally, and tears rolling down her cheeks. "You're a good man, Jimmy Kerrigan, despite your wicked ways."

Kerrigan hangs his head, grimacing.

"I promise to look in on you more, it's the least I can do while Michael's at the war. You know his regiment was at Gettysburg, have you heard anything?"

"He's missing, presumed dead. I haven't told the boys yet. I wanted them to have a bit of fun before. That's why I took them to the Island today," Catherine admits, a profound sadness settling on her tired features. Jimmy nods, the sadness overtaking his big frame as well.

"He'll turn up, with that crooked grin and another fish story."

Catherine holds his dark brown eyes for a long moment and a hard understanding passes between them. Jimmy the Bracer is at loss for words before the petite Catherine McCarty. He looks away toward the docks and the sea, then back toward the sound of rioting. There's a touch of anger in Catherine's voice as she bids him goodnight.

"There's enough devilry out there tonight already Jimmy Kerrigan. Well, be off with you then, and God bless you."

GETTYSBURG JULY 6, 1863

The armies of Lee and Meade have retired from the field, leaving the fallen in rows and heaps. A massive stench lifting to the heavens and barring forever all trace of normalcy from the prudent little college town.

Grim-faced men are hard at the terrible work of identifying, removing, and interring the dead—with many a poor son going into an unmarked grave. Whole regiments of southern boys shoved in a common hole and covered over with the blighted soil of Gettysburg.

A wagonload comes in from Seminary Ridge and passes another crew heading out the Chambersburg Pike. The road leads to a crowded trail heading into the woods, to the place where the Iron Brigade held their ground. Heads down, a ragtag group of black contrabands trundle into the shattered forest, stopping at a ravine to assess the next cruel task.

Down below a twisted mass of bodies lie at the bottom of the shallow cut. Young men from Virginia, Michigan, Wisconsin, and a few from broken New York regiments—all in a final embrace.

"Look at dat fellow down thar wid his eyes open."

"He's seein all de way to glory."

"Least he got a head still."

After a silent moment, they cover faces and descend. Their minds had numbed to the task after the first day, it was the only way such unimaginable work could be accomplished. The horror of the cut was just another job now to set to and get done.

At the top of the mound one corpse gazes up at the summer sky. Only the head and one arm visible, as if he'd clawed his way up from the bottom for one last breath of air, one last look at the world. The puffed face still clinging to a handsome past, and eyes a light mystic blue.

9

The deep blue sky is dotted with legions of clouds like little puffs of cotton. Under the softened firmament a horseman slowly negotiates the high desert—traveling south on a dirt two-track near the base of a jutting mountain range. Another scapular range to the west almost like a mirror image, save for one detail.

On the eastern side of the basin horse and man pass close to the White Mountain, its enormous bulk plunging from snow-capped pinnacles straight to the floor of the chaparral. A gallery of petroglyphs rises along a tumbled basalt ridge, its chiseled animals and humans forever watching the road below.

Head down, the rider seems unaware of his grand surroundings and unsteady, perhaps asleep under a wide-brimmed hat.

Jesse Evans lifts his ashen face to peer ahead, looking for the river. His white shirt stained dark red by the blood oozing from a bullet hole in his chest, and a wound along his broken left arm had trickled a blood trail for miles. In the saddle now for fourteen hours and drawing breath in a ragged hiss. A tight grinding clench of jaw and the hat dips down again.

Another half-mile and he reaches the little river, flowing at a right angle away from the Mountain. The horse stops to drink and Jesse lowers himself out of the saddle, gingerly reaching the ground and a quick stumble to water's edge. He removes his hat to dip and fill, pouring the contents over himself. Jesse sits and looks at the water flowing for a long moment before leaning forward and easing himself into the shallow river. Maybe a dip will break the fever.

Lying in the cool water, all weight taken off his wounds, Evans is not thinking of revenge, or redemption, of the future or the past—only of survival.

Slowly reemerging, he drips up out of the baptism and grabs the saddle horn. His eyes lift toward the basalt ridge.

Back down the track a rider is paused, watching him.

Five Days Earlier

Olinger hovers around the stove, feeding and poking the fire within and watching his boss out of the corner of his eye. Secretive and cagey as always, and sporting a furtive smile—always the tell. Jimmy pours out two healthy shots from a jug.

"Frank and Billy have made themselves scarce?"

"Headed to Texas," answers Jesse.

"Good."

"Not so good for them, they have a bad rep there, but as a choice its better than staying here."

Evans looks at the amber and notes its color. Jimmy had poured from his reserve and not the busthead they more routinely drank.

"An interesting story has come my way," Jimmy confides.

Olinger gazes into the fire, an acid grin at play.

"There's a sheepherder on the south end of the Malpais, I've been told he's sitting on a strongbox with a fair amount of Mexican silver and gold in it." Dolan places a worn twenty-peso gold piece in front of Evans. "I'll pay you extra for the trip, and if there's loot—we can talk about how to split it up when you get back. I need capital...and so do you."

"Why not send him?" asks Jesse, nodding toward Olinger.

"Bob stays at my side until things settle down here. And besides, we're meeting the governor on the seventh, when his stage arrives in Mesilla, escorting him to Lincoln. Brady's letter has had the desired effect. Our version of the Tunstall affair is known where it counts, and the governor will be setting things straight."

"I wouldn't be so sure about that, and that doesn't sound like any goddamned sheepherder to me," Jesse concludes and Dolan does not disagree.

"He's some kind of hombre for certain. That's why it needs to be you."

Evans looks away.

"Does sound more challenging than sitting on a powder keg waiting for some idiot to light a match," says Jesse, glancing over at Olinger. "You'll pay me extra if there's nothing and I'll take a seventy-thirty split if there is."

The Regulators, as a hunting and fighting unit, are an unproven lot—but dogged. Their first sortie has delivered them to what they hope is a hot trail down in the Pecos River country, a two-day ride from Lincoln.

Baker and Morton had slipped down into the lowland nether world aiming to continue slipping all the way to Texas. They aren't quite there yet.

"I sure hope that campesino told you right, Mr. Bonney. It's a long way to come on the word of a farmer," Brewer protests.

"Horacio steered us right. Frank and Buck are in this bunch we've been trailing, I'd bet my bottom dollar on it."

"Seeing as that's the only dollar you got, it better be a good bet," Charlie says.

"I can't quite get comfortable calling you William, how 'bout Billy Bonney, or just Billy?" Tom asks.

"Naaah, don't fancy that much. William Bonney…now that's dignified, lighthearted and Irish, all at the same time. But just call me Henry, or Kid. William Bonney is for the world, not us."

"Sounds to me like you got an issue with being unknown," says Frank McNab, a new man sent by Chisum.

"Who doesn't want to be famous?" Henry asks, a twinkle in his eyes.

"You won't be getting famous out here," McNab states, blunt as a hammer.

John Chisum had finally been released from the Messilla jail and Catron's clutches. He'd come back to the Southfork and decided to ante up—sending his two best fighters to hunt down Tunstall's murderers—Frank McNab and Doc Scurlock, the former a hot-headed Scotsman and first-rate cattle detective and the latter a seasoned range fighter.

Now they were nine, including the emphatic Chickasaw cowboy Fred Waite, apple farmer George Coe, and failed West Pointer Jim French. A formidable posse in all, and when not riled, a good-natured lot.

Today there is one more as well.

"I don't like that McCloskey turning up out of the blue, wandering was we hunting Frank Baker and could he ride along? There's something not right about him. Probably a goddamned spy," says Charlie, looking back at the Johnny-come-lately.

"Baker and Morton are crazy as a couple of shit house rats, maybe they all deserve each other," Henry replies. The trail turns into the Pecos River bottoms, and one by one they disappear off the bluff and down into the Seven Rivers outlaw country.

"Yes, it's a very long and famous road and you seem to know a lot about it and everything else. Now, will you please shut your endlessly babbling yap," the man blurts out lowering his newspaper, the cruel line of mouth and nose matching the bite of his cold gaze.

"And just who might you be?" the drummer asks, suddenly timorous after a long burst of unchallenged flapdoodle. He'd gone on and on about the new vertical lift in women's fashions, the best places to eat in the capitol, the poor quality of canned milk available and the ancient road they're traveling on.

"I am the governor of New Mexico," Axtell announces in a tone meant to convey the authority of his office, and to shut down all further talk in the tightly packed coach. It succeeds.

The governor sinks back into his paper—the header shouting the slaughter of a British citizen in Lincoln County.

A journey to the troubled region has become necessary. That impetuous hothead Dolan had his rival killed and an all-out range war would surely follow, just as murder had proceeded war in Colfax County. He and Thomas Catron were able to put that uprising down, and though the situation was different in many ways—similar tactics were called for now.

The Colfax troubles between settler vigilantes and the Ring-supported Maxwell Land Grant Company—were egregious. There had initially been far too many *pro-settler* verdicts by local juries and *pro-settler* actions taken by local judges, partially in response to a reign of terror brought on by one man. The Governor had swooped down on that violent place and suspended judicial powers—and would do the same now, before matters got out of hand—though he was greatly irked by the tiresome journey that lay ahead.

He was comfortable and happy in grand places like San Francisco, Salt Lake City, and now Santa Fe—but detested the little godforsaken outposts he was required to visit from time to time. The Governor is not fainthearted and certainly accustomed to having and handling frontier power; but he hated the rough travel, the hurly-burly at the edge of civilization, and had developed a healthy respect indeed for the delirium that could inhabit men souls in such outposts.

Axtell shuddered to think of the violence and chaos he'd witnessed in Colfax County. They responded late and crazed gunsharks on both sides had run completely amuck. That demented firebrand Clay Alison stood out from them all. He still haunted the governor's tidy and judicious mind like a demon from some gothic nightmare.

To begin his war, Allison had cut a man's head off and stuck it on a pole in front of the St. James Inn in Cimarron. St. James was the first of the twelve disciples of Jesus to be martyred, and the head piked in front of the Inn was Alison's way of saying *here* is the first martyr in *my* crusade. A nuanced bit of symbolism lost on many—but not on the Governor.

Clay Allison, along with the rest of the vigilante uprising, had eventually been overwhelmed and subdued—but it had taken military intervention to finally put a cap on it. He would act quicker this time, before hell opened up.

The first stop on Governor Axtell's itinerary is Fort Stanton—only a few miles from Lincoln. There to make matters clear to the Fort's new commander, Nathan Dudley.

The Governor knew of Dudley's checkered past, *and* his friends in high places. A heavy drinker for certain, cantankerous, and a mite too sovereign for his own good—but Catron had recently brought him into the fold and vouched for him completely.

"Pardon me for asking, but are you going to see about that British fellow killed on his way to business in Lincoln. Murdered no doubt. That's how things are done out here." The drummer had found his tongue again, much to the Governor's chagrin. He brings the paper down enough to bore a look at his gabby traveling companion, there's knees touching.

"According to Sheriff Brady—it was self defense."

The paper goes back up.

Brewer raises his hand to the five men on the opposite bank. They were a hundred yards away. Three of them unknown to the big foreman, but Baker and Morton are there for sure, hanging back.

"Goddamnit, it's that fuckin Dick Brewer. I knew'd we shoulda kept moving," Billy hisses.

"We ain't caught yet," Frank says, wheeling his horse.

The rest of Brewer's men come charging up around the bend and, to his chagrin, immediately release a hail of bullets across the river. It scatters the five into two groups.

"You fellows have got to learn some discipline. We might could've taken'em without a shot." Brewer shouts at the Regulators as they splash across the dark waters of the Pecos.

"You're dreaming Dick," McNab shouts back.

A running battle gets under way along the winding river bottom, with a healthy lead separating the two parties and ineffective bullets flying in both directions. The Kid is the best mounted and takes the point, determined to run the two to ground.

Baker and Morton keep looking back and offering various gestures, and an occasional bullet or epithet. Finally, they disappear around a bend and without the slightest hesitation, The Kid turns Slippers and follows a game trail up the steep embankment to his left, almost going down when a crumbling patch of loose sod gives way.

It's a wide bend and, taking a generous mark on where to angle across, boy and horse make for the opposite side. Slowing only a little, Henry works along the rim and then choosing a place—commits to an almost vertical decent. Slippers hits the bottom with an intense burst of energy, his back legs splaying out and an avalanche of dust following them down.

"Ah shit," Frank groans out at the spectacle of rider and horse slamming down the embankment in their front, and at the bottom—The Kid has his Winchester out and drawn. No choice for the mummers but to stop on the narrow trail, their horses blowing hard and the black river flowing to their right. It's shoot it out are give it up.

"Kid you ought to jine the circus, almost worth getting caught just to see that," Billy says. Frank pulls his side arm but hesitates, remembering all he knows about Kid Antrim.

"Well hell, our horses are played out anyhow, don't suppose you'd loan yours. She'd carry both of us," Frank pleads.

"This is the end of the line."

"Whoa, now that sounds awful heartless. Surely you have some feeling for us."

"I might have once, back when I mistook you for human beings." The Kid has both pistol and riffle leveled on the mummers as he watches the Regulators approach.

"Don't take on so Kid, it was just a job," Billy says in protest.

"You won't be no different'n us fore long," Frank adds.

In another minute, Frank and Billy are surrounded by a circle of angry men. An argument ensues over whether to dispense summary justice—or risk turning them in.

"If we take 'em to Lincoln, the sons-a-bitches will just get away. One way or another, release or escape, that Fenian cunt Brady will not hold them—and they'll skip," McNab says, ready to end it right there.

Brewer is equally passionate.

"If it were just up to me. I'd beat these two snakes into hammered mule shit right now, but we've given our word as sworn deputies to arrest, not assassinate. We must hold for what little is left of the law out here," Brewer warns, his baritone once again unassailable.

"McCloskey what the hell are you doing out here with these cunts, here to settle that debt I'd guess?" Frank snorts, eyeing his sometime accomplice, and ignoring Brewer's pronouncement.

"I'll tolerate no back-talk. If you want to stay alive you'll keep your mouths shut," Brewer roars.

"You can kiss my granny's lily-white ass, Sheriff Brady would disagree with this arrest," Baker spits out with a sneer.

Brewer's right fist leaps out and knocks Frank Baker on *his* ass.

"We aren't going to Lincoln we're taking these boys to Fort Stanton. Now holster your guns," Brewer announces. Frank rubs his jaw and gets back to his feet with a smirk.

"Dick you're in command, but with all due respect, you shouldn't fight with pigs. You both get dirty and the pig likes it. The cleanest plan is for these two sinners to pay up right now," Henry says, grinning wide.

"Tunstall fired on us or we never would have shot him," Billy Morton says.

"You forget, you lying shitheel, we were there. I was up in the pines and saw you two lift riffles. You shot Mr. Tunstall like a dog," Tom says, reminding him.

"Well, then, you were deceived you sorry peckerwood."

"Don't waste your breath, Tom. It's a long ride ahead," Dick councils as the Regulators remount. McCloskey helps Frank Baker onto his horse and the two men exchange a heated glance.

Jesse watches as two dust devils form and sweep across the basin. They nearly collide before disappearing in a last explosive burst, as if heralding their approach to the dark valley and its long spew of obsidian.

"What do you suppose we're getting ourselves into?" asks Tom Hill, breaking a silence of nearly two hours.

"The malpais's getting to you already?"

"It's a strange place, why would anyone live here?"

"Natural defenses and few prying eyes I'd guess," Jesse answers. He squints at the mountains to his right for a long while before returning his gaze to the blackened valley.

"We'll stop in over to Anton Chico on the way back, I'd like to see Gold Shoes. If she's still there," Jesse says, a hint of wistfulness clinging to the way he'd said her name.

"That ain't on the way back," Tom says, smiling.

It was a long ride out of the Seven Rivers nexus and back to the high country. Brewer had to work hard to keep his men from flaying their prisoners alive. They regard the two murderers as living on borrowed time, and the trip to Fort Stanton as a futile exercise. There's no guarantee Colonel Dudley will allow Baker and Morton to be placed under guard, or even if he does, that he won't release them if pressured by the Ring.

During all the long hours on the trail, Frank and Billy had been working a steady game of needling everyone within ear shot. Especially the big man, just as they had Olinger. Several times Brewer had to lay hands on one or the other, and both men sport the purpling effects. A beating is one thing and killing another.

Henry is a favorite target as well, and he'd quickly decided to keep his distance from them. At the Chisum cow camp, where they'd stopped for the night, he sits well back from the fire—and away from the poisonous invective.

"You might as well quit acting like your shit don't stink kid, I can smell it way over here. Come on to the fire now and be sociable. How about singing a round of Tobaccy Posey at least," Frank yells to Henry, fifty feet away.

"I'm fine where I am," says Henry, keeping his eyes down. McNab and Scurlock and Bowdre and French share a look—something hard and hot seems to pass between them.

"Ah hell...you ain't no better'n us, just younger," Franks yells back with a wicked grin. The flickering light had been playing oddly with his features. Looking up he seems harmless enough, but looking down, the shadows lengthen and the mummer becomes the Devil himself.

"Frank's right kid," McCloskey adds, looking at Baker with a smile that was neither genuine, or truly false. For he was very happy to be amongst the Regulators and near to Frank Baker, but no one knew why—save Frank.

"Shut your pie hole McClosky, nobody asked what you thought," Frank hisses back, suddenly gone surly.

"Tell you what, you can shut up yourself Baker and not say another word tonight, or I can start knocking out your teeth and you can be an old gummer the rest of your life," Brewer says, his patience worn completely out.

Frank communicates his desire to keep his teeth with an elaborate pantomime of sewing his mouth shut but finishing with a one-fingered gesture. Dick Brewer looks down and spits, then gets up and walks over to the fire untying his bandana. He jerks Baker up to a standing position and marches him over to a scrub oak.

"Listen sheep dip, I'm the only friend you got in this camp. You need to quit working these men." Baker is shoved to the ground and tied securely to the little oak, Brewer handling him about like he would a calf in a roping contest.

"I don't suppose you'd leave my pecker out, so's I don't have to piss my britches?" The bandana goes around Baker's mouth, then jerked back tight and knotted.

"Now, let's get some sleep."

Within fifteen miles of Fort Stanton they string out along a brushy, boulder-strewn trail at the bottom of Black Water Canyon. There was a much more direct route, but they'd heard the Boys were laying another ambush, just as they had for Tunstall, so had diverted onto a much longer and less well-known track.

Everyone has been waiting for just this opportunity. Suddenly, when their leader is riding drag and separated from the prisoners by a long bend—there is a confusion of shouts, a sudden rush of pounding hooves, and an intense burst of gunfire.

Brewer spurs forward frantically and the fusillade continues.

He finds the Regulators dismounted and standing over the bodies of Baker and Morton as if they meant to protect him from further harm. McNab speaks first.

"Baker somehow got his hands loose, caught McCloskey napping and managed to pull his gun and shoot him. He's lying dead back there. We had no choice but to open a deadly fire."

"Well, that's just a fresh load a horse shit. These men are shot all to hell. I'm counting eleven holes in Baker alone. So now we're executioners," Brewer shouts, furious.

"McCloskey and Baker got the dance started. There was some kind of score settling going on between them and it got settled, and no matter how you sing this...it's done now. It won't bring back John, but I'll not deny that it feels good," Henry declares.

"Hell of a message to little drummer boy Dolan—and to God almighty his self—Jesse Evans," Charlie adds with a whoop. Henry nods slowly, clucking his tongue.

Brewer looks them all over, including the bullet-riddled corpses, before turning away.

"Hell is right. Go hide yourselves around San Patricio and wait for me. I'll head on to Lincoln and talk to McSween."

"What about them?" McNab asks, nodding toward the two mummers.

"Find a place and bury'em, damnit, deep as you can."

They'd followed the edge of the Malpais until sighting sheep out in the buffalo grass, and through a pair of field glasses—a man walking the far edge of the herd. They dismount and lead their horses through a gap into a large circular opening in the volcanic landscape, its caves and fantastical spirals of frozen lava incorporated into pens and sheds, even the living quarters. An eerie silence hangs over all and Tom Hill wishes they were a hundred miles away.

Jesse opens the cabin door. A stove in the corner fired and pot of beans simmering, ratcheting up their caution as they peer into the gloom of the interior.

The low-ceilinged hovel is cluttered, foul-smelling, and somehow perverse; more like the lair of a twisted brujo maybe, or some deviant Mexican outlaw. Judging from the preternatural things hanging from the rafters, and the shrine to Salais, patron saint of thieves in the wild mountains to the south—he's some execrable combination of both—and probably on the run from something worse than himself.

"This hombre is from the Sierra Madres," Jesse says as a warning. He is about to make a further judgement when they hear a sob. The two men advance with pistols drawn. They discover a young girl in a rags, chained to the lava wall at the back of the rambling enclosure and pitiful to behold.

"*Llave? A donde?*" Jesse asks. The girl shakes her head and points outside.

"*El oro, dinero?*"

"*Allá, allá,*" the girl whimpers, pointing to a corner. "*Bajo la roca negra.*"

They root out the metal coffer from under a ledge of malpais, bound by a heavy padlock. Jesse holsters his pistol and begins to work the lock with two iron pins plucked from his coat pocket. He inserts the first pin with his left hand, pushing it all the way to one side of the keyway, and inserts the curved end of the other pin to probe. Both men are focused tightly on the lock.

Suddenly a man enters through the open door like a silent predator.

From a distance he would look like any New Mexican sheepherder. But up close—the well-oiled guns, the gold teeth, and the eyes—are tells of something poisonous and evil.

"*Hola, muchachos.*" Evans and Hill drop the box and wheel around.

They lock eyes with the man in the doorway. In one hand is a sawed-off shotgun pointed at Hill and in the other a heavy Colt pointed at Evans.

Jesse sees a very narrow opening. Hill has his pistol up and the malo will favor to the left.

"*Qué paso?*"

"*No mucho.*"

"Pardon my temper, hombres, but I do not like to see two extraños in mi casa."

"You weren't here to let us in amigo."

"And now the rats have found the cheese." The malo's eyes move between the two hombres, back and forth—watching for the slightest sign of intent.

An epic standoff stretches into deep silence. The malo has the drop on them, but knows he must kill them both to survive. A long minute passes.

"You're no damn sheepherder," says Jesse, the eyes unwavering.

"A man can be many things," the Mexican answers back. "I knew men like you would come." He spits and Hill fires, without a tell, buying an important split second.

Five shots roar out in rapid succession and all three men go down.

Evans lets out a choking cough and struggles to his feet, gasping for air. He had leapt away and pulled, waiting a crucial split second for his aim to lock on—taking a bullet but to the left of its mark, and firing his own kill shot. The last bullet fired had clipped Jesse's left forearm.

He staggers toward the *pistolero,* firing two more rounds into the body as he approaches. The girl lets out a shriek and pantomimes the necklace of keys hanging under the malo's shirt.

"*Las llaves.*"

Evans stoops down and grasps the leather chain of keys, pausing to look at the other strange milagros attached to it, then wrenches it away. In the corner a reredos of St. Jude, patron saint of impossible lost causes, catches his eye as he fits the key.

The strongbox opens with a rusty screech. He stares at the contents, disappointed and disgusted, then looks over at his man, Tom Hill. Tom was the best of the Boys and he'd taken the shotgun blast. Standing over the dead with eyes closed, meditating on his own lost cause, the pistolero sways slightly and gathers himself.

"Goddamnit," Evans whispers. The handful of gold coins go into his coat pocket and the box smashed against the St. Jude.

There was some vile alchemy of God and Devil here, birthed in the hold of the Sierras. And like the dark pinnacled mother herself—the work of centuries. Well, now the bastard is *muerto* and the spell broken.

He returns to the hombre malo and kneels suddenly, as if overcome by an urge to pray. Jesse inserts his knife and pries out a clump of gold teeth. He wobbles back to his feet and goes to the girl. The keys are released into her hands along with drops of blood from his wounded arm. She lifts her eyes to his.

"*Le puedo ayudar.*"

"No."

He turns to go but the girl is up and running to a wooden chest and pulling out cloth to rip into pieces. Jesse sits down, hard, the strange cabin starting to spin. The bullet went through a lung and each breath drawn is a ragged thing. The girl removes his coat and shirt, the hard-muscled torso white below the neck and welted with a dozen vicious scars. A map of his battles won and lost, and now two ugly red holes and a long rip to join the fray.

From the stove she pulls a hot poker, hiking up a ragged skirt to grip the iron. He eyes the red orange of the point and looks at the girl for a long moment, then nods.

"Goddamnit," Jesse grunts, flinching when she does the front, arching his back when the exit wound is gouged. She snatches a handful of cobwebs from the low hanging soffit, then balls and rubs it into the sizzling flesh.

Wrapping absorbent material hard against the wounds with strips of cloth, she looks at the pale face of her savior and smiles. There is a missing tooth and streaks of grime on her cheeks and forehead. The hair is wild and soiled and all of her defiled and bereft—yet there is strength in the dark eyes.

When she takes the wounded left arm, there is another groan, worsening as she feels along the ulnar bone.

"*Esta roto,*" says the girl and he nods. Nothing she can do but wrap it.

Jesse struggles back into his shirt and coat. There is gratitude in his own dark eyes. He stands and looks once more at the body of Tom Hill then staggers over to the stove. Placing one boot against the oblong belly, he pushes it over and turns to the girl.

"*Vamanos.*"

She hustles a number of useful items into a bag, including the malo's pistol and knife, and follows Jesse outside. The cabin is already alight as he struggles into the saddle. Evans gives the flames, and his chances of survival—a cold professional reckoning—the cabin and its black secrets will quickly burn to the ground and not more than a fifty-fifty chance of making the sixty-mile ride ahead.

The girl stares at him sitting there like some stone-faced guerrero, wondering what the strange gringo will do next. Jesse reaches into the pocket of his coat and motions to the girl.

"*Aquí.*" He leans over and places a gold piece in her hand.

"*Gracias, Señor.*"

"*Cómo se llama?*"

"*Rosa.*"

After a few moments he puts his head down and spurs ahead. Rosa watches him ride through the opening in the malpais. In a moment she is on Tom Hill's mount following at a respectful distance.

Built of stone and placed on a high plain, Fort Stanton is both an impressive rampart against the Mescalero Apaches, and a massive engine of commerce. The Fort has brought all else into being in Lincoln County, and even the Apache tend to think of it as an opportunity.

A platoon of black soldiers marches crisply at quick time on the Fort Stanton quadrangle. They display an impressive snap and energy in all their movements, as if they have something to prove. They are soldiers of the 9th calvary, a vaunted regiment of buffalo soldiers. Organized by Phil Sheridan just after the Civil War, mustered out of Kentucky, trained in New Orleans and San Antonio—and from there brevetted to the Indian Wars.

Their motto is, "We Can, We Will."

Uneasily shoehorned into Fort Stanton's white soldiery, they take every opportunity to show their value. The 9th could field a soldier worth two of its white counterparts, at the drop of a hat. The officers were well aware of the disparity and used it to their advantage. If the job was a tough assignment—it went to the 9th.

Inside headquarters, commanding officer Colonel Dudley knocks back a silver cup full with hasty relish—glancing at the dedication on the rim after draining its contents. The colonel has a great nose for trouble, and he'd been smelling it for weeks now. In fact, since the first day he took command of Fort Stanton.

There is only one question in his mind now—will I be able to avoid it this time?

The cup was a commemorative gift during his salad days of the Civil War, between the first and second court-martial. Colonel Dudley sailed through both proceedings relatively unscathed. In the second court-martial he'd been accused of drunkenness and conduct unbecoming an officer, among other things. The rumors and innuendos were difficult to prove though—beyond a reasonable doubt.

For many reasons both judge and jury were prepared to be doubtful. Perhaps overly so given the preponderance of evidence. But it was New Mexico, and Thomas Catron himself was defending him.

Colonel Dudley a devoted Mason and so too the fat man, as we're many of those sitting in judgment. Tecumseh Sherman, Commanding General of the United States Army, weighed in from afar as well. For Sherman, drunkenness was not a career-ending offense.

Dudley was demoted to Colonel and given the troubled post of Fort Stanton.

The newly installed commander takes one more bracer before going into a meeting he knows will be prickly and trying. On this 11th day of March, Governor Axtell has finally arrived from his tedious journey and Dudley's adjutant has forewarned the colonel of Axtell's sour mood. Dudley knows his eminence is here to try and halt the brewing range war, and that he and his little army will more than likely be asked to take sides.

"A pleasure Governor Axtell," Dudley exclaims, with moderate civility. The greeting is masonic and perfunctory. Colonel Dudley does not like meddling in civil affairs, or being steered by politicians to do so, even a brethren.

"I've received orders from District Commander Hatch saying I'm to assist civil authorities...but which ones, and against who?" Dudley begins, dropping the civility and allowing his annoyance to spill over in his first statement.

"Let me be clear on four matters particularly, as will be spelled out in my written proclamation. Squire Wilson's appointment as justice of the peace is illegal and all processes issued by him are void. Henceforth, the only *legal* processes to be enforced are from Judge Bristol and District Attorney Rynerson, the only civil officers to enforce them are Sheriff Brady and his deputies—and lastly, that McSween bunch are all outlaws," Governor Axtell proclaims, poking the air with his cigar.

Dudley is silent for a moment, but then begins to chuckle.

"Well from one scoundrel to another, I believe I comprehend your plan, Governor, and I agree, McSween and Chisum are a couple of horse thieves. But with all due respect the interim appointment of Wilson *was* legal and the Englishman was likely murdered. But of course this proclamation you're planning fixes all contingencies. And that's *all* that matters, lest the heavens fall. Now, may I offer you a drink."

The aging windmill sings out, its pump rod rattling in the standpipe and gear box whining. A weary rider approaches and passes into stock yards, ignoring the cowboy waving from behind a fence.

Jesse dismounts. Arturo looks up from the dough he'd been kneading and out the window, issuing a curse. He raises a call and runs outside.

Evans makes it to the porch and crumples onto the boards.

"*Señor.*"

Arturo feels for a pulse. Looking up, he sees the girl.

10

Somber March rains sweep the open highlands to the east of the White Mountain. Their wide outstretched arms run at a benevolent grade to where the broad steppes slowly give way to deep canyons and lush valleys. Fort Stanton sits brooding there on the edge like an old campaigner.

Kit Carson had been its first commander. The frontiersman's understated genius made a profound impact, both with the dispensation of the Mescalero Apache, *and* in setting up the nature of commerce in what would become Lincoln County.

The Mescalero survived with a portion of their homeland intact, and the wild country began to prosper in a sudden burst of economic opportunity. Two of Kit Carson's best and most highly promoted officers, Captain Laurence G. Murphy and Colonel Emil Fritz—stayed on after the Indian Wars to begin a profitable monopoly—built around the grind wheel of the Fort's sustenance.

Murphy was Kit's trusted adjutant in the New Mexico Volunteers, and Fritz won a commendation for staunchly defending Carson's right flank during the battle of Adobe Walls. The two somehow made a formidable team despite being polar opposites; the Irishman of County Wexford was personable and charming, if given to tippling the ardent, and the German from Stuttgart was pragmatic and shrewd.

Their newly born enterprise, Murphy & Co., enjoyed a good balance of thievery and profit from the beginning. Fort Stanton made a show of protecting Indians and settlers alike, and required huge allotments of beef, corn, grain, hay, and horses. Indians stole from the settlers and ranchers, who stole from the Indians, and each other, in return.

Everyone worked hard and most were eventually gouged by Murphy & Co, and all was ultimately sold and traded at the Fort. And just about everyone, including the commissary officers, cheated the US government. A wink and a nod and devil take the hindmost being the order of the frontier.

The Apache regarded it all as not unlike their long war with the mighty Comanche. The white eyes were far more plentiful but not as intelligent, or as mean. And the white traders had opened the whiskey trade. Amber fire flowed in all directions and many sins were committed and forgiven because of it. When queried on the illicit subject, Chief Santana was fond of stating that he'd found a spring.

Driving his mount at a fast trot, Dick Brewer reaches behind the cantle for a rain slicker. He pulls it over his big shoulders and snugs the hood down. The Blackwater trail deposited him onto the muddying highland road. He'd passed the Fort a half hour before, with a shrug and a spit.

The tight entrance of Bonito Valley lay just ahead. Halfway up the western ridge a cleft leans outward like some ancient menhir guarding the way. It had always given him a moment's pause. Passing under the stone invariably felt like an omen of ill-fate—for the dark rock leers ominously and seems to pass judgement, and to ascribe some cursed deadfall ahead.

But just beyond the gate benevolent farms and orchards open out along the Rio Bonito to the east and inspire different perceptions entirely. The leader of the Regulators continues on into the graceful vale and the worsening rain, finally arriving within the agitated heart of Lincoln.

Dick stands on the porch stomping his boots and trying to shake off a little before entering. In the McSween parlor, Brewer exchanges an avid grip with the councilor. Susan starts with a handshake, but under the influence of one of her strong emotions, pulls him into a hug that lasts a little too long.

"Thank God we're all still alive Mr. Brewer, I feel so much better with you here. I wish you would stay with us until this is over. I well understand now why the natives call you the Lion," Susan adds, more than a little rattled by John's murder and the ensuing chaos.

It's been a difficult adjustment; the violence and hate and palpable danger that now surrounds she and her husband at every move. Susan longs for their former life. The one where Alex sharpened his angles and she was left in peace to run the household and contemplate her music, or the next shopping spree in St. Louis.

"You must forgive my wife. Susan speaks her mind," McSween adds. Brewer nods back with an uncomfortable smile. "What news have you?"

"I'm afraid I have nothing comforting to share. Just the opposite. We caught Morton and Baker, but both were killed attempting to escape," Dick admits, as McSween lowers his gaze to the floor.

"Well, it would have been far better to put them on trial. My news is no better. The governor has issued a proclamation and it couldn't be more partisan if Jimmy Dolan and Brady had written it themselves."

"I'm sure they *did* write it Alex," Susan fumes, the color rising up her neck, one vein in particular bulging slightly and distracting Dick's eye for a moment.

"Judge Wilson's appointment has been revoked, his warrants invalidated. The Regulators have been declared outlaws, and we must all of us go into hiding."

"I'm sorry to hear that," Brewer admits, heaving a tremendous sigh.

"Susan and I will head to the safe haven of the Chisum ranch, and perhaps you would consider escorting us there."

"Are we finished then, with nothing to do but run and hide?" Brewer asks.

"No, we are not finished. We *will* get a fair hearing, and in the meantime, I'll fight this in the territorial press, and beyond. Believe me, I am not finished by any means...there is much I can and will do," McSween declares, revealing the depth of his pride, the lawyer's supreme conceit—that he is smarter and more ruthless than everyone else.

"Is the governor still here?"

"Ha! Yesterday our fine and distinguished governor spent all of three hours in Lincoln, and most of that time with Dolan. He only stopped at our door for a moment. Mac was in Messila, seeing about the summons. The governor told me he wasn't here to speak with my husband, but only to warn us," Susan spit this out with the vein bulging in her neck again.

"My God," Dick offers, not knowing what else to say.

"Yes, there will be no help from Santa Fe. They'll seek to bury all of this, and quickly, just as they did in Colfax County," McSween reveals.

"Bury *us* you mean," Susan snaps, a second vein bulging now. "The rumors of what Dolan plans to do next are...despicable."

"No Susan, I will not allow that to happen," her husband corrects. "I *will* protect us. I plan to reach well beyond Santa Fe, to Washington. They will know our side of the story and soon. I've written to no less a person than Secretary of the Interior Carl Shurz. He's a dedicated reformer and pressing hard for higher moral standards in government. We just need to buy ourselves some time."

"I'd say there's little or no moral standards, at all, in our precious territory of New Mexico. Those scoundrels in their fine suits are just so many black-hearted thieves who care nothing about morals—only business and money and cheating. If they'd kill a fine young man like John Tunstall, as if he were some reprobate common criminal," Susan weeps, tears starting from acutely disturbed eyes, and her face now plainly wearing the terrified expression of panic.

"Susan you must calm yourself, it won't do. Dick will be scandalized if you get any more worked up," McSween pleads, truly concerned and also embarrassed by his wife's frenzy of emotion.

"What of John's parents, I suppose it will take more time before you hear from them," Dick asks, hoping to change the subject enough to keep Mrs. McSween from sailing over the edge, and deeply curious as well—about his friend's family and what could only be the deepest kind of bereavement.

"Late April is the earliest we can hope for a response."

"The poor Tunstall family...I can't even imagine," Susan pronounces, suddenly far more tranquil. As if contemplating a disaster greater than hers—had suddenly stilled the roiling waves.

Upward of eighty thousand head of cattle roam the vast prairie surrounding the Chisum South Spring hacienda. Cows and calves low in the distance from dawn to dusk. The murmur of it hypnotic and somehow reassuring.

Despite the large presence of Dick Brewer cantering along beside them, both husband and wife are very much unsettled. They roll on across immense grasslands in silence, Susan grinding her jaw and a desperately bold scheme blazing to life in Alex McSween's head. It's strictly a game of high hand stud requiring a fatal show of royalty, a glacial poker face—and a load of intestinal fortitude. He'd feel better once he had Chisum's council, and hopefully his support.

At sundown the thick-walled fortress and its grove of cottonwoods finally comes within sight. Susan breathes a deep sigh of relief and Brewer spurs ahead with a whoop. All of them grateful to be at a far remove from the violence of the mountains.

John Chisum himself had been watching their approach with sharp eyes, levering back and forth in his favorite chair—a huge porch rocker with an Indian blanket draped across it's back. He'd sat there many an hour; contemplating the day ahead and sipping coffee, or the day just passed with its work well-done or found wanting, a pipe clenched in his strong teeth and smoke wreathed about his head.

He'd only just returned from three months in jail. Tom Catron had set a trap that Chisum could have bought his way out of—but choose not to. The telegraphed writ came directly from Catron's office in Santa Fe and cornered him neatly on a Las Vegas business trip.

There was plenty of money on hand, McSween had brokered a deal for his Bosque Redondo ranch and herd, two years before, worth a quarter million dollars. But being stubborn as hell and tight as the bark on a tree—Chisum refused to make payments on the list of debts. He regarded them all as scurrilous and paying them was unthinkable.

Catron had counted on that. It was his way of keeping the cattle baron out of the fray, and it had worked.

This day, as the sun sets and tobacco smoke curls around him he's just glad to be home, with his brothers and his niece Sallie, and the cattle in their thousands spread out over the valley. John Chisum is a shrewd man, and one for the long game—and the Ring would pay for their almighty arrogance, in time.

He rises to greet his guests and walks toward them with a pronounced limp. A broad smile crinkles his weathered face, lifting the handlebar mustache as he extends his hand. Both McSween and Brewer tower over the cattleman, but in truth, the world looks up to John Chisum.

"Good to see you safe and sound. Susan you grow prettier by the day."

"Thank you John, but I'm quite sure you exaggerate," Mrs. McSween objects as she reaches for Chisum's hand, smiling into his dark brown eyes. "A day in that infernal buggy hasn't done me any favors."

"There's a lot to be said for the rouge of the sun. Dick it's good to see you too."

"Things have gone hard against us since last we spoke," says Alex.

"We've had the devil's own time of it for certain...I sure hate what happened to John, God rest his soul," Chisum replies, looking at his guests with a percipient squint. Brewer nods his head slowly and looks away.

"We have indeed John, and I fear it only grows worse," Alex replies.

"There's someone stopping at the ranch who may be able to help us, in Washington. He's both an Englishman and an American citizen—and a prominent man to boot," John declares. The statement draws a sharp look from his guests. "Mr. Montaque Leverson, a successful Colorado businessman, with powerful friends," Chisum announces.

"That is excellent to hear and I look forward to meeting him, but you and I must have a talk in private, later this evening," McSween says this gravely, with a quick look almost of panic. Puzzled, Chisum nods and they follow the others inside.

Dinner at the Chisum ranch is always tumultuous, particularly so this night. John's favorite, his comely niece Sallie, sits to his right, and the honored guest, Montague Leverson, at his left. Next, the McSweens and Dick Brewer, followed by the brothers James, Jefferson, and Pitzer Chisum—with various and assorted children and wives stretching down to the end of a long cottonwood table.

After listening to a full partisan recital of Lincoln County troubles from the councilor and the baron, culminating with the murder of a fellow countryman—Leverson is stirred to great passion, somewhat abetted by a generous pouring and downing of good bourbon. An ample supply, freighted all the way from St. Louis, is at the ready in a line of oak barrels stored in the cellar.

"I do not understand how such outrages can occur and be countenanced by the authorities."

"The authorities are the ones who committed the outrages," John says, and Alex shakes his head.

"Dying in a foreign land is one thing, something we English have grown accustomed to. But a young man cruelly murdered under the guise of American law is another thing entirely. What a ghastly trial for the family."

"We were all quite fond of him as well, he was a fine man. Different, even amongst the Englishman I've known, but very fine," Sallie Chisum offers, a sadness breaking on her last words.

"Yes of course, what a horrible thing all the way through," Leverson replies.

"I have written a letter to Washington, to Carl Shurz, Secretary of the Interior," McSween allows.

"I know him, and President Hayes. I'd say he owes me a favor in fact. Both men shall be hearing from me."

"I can't tell you how pleased we are to hear that Mr. Leverson," says Susan, a little catch in her voice drawing Montague's attention.

"It seems the stench of the Grant administration continues to waft across the West. Governor Axtell and this bullying Attorney General should be removed from office—immediately."

"Bully for that!" Dick Brewer says in his loud baritone, startling the Brit.

"Mr. Leverson I hope you've saved room for some apple pie," asks Sallie.

"Yes, I believe I have," replies the bewhiskered Englishman, discreetly eyeing the blond twenty-year-old woman of the house. "But the apples, are they sweet or tart?"

"The apples are a tart variety, but heavily sugared, and I'm known to be very free with butter and cinnamon," Sallie states confidently, her smile lifting to high cheekbones. She is a striking girl with eyes the color of the prairie and enough moonstruck cowboys trailing along behind to fill a dance hall.

"Ah, then perfect, and gentleman, I will write letters this very night," the Englishman announces, wrapping the table with the knuckles of his left hand and a moment later, draining the remainder of his bourbon and nodding to his host and all those seated at the table.

Alex McSween, though relieved by the promise of help from Leverson—is nonetheless in a panic. He's waited throughout the long evening for a private talk with Chisum and they are finally seated before the embers of a fire, alone.

"Alex you sure seem tight, things are pretty bilious I'll admit, but now is not the time to lose your nerve. Not like you, we've done a lot of...*hard* business, nothing's ever rattled you before."

"I hate to say it, but I am a trifle discomposed."

"I suppose its John's murder, it's a goddamned shame Alex, and they will pay for it. But you need to set fear aside and think clearly," Chisum acknowledges with a fierce glint, stoking up his pipe.

"The House intends me to be dead as well, they will arrest me for certain, and once I'm incarcerated I may never see the light of day again. Or they will shoot me down on a lonely stretch of road as they did John...both rumors have fallen on my ear, amongst others even more appalling."

"You are not without friends, and there are prudent steps to take every time you step out the door," Chisum argues.

"You mean I'm to move about in a phalanx?"

"Possibly, it surely means you keep your eyes and ears open and men about."

"I doubt I can count on much help from the citizenry. I'm no champion of the people, like John was, or Mr. Brewer. They regard me as a glorified bill collector."

"Well maybe," Chisum says, chuckling into the fire. "But you're also one hell of a lawyer. A master of hard deals and delinquent accounts, collected more money for me than some men make in a lifetime." John's dark brown eyes seem opaque. "You just need to buck up, and we need to buy some time."

"That is for certain. I'm thinking I should play by House rules now. Discreetly offer the Regulators a cash reward for killing Brady, and his deputies. It would cripple the application of Ring law, for a time at least and buy that time." Alex looks at Chisum with uncertainty. Chisum is silent longer than Alex would like.

"Been thinking along similar lines. There's sense to it. Even if you *just* get Brady, those deputies would be pretty helpless without him, not to mention toothless."

"I would err on the side of caution."

"It's a bold move, and if you're looking for my blessing...I don't know a thing about it."

"Well, agreed then, I'll send Brewer back to the Regulators in the morning," says Alex, sinking back into his leather chair. Chisum looks into the embers and pulls at his pipe again.

"He won't want to get involved, but the others, how much will you offer them?" says Chisum, after a cleansing birth of smoke.

"Five hundred a man?"

"Too rich for my blood. Just how much are you willing to pay out? The whole lot of them may answer the call."

"I would again err on the side of caution, besides, there may be some difficulty in getting the money right away." Alex gestures by opening his hands out and lifting his eyebrows. Chisum nods.

"Those Regulator boys are roostered up enough to start their own war anyway. All they need is a little nudge, and Brady's demise *will* buy some time. I have a notion the spring term of court in Lincoln will favor us as well."

"It's Judge Bristol and he's a Ring man for certain," McSween growls.

"But the grand jury will be Lincoln County men," Chisum adds, while rubbing his leg and grimacing.

The little river arches around and through San Patricio's quiet valley. It hugs the sharp hills that protectively enclose the vale. The Regulators have taken safe harbor nearby, in a pine cleft, above the river and the village. They've all developed close ties to the community.

Some ties are very close indeed.

Reclining against a piñon, Henry's lost in the second book John Tunstall had loaned him, back before the murder, before their lives had all been dropped into a hurricane. It was another fine talent of his; to be able to create a sanctum wherever he was, a relaxing carefree moment—even as the hurricane picked up wind speed.

The others are engaged in a variety of activities from gun maintenance to nothing at all. Tom looks up from mending an old hackamore and over at his friend, a grin coming up on his freckled face.

"How many times have you read that book?" Tom asks, shaking his head. The Kid holds up two fingers. "Another time or two and you can read it without the book then."

They hear someone approaching from the river and Fred Waite, nearest the trail, pulls his pistol—but it is only Adelita, carrying a basket of freshly made tortillas and a spicy bean paste.

Henry suddenly jumps up to help her, the happiest smile adorning his handsome face. They immediately begin flirting in a rhythmic trilling of Spanish pleasantries. Henry takes the basket and hands it to Tom with his right hand, taking Adelita with his left and begins a lively danza.

He sings and hums the old Mexican waltz *Alma Angelina,* twirling her for a spin in the dirt. His friends and comrades whistle and hoot and sing along themselves. It's a moment only the young Irishman can deliver.

Since the night of the baile Henry had fallen deeper and deeper into the magic of San Patricio, returning there often to visit with Adelita and her family, and becoming known to all. The oldest man in the village had honored him with a nickname—*el chivato,* the kid—and everyone had picked it up.

Chivato had begun to teach some of the children English, and they in turn taught him songs of Mother Spain and of the Stepmother—Mexico. Venerable songs of poets and Kings and bandits, and he'd come to regard these heirlooms as an inexhaustible treasure of the greatest beauty. He learns them quickly, stores them away carefully, sings them frequently.

While the Regulators sit with their tortillas and beans, the spinning and flirting continues. But a rider moving briskly up the trail puts a quick end to the little noontime fiesta.

"Hallo to the camp!" Dick yells out, a moment later thrusting up out of the brush with a sweating mount and a grim look. He dismounts and realizes that he and his horse have trod on a happy moment.

"I hate to break up the party, but I've some news."

"Bad news I bet," Henry adds.

"Is there any other kind?" says Frank McNab, before swallowing his last bite.

"Don't keep us in suspense big fella," Fred encourages, after wiping his mouth on the back of his sleeve.

"The governor has been to Lincoln and issued a proclamation... Justice of Peace Wilson has been removed, and we've been outlawed," Brewer announces with a baritone as grim as his face. No one speaks at first, it takes a minute for them to digest the information.

"That's a hard chunk to swallow," says Doc Scurlock. "I don't recall telling Uncle John it'd be all right if we got outlawed."

"Don't matter now, sounds like we *are* outlawed," Frank says.

"Brady penned a letter to Boss Catron saying how John refused the warrant and fired on members of the posse. And all our actions have been illegal ever since."

"Arrogant lyin bastard."

"Goddamned Fenian cunt!" McNab spits out in his thick Scottish burr.

"I do have one bit of good news, the gossip I've been hearing in Lincoln says Dolan sent Jesse Evans down into the basin on some errand and he didn't make it back. Hasn't been seen for a while." Again, the news takes a minute to swallow.

"Well Dick, ain't you a one for surprises today," Henry says, meaning to sound lighthearted, but somehow failing.

"I'm riding on to my ranch, got to see to things there. Henry, ride along with me for a little ways so we can talk," Brewer asks.

Brewer, George Coe, and Charlie Bowdre slipped off to see to their own small ranches—leaving McNab and Scurlock to grouse with the others as the day sails into the afternoon, and then into the evening.

"Do you ever miss Scotland?" Doc asks.

"No. Scotland's got just two kinds of weather, cold and colder. I miss my family though," Frank answers, and the admission seems to have a solemn effect on the others. Several minutes pass in silence. "Wonder what the kid's up to, he's been gone all day."

"Ain't no telling. Inventing a fancy of some sort," Fred replies, staring into the flames.

"We've been declared outlaws by a gang of criminals, can you fuckin believe it?" Doc Scurlock fumes, before taking a generous pull from the jug making its way around.

"Shut it Doc, you've been sayin that all afternoon. Out here there's no justice but what you can make yourself, you know that, and this writ from the Governor ain't any kind of due process," McNab replies, his burr thickening further with the liquor.

"It's *war*. They've won the first battle and they're hoping we turn tail and run. And they're counting on the world forgetting about John Tunstall and Lincoln County and it will, if we let it," Henry offers boldly, walking up to the fire. He'd been thinking all afternoon about what Dick had said and had been hanging back in the shadows, listening.

"What the by god hell are you saying kid?" asks Fred Waite, perking up suddenly.

"I say we do something *big*," Henry responds, deadly serious now.

"Well okay, and just what the fuck did you have in mind?" McNab inquires, his ear caught now as well.

"Let's kill that letter writin son-of-a-bitch Brady. Give it to him just like they gave it to John," Henry levels, his voice steady as the south wind. "Cut the head off the snake."

"I'd gladly send that torturin windbag to hell, with a smile. Always bragging about his glory days with Kit Carson, you'd think he settled the West all by himself. He spent a half hour needling me with a red hot gun barrel last time I was in his jail," says Jim French. He lifts his shirt and reveals the welts. "No doubt he was upset about the colorful remarks I made about his wife. But still...executing the sheriff might be a bit extreme."

"I like it. Take the fight to them. They'll be crippled without Brady," McNab says with enthusiasm.

"Now hold on, you're not thinking this thing through," Doc Scurlock declares. "We ain't a bunch a kids playin Shiloh, you ring this bell it cain't be un-rung."

"The bell's already been rung," Henry answers.

"We killed the triggermen, don't that count for something?" Doc replies, insisting.

"Yes, it surely does, to us. But nobody will ever give two shits about them, or their sad demise. Just two lowlife cunts and no eyes on. It sure as hell won't tip any grand scale toward a federal investigation—*comprende*?

"Maybe," McNab replies before taking a thoughtful pull on the jug.

"What if I told you there's been a purse put up for Brady and his deputies. Five hundred dollars for anyone willing to stand up and fire a righteous bullet."

"Well fuck me," McNab spits out, stunned.

"Dick and Charlie and George have bowed out, but we could sure as hell do it."

"Sure, wouldn't be no trouble," says McNab, the burred sarcasm thick.

"So, we wait for him on the road somewhere's, like they done John?" the Chickasaw cowboy asks. He tugs at his mustache and makes a peculiar expression before taking his own long pull from the jug.

"No. Not bold enough...we shoot'em in broad daylight on the street. That will shine a light gentleman. The world will have to know—*what the hell* is going on in Lincoln County?" The Kid offers this resolutely, as if it were a completely logical conclusion. "They're going to try and rub us out, one way or another. It's get the hell out of Lincoln County or stay and fight. We get Brady and it kills two birds—and the outcome will justify the means."

"Well you count me out on this one. Ain't worth the money or the trouble," Doc answers back. "This across the street war reminds me of something that happened in Mexico. Had to shoot my way out of game of chance. We both stood up and fired across the table, only he tried to get slick and go for a head shot. I just aimed at his belly. He got me all right, shot went through my mouth, took out two teeth then out the back of my neck. I survived and he was dead. Recovering from that wound was the misery of my life, but I was lucky, profoundly lucky. Do y'all feel that kind of luck?

"Yes, I surly do," The Kid proclaims.

The others; Fred Waite, Jim French, Frank McNab, and Tom O'Folliard—fall silent. They concentrate on the fire, as if the answers to their questions were buried somewhere in the flames.

"I'm in," Tom states, breaking a silence that had lasted through the past half hour, while the others had jawed and groused. His mind hadn't quite grasped the scope Henry was reaching for, but he'd decided he would follow his friend come what may, and that was a sight of money.

"So Mac wants Brady dead, that means Chisum does to, and who are we to gainsay the high and mighty," the Scotsman answers.

"If it all goes south afterwards. I guess we can just disappear," Jim French says, looking up and tipping his hat to the kid.

"We cain't disappear, but we can sure as hell go to Mexico," Fred Waite argues. A broad smile gaps his face as he sticks up a thumb, causing his thick horseshoe mustache to spread and out comes his tongue to complete the picture. They had all gotten used to this extraordinary expression. He seems to love making it, but it took a particular occasion.

"You got brains Henry, now we'll see if you got *balls*, and I still say you got a problem with being unknown," says McNab, looking square at the kid.

The men glance up from the fire and at the boy they know as Henry McCarty; a fine singer and storyteller and horseman, a generous goodhearted fellow and crack shot—many other things as well. But there's something else besides, something none of them can quite fit their hats around.

"You fellows have all lost your minds," Doc continues.

"Ease up Doc and pass the jug," says McNab.

"For John," Henry toasts, taking the jug himself and the big grin returning.

"And the money...*Mr. Bonney*," McNab adds with a wink.

His eyes open, slowly. They'd been closed for an eternity and he'd grown to appreciate the darkness and the peace of it. Only with the greatest reluctance does he allow them to open now.

The gun and coat hang on a chair.

Through the open window he can see the desert is still there as well, and the saw-tooth mountains beyond. Some strange fate, or miracle, had occurred out in the malpais. Whatever it was, he was not one to apotheosize it. He would tuck it away somewhere and ride on.

"There you are, good to see you back Mr. Evans," says the camp boss, Leighton Shed.

"I survived," Jesse whispers, not quite a statement or a question.

"You did, I sent word to Dolan. You had some help all through it," the man answers, getting up from the chair and revealing the girl standing behind him, in clean homespun and making a close study of the floor, a milagro of some sort clutched in one hand.

"What's she doing here?" Jesse asks, coming fully awake.

"I'll let her tell it, if you can get her to talk. She's been tending you, ain't left your side. I got work to get back to Mr. Evans," the camp boss adds.

The door closes behind him.

Jesse looks at the girl a long time without speaking; taking in her big haunted eyes, the wild black hair pulled back now, the skinny little neck with discolored bruises working up the sides, the long fingers and the dirt under her nails.

"*Cómo está*?" he asks at last.

"*Buen.*"

"*Gracias.*"

"*De nada.*" She ventures a fragile little smile, reminding him of a stray cat wanting to come in out of the cold and be fed.

"*Dónde tu padres*?"

"*Con Dios...el hombre malo los mató.*"

"*Lo siento.*" Jesse closes his eyes, wishing the darkness and the peace could flood over him again. Eventually he opens his eyes. The girl is still there.

"*Tienes hambre*?" she asks softly. Her eyes lift from the floor.

"Yes," says Jesse Evans, sitting himself up and nodding. The expression remains stoic, but there is a wink. "*Mucho hambre.*"

APRIL 1, 1878

A benevolent morning sun shines over the ridge like an old friend. People are up and about and shouting greetings to each other. A pall had settled hard after the Tunstall killing, but the arrival of spring and the scent of verbena work a kind of magic over the little town.

The constabulary are abroad as well—at nine o'clock Sheriff Brady leads his men down the street with an irritable swagger. The balm and fragrance of April stirred up a different response in the sheriff. Cockcrow and the red sky morning had brought to mind a Navajo raid gone wrong in the bloody spring of 63', and his mood soured headlong.

He'd been on picket duty that night and fallen asleep sometime before dawn. It cost the Volunteers dearly. His full redemption came in subsequent encounters, yet the disgrace still jutted out from time to time like a broken bone.

Brady looks at the Tunstall store as they pass, shuttered and silent, and spits.

"I doubt we'll see any more of those addle-brained Regulators, but keep your eyes open. Their blood may be up, but I'd bet their peckers are down," Brady says, pointing suggestively with the Winchester he'd confiscated from William Bonney.

"They're on the dodge, shading down toward the border I'd bet," Deputy Peppin says.

"Top of the morning Sheriff," says a kid poking his head over a high wall fifty feet away. Brady turns and recognizes the boy he'd thrown in the hole. Four other men have guns leveled over the adobe bricks, all aimed at him.

"Goddamnit," yells Brady, trying to bring the rifle up. But in the time it took to curse—all five men poured forth a hailstorm. Brady, and Deputy Hindeman, collapse onto the street. Deputies Peppin and Long, escape the fusillade unscathed. They dart off the street as another erupts.

The sudden violent tableau engraved itself onto the souls of all those who'd been enjoying the air a moment before. No one quite understands what it is at first, and all stand motionless, staring. Then just as suddenly, the tableau erupts into a screaming melee.

"I'm gonna get my Winchester," Henry announces, jumping down from the wall.

"Come on kid," McNab hisses.

"Let's ride Henry," Tom pleads.

"You boys fog it. I'll be along," Henry shouts back. McNab, O'Folliard, Waite, and French are already mounting up. In another breath they take off in a hurtling clump, flying for the river.

Henry runs out into the street, pausing a moment to look at the sheriff—light fading from his eyes and a fleeting glimpse of eternity escaping like water down a drain. He keeps moving, quickly jerking up the

Winchester. Another shot roars out and strikes Henry in the left thigh. The boy pitches forward and rolls, pulling his Cooper.

"Fuck you *Bonney,*" Peppin shouts out as he fires another round. A shot comes back at the enraged deputy and takes off a chunk of the adobe wall next to his head. Henry is running and firing, still in possession of the prized Winchester. He triggers one more shot before disappearing around the corner of the Tunstall store, blood coursing down the inside of his pants and into his boot. *Still worth it to get the Winchester back,* he thinks—*if I can get away.*

"*Amigo...sígame,*" says Ygenio Salazar. Henry wheels around and finds his friend from the pit running along the wall toward him.

"*Ygenio! Ta Bueno.*" Henry follows him around another corner, down to the river and into the weeds. They start toward the southern end of town and his family's home.

Townspeople begin to gather where it happened, staying well back as Deputies and the Dolanmen hoover over the bodies.

"Brady's dead. Hindeman too."

"I can see that," says Peppin.

They lie in red pools, their blood coagulating and mixing in the dirt. A sharp smell of iron, and of shit, wafts from the bodies. It wasn't the only street murder in Lincoln's short history. Captain Murphy, personable and warm-hearted though he was, had seen fit to have his only serious rival killed—not a hundred paces from where Brady lay this morning.

Peppin throws himself into the aftermath in a blind passion and a search begins door to door; an angry, unruly mob of partisans bent on some measure of revenge. The shakedown roars from one end of the winding town to the other. Within the hour, a detachment of twenty-four soldiers from the 9th Calvary arrive from Fort Stanton. They fall in line behind the mob with a shrug, more than one of them rolling his eyes as they surge forward.

Over forty men swell into the yard of the lawyer's compound, between the fence and the front door. Brady had meant to arrest McSween that very day, and shoot him if he resisted. Peppin was well aware of this as he approached the front door at the head of the mob.

Alex and Susan had only just arrived the previous evening from Chisum's ranch. Montague Leverson accompanied them with an escort of Chisum cowboys, and the fusillade erupting over their morning coffee. The concussion of it startled their English guest enough to drop a half-full cup into his lap. Susan screamed and the vein rose up and Alex took a deep breath.

"Open up McSween, I demand to search the premises for that damned murdering coward Bonney. I also intend to arrest your sorry arse!" Peppin yells, adding a touch more salt than needed.

"Deputy Peppin I do not recognize your authority, and furthermore... from the sound of your voice, I'd say you might well be under the influence. In any case you have no legal basis to make an arrest or a search."

"Mr. McSween, will you surrender to me? I'm Captain Purrington and I'm here with a detachment. I will see you safely to fort."

"Yes captain I will surrender to you. I'm coming out. But I do not give these men leave to search my home." The lawyer emerges, marching coolly by Peppin and his men. Susan follows with her sister and family, then Leverson, and finally, Zebrion. They stand awkwardly in the front yard for a moment, not knowing what to do. Captain Purrington motions them through the gate and toward a wagon.

"Captain these men have no warrant and in their condition, will make a wreck of my home. It is full of expensive furnishings."

"That is not my concern Mr. McSween," Captain Purrington snaps as he again motions with his right arm. The black soldiers under this white officer's command, again regard each other with a resigned look.

"Captain, my name is Montague Leverson of Colorado. I have prominent business concerns there and perhaps soon in New Mexico. I really must protest. You are flaunting this man's constitutional guarantees. I may have a British accent but I am an American citizen and I know the constitution very well indeed."

"Damn the constitution and you for an ass. You are impeding my business here sir. Now move back," Purrington answers hotly as Peppin's drunken search party enters the house with a clamor. A table is overturned, and crockery breaking is plainly to be heard, along with curses and the clomping of heavy boots.

"I will be writing a letter, young man—to the president of these United States, about the outrages I've witnessed today. Among other things I will include your statement, you may count on that."

"Sir, you have my permission to fuck yourself," the good captain barks as he turns on his heel. Leverson is astonished at the indelicate disrespect and lack of discipline shown by an officer of the United States Army. Clearly this man is no gentleman. His eyes are ready to start from their sockets as the captain marches off.

McSween looks on from the wagon—in fact it all goes accordingly and better than he could have hoped.

When the mob draws closer to the Salazar home Ygenio pulls up a floorboard and smiles, pointing down into the hole. "*Por favor.*"

"*No hay problema,*" says William Bonney with a grin, but looking down into the space the grin becomes a grimace—it's like looking into his grave. Climbing down, he remembers Slippers. "Can you find my horse?"

"Of course." Ygenio nods his head. "And a doctor."

"*Gracias amigo.*" Henry goes into the cobwebbed slot between the joists and Ygenio places the board back over him, giving it a stomp and pulling the throw rug back into place. The tight space is dark as the inside of a tomb. A spider crawls over his face and something else goes up his pants leg, which he manages to crush. His wound begins to throb.

In the blackness he sees the shooting again and the look on Brady's face as he slipped away to the infinite. It had felt terrifying, and somehow good. But lying there sepulchered, Henry begins to feel that tug in his belly again, like he'd felt out on the barrens. A continuous shiver starts to run from head to foot and back again.

Henry finally hears them stomping and cursing just above his head when the mob reaches the Salazar home.

"He ain't here either goddamnit. That little bastard will pay dearly, and the rest of'em."

"Who is he again?"

"Just some little tramp, worked for Tunstall—calls himself William Bonney. I think Pecos has it out for him, now Peppin too."

It all brings a smile to Henry's face, and an end to the shivering.

Two hours later, Dr. Ealy tends to Henry by lamplight in the Salazar root cellar. The round had passed straight through his leg, just missing the bone.

"Another inch to the right and your dancing days would be over young man." Henry sits with his britches around his knees, biting down hard on a wooden spoon. "I'm going to pass this handkerchief entirely through the wound. Silk has amazing curative properties."

The silk handkerchief is pushed in with a thin rod, and pulled through slowly by hand. The kid's other leg trembles and sweat runs down his face, the eyes bulge and his jaw clenches down tight.

"I do not understand how respect for human life is so entirely disregarded in Lincoln," Dr. Ealy says, almost academically, as he finishes the procedure and pours alcohol onto the wound. The Kid grins back at him, pain searing through the bullet's path like lightning.

"I'm sorry Dr. Ealy, I know this is probably incomprehensible to you, but those men had it coming to them," Henry says.

"You don't get to decide that son."

"Maybe not, but we did anyway. Dolan and Brady and that Santa Fe bunch behind'em have already decided against us, and plan to make us just as dead as Mr. Tunstall. John was worth more than everyone on the other side put together. The Ring does not recognize the laws of God or men, except where it suits them."

"That can't be true."

"This is stony ground sir...and this is a war."

"It sounds more like like anarchy and madness."

"Maybe, but it's part of the plan. I believe it is salvation and will bring on a federal investigation of the Ring," Henry declares proudly. The Presbyterian looks down at his patient, through his glasses and eastern proclivities.

"I see. God does not show man the tree of gold or a camel going through the eye of a needle...but miracles *do* happen, I suppose," says the doctor of divinity and medicine.

"Amen, I'm counting on it." Henry grits this out as he stands and pulls his pants up and puts weight on the leg.

"That leg will take some mending," Dr. Ealy finishes with a solemn nod. He stands and looks down at his patient with a sternness born of concern, and doubt.

"*Vámanos amigo,*" Yegenio hisses as he throws open the door.

"Thank you, professor, and god bless," Henry concludes, with a firm grip of the clergyman's hand. He'd become well-aware of Dr. Ealy's lettered and philosophic mind in the short time he'd spent with him. "I'll look forward to hearing your first sermon. You'll find me a strong tenor."

"Well...I hope to somehow see you in church young man, there may be hope for you yet," Dr. Ealy says.

"*Andale muchacho,*" Ygenio yells, as Henry limps up the stairs and out the door. Slippers is right by the cellar door.

"Mil gracias," he yells back over his shoulder as he gallops off down the street. Deputy Peppin and a host of armed men are drawn forth at the sound—running from various points to the north.

Henry McCarty, alias Kid Antrim and The Kid, also known as William Bonney thunders up the ridge just east of the Ellis store. He pauses at the top, full in the afternoon sun, out of range but plainly visible to the hectoring mob a half mile away. The provocateur dismounts and fires his pistol into the air. Then with a great flourish, bows low and doffs his hat, vanishing from the hill a moment later like a wisp of smoke.

Leaning down from the saddle with left hand on the horn, Jimmy Dolan plucks up a handful of mint at water's edge. The little river runs clear and cold over granite rocks, following along the two-track. Trout are to be seen in the deep pool formed behind a fallen tree. He strips the leaves and balls them into his mouth, figuring to make a mint chaw and hoping to mask any lingering hint of last night's alcohol.

Morning sun shone warm on his back and Jimmy Dolan's heart almost skips a beat. For eight miles he'd ridden east from Lincoln, thinking of the Fritz Spring Ranch all the way. A relief to ponder something besides the game, something completely different and equally compelling. Another track turns off the road up ahead and Dolan gives his horse a kick.

"Bob, find yourself a shade tree. I'll be an hour or so," says Jimmy, turning in the saddle to face his persistent shadow. Pecos nods.

The hatchet man cracks his neck and slides off his mount. The big knife pulled and a moment later sticking from a post, the handle vibrating still.

Dolan's spotted gray carries him over the wooded ridge and down into the little valley with light, quick steps. A sturdy, comfortable home sits at the end of a green field. Dolan smiles as it comes into view. Emil Fritz had planted a line of Poplar trees along the arch of his drive ten years before. Now Emil's Poplars stand quivering in the morning breeze, as if to welcome an honored guest.

Colonel Fritz had poured all of his fastidious care and a good deal of money into this handsome property. He'd made it a home and ranch worthy of the twenty efficient years he'd put into taming and building up Lincoln County. Fritz soldiered well for ten of those years, and managed the practical end of the House for another profitable decade.

In all that time, the hero of Kit Carson's right flank never made a false move or an untidy gesture, until he betook himself to the homeland and died there with his will intestate—and the dispensation of a life insurance policy in a muddle.

The colonel's sister and seventeen-year-old niece inhabit the stone and clapboard grange now, awaiting developments with the will, and other matters. This morning mother and daughter take the air on the home's generous front porch. Both work diligently at their embroidery, smiling at each other as the rider approaches.

"Good morning ladies. Nice to see you both," Dolan sings out. He dismounts and climbs the steps with an eager bounce, trying not to ogle the petite and very pretty, Caroline—forcing himself to give equal attention to the mother, Emilie. He is all smiles and polite deference.

"Well, Mr. Dolan, how pleasant for you to come calling on such a lovely spring day, whether you've got matters settled for us, or not," Emilie states plainly, her German accent distinct.

"I wish I had good news for you. But I promise you, it will all come right in the end," says Dolan. His lilt tends upwards before the two ladies, otherwise it was strictly down.

"I do hope so, Mr. Dolan. I've been at war with that swindling lawyer far too long already. If I could see him in irons and on his way to prison, I believe I would give up that money."

"I'm afraid the news is bad. Sheriff Brady's been murdered."

"So we've heard, a horrible business," Emilie replies, the color rising in her cheeks. "At least McSween's under guard at Fort Stanton."

"I doubt they'll hold him for long, but he'll get what's coming to him in the long run, I can guarantee it."

Caroline looks up and meets his eye. Jimmy Dolan, arrogant and brash and cocky as a prizefighter—skewered by a glance of such charming coquetry that he is stricken and befuddled.

"Perhaps we should talk of happier things," Caroline suggests while looking back down at her needlework, eager to turn the conversation to more personable topics. When she looks up again her precocious eyes have recovered to a state of innocence.

"You and your mother are comfortable here I hope?" asks Dolan, after an awkward silence. He looks directly into her eyes, noting how she had just flirted like a seductress, and then seamlessly withdrawn into youthful chastity. He might well get more than he bargained for in this little ingenue.

"It's a lovely home and snug, and the yard is so pretty. Our drovers work the ranch to our satisfaction. The fruit trees are a wonder and keep us busy...but it gets lonely." The green eyes flash again.

"She's always complaining that we're too far from town," the mother offers as she continues to guild the appliqué in her lap.

"It's only natural," says Dolan, happy to take Caroline's side. "I have plans to build the grandest house in Lincoln, near the church. Already have the lot purchased. No half-wild adobe but a fine house with a pitched roof, lots of windows, green curtains, an elegant parlor and a long dining hall. Ah lass, I can see it very clearly," Dolan elaborates and beams, all through his castle in the air.

Caroline watches her guest closely. Jimmy Dolan is not a handsome man, but his confidence and persuasive powers are hypnotic. Caroline felt certain Mr. Dolan would use those abilities well, and one day become the uncontested boss of Lincoln County.

All of that more than made up for his looks. She also knew a marriage proposal would come, sooner or later.

April 4, 1878

The big white sky boats have begun their stately journey over the mountains. Patches of intense blue in between the massive ships draw the eye even more.

Dick Brewer removes his hat to wipe the sweat from his forehead and veil his look down into the Tularosa basin. The presence of a highland warrior, fearless and invincible, more than ever graces the broad-shouldered man who leads the Regulators.

White sands beckon from the desert floor in a long glimmering sheet, both softening and exalting the saw-tooths just beyond. His gaze extends to the south of the iridescent dune-field, wondering if they'll overtake the herd or will they have to ride all the way to the Organ Mountains. And either way, will he be able to control his men when it comes to it.

Anger had ruled his mind since Tunstall's murder. The broken heart he'd carried for two years transmuted overnight into a white-hot passion of revenge and retribution. He'd finally let go of sorrow and taken up the cudgel of justice.

It would be done lawful and righteous, if he had his say. Those quaint notions were deeply compromised now by his men, and by McSween, and even by John Chisum.

Still, he would hold the line.

"Brady shot down in the street, god rest his soul, and you hotheaded assassins still on the prod. Well, today we're going to bring the cattle back and you lot had better follow my lead. Understood?"

"Hell yes. You're the boss Dick," snorts Fred Waite, the big grin coming, but this time the tongue stays in.

"They'll be no bloodshed at the ranch, just non-combatants out there," Dick announces.

The Regulators, eleven men strong, ride through the pass and into the lowering divide. Blazer's Mill is visible further on, down in an open valley.

"I vote for dinner at the mill. It's right on our way," says Henry, gay as a rover on his way to the fair, whistling *Silver Threads* as they trot along. "Also wouldn't mind for Dr. Blazer to take a look at this leg."

"You fellows sure took Mac's bounty to heart," Brewer states with a bitter edge, his eyes on the blood-stained pants Henry is still wearing.

"If the powers that be wanted Brady dead, who were we to gainsay?" McNab answers back. Brewer shakes his head at the callous sarcasm in the burr.

"Reviews of our little show-stopping performance will no doubt be going all the way to the East. Letters have been written to President Hayes and the Secretary of the Interior, as well as to the press all over New Mexico, and in Colorado. From there it will travel on and on, and just maybe, there'll be a federal investigation and the Ring will have to close up shop—you said so yourself," Henry states, sounding more like a politician than an outlaw.

"That kind of sheriff murderin anarchy is likely to hurt more than help."

"That's a risk Mac was willing to take," Henry reasons. "Besides...I believe it's going to make the investigation an *imperative*!"

"What the hell's an imperative?" Tom asks.

"Means it's going to happen," Jim French answers.

"I think the Kid's right," McNab says in agreement.

"It could be he's wrong, too, and everybody goes to prison, or the scaffold," Doc Scurlock says.

"Cain't hang a dead man. Nor jail a corpse," Fred interjects with grin and tongue.

"What the hell's that supposed to mean?" Tom asks, bursting in.

"I don't know, but I'm making a song out of it right now," Henry says, giggling. "Here it is boys—one stanza anyway." A slow and haunting dirge follows. The word *mighty* ornamented, and *forth* hung on in a long plaintive moan.

Can't hang a dead man
Nor jail a corpse,
And the mighty will fall
When the inquest comes forth...

The Irish singer makes one of his grand dramaturgic gestures and Fred returns the bow with his own idiotic salute. Dick rolls his eyes and smirks back at the two comedians—first Henry, and now Fred Waite. It was like a virus.

Henry enjoyed a thorough appreciation of the Chickasaw cowboy. His skills were honed and serious, but Fred came at everything as an opportunity to let the air out of it. His sense of humor exhausted most, but suited Henry just fine.

By noon the Regulators reach the comforts of Blazer's Mill. It's practically a village unto itself, spread out in a bustling valley like a castle and its ward. A big main edifice of stone surrounded tightly by the manor house, a dozen smaller outbuildings, corral and pens filling the vale.

Dr. Joseph Blazer watches the men tie up at the corral and goes out to meet them. The well-armed company approaches on foot, by way of the inclined street between a row of out-buildings. Dr. Blazer's face is stern but the eyes are welcoming.

"Hello Mr. Brewer, always good to see you. What can I do for y'all today?"

"Mr. Bonney here has a wounded leg. And we'd like to eat a good dinner," Dick answers.

"Certainly, you fellows go on in to the long table. If you'll follow me Mr. Bonney, I'll take a look," replies Blazer. Known all over the mountain for his supply of medicines and curative abilities, and for much else besides, he glances at the blood-stained boy and turns, leading him into his office.

As he works, Blazer regards more than just the wound, fully aware of what the young man before him had recently taken part in. The mill was a hub and the doctor well-informed.

"I know there was provocation, and a continuing threat. But shooting Brady and Hindeman like that was just as bad as the Tunstall murder. It was an execution, plain and simple," Dr. Blazer offers, bluntly, looking up from his examination. An intelligent fellow, still handsome and youthful at fifty-five. His mill is a hive of county activity and the people often come to him for council and guidance—even the Apache.

"I know how it looks, but that's a gamble I was willing to take. For John Tunstall."

"You know Sheriff Brady had a Mexican wife, and nine kids?"

"I did not know that," Bonney replies, his light blue eyes suddenly serious.

"You're a healthy specimen Mr. Bonney, I'll say that for you. Your wound is not infected."

"Thank you, Dr. Blazer, I know I must be a sore trial for your patience and your...ethics. I guess I *am* a bit of an anarchist. But I have a good heart. When the dust settles, I'll see if I can't help that family."

"And do you plan further mayhem and reprisals today?"

"No sir, we plan to retrieve Mr. Tunstall's cattle from Shed's ranch and bring them back to the Rio Feliz, and right now I'm powerfully hungry," says Henry, pulling up his pants and smiling.

"Well go on in and have your dinner then," Dr. Blazer replies. His eyes follow the strange little fellow out the door. *That boy is no common thug for certain.*

Henry alternately limps and dances to the table, flashing the crooked grin. His bowl is soon under attack and a silence settles over the ravenous company.

"God damnit boys, Buckshot Roberts just rode up," Frank Coe yells out busting through the door. George Coe's cousin had joined the company for the day and had been out keeping an eye on the horses.

"They hell you say," yells Charlie, jumping up and running to the window with the others.

"I'm telling you Roberts just rode in on a bay mule and he's tying up at the corral," Frank answers back.

"That's him all right," says Henry, getting excited.

"That gimpy-armed bastard kept us pinned down singlehanded, the son-of-a-bitch, while they killed John," Charlie spits out.

"Now you listen up, we are going to take him under arrest, peacefully. I want no disagreement on the matter," Brewer orders.

Buckshot Roberts looks up toward the big building, he was near being gone from Lincoln County when he'd passed the mail rider. Deciding to turn back to the mill, he'd hoped a check for the sale of his ranch might be in the day's post. It crossed his mind that he should just keep going, but the man was stubborn as a Missouri mule and resolute once his mind was set.

A Texas Ranger in his youth, Roberts later turned to hunting buffalo. For a time, he was an associate of Buffalo Bill Cody—though he didn't share Cody's ambition for the stage. There was little in the West he'd not seen or done, and no man he feared.

His moniker derived from the load of buckshot embedded in his right arm; unable to lift his rifle higher than the hip, he had no choice but to rework his formidable skills entirely—and Buckshot Roberts did just that. In time he was as formidable as he'd ever been. For those privileged enough to see him throw down, it was an unforgettable thing to behold.

The aging sharpshooter had purchased a ranch the year before, and entertained the idea of settling down, permanently. He'd picked a fine spot up mountain but was determined now to get out of Lincoln County, and away from Dolan's war. First Tunstall murdered—the ignition point, he and the Boys had seen to that, then Morton and Baker shot out of their saddles a month later. Now Brady and his deputy assassinated in the street.

It was time to move on.

"He's an old man with a bad arm and a big rep, and he's carrying that damn Henry. He won't surrender and I would not cross him," says Charlie, offering the best advice he has.

"You know him Frank. Why don't you try talking to him?" his cousin George suggests.

"I'll give it a twirl, but I doubt it'll be worth the trouble," says Frank Coe with a shrug. He steps out into the yard and ambles down to the corral.

"Hello Buckshot," Frank begins. Roberts stopped by the Coe ranch on more than one occasion, to water his animal and himself, and have a visit. He was loquacious when not pressed. Buckshot motions to a door stoop and they sit. The weather and other important topics are framed in a desultory manner, as if they had all day to chew it out properly.

"We've got a warrant for you Bill," Frank admits suddenly.

"Oh, who is *we*?" Buckshot replies, still sounding as if the weather might be the subject.

"The regulators are here, eating their dinner and figuring on arrestin you. You'd better come on in the house and see Brewer. There ain't no way out of it."

"Well, we see about that."

"Ain't no sense in resisting and getting killed for your trouble."

"Ha! That's about what they said to Morton and Baker I'd bet," Buckshot allows—the old man beginning to get riled and working a chaw ferociously.

"Brewer has made it plain as day, no more killin. You surrender and nobody will hurt you," Frank replies.

"Dammit, I admit I regret what happened to Tunstall...sorta...but not to a particular. Ain't the worst thing I've seen or done by a long shot. Fuck it, I rode with Jesse Evans when asked and no hesitation, he's as formidable as they come, and a smart fellow. And I've known Captain Murphy a long time too, a terrible drunk but a decent man. But I'll swear to this—I'm done working for Jimmy Dolan, and I'm done with Lincoln County. I've sold my little ranch and I'm leaving and no one will be stopping me." He'd finally worked himself into a fine temper and stood up abruptly, grabbing the rifle he'd leaned against the steps. Frank spits and rolls his eyes.

"Now hold on, there are men here who might be getting in your way."

"Well by god they best show their hand."

"Mr. Roberts, I have a warrant for your arrest. You need to put down that Henry and come with us," orders Dick Brewer.

The other Regulators have moved into the yard from around the back of the mill.

"Drop that *goddamned* Henry, if you want this to end peaceably," Charlie Bowdre yells.

Roberts looks over the men approaching him from fifty yards away and notices a weakness in their haphazard alignment—they were not line-abreast and if he could pick off Bowdre on the left and Brewer on the right, they might fold up. That would buy some time and he could slip back to the corral and 'lope outa here. Maybe get off the street at least and to a defensible position.

But he had to act now.

"Not much, Mary Ann," Buckshot replies and in a deadly blur of motion, jerks the rifle up and opens fire.

The first bullet severs Charlie's gun belt and a second shot slams into his left shoulder. Bowdre recoils, pulls and fires, definitively thumping Roberts in the gut.

The first round had continued on from Bowdre's gun belt and knocked George Coe's pistol out of his hand—taking his trigger finger with it. The Kid watches it sail over him as he, Tom, and Fred pitch to the ground.

Brewer, McNab, and Scurlock stand to the right almost frozen and Roberts blazes a spray of bullets in their direction.

Brewer refusing to fire—McNab and Scurlock shoot wide and all dive for cover. In a matter of seconds one man had indeed folded up the Regulators, and then scrambled downhill to a little adobe.

"Well, shit...that went well," growls Charlie. He glances at the wound and at Buckshot's redoubt. Roberts drags an overturned bed into the doorway and is levering the Henry across the frame.

"Oh fuck." Charlie rolls behind a trough as the Henry speaks again and another .44 slug kicks up the hard pack where he'd fallen.

A few made it to safety behind the mill. The rest sheltered on two sides of the yard. Four were variously wounded, Charlie the worst. Directly across from him and behind a stone porch stoop, Fred, Tom, and Henry piled up in a huddle. Waite looks over at Charlie with the big grin and the tongue sticking out.

"Hell of a shot for a wounded cheesemaker," Fred offers. Years before Charlie had briefly gone into the cheese business with Doc Scurlock, and they'd made good cheddar but poor business decisions.

Charlie lifts his middle finger.

"That was something Charlie," says Tom, dumbfounded by what he'd just witnessed.

"I'm just gonna lay here until y'all figure out how to finish the job," Charlie announces.

"I don't know where the hell you'd be going," Fred says wryly.

"Charlie stay put, and we'll get to you. That damned old buffalo hunter has got us pinned down, again...and he's gonna punch the big ticket for his trouble," Dick raves—once more it had all gone wrong. The men should not have moved up on Buckshot like that. They had slipped out the back and gone around the minute he'd walked out to parley.

"Hell, if y'all'd just waited a little longer I might'a gotten the gun away from him. And my cousin might still have his damn trigger finger," Frank Coe yells from behind the mill, where he'd hustled and scrabbled to safety—next to George.

His younger cousin sits looking at the maimed hand grinning. The index finger torn off and gone, as if by some hungry animal. A ragged stump and a sharp sliver of white bone sticking out was his plum for the day's work.

"I can take that little nub of bone off with my pruning snips. Then I'll sew it up pretty as you please," Frank continues. "Meanwhile...I'd not look at it."

"Buckshot Roberts you can kiss my ass!" George yells at the top of his lungs, the woozy grin still in place. It made his vanished finger hurt all the worse to think of being pruned like a rose bush.

"I'm fixing to open up on the son-of-a-bitch," The Kid says. "I can get a bead on him if he pokes his head up."

"Just remember he's waiting for you to fire and give away your position," Jim French says.

"He's going to have to sprout wings to hit me."

The Kid found an excellent perch for the Winchester, behind the stoop and between a large flowerpot and an iron boot scrape.

"Don't be too damn sure about that Kid," McNab says.

"We should all let fly at once. It's called firing for effect. Then we'll see what kind of shape he's in down there," says Jim French.

"All right West Point, have it your way. On my say then, Henry you're the one with a rifle—make it count," Dick commands, his voice lowered. "Okay...fire!"

The barrage opens with a roar. The Kid waiting on his second shot and able to place it tight. He was pretty certain it hit. A few seconds go by and Buckshot returns the favor—making the regulators wonder who had the high ground and the advantage.

"How many rounds you suppose he's got," asks Tom.

"Enough or he would not have blistered us like he just done," Charlie answers.

"I'm pretty damn sure my second shot hit home."

"Oh well, a few more'n we'll have him then," mutters Doc.

"Sure wish I'd taken a big drink a water before we all stuck our heads up his arse. That salty stew has left me with a damn parched throat," McNab says. He drops his head back onto the dirt and looks up at the sky. "Shit."

Down below Roberts pulls his shirt open and looks at the hole, probing just a bit. The bullet was in there somewhere and had not gone through. He lets out a low groan. Nothing worse than dying this way—or just about, anyway. In his long life on the plains he'd seen ways to die that shaded this, and he's quick to remind himself of that.

Death was something you want to watch come with body in one piece. He'd be granted that but by god this was going to be a hard row to hoe.

Another groan escapes his gritted mouth. Buckshot felt certain he was about to shit a bucket load of broken glass.

He *was* determined to take one of those shitheels with him—something to focus on besides the burning misery. The old hunter's patience coming to him as he keeps the Henry propped and eyes peeled, firing off a tight pop every now and then just to let them boys know who was the bitch and who was the bull. All the time his life blood oozing out onto the floor and his bowels in a blazing roil.

An hour passes and Brewer decides enough is enough. "All right, this is just stupid. We need to at least get ourselves outa this shootin gallery and behind the mill."

"We are damn sure on disadvantageous ground, perhaps outmatched. A tactical withdrawal is called for certainly," Jim French volunteers with a curious smile.

"Okay West Point, it's your show," says Brewer.

"We'll open up on the right, you on the left fall back. Then do the same for us. Simple. You fellows in the back find a place to shoot." In a few minutes they accomplish the retreat, though no one is inclined to admit it *was* a retreat.

"We wait long enough the old fart'll just die," says McNab, pulling up a bucket of fresh water from the well and practically emptying it all down his throat. "Of course he may be at it a while yet."

Another hour crawls by with Roberts suspended between worlds. And for all the noontime mayhem, he drifts in a quiet afternoon of sweet spring air; with the soft *hoodle hoodle* of a Stellar Jay somewhere in the valley, and the sound of waves lapping the other shore.

Two rounds left.

Brewer starts to move in—crouching down and working his way out along a stack of split pine. He sent four of his men to flank Buckshot intending to draw his attention to the front, if the old coot was even still alive.

Seeing a bit of movement up by a long woodpile the frontiersman is recalled to life. The moment he'd been waiting on for an eternity at hand now. Brewer lifts his head up slowly to get a look.

A round explodes through the door and they hear a sickening thwop, as if someone had cracked a giant egg. They all knew what the sound meant. McNab and Scurlock crawl out around the corner and both are flattened by the horror they see there. They move out along the wood pile and pull Brewer's heavy frame behind the mill, the head flopping back and trailing a gout of blood and tissue.

The Regulators approach his body reluctantly. Dick is lying there handsome and warrior-like as ever and eyes open—but the top of his head gone. The .44 caliber slug caught him right at the hairline. Henry looks down at a jagged crater of white bone and dark red tissue—the bullet's path a monstrous cleft and his stomach a hard knot.

"Blazer sent a rider first rattle out of the box, we can't stay here, and I'll not let that bastard have a crack at any of the rest of us. He's gut shot but he's not done for yet, not by a sight. We are going and right now," says McNab.

"We can't just leave Dick like this," The Kid objects.

"Look at him, I'll not scatter what's left of his brains over the road to Lincoln. Blazer will see to a proper burial. We can settle with him later." McNab was right, and nothing for it.

Henry kneels beside Brewer and takes his hand, crossing himself and offering the Lord's Prayer. The others join in one by one:

Forgive us our trespasses
As we forgive those who trespass against us
And lead us not into temptation
But deliver us from evil. Amen.

Henry continues alone...

A Naomh-Mhuire
a Mhathair De
guigh orainn na peacaigh.

Fred covers their leader with a coat, his face grim for once. The butcher had come to collect his bill again, and to claim their best. It was a burden they all had to shoulder and it clung to their young minds and hearts like the lost battle it was.

Frank Coe and Jim French ease down to the corral and swinging out wide—manage to bring the horses in one trip. They saddle up; Tom and Fred helping Charlie, George with his hand wrapped in a rag soaked with coal oil, and all taking care to keep the mill between them and the old timer.

The attempt to arrest Buckshot Roberts is abandoned without another word.

It had happened again. The person Henry looked up to most had been violently taken—across the veil and gone—and no amount of playing Kid Antrim, or The Kid, or William Bonney seemed worth it just now.

Joseph Blazer watched it all unfold from the second floor of the mill. He'd kept his family and employees away from the windows, and shook his head when the Regulators finally rode away.

"It's over," Dr. Blazer sighs.

His oldest son and the cook went with him to move Dick Brewer into the root cellar. The boy threw up as soon as they had come back out into the sun. Blazer shakes his head again and closes the door, knowing another hard job had to be done.

"Buckshot, they've all gone. I'm going to come in," Blazer yells out as he approaches.

"Well come on then."

Dr. Blazer rights the bed and mattress and helps Buckshot up. He'd been miserably uncomfortable during the last several hours, hunched behind the bed frame. Lying down was a little better for sure.

"Joseph could you bring me some water and a jug, I'm powerful thirsty for both the clear and the amber."

"I'll be back in few minutes, and we'll take a look."

He returns with a bucket of fresh water and a cup, a jug of whiskey, and a half-full bottle of laudanum. Roberts tosses back a glass of whiskey and laudanum.

"I don't think there's much hope," Dr. Blazer says flatly.

"They ain't no hope a'tall, I've sat with enough poor gut shot bastards to know, now's my time to be on the other end of it," Buckshot pants out, reaching for another pour of laudanum and rye.

"You are going to make the history books Mr. Roberts. I saw it all with my own eyes and still don't believe it," Blazer proclaims, an undeniable sense of wonder and pride in the stentorian utterance.

"Ha...the last stand of Buckshot Roberts."

"I'll stay with you, if you like, unless you'd rather be alone."

"Company suits me. Thank you, Joseph, you're a good'n. They ain't that many in this country but you're one of'em certain," confides Buckshot, looking at Dr. Blazer like a man about to go over the edge of a thundering waterfall.

"There's a lot of good common folk on this mountain, all colors and beliefs."

"There, you see," says the frontiersman, managing a sly squint. The doctor nods his close-cropped head and tups his pipe against the chair leg.

"You got a letter in today's mail," says the doctor after refilling his pipe and firing the bowl.

"That'd be my check for the ranch. I have a niece in San Antonio, her name is Delphia, lives on Flores Street, send it on to her."

"I'll get it done."

"Sure is a pretty day. Warm air, soft wind," whispers Buckshot. He'd won the battle of Blazer's Mill and now there's time to die. He notices afternoon shadows dancing on the wall and the *hoodle hoodle* echoing again, a depth of remembering setting in with the ardent and the opiate.

11

"The rats have been at the corn," suggests Judge Bristol, leaning over to spit a stream of tobacco juice. He'd developed the unpleasant habit, and many others, during his tenure in New Mexico. It helped him pass the interminate hours of travel and court, and required no relighting.

"Time then to set the traps and lay the bait," District Attorney Rynerson replies. His booming voice carries back down the line of troopers and stands in marked contrast to the judge's reedy tenor.

Warren Bristol had passed through many changes in a long and contentious life and each passage seemed to leave him ever more isolate and cynical. His time in the New York hamlet where he'd grown up, kissed his first girl and attended law school—was marred by a broken heart. By age thirty he'd moved on, been elected District Attorney of Goodhue County, Minnesota, and had comfortably settled into a marriage. He was a widower one year later morning the loss of wife and son—both taken in childbirth.

At age forty-two Judge Bristol rose to some prominence as a fire-eating Republican. He was a passionate supporter of William Seward at the dark horse convention of 1860, and devastated when Abraham Lincoln clinched the nomination in the third ballot. Eight years later Grant sent him West to be a justice on the New Mexico Supreme Court—there he fell into the orbit of democrat Tom Catron.

Grant's appointee mounted a weak defense against the inexorable pull of gravity and underwent his final metamorphous under the watchful and covetous eyes of the fat man.

Catron had plans for Judge Bristol. Plans that involved the sprawling new district of Lincoln County. And whatever disposition the judge may have had toward an honest career, whatever bright and shinning ideals he may have held high in his youth—were far behind him now. Far enough behind that he tended to forget they ever existed. Bristol had gathered the reins of Lincoln County's legal processes in a tightfisted clench and gave Tom Catron no reason to be dissatisfied with his service to the cause.

On the 8th day of April 1878, Judge Bristol and District Attorney Rynerson proceed to Lincoln like the grand inquisition—ready to prosecute the spring term of court with brutal efficiency. There is much to be decided there with regard to high crimes, real and imagined, and much to ensure goes the right way.

Every day of the session a spectacular pilgrimage is made from the safety of Fort Stanton; District Attorney Rynerson dwarfing the large horse he rides—his long legs nearly bent double, Judge Bristol in his wrinkled suit on a spotted pinto, Black cavalrymen following smartly along in paired formation.

"The damn rats are always at the corn, and the traps sometimes fail," says Judge Bristol, his horse snorting loudly and taking a rut which bounced the spindly judge more than he would have liked.

"There's no reason to despair," Rynerson replies.

"I *am* worried about the Grand Jury. I have an uneasy feeling about this session, don't trust Patron and Dr. Blazer in particular—too damn well-read, accomplished, and open-minded."

"Judge you will instruct them, as you always do, with perfect clarity. And inform them whereon to hang their balls," Rynerson assures. His voice trumpeting from the outsized body like a clarion call. Sergeant Terrell, riding just behind the right and left hand of Ring Law in Lincoln County, has to stifle a guffaw.

"Sergeant, do you have something caught in your throat?" Rynerson asks, his enormous head swiveling to cast a scowl back at the dark-skinned trooper.

"No sir. Just a little dust," Sergeant Terrell replies, not intimidated and determined to show it with the evenness of his gaze.

"First order of business will be to elect a new sheriff," Bristol continues. "Got to stop the bleeding."

"There's no one to replace Brady, not even close," Rynerson answers. The impossibly tall District Attorney had also ridden in the Volunteers with Brady, Captain Murphy, and Colonel Fritz. That kind of brotherhood and loyalty, bound in blood and battle and christened with masonic mysteries, had no replacement.

If Rynerson and Bristol were the right and left hand, Murphy and Fritz had been the heart and brain of Catron's pet County—and Brady—the erect phallus.

When the parade reaches the outskirts of Lincoln people gather to watch.

"Now there's a sight," says Dolan from the vantage of the second floor House porch.

"Looks like a goddamned circus," Olinger says.

"It better *not* be a circus for fucks sake," Dolan replies.

The column soon comes to a jangling dismount at the Monsano store and saloon in midtown. The Judge and the Giant head inside to preside over the Grand Jury and their secret proceedings. Bristol takes his seat, making sure to have a spittoon installed next to his chair.

"All right men, at ease, no drinking and no cards," barks Sergeant Terrell. The men fall out under a giant cottonwood and the long day of waiting begins.

Judge Bristol surveys the faces of the seated elders of Lincoln with a withering bore. Dropping his eyes to various pages of written statements, the judge launches into a gratuitous and partisan tirade; railing against the murderous violence of recent weeks, quickly passing over the killing of Tunstall (an act of self-defense), and emphasizing with acidic clarity the specific contributions of the McSween faction in all events, particularly the alleged insurance embezzlement—more like a fire-eating prosecutor delivering a final slanted argument than a judge beginning an impartial hearing.

"...finally, you gentleman are to set your minds to the task of weighing the evidence and finding what truth and enlightenment there may be in the voluminous testimony we will no doubt be subjected to, and with your unbiassed judgment, bring the nobility of law to these lawless times."

His eyes lift now to engage his Grand Jury.

"You must root out the rats who are at the corn, you must find for the innocent and you must indict the guilty." Judge Bristol finishes and drops his gaze with a dramatic nod.

The message is heard loud and clear, and some of the jury members nod slightly with a begrudging air. Juan Patron and Dr. Blazer sit toward the front with blank expressions. One man toward the back looks out the window with a smirk.

Alex McSween grew up in the grand Scottish tradition of Presbyterianism, on the faraway coast of Newfoundland. His letter to the Presbyterian council of elders in Philadelphia brought forth Dr. Ealy and his family—all the way to Babylon. And whatever the lawyer's transgressions in the past and present, he thought sincerely to improve the county with spiritual guidance from a properly educated minister.

One more tenon into the mortise of civilization, one more potent reason for men to refrain from sin. Even if Alexander McSween still withheld that prideful choice for himself.

Taking responsibility for the minister—McSween had put the Ealy's in the Tunstall store soon after their arrival. The building being empty, and the spacious private rooms being more than sufficient for their needs. Although he and his wife found it strange sleeping in the dead man's bed. One more test of faith in a bewildering hinterland of challenges.

Dr. Ealy emerges at midday on the 8th to take the rising temperature of the parish, feeling the imperative of worship approaching and the call of duty. He pauses in the midst of an agitated huddle of men, listening to the profane arguments being put forth in the Tower of Babel.

"William fockin Bonney, indicted for murder. Alexander fockin McSween indicted for embezellment. Now that's what I want'a hear. And I'd be glad to carry out the harshest sentence and skip the damn trial," Deputy George Peppin boasts.

"Hell yes, it's plain to see and don't know how they could find other wise. We should just hang the bastards and be done with it," says Olinger in his needling rasp.

The Reverend notices Juan Patron on the opposite side of the street and moves off toward his friend and supporter. A territorial representative, Juan left for the capitol in early March and has just returned.

"Good to see you back in Lincoln, I'm told you've just been nominated Speaker of the Territorial House. And at an age when most men are still finding their way."

"Thank you Dr. Ealy, I'm afraid it makes me quite an easy target, but it *is* an honor, and a privilege."

"Yet you've returned to bedlam, I'm sure there must be an excellent reason."

"My family. Our roots go deep in this soil. *And* I needed to be on the grand jury. But I will return soon to the capitol and gavel in," Patron answers with a smile. The minister nods, acknowledging the intelligence and ambition behind such proud achievements at such a young age.

"I would open a school here, and a church, as the council has directed... if men would stop shooting each other. I cannot understand this unbridled violence. Eight men have been killed since I arrived in Lincoln, murdered, executed, everyone of them," Dr. Ealy says, dumbfounded.

Patron looks away to the ridge line surrounding Lincoln before looking Dr. Ealy in the eye.

"You were expecting fair play, moral judgements, perhaps at the very least an honorable duel in the middle of the street? Out here, when matters are settled with a gun, nine times out of ten there is no fairness or honor or morality involved—it's only about killing."

Patron's unflinching assessment comes as a hard revelation to Dr. Ealy. He'd been approaching the horrible truth by degrees. Hearing it confirmed so bluntly sees him the rest of the distance.

"I've often heard the great War described in exactly those terms," the doctor admits.

"These hard times will pass, and we *will* have law and order. Your presence here confirms that to me. Open your school, hold your services. The good, common people of this county, and their children, are in the majority and we need you," states Patron with all the passion that had just won him the gavel.

The Flat isn't much to look at. Just another pathetic scatter of shady enterprises and viperous saloons nearby to a Fort; in this case, Fort Griffin, Texas. It lies up on the northern edge of Shackleford County and the nearest real town is Abilene—a long day and a half ride to the south.

In the middle of town an enormous pile of buffalo skulls rises fifty feet, and the stink of hides drifts in the air like a curse. There is a bustle of hard-scrabble humanity here, and despite the crumbling presence of the Fort and soldiery—men conduct themselves with a bare minimum of civility and restraint.

Standards are low on the buffalo plains for certain, but three saloons offer a degree of salvation. Dave Rudder's White Elephant sits prominently in The Flat and boasts refinements unavailable at The Wayward or The Jug. A skewed chandelier hangs near the front window, and the proprietor sees that its candles burn brightly all night. The abused corona has seen better days, but is a marvel nonetheless. Torn red velvet curtains adorn the back wall, along with an old German upright that seems to never stop resonating.

The White Elephant; catchphrase and proverb, exotic Eastern icon of the richest opulence—a trickster god in chapter and verse of *the religion*. And an alabaster pachyderm in every city and practically every hellhole in Texas, the rubric alone twisting the minds of its devotees; for Blacks are disallowed and the emanations of an unfettered delirium are to be found within. It might be a blessing and then again, it might be a curse. Either way you'll be baptized, know the glory, keep it pure and *see the elephant*.

John Selman, heavily-bearded and tight-lipped, sits regarding the pendulous scrolls and prisms of the battered chandelier with intensity—as if it held the secrets to his deepest concerns.

"Do not gainsay me, little brother, I say we head to Lincoln County. They are at war there and the back door is wide open."

"That would not be to my taste," Tom begins. His eyes wonder about the room as he cracks the knuckles of his right hand.

"Everything in the letter from Ed Hart says its perfect country for us. We can be as proddy as we want and no goddamned law to bother us," says the elder brother, in a drawl that rose up and down like a preacher feelin it on Sunday.

"Hell, I don't trust him. Ed Hart is apt to kill you one of these days."

"Every man's got ambitions, Ed's just doing his job right now, over on the Pecos. And the word is to come on to Lincoln County."

"I've told you before that would not be to my taste. Bean eaters everywhere, nigger soldiers, and Indian country to boot. And no sure thing which niggerun heathens I hate most in that sorry bunch." Tom leans over and aims a stream of tobacco juice toward a spittoon.

John grabs his brother by the shoulder.

"Well Tomcat, I guess I don't give a goddamn what kind'a nigger you hate most. You need to set aside your passions and rooster yo'self up, it's about time for us to skin outa here. There's choice swag to be had in that *heathen* territory, and besides—I've already decided goddammit—Selman's Scouts will ride west. We wait for Jake and Roscoe and the rest, but we're going to New Mexico, *for certain,"* John declares with a glazed passion.

He continues staring into his brothers wobbling eyes until they still, finally letting go of the shoulder with a hefty shove and a grin. Tom shrugs and manages a half-hearted nod.

"I wish to god you'd not call me by that name."

"Tomcat is your name and always has been. Now light'n up you little shitheel and quit looking like I just shot your puppy," John demands, his thick gaze shifting to the back of the room.

He'd recognized a scruffy little fellow in a plaid coat, drawing his mind to more immediate concerns. Selman's eyes narrow and the man abruptly leaves the crowded Faro table, as if he'd a sudden urge to visit the privy.

"There's that fucking rat, Cuddy. Tomcat you stay here and keep our table. I'll be returning in a bit with a trophy."

Selman is up quickly and out the back door. He sees the yellow coat drift through a shaft of lantern light and follows at an oblique angle. In two hundred feet he rounds a corner and comes face to face with the man.

"Hello Cuddy, where you headed?"

"Oh just down to the Wayward, Mr. Selman."

"You weren't trying to avoid me just now were ya?"

"No sir Mr. Selman. I just had a thought I might drift to the Wayward."

"Well now that's not how it looked. It looked like you saw me and remembered the payoff I ain't seen yet and lit out."

"I swear Mr. Selman that's not how it is. I'll have your money, just need a little more time, that shipment did not arrive as I thought it would."

"Or maybe it did arrive and you stuck it all up your ass. You don't mind if I have a look do you." Selman grabs the panicked hustler by a shank of hair and thrusts a knife up to his head. "Or maybe I'll just take an ear for safekeeping until such time as you do have the scratch. You took my money promising to triple it at forfeit of your very life, so an ear is mighty generous considering."

"Please Mr. Selman, I will not let you down, just give me another chance."

"Maybe a finger, instead." Selman forces the man's hand out flat against the timbered wall. The big knife, flashing a little as it catches some light, goes between ring finger and the pinky. "You've got ten, and a dingus—plenty to whittle away at."

"I don't have the money and I don't have the hop, but I'll, I'll make it up to you I swear it."

"So you took the hop and did it all yourself, you worthless son-of-a-bitch."

"No sir, no sir I did not...please don't take my finger. I did not purchase the hop as I was supposed to. It's true."

"Well Cuddy, what the fuck *did* you do."

"I gave the money to Addie and sent her to Abilene to live with my sister. She's pregnant with my child, I love her and this ain't no place for our child to be born. She's starting to show big and I could feel the baby moving," Cuddy pleads, the words rushing out in in a heap and tears starting from bloodshot eyes.

Selman lets go of the hand, and rams the knife back in its scabbard, his venom abruptly transmuted into something human. He gives Cuddy a hard, searching bore, as if he could see truth or falsity wandering around inside the unkempt head.

"A child born to man is a precious thing—like an arrow in a warrior's hands. A man has to take care of his family Cuddy. It's goddamned sacred. You get on after your girl now," Selman proclaims, directly into Cuddy's face—the matter resolved to a fine but unexpected point. "I see you around here again, I'll cut yer plums off."

Selman walks off like some twisted oracle shading back into the dark.

Recovery is a slow thing, Cuddy felt sure Selman was going to maim or kill him. He'd seen the look before, and always before it meant a sacrifice, an offering—to whatever insane god ruled the man.

But Cuddy was telling a truth and it somehow had broken the spell. *Wait till I tell Addie what happened.* Breaking from the wall he starts to run.

"So where's my damned trophy?" Tom asks. John takes a chair without replying and his eyes return to the glittering pendalogues, settling on one in particular. There's a crack and a chip in the imperfect lobe, and the way it prisms the light into a tiny rainbow is a fascination.

"Things ain't always what they seem Tomcat. Naked I came and naked I shall return, the lord gives and the lord takes away," John says, at length.

"Goddamnit John, yer soundin more and more like a fuckin loopy-headed church-man."

"Don't you worry about it Tomcat. Momma's preachment still rattles around in my head is all. I enjoy letting it out now and then, and it does occasionally bind," says John, tossing back the busthead and pouring another round. The light fell on his face strangely and he looks to Tom more crazed prophet tonight than bearded outlaw.

APRIL 27, 1878

The grand jury having finished its deliberations, Lincoln is in a state of fevered anticipation. Everyone, high and low, awaits the blowing of the big wind to follow. In a room thronged with partisans of both sides, jury foreman Joseph Blazer rises to deliver the findings to Judge Bristol. Eye contact between the two men is like a meeting of flint and steel. There is no expression on either man's face to give away the intense flare, but District Attorney Rynerson had seen the subtle spark and his officious scowl deepens. Jimmy Dolan's pig eyes seem to narrow. Olinger silently works his mouth and fingers the bone handle of his knife.

Alexander McSween, the most intellectually arrogant man there, alone appears confident and relaxed.

Judge Bristol clears his throat and begins.

"As to the murders of Sheriff Brady and Deputy Hindeman, the jury finds for an indictment of William H. Bonney, Frederick Waite, and Jim French...as to the murder of Andrew L. Roberts, the jury finds for an indictment of Charlie Bowdre, Frederick Waite, Josiah Scurlock, and William H. Bonney. Bond is placed at five thousand dollars."

No one is particularly surprised at any of that, and the buzz remains relatively low, no more than murmurs passing from man to man.

"Wonder who in hell will serve it?" one man whispers to another.

"As to the charge of embezzlement against Alexander McSween, the jury is unable to find any evidence that would justify that accusation. (The judge pauses, looking as if he'd swallowed a turd). We fully...exonerate him of the charge and regret that a spirit of persecution has been shown in this matter." Bristol reddens, as if he'd swallowed some peppers this time. A tittering of gasps and excited whispers suffuse the room, settling as the Judge continues.

"As to the murder of John Tunstall...indictments were found against Jesse Evans and Jimmy Dolan—bond is placed at five thousand dollars." The Judge places the last sheet of the indictments back on the stack and removes his glasses to rub his eyes—finally banging down his gavel with disgust—the spring term of court had delivered an equitable assessment of crimes.

His face is the color of a beet and if he was trying to hide his disgust, he may as well of not bothered. The old judge says nothing more, and rises to depart. Unused to such shocks, Bristol is seeing past the crowd and already thinking ahead to his main fear—Catron—the center of his universe.

Stunned murmurs build to a full-scale chorus of cheers and whoops as McSween stands and his partisans react to the bombshell. Principals of the House quickly exit, leaving District Attorney Rynerson to rise last, bristling and glowering over the celebrants.

Alex McSween extends his arm with a gentle nod and a wink, his wife Susan touches his coat sleeve and they step out into the street. Bountiful trees overhang and festoon their promenade, soughing in a vernal breath of the softest and most generous quality.

Even the sight of Jimmy Dolan, standing across the street and fixing them with a hard stare—can do nothing to alter the flush of victory. Looking down at his wife's carefully made up face and genuinely happy smile, Alex takes a deep breath as they stroll homeward.

The Kid sits with a newspaper in his lap, reading out its brief and solemn account of the Blazer Mill shootout. Survivors of the battle are gathered around in the cleft above San Patricio, receiving the chronicle with a strange sensation in their bellies, for the word had spread quickly; they'd been officially outlawed.

"At a coroner's inquest held on the body of Andrew L. Roberts, who was killed at Blazer's Mill on the fourth of April, it was found that the deceased came to his death at the hands of Richard Bruer, *spelled with a u*, Charles Bowdry, *with a y on the end*, Frank Mcknabbe...*m-c-k-n-a-b-b-e.* 'Doc' Scurlock, Fred Waite, both correct, Tom *O'Falaran*—sorry Tom. George Coe, correct, and W. H. Antrim, alias 'The Kid.'" William Henry McCarty delivers his name with the biggest of grins.

"Saved the best for last, so there you go, you're on your way," says McNab. He scowls and shakes his head when The Kid tips his hat back. "Well, William Henry Antrim, or is it Bonney, alias The Kid, whatever the hell it is—you mind if I just shorten that to Billy?"

"Billy Bonney! That's a rip snorter of a name," Fred says with a grin.

"How about Billy the Kid?" suggests McNab and the whole company falls silent.

"Now wait a minute, no sir, its short, catchy I'll admit...but I don't like it."

"Cause you didn't think of it!" Doc shouts out.

"Because it makes me sound like a runty little circus clown," The Kid replies and McNab laughs, hard. "I prefer William H. Bonney, dignified and light-hearted, in the same breath."

"And regal," McNab adds.

"To the fucking manor born," Fred grins out once more and everyone agrees. There's a round of laughs, but The Kid sits down again with his newspaper, face clouded.

"First time my name's in print and they get it wrong, just my hard luck," Tom complains.

"Maybe it's good luck your real name ain't mixed up in it yet. Myself—I do not like the glare of public attention," Charlie grouses, reaching up to rub his shoulder, it healed up well enough since the Blazer Mill fracas, but ached still.

"Of course not, you like sneaking around. Me, I like seeing my name in print," says the Chickasaw cowboy.

"You need to watch that smart Chickasaw mouth of yours. I'm liable to dig up the hatchet one of these times," Charlie warns.

"Ease up amigo. Whether you like it or not, our names are still going to be there a hundred years from now, and as for the things they didn't get right, it's all in the price of doing business,"

"What business?" says Charlie, getting testy.

"The business of fame. The more of it we get, the worse it is for them. If you would reap in the fall, you must sow in the spring," The Kid says with a gleam in his eye.

"Well I've a notion fame is like a wild horse, maybe you can tame her, and maybe you can't," Charlie answers back.

"What say we leave off on all these matters for now. Let's have some action, cards or the bones?" asks The Kid.

"Find The lady," Fred says.

"Damn Fred you know I always win at that, how about Birdcage or High Dice," replies The Kid.

"Find The lady first."

The discussion of monikers had not pleased Henry. *Hopefully running some games will put me in a better mood,* he thinks. It'd be a cruel joke if that *Billy the Kid* handle stuck. And Charlie had a point for sure—it could all spin away from him.

Not that he had control over any of it, but Henry liked to think he did. He could talk to the cards and the bones and make them come out laughing—he has the touch. They all thought of his gaming abilities as just about supernatural. But it was mostly skill and being quick and sober and having a bit of luck.

Henry loved dealing out the powerful face cards, and the cut and shuffle of pips is another keen pleasure. But today royalty only brought to mind the lost, and the *cost* of it all.

In the Queen of Hearts he saw his mother. The Ace of Spades brought John Tunstall to mind, and Dick was the King of Clubs. Jesse Evans could only be the Ace of Diamonds, and that card had not showed itself at all.

Worrisome clouds obscured the larger enterprise as well. The big pursuit relied on skill and intelligence, for certain, and luck, but there was something else besides—moving silent down in the pitch-black dark. Something that maybe he'd hooked and maybe he hadn't. And whatever *it* was—was big, fucking enormous. He'd felt a mighty tug when he read his name at the very end of the newspaper story, like some colossal leviathan had struck the line and slid back into the deep.

"You look like an old topper who's just pledged an oath to the sons of temperance," says Murphy, sitting up and enjoying the moment, realizing just how desperate his former protégé is. Dolan had come to see the captain and take his lumps, and hopefully get some useful advice as well.

"Catron's got your business, McSween's got your balls, and Chisum's counting his cattle and having a good laugh...ahh Jimmy Dolan, you're a proud man, a proud little gamecock." Dolan had heard this many times before and it was making him crazy to hear it yet again. "That lawyering gobshite McSween has the insurance fortune tucked away in some bank. Caroline will not see her inheritance, I'd bet on that."

Dolan's eyes lift and blaze and Murphy smiles. "That bothers you more than the indictments." The captain laughs. "Never saw you as a romantic Jimmy, you *are* full of surprises."

"I hope to marry Caroline when this is over. Build us a proper house here in Lincoln, with a pitched roof—right across from his Lordship."

"Why not, he won't object, you'll come out of this yet lad, and smelling like a rose."

"My luck seems to have vanished boss—Jesse laid up and both of us indicted for murder, Brady sharked and McSween strutin like a rooster, the Regulators on the loose, the Boys all but disbanded, the House mortgaged to the fatman and I'm just about broke. It's a goddamn dry shite bag of rocks."

"And I'll be gone before the snow flies…but I'll wager *McSween* goes before me," insists Murphy, managing a chuckle that turns phlegmatic and choking. He leans over and spits into the pitcher by his bed.

Sitting up, the captain takes a pull from his flask and pushes back the lank auburn hair that once had shone and been a point of pride. It now bore the flattened quality of a dead houseplant.

"I used to see the future, but I can't see much of anything just now," Dolan admits.

"Well, you still see that house with the pitched roof, and the *girl* that goes with it," says Murphy, a hint of the old fettle peppered onto the way he'd said girl. "Rynerson will never sign those warrants on you *or* Jesse. You'll outlast McSween I know for certain, Jimmy boy, you are a genuine son-of-a-bitch Irish bulldog. Once you hate a man you never let up, and god love you for it."

"I need more'n hate."

"There's a strongbox under the bed. Lift it up here for me." Jimmy fishes it out and hands it to the captain. "There's about two thousand, from the sale of Fair Oaks. Take it and finish this little war, you'll have to take care of me now until I pass." Jimmy undergoes a transformation as he takes in the captain's offer. "That's your last play, and mine, you damn well better make it count."

"Sure as the sun comes up. Thank you, Captain," says Dolan. He raises grateful eyes to the man in his soured bed.

Jimmy took the abuse of the past half hour, as he always had, not expecting anything but sarcasm and sound advice. But he'd just been given the means of survival and revenge as well, just when he needed it most, and with it—a strong indication of the captain's true feelings for him.

"You need to whittle down on the other side. Send Bob and Jesse to get that Pecos bunch stirred up against the Regulators, they hate Chisum as much as we do—that'd be my next move."

"Yes sir, I'd thought of that. But I can't send Jesse. He's recovering out at Shed's ranch. Took a bullet through the lung down in the malpais. Somehow made it to the ranch."

"Jesse's tough as an iron door, not many of his quality around anymore... he reminds me of Kit."

"I'll be glad to have him back. I sure wish he and Bob could get along though."

"Bob's an insufferable shitheel and I wished I wasn't dying. Now what the hell was Jesse doing out in the malpais?"

"I sent him."

"You sound like the man who got caught tupping the judge's wife...are you going to tell me the story?"

May had arrived with a flair and Frank McNab felt damn near invincible. He'd come through all the mayhem of the previous months without a scratch or a legal blemish. The indictments against the House and the clearing of McSween emboldened Chisum as well, enough to set his hard-nosed cattle detective on the righteous prod. Today the Scotsman means to start another offensive.

"I'm gonna close John Kinney out, are you boys up for making some money? Uncle John smells blood," McNab begins.

"Hell yes, but we need a better plan than just wading into Seven Rivers with our dicks out," Fred answers back, without the grin and the tongue. Taking on John Kinney down in the roughs was no joking matter.

"Well that's frying pan to fire by god. Frank you need to put a lid on all that. The word is out," Doc Scurlock answers with his usual skepticism. "You and the boss sure seem worked up, dangerous I say, what you're planning. Me, I can't get my hat around how those damned indictments put some of us in and left the other half out."

"They damn sure should'a left you out, Josiah, see'n as how you argue against everything," Charlie grouses.

"Those indictments don't matter, Uncle John says Copeland will never serve the warrants," McNab says, counters.

"He's right. Copeland will protect us, just like the Giant will never sign the warrants against Dolan and Jesse Evans. Kind of a stalemate, meanwhile we keep fighting. So, let's come up with a plan," says The Kid. He'd been sitting back and listening to the arguments and seeing the rise of another opportunity.

The few honest ranchers in the Pecos country hated John Chisum lording over their range the same as the Seven Rivers boys. And even the Jones family, best of the ethical crowd, are not above sending a son or two to join with the roughs—if it was in defense of the southern end of Lincoln County.

Sure enough, when word got around that Chisum's detective was planning to scald out the Pecos country—they sent Buck and Jim over to Seven Rivers.

"I'll give this a go, but something tells me we're both going to regret it," Buck says.

"It beats the hell out of our normal routine," Jim replies with a smile nearly as big as his face, more than a little excited to be on a spree that involves guns and no doubt some drinking and gambling.

"Well maybe, I don't know what these fellows have planned. There sure as hell ain't no missionaries amongst them. Standing off a gang of hot-heads is one thing, starting a range war is something else," says Buck, showing that being circumspect and thinking ahead is still his first inclination. "Besides, Henry is mixed up in this on the other side, least he was when the Regulators stopped by the ranch back in March. And that sure enough does give me pause."

If you've a mind to work stolen cattle on the Eyebrow, you can run them down into the southeast lowlands and haven at Seven Rivers, there to deal and trade. And if you don't mind a rough godforsaken camp, Seven Rivers might treat you tolerably well.

The name calls to mind a host of Arcadian notions, but reality sings a different kind of song—about a windswept shit hole of a rustler's camp, a degenerate nexus of seven brown-water creeks dumping into the Pecos—out in the ass end of nowhere.

And of course, there *is* the "Colonel," John Kinney, to deal with. He can be capricious and mite inequitable. Colonel Kinney rules over his half-wits and hard cases with a sawed-off shotgun and an erratic and subtle kind of hypnotism. Like it or not, he's the undisputed boss and everything goes through him.

The camp sits down in a wide draw just up from where the muddy creeks run into the black river, well-hidden from the view of anyone up on the prairie. A rude and stinking place, with nothing of permanence about it.

Olinger and Peppin arrive in the early evening and the two men stand before a fire of cow chips—talking of a pay-off from Dolan if they wipe out the Regulators—and goading the Seven Rivers men with McNab's boasts and taunts: "McNab is a Chisum detective first and foremost and means business. He and his men shot down Morton and Baker on the trail, Sheriff Brady in the street, Buckshot Roberts at Blazer's Mill, and now he's made a boast of putting you fellows out of business," Olinger says. His eyes work the crowd of ragtags, looking for those he can push.

"The hell you say," says the colonel, patting the barrel of his scattergun. "Feller sounds like a genuine brass-balled bastard."

"He ain't no fuckin piker I can tell you that. And now that Brewer's dead—he's the boss," says Peppin.

"We could wait for these *Regulators* to come for a visit, wouldn't be no trouble to take care of'em all out here. I've set many a trap and this is good ground for it," suggests a man in a ripped coat. The rip had been clumsily mended with string and for the most part had come undone again.

Olinger stands up and saunters over, something about the man immediately put him in a suspicious snit.

They stand soured face to soured face, neither flinching.

"Think so? I know these other fellers here...who might you be?" Olinger demands. This scud in a ripped coat was up to some weaselly dodge, he'd felt the same thing when Kid Antrim showed up out of nowhere.

"Name's Ed Hart, come from Texas with my friend Caleb." Caleb steps out of the shadows, closer to the fire, much like a wild animal of some sort—careful and bold all at once.

"I'm Caleb the Prowler. We crawled out the asshole a Texas and straight up the backside a Seven Rivers." He snuffs at the air. "Just to take a whiff. What about you *payaso*?" The Prowler says all that with his head lurched to one side, staring at Olinger and waiting to see what effect his clever little speech might have.

"Shut up Caleb, where's your manners?" Hart admonishes, but a sly grin at play. Olinger could see a livid scar running from jaw to ear and his hand strays to the bone handle.

"Must a left'em at the White Elephant," Caleb answers back. The crooked smile he brought forth put on display a row of missing teeth, behind a sharp cuspid. "Bet that sombrero'd make a good boat if it came a flood."

"You boys are awful mouthy for a couple a cunts from Texas," Olinger says, his face dark.

"We done proved ourselves to the colonel, didn't mention we'd have to prove anything to you," Ed Hart levels back, if either scud was the least spooked it didn't show.

"You might have to learn some New Mexico manners is all," Olinger answers back, his voice stiffening. He'd not lost any of his sass or bile since the big fight with Brewer. Olinger regarded that as a win he'd been cheated out of.

The Prowler's head had straightened at the word *cunt*, then lopped to the other side. Ed Hart grinned bigger, rippling the scar. Another comment and there would have been quite a show—but two riders come up out of the dark and hallow the camp—breaking the spell.

"Buck and Jim Jones here, okay to approach the fire?" Buck yells out.

"Hell yes boys, come on in. Anyone from the Jones family is welcome here," Kinney shouts out. "Come on down, things are just getting interesting."

He backs Olinger away from the two cohorts, casual-like, the big gun resting in the crook of his arm and his eyes hinging back and forth. Olinger returns to the fire and sits down next to Peppin, gesturing toward the Jones boys with a self-satisfied smirk.

"I've been thinking up a plan," continues Colonel Kinney. "We could wait here and have us a nice little ambush, like Ed suggested, or we could go up mountain and shoot this Scottish bastard out of his saddle. I say we choose high ground for the deed. *Then* deal with the rest, and maybe have a little holiday up where it's cool," Kinney argues, working his men with another spell, walking amongst them with his eyes moving in a kind of dance that parsed every man then coming to a dead stop on one in particular. It gave some the shivers and never failed to rattle everyone into a serious mood. Last moving up on Olinger and holding a moment before he speaks. "What say you...*Pecos* Bob?"

"I say let's ride at first light, Colonel," Olinger responds with a wink—as if to say—I'll play along but don't waste that horseshit on me.

Little by little the camp began to regain its former devil-may-care esprit de corp. Caleb the Prowler and Ed Hart jumped right back into a raucous game of chuck-a-luck, one they had going before that long-haired bastard had showed and started running his mouth, but they kept a wary eye on him the rest of the night.

Under the influence of a close brush with the Devil and Death, a man might be compelled to seek some manner of exculpation for past sins, some atonement, some reparation to a higher power—for seeing him through the ordeal and setting him down on the side of the living.

But no such spiritual contrition had occurred. Nor did Jesse Evans plan revenge for the fool's errand he'd been sent on. He came back with a gain and didn't worry it further.

"It's good to see you up and about Mr. Evans," Mrs. Shed offers, working steady at plucking a chicken and carefully stowing away the feathers.

Jesse sits at the kitchen table working a plate of biscuits and eggs. The left forearm splinted and wrapped in a sling, the right busy chopping the yokes into the white and peppering it all black. He looks up and nods with a tight smile.

"You'll be going up mountain soon I suppose?" she asks and Jesse nods once more.

"You can't leave Rosa here," Mrs. Shed states flatly.

"She'd make you a good hand."

"No doubt. But I'd spend all my time keeping the men off her. This ain't no place for a stray girl—besides, she deserves better and I think you know it. That poor child has a lot of healing to do. Rosa needs her own people, a family," Mrs. Shed continues, the chicken nearly bald and Jesse staring into his plate. He looks up into the woman's eyes.

"Is she..."

"Yes she is. Take Rosa up mountain with you Jesse, there's a Mexican family in Lincoln or the Hondo Valley that'd take her. It's not your usual line I know, but I believe you'd do a good job of it."

Jesse remains silent and she goes back to her plucking.

"I'm going to miss your cookin Mrs. Shed," says Jesse, finally. The last few feathers come out and Mrs. Shed looks up again, smiling.

"Jesse's a big name in the Bible."

"Father of David, grandfather of Solomon. Growing up I always wondered how a fine Virginia name wound up in the Bible. I still don't think it belongs there," Jesse protests.

"But its t'other way around."

"I know."

Jesse stands and goes out the back door, there to sit on the stoop and look up at the saw-tooths—and consider the young girl he'd saved, or who had saved him. He wasn't sure which and it didn't matter.

April 29th, 1878

Some thought Frank McNab as handsome as Dick Brewer. Well-built, square-jawed, a fine aquiline nose, and the dimple in his chin had fascinated many a girl back in the highlands.

To a man, the Regulators were a fine-looking bunch. Susan McSween wanted them all to pose for a vignette, when a photographer came through two months earlier—before the killing of Morton and Baker and all the killing that followed.

"Now we'll see who's the smartest of the lot," The kid had said.

"That'd be Mr. McNab for certain," Brewer replied.

"My money'd be on you Dick," Frank answered back and the big foreman, not used to compliments on his appearance, looked away and reddened.

They were ready to consent to Mrs. McSween who was to pay the photographer, but a friend of The Kid's rode into camp with news of Morton and Baker and the opportunity passed. Much blood had been spilt since. But today three partisans head out of Lincoln with only farming in mind, looking forward to being home and cantering along with a smile.

Frank Coe and his brother-in-law Ab Saunders were longtime tillers of the soil and good fruit growers, but McNab was new to the ground and had only recently purchased property and no real work done yet. He's delighted to have a day to just wander around on it and dream of what he *might* do.

They would all reconnoiter tomorrow back at the Ellis store in Lincoln—and he'd plan out the Pecos raid. But today is a day to take stock, smell the air—devote some time to thoughts of family.

Frank McNab had fallen in love with his adopted homeland and the farther he traveled into the West, the more at home he felt. It was an unending, untidy wilderness—and he was beginning to find his rightful place in it.

But there was something from his past that wouldn't let go, a persistent guilt had dogged him all the way from New York, like a bloodhound; he knew he'd never go back home to Scotland, would never see his mother again.

No matter how fierce a man he'd become, her letters had always broken his heart just the same. The simple straightforward words conveyed suffering far more than she intended, and there was *nothing* he could do to relieve it. She'd always closed with a mother's wish to see her boy again, well and happy and sitting by the hearth. Frank would then summon the cheerful lad he'd always been and write back of his adventures, closing with a promise to sail home someday, maybe next year.

But he'd never told her the truth; having made that terrible crossing once—four weeks on stormy seas—he knew he could never make a second. His courage is a solid thing on land, but the wild ocean was another matter. He'd *seen* it, the monstrous deep in all its fury, and the great waves still crashed in his mind like some epic nightmare.

Frank had received the sad news of his mother's death in January. Now he needn't worry about hiding his secret, or disappointing her ever again. There was that at least.

"Mr. Coe do you expect to have apples come fall?" asks Frank, wanting to bring himself back to the present. Food was also on his mind. They'd had a good lunch at Wortley's but the cook ran out of pie before they could get their share, and now on the road to the Hondo valley—he's regretting it more and more. Something sweet was the perfect way to end a meal, and it always had a way of getting his mind off a sadness.

"Well maybe, that's a big question. If they make, it'll be the first crop. Takes several years after you plant and a lot of pruning and cross-pollinatin and praying. Once they come in though." Frank's face stretches into a congenial bloom of hope, and joy.

"I admire your patience."

"Takes more'n a little."

The three men round the bend just past the Fritz Spring ranch and continue on in the mid-day sun. Up in the piñons he notices several flashes catching the midday sun—and Frank's thoughts suddenly snap back to his profession. A stir in the shadows back up in there on the right. The hair on his neck stands straight up.

"Fellows..." But he got no further.

A tremendous volley, thirty guns strong, detonates from above. McNab's horse rears and he tumbles backwards out of the saddle, flipping onto the road with a resounding thud. Saunders is shot through the hip and two mounts are killed, all in the first seconds.

Frank Coe suddenly finds himself sitting atop a dead horse, his gun out and McNab trying to crawl away in a gout of dark blood, Saunders trapped and moaning. A hoard of roughs come down out of the trees to surround him, and to celebrate.

"*Frank* Coe. You aren't one of the *official* Regulators," Olinger admits.

"Neither is Abe Saunders, lying there with a bullet in his ass, he'll be lucky to walk again," Frank answers. The posse mills about with little intention to help.

"Guilty by association, and you are one lucky son-of-a-bitch. To have come through a firestorm like that without a scratch," Colonel Kinney announces, pulling the shotgun into the crook of his arm again. "I do require that you stay with us."

Manuel the Indian, one of the last of Jesse's Boys, walks over to McNab lowering his shotgun and pulling the trigger at point blank.

"He was still alive," the Indian says.

"Not no more...a handsome feller, you can kinda tell that," says Caleb, standing over the body with his head in that awkward tilt.

"Alright you sorry-ass river rats, we managed that well enough, we'll be riding to Lincoln now," the colonel bellows.

"Are we going to leave the horses and body in the road?" Jim Jones asks, a queasy look torturing his young features. "And what about this other feller."

"The Fritz boys will take care of it, why don't you ride over and tell'em there's a wounded man out here in the road. Yer a good man for the job, one of us gun thugs might spook'em."

"Yes sir," Jim answers. He wished now he'd lit out and gone home that first night like his brother. Buck refused to have anything to do with a posse that included Bob Olinger. The look of many of Kinney's new recruits didn't set well with Buck either. They were a grim bunch and no mistake but Jim was eager to see the elephant, and that desire outweighed all other arguments.

A little ranchero burrows into the foot of the hill like a natural offshoot. The casita and out-buildings look as if they had somehow risen up from the earth. Blooming chokecherry trees define the yard with a border of white flowers and dark red berries.

The Chokecherry has many gifts; the bark can be made into a medicine to treat stomach maladies, colds, and fevers, the berries make good wine and jellies, and the pure white clusters give off a heady aroma. Some find the smell unpleasant, but others swear by its powers as an aphrodisiac.

Inside the snug little adobe, Abuelita Jimenez sews by the window. She looks up from her work and a smile brightens her wrinkled face. Seated across the room are grandson Mateo and the blue-eyed charmer the people are beginning to call *El Chivato*.

An English lesson in progress at the family dinner table consumes teacher and student. The lessons have been underway for a few weeks. Today a few simple sentences have been written out in large letters. Mateo must read them out loud and write it out—in English.

"My name es...Mateo. I am...ah...gift from God."

"Good. *Bueno*...continue." Chivato smiles at his student.

"Today es... Tuesday...nueve, veintinueve... Ahpril twenty-nine."

Chivato reaches out and pats Hilario on the top of his head and motions grandly for him to proceed.

"The air...is warm and sweat."

"Sweet, two e's make a long e...eeee...vowel sound." Chivato laughs this time.

Next Mateo must copy the alphabet and the sentences, and while he works The Kid is busy himself. First, he helps Abuelita Jimenez by threading a needle and neatly tying the knot. Then on to a complicated dance step, and finally, the quick-draw from a variety of unusual hideouts—humming and whistling all the while.

Mateo completes his task only to find Chivato busy writing out another one, this time twice as long. Chivato goes back to his quick draw—he is lightning fast, not only from the front or back of his waist but also from boot.

Chivato still carries the Cooper Double from his days in Hopville—it made an excellent hide-out weapon, but now he proudly sported a colt pistol and Winchester as well.

Over by the open window, the abuelita is beginning to doze in the scented air. Mateo looks up from his work, occasionally, to admire his teacher's skill. "*El Chivato, es un pistolero fantastico...pero*...are you a bad man?"

"No, but there are bad men who want to kill me...so I hide out here while they chase their tails, and I teach you English," Chivato answers, performing a pantomime of men chasing their tails. He stops when Mateo's sister enters the room. El Chivato immediately bows low and doffs his hat in exaggerated salutation. Adelita giggles at the buffoonery and he raises a forefinger to pursed lips, nodding toward her sleeping abuelita. They slip outside, the teacher motioning for the student to continue as he closes the door.

"*Quieres atrapar a me*?" Adelita whispers backing away.

"*Si.*"

"*No soy un animal salvaje.*"

"*Esta seguro*?" El Chivato asks, an innocent smile gives way to something more mature as he chases her around a corner.

Adelita's eyes blaze back at him, but soften as he moves the last fateful distance and presses her lips. The maddening taste of her rosebud mouth like an unknown fruit and the tang of Chokecherry blossoms heavy in the air.

The word jumped through the valley like ball lightening. Adelita's father brought the news from the next village over. Fortunately for all Henry was finishing Mateo's lessons, and Adelita had taken up her grandmother's sewing when the father rolled up. Mateo knew there was some secret to protect, and if Abuelita Jiminez was on to them, she kept it to herself.

Henry had planned to ride to the Ellis Store the next morning but was already busy saddling Slippers in the dimming light. He'd take the shortcut over the mountain and watch all the way for the ragtag posse that had taken Frank McNab's life.

"*Enrique, con cuidado,*" Adelita pleads.

"*Si, corazón,*" he says, softly, almost inaudible. Then onto his mare and off across the fields, heading for the road to Lincoln. He keeps Slippers at a good loping pace as long as possible, god knows what that bunch has in mind for tomorrow, or even tonight.

Whatever it was, he would damn sure be in the middle of it.

From the top of the ridge he spots an encampment near the main road, just outside Lincoln. Working down to within a hundred yards he recognizes Peppin and Olinger, and Manuel Segovia—the only one of the Boys he truly feared, also Frank Coe bound to a tree, and Jim Jones off by himself.

Thirty men in all, jawing about attacking the Ellis Store in the morning. Henry withdraws, figuring now the war would truly begin.

He sure hated to see Jim Jones amongst that rabble.

Issac Ellis is the Regulators most partisan supporter amongst the burghers of the town. His home and store had become their supply depot. The Regulators were forting up there right now, but mounting back up, Henry doubted there were more than a handful to defend it tonight. One more at least. The Kid's heart skipped every other beat as he careened down the steep switchback into Lincoln.

Under the direction of Jim French, they were finishing a solid defensive redoubt as he rode in; emplaced at a salient angle in front of the thick-walled adobe, with two more arms protecting the north and south facing ends. The perimeter fence in back was solid and the roof sported an improvised curtain wall. All approaches were covered and good sight lines. Henry lights down off Slippers and inspects the earthworks—impressed, amazed, and eager.

"Well hell look what the cat drug in," Tom yells out.

"A genuine hellbent outlaw loaded for bear," Charlie adds, and Henry pumps his rifle in the air.

"That is a beautiful redoubt gentleman."

"About time that education came to some use, and we aren't done—still time for you to do your share," Jim replies.

"Mr. Ellis, your fine establishment has become a Fort." Henry reaches for Mr. Ellis's hand, and the hands of his two sons, Ben and Sam. "It will be an honor to fight here. I just snuck by their camp and had a listen—those fellows are on their way first thing tomorrow."

"The bastards shot Frank out of his saddle, then shotgunned him," Charlie tells them.

"They're fix'in to get what's coming to'em," raves Doc. All those present are in agreement on this; Mr. Ellis and his two sons have their own grievances with the House, and the Regulators are a tight and angry field unit—they've given blood for blood.

They came sneaking through the campo santo at first light, startling Mrs. Montano at the privy door, and Mr. Salazar, who had stepped outside to urinate.

The ragged hoard was bristling with arms and filing carefully into position opposite the store—creeping through the graveyard in half-light, they looked also to be minions of the Devil risen up from the crypt.

"Fuck me, that's a nice-looking redoubt," hisses Caleb from behind a gravestone.

"Damn sure is. Looks to be tight as a drum, if anybody over there can shoot we *are* fucked," Ed whispers back. He breathes a heavy sigh and pulls out a plug of tobacco, biting a chaw and handing it over to the Prowler.

"Well shit. The Indian is signaling to move in tighter."

Seventy-five yards opposite the regulators are at the ready, with men in the salient, the south and north arms, and on the roof.

"Wait just a bit now, if they move any closer—open up. Most likely be our best chance," Doc orders and the rest check their weapons a last time. The Kid has the Winchester primed and resting in the firing slot on the right side of the salient.

"Here they come."

Suddenly the Ellis compound roars to life with a sheet of flame and smoke. Several Kinney men are hit and a stunned moment passes before a consistent return fire begins from the Campo Santo. After a hard fifteen minutes smoke fills the little battlefield and acrid scuds drift through the frightened town, along with groans of wounded men.

"Well shit, Walter and what's his name is gut shot, man next to'em is winged, a leg wound next door—and two is most assuredly dead," Caleb barks out as he rolls from left to right, reconnoitering the field.

"They's more'n one marksman over there," Ed replies.

"Alright Pecos, what say we go find Sheriff Copeland. Tell'em we're ready to help him arrest these bastards," says Kinney.

"Suppose it's worth a try, we ain't doing no good like this."

"Send that Jones boy, he's back there with the horses," Kinney answers, frustrated with his options and perusing the sorry state of his tactical position with blood running down his face. A near miss clipped a gravestone and splintered a piece along his forehead. But to panic had not entered his mind, he merely pivoted.

Behind the redoubt, men are jubilant as only victors in battle can be. They reload and check in with the four men on the flanks and the two on the roof—all in good health and the highest spirits.

"I count six men down over in the campo santo and the rest buttoned up tight as you please," Charlie declares.

"They'll not underestimate us again." The kid laughs, spinning the chamber of his colt and placing the gun next to his firing port. He levers his rifle back up and grins. "Suppose they thought they'd just waltz in and catch us sleeping."

"Sheriff Copeland sent a man to the fort first thing. They'll be a detachment here in an hour or so," Mr. Ellis calls out from up top.

"Then we best cut'em off from their horses. I want Jim, Charlie and Fred to slip out the back and flank'em," Doc Scurlock orders. The chain of command had quietly passed to him, and it rested on his shoulders now like an old coat.

"Aaoooh!" Fred crows out a jubilant howl. The mustache lifts, the grin returns and the tongue emerges.

Before lunchtime the Kinney gang is arrested—and all of them paraded to Fort Stanton by a detachment of the 9th calvary. And Frank Coe at liberty again, after an ordeal lasting a full twenty-four hours.

"Of all the outrages of my life, this tops it all," Caleb groans. He is surrounded on two sides by black soldiers, close enough to see and smell their muscled bodies sitting prideful and easy in the saddle. The 9th riding stoic and silent alongside two bigots of the old school, occasionally allowing themselves to grin at the strange little man's obvious discomfort.

"Quit running your goddamned mouth Prowler, you're just pissin up a rope," says Ed Hart, the eyes staring straight ahead.

But things soon change again. Within another few hours, McSween and the Regulators are also surrounded by the 9th, and likewise, escorted to Fort Stanton. There to face off with the Kinney gang from across the great quadrangle. Two days later yet another hand is dealt and the Pecos men are freed while the Regulators remain in custody.

Discretion being the better part of valor, Colonel Kinney and his men saddle up for the Pecos, and the Regulators once again claim victory at the Battle of the Campo Santos.

"Come see us again Colonel. Next time you best bring more than a lick'n a promise!" The Kid shouts out and Charlie lifts his middle finger to laud their exodus.

"Listen up you biggity sonsabitches and *regulate* this...we'll be coming back all right and next time we'll catch'ya when'ya ain't hiding behind a goddamned wall!" Colonel Kinney roars, he'd stopped and reined toward them holding there a moment. "Tell your mouthpiece he ain't got much time either."

"I believe he means to rattle us."

"Yeah I might have to go clean my drawers now."

Alex McSween joins the others to witness the inglorious departure. He knows *their* warrants will fall apart as well and the Regulators will soon be released, but something else is on his mind. While the Regulators taunt and the Kinney roughs reply in kind, Mac stands apart and strokes his mustache, piqued over a dispatch that had just reached his hands. Two weeks before, McSween had sent a terse and high-toned letter to District Attorney Rynerson—about the warrants for Dolan and Evans gathering dust—and Rynerson had now responded with his own condescending diatribe. He spoke from an Olympian height, declaring that he needed no assistance from a third-rate lawyer and that he should mind his own affairs, for they would soon catch up to him.

"It was a nice visit!" Fred yells. "Next time you want to get shot all to hell...come on up."

"Fuck you peckerwood, you can suck my dingus dry!" Caleb yells, punctuating the thought by pumping a fist over his rank mouth.

McSween looks at his men and the sorry bunch making their exit, and turns away. He allows himself to despair only a moment longer. *His* letter was a tight and legally astute warning, and Rynerson had returned a swaggering pretentious threat—but no one would get the better of him in the long run, for he possessed the most brilliant mind in the territory and that was certain.

Another Sabbath arrives in Lincoln on a breezy May afternoon. The town is at war but the church, normally quiet and visited only infrequently by itinerant preachers—is blessed with both a congregation and a Presbyterian minister in fine form.

"I look out on you all today with both a joyous and a saddened heart. For in my first few weeks in Lincoln I've witnessed the lowest depths of sin and also, the greatest kin of Christian fealty likewise spread generously across different races and different faiths. And I conclude, in hope and in love, that when man is at his worst...so too is he at his best...let us pray."

Finally, brothers and sisters, rejoice.
Aim for restoration, comfort one another,
agree with one another, live in peace;
and the God of love and peace will be with you.

Dr. Ealy delivered this sermon with more passion than any gone before it in the civilized East. The assembly of partisans from both sides and a good many caught in between, had listened hard to the words and every man and woman present hoped some good could be done against the balance. All join now in the closing psalms with a flair, regardless. The minister's wife pounds the piano in a state of high transport and at her side is the Irish singer, Henry McCarty.

There's not a plant or flower below
but makes your glories known,
and clouds arise and tempests blow
by order of your throne;

The full-throated hymn pours out open doors and windows. A rider on the street lifts his dark eyes, head turning to the girl trailing behind. They enter the church yard and dismount, seating themselves in the shade. Above the ragged thrumming of voices, a clear tenor begins to rise, catching and gracing the refrain like a trumpet shouting to the heavens.

Sitting next to Jesse with a smile, Rosa folds her hands, as if maybe to pray.

12

Reveille sounds out across the quadrangle like the hammering of fate. The melody forever caught in the mindless wheel of a major triad—tonic, mediant, and dominant—those three and no more are all a soldier is given to begin each day with.

"I hate that fuckin song," moans a private while rubbing his face.

"That ain't no song."

"Sounds like a damn bee stuck in a can."

A full company of the vaunted black 9th roll out of their bunk beds with a collective groan. Sergeant Terrell, already crisply dressed and wide awake, is in amongst the bunks encouraging his men with a slap here and a kick there.

"Come up out of those dreams boys, your period of silent reflection is over. Rise and shine, it is a new day."

"I'd like to shoot that goddamned bugler," another complains as he stretches into his blues and boots.

There's a new recruit in their midst, a malcontent. He rolls over and issues a far more insolent challenge, not quite under his breath, "Y'all go on ahead, I just skip breakfast and sleep."

"Private you will turn out for the colors! This ain't about breakfast," orders the sergeant.

He is on him quickly, grabbing an ear and giving it a vicious twist. The recruit, a big man, comes boiling out of his sheets:

"Oh yassir, Uncle Tom, yo *shore is* some kind a black martinet, just a prancin for the master like a minstrel show." Sergeant Terrell, a half-head shorter, stands his ground and the two men face off. The separate forces of their hardened lives ready to spill forth, but somehow forestalled. A hush falls over the barracks. The sergeant begins to work his way into the thick skull of Private Burton.

"You see these three stripes, that means I'm a sergeant, a *black* sergeant. There's a white private in the Twelfth just as big as you, and when I walk by he has to salute my black ass. I've been twelve years on the frontier and each one of those stripes cost me a life. Now...it's *me, not some white master,* that's gonna bust you down you dumb Georgia boy."

"Tell'em Sergeant."

"Scripture and verse."

"There's all kinds of war going on out here, white and brown folk killing each other every day. And the red man—mean and wild and more guts than you can hang on a fence—he's fighting for his life, too. There's a lot of work to be done and a chance for us to prove our worth to the country...to ourselves. Now, Private Burton, turn out for the colors."

"Yes, sir." The big man knows he's lost the test of wills, and his head drops.

"Good, I got plans for you. This day is like any other, my company of buffalo soldiers will prove itself the equal of any company of white men in the whole goddamned army, or die trying. Your job is simple. You do what I tell you to do and you do it well! And any man who fails me...will regret it."

It's not what he'd expected to hear, but what he *did* hear was worth considering. Private Burton joined the white man's army for the chance to see what a buffalo soldier's life was like—it had to be better than what old Jim Crow allowed.

"Is this company ready to fall out?"

"Yes Sir!"

A soldier's discipline is a hell of a hard thing, white or black, strong or weak, broken or whole. But the big man wasn't going back to sleep. His eyes were open and the sun well up.

After an absence of two months, Jesse sits across table from Jimmy Dolan with his hair grown long and another glass of true rye whiskey before him. Jesse definitely had been through hell. There was something more angular and haunted about him now, and he already far gone in that direction. And returned with a child in tow—the strangest thing of all.

"Glad to have you back with us and reasonably healthy," says Jimmy, counting out some of Murphy's donation and handing over Jesse's back pay with a little extra.

"It was a narrow thing," says Evans and Dolan looks away.

"I'm sorry about Tom."

"So am I."

"And the girl?"

"Her name's Rosa, the hombre had her in chains. She gave my wound an excellent field dressing, followed me back to Shed's. Might not have made it without her."

"I'd say Rosa's good luck then and a good hand, and you came back with something after all."

"Need to find her a home."

"Maria can look after her for now, she can help with Captain Murphy," Jimmy suggests and Jesse lifts his chin, placing on the table what he regarded as Jimmy's take from the malpais expedition—a dental framework that enclosed two gold teeth.

"Thirty percent."

Jimmy Dolan looks at it and nods, edging the gold into an open drawer with his glass. He wonders if it might be accursed, or possibly, a token of good fortune.

"Now, to other business, we've both got an indictment hung on us for Tunstall."

"Rynerson will take care of that."

"Yes, eventually. We'll go pay him a visit over in Messilla. He sent word for us to come. Meanwhile business as usual, down to it. McSween or me. I'm gonna put a bounty on his head for five hundred—Rynerson himself laid out for it. Don't suppose you'd be interested?"

"No high-profile killings—you know that. That's what the troops are for."

"Just thought I'd ask. I'm running out of time."

"We'll get'em."

"We're also gonna have to give a statement to that damn investigator. He's the President's man and there's no gettin around it."

"I'm not worried about it, I sure as hell didn't kill the Englishmen."

"So there's that, as soon as Detective Angel leaves the territory we'll get Copeland' out of the way, and Peppin appointed sheriff."

"Peppin's a good carpenter and that's about all."

"He's *ours* though and he's bloody. And we're still gonna need more men."

"I'll go on the scout, see if I can make a raise—there's always Kinney and his ragtags," Jesse suggests, as if to say you could always shoot yourself in the ass.

"Don't know that he's ever forgiven you for deserting him. Or taking his best men. Can you two get along?"

"I suppose," Jesse growls, still bothered by what had befallen them two years before.

Kinney had started a saloon fight one wild night in Messilla, with practically a whole company of black troopers. Jesse had no choice but get his ass kicked good and proper. One of the soldiers died the next day and other troubles followed closely attached. Evans parted ways and the two hadn't spoken since.

It was a deeply offensive affair, not so much to Jesse's politics, but certainly to his sense of logic.

"I'd soon leave him out, but times are hard," Dolan says, shaking his head.

"Where's the Indian? He's the last one, and the most lethal."

"Down at the Black River cow camp, I think."

"Let's keep him close, that camp's halfway to Mexico...he's your man to get McSween."

May 14th, 1878

Johnny sat by the cook fire, his fifteen-year-old eyes impatiently watching the son-of-a-bitch stew with the sun reaching its zenith and the air hot. *Damn another long one*, he thinks to himself—breathing out a sigh. Time passes slow out in the grasslands and noon time is the worst.

He had agreed to work the camp with his uncle quick enough, there might be something out there more interesting than the deadly boredom of farm life. After a few weeks he reckoned it to be a little better at least. At times there was plenty of work and quick-witted banter, and those days were better. Other times he sat and watched the fire wishing something would happen, thinking about the girl whose family lived down by the spring—

wondering what she looked like with no dress or bloomers. He'd sell his soul to see that.

At least there was a gun shark amongst them now. His uncle warned him to stay away from the Indian, but Johnny tried to get him talking anyway. The fellow just looked at him with those dead flat eyes and spit, told him to shut up—that he was listening to the wind and needed to be left alone.

When asked what he was listening for, the Indian stood up and walked away.

Manuel the Indian heard things others couldn't for a certainty. It was a habit he'd picked up from the Chiricahua who'd abducted and enslaved him as young boy. They'd taken him from his little village out on the Sonoran plains, and killed everyone else. When he finally returned nothing was left of the place. The burned-out jacals effaced by time and by wind down to nothing and all of it grown over like it had never existed. The wind whining over a sharp ridge line a half mile away was all that told him he'd come home.

That wind had followed him ever since like a shadow, like a ghost. Warned him of things to come. Told him stories of the old world. And sometimes was just an ache in his head, a vibration thrumming in his ears like madness.

Today the wind had picked up at daybreak. Its trickery began straight off and continued all morning. At mid-day Manuel angles up from the Black River toward the fire, in a kind of delirium. Johnny's eyes go from the pot, finally starting to boil, to the frenzied look of the approaching gun shark. It occurred to him that his uncle was right—the man is crazy as a shit house rat.

Manuel looks past Johnny out into the tall grass and to the low rise. His eyes abruptly focus on something and the delirium empties like an overturned pot. The boy gets up to wood the fire and an immediate roaring sheet of flame bursts from the ridge.

A riffled bullet tears through Johnny's left arm, the length of it suddenly dangling by a piece of skin and muscle—the round continuing on to clip the Indian's rib cage. Their eyes locked at the moment of impact, a terrible understanding flashing through them.

The Indian scrabbles away and Johnny falls to the ground trying to hold his arm on. Another ear-splitting burst rakes from the high grass, as if the prairie itself had risen up in anger. Others wounded now, but one terrified scream rises above the din like a dying fawn.

The shotgun and pistol were left by his saddle—Manuel had meant to clean and oil them once his head cleared. Hang me for a fool he thought, scuttling back toward the river with the guns left behind and only a knife in his belt. In a few minutes he's splashing across and up a draw, finally hoisting himself onto the prairie.

"Hold up there hombre," Fred Waite commands with pistol leveled. The Chickasaw cowboy had been waiting for him to top out and stands a few paces away.

"Better be a kill shot," says the Indian as he gets to his feet, slowly. "You miss I'm gonna cut your throat and go right on."

"Your welcome to try."

His knife comes out and the trigger hits on a fully-cocked hammer—slamming a .45 cartridge into the Indian's chest. Fred catches the knife hand with his left and over they go.

A second cock, pull, and explosion before they hit the ground. Their faces inches apart and the knife close to its goal but the Indian's strength fading out. The point of the blade goes in as a third bullet puts an end to it.

Fred shoves the body off him and pushes away, eager to be well back.

"Hey cowboy, you all right," yells Charlie running up on foot. He'd been fifty yards to the west. They were the rear side of the operation, along with Henry and Tom to the east.

"Yeah, I think so," Fred allows, voice a little unsteady while pulling his bandana to staunch the inch-deep cut in his neck. The Kid and Tom waltz up in time to see the Indian face down and Fred sitting a few feet away.

Shaking and plainly rattled, the olive skin and thick mustache giving him more the appearance of a sturdy Italian brick layer than a fierce warrior of the great plains—he'd nonetheless held his ground and the honor of stopping Manuel the Indian Seguro belongs solely to Fred Waite.

"Hopmagundy...we have a hero in our midst."

"We got'em Doc," Charlie yells out through cupped hands.

Doc Josiah Scurlock had come down from the mountain with plenty of men but hadn't expected any kind of shindy. They'd figured to hit Dolan's camp and take back Tunstall's livestock and nothing more. But the Indian had been spotted and the mission immediately shifted to a deadly serious manhunt.

At the conclusion it became something else again.

"What's your name son?" asks Doc, looking over the wound and planning his cuts and sutures.

"Joh...Johnny," sputters the terrified boy.

"Johnny you're a brave man. I can't save your arm, but I can damn sure save your life...now bite down on this."

The boy's eyes gone wild, teeth clamped hard on a wooden spoon and skin pale as milk. Thick blood had poured out in a pungent gout. The mangled arm lay in a festering red pool, and while the guns roared Johnny'd somehow smelled iron and molasses—and something rotting.

Doc fashioned an excellent field tourniquet and that stopped the bleed out, but the arm would have to be cut away and the skin pulled and sutured over the stump.

"Now you just keep your head turned...look at your uncle there."

"You're gonna come through just fine, and marry that girl you're sweet on," his uncle promises.

"Learned my medical skills in New Orleans. I'd go to the Quarter at night and dance with the most beautiful girls you ever saw. The naughty things you could see on display there—shameful as they were magnificent. There were girls in silk dresses kicking their legs high and showing all kinds of things underneath."

The others had all gathered around, intent on the unexpected drama overtaking the day. No one looked for a skinny little kid to be there, let alone get in the way of high caliber bullet and lose his arm.

Getting that goddamned Indian was a good thing; he'd been in on Mr. Tunstall's murder, emptied a shotgun in Frank's chest, and no doubt done more evil than a pack of devils—but to a man they had forgotten the Indian and now stood watching and hoping for the boy to pull through.

"Private Burton," barks Sergeant Terrell. The big recruit takes one step out from parade rest. The others in line look straight ahead, as if nothing of interest were occurring to their left. "Are you ready to fire the big gun and demonstrate the marksmanship for which you Georgians are famous?"

"Yes Sergeant!" the big private shouts, loud enough to be heard on the quadrangle a half mile away.

"The Gatling was invented in eighteen sixty-one...but it saw little action in the big war," Sergeant Terrell recounts, looking over his men. "The Gun was underestimated, misunderstood, just like the black soldier. She also had a limited magazine capacity, often jammed. Now we have the Broadwell Drum and four hundred rounds. But it takes one hell of an arm. Private Burton, are you up to that task?"

"Yes Sergeant!"

"Carry on then," Sergeamt Terrell answers back softly, as he spins to face the gun and the open firing range.

Private Burton takes another step forward, executes a right face and marches up to the shining ballista mounted in its caisson. The mighty Broadwell Drum cylinder, with its twenty stacks of twenty rounds each, sits atop like a giant colt cylinder pointed at the heavens—ready to drop a full load of 45-70 missiles into ten rotating barrels.

Arms bulging against his uniform, Private Burton grabs the crank handle with his right hand, the steady bar with his left and starts to grind out a fearsome volley. First a bit wide but then obliterating the wooden target. After two thunderous minutes without a pause the big private empties the gun's magazine to a rattling spin.

A wild yell breaks from the men at parade rest. Glistening with sweat, Private Burton turns to his sergeant. The black soldier and gold weapon stand amidst a tremendous cloud of gray smoke—and every man on the field has a Georgia-sized grin.

"Well done Private."

"Jest like crankin ice cream, Sir."

He was two weeks out from New York. Most of the time spent with his rear-end on a hard seat and the great expanse of America slowly advancing and retreating. Harvard educated, well-trained, supremely disciplined; Frank Angel brought as much to read and study as he possibly could—and it wasn't near enough.

Angel's prestigious law firm is a well-connected bastion of Republican concerns, and the senior partner a personal friend to President Hayes. When word arrived from Washington that a special investigator was needed, Frank Angel's name came up immediately.

He was both excited and apprehensive to except the appointment. Working for the President of the United States was the highest of honors. But dear god, to get there was six days on a train and nearly as many in a coach. It would also be dangerous. Men in power do not like to be toppled, and he was going to the territories—the man from Washington had called it the *nether world*.

For much of the journey he was left to contemplate the immeasurable void of America's hinterlands. It felt lonely and bereft, oppressive—in a way he'd never experienced and could scarcely put into words.

And every now and then he'd be forced to acknowledge the stunning beauty of it all.

Santa Fe was an immense relief, for he could finally get off the endless rails and dusty roads and away from the great emptiness. Bustling in an exotic clamor of languages and color, the capitol seemed like a foreign city. He could imagine himself to be in Mexico and hoped there might be a little time to explore.

But Frank Warner Angel did not come to sightsee. He'd come to untangle a riddle—the truth of what was happening in this *nether world*. Governor Axtell and Attorney General Catron would not help him, that much was clear, despite his Presidential seal. He saw the first day that the two highest ranking individuals in the territory would only obfuscate his task. Sleuthing out a lawyer and a U.S. Marshal in the Capitol who *were* willing to talk was an easier proposition. One led to the other, and they both painted a very clear picture indeed; Tom Catron sat in the middle of the portrait with his hand run up the back of a diminutive Governor Axtell like a ventriloquist, while he squashed everyone else with his giant rear-end.

When Warner finally arrived at Fort Stanton, Colonel Dudley provided another telling angle—one that sharply cut cattle baron John Chisum and the lawyer in an unflattering light. It all led to a key deposition in Lincoln of Alexander McSween. By the time the New Yorker was shown into McSween's home, he figured he'd arrived in the heart of the Gordian knot.

Warner sat quietly regarding the showy Scotsman, and listening to pleasantries while adjusting his mind and his tools. Angel's approach to the hard work of deposition is meditative. The words flow out like a parade of boats on a calm sea. You capture them one by one and in groups. Critical cognitive moments rarely lift above the fleet and only later does it settle into a narrative. But John Tunstall's case was different, in just about every way.

The real story had a way of emerging even as he was writing. It would tingle the back of his head, and after the jolt, he would sail on.

McSween talked for hours, or so it seemed to those waiting their turn in the parlor. Angel wrote every word, and even with McSween's practiced equivocations and self-serving invectives—the truth often peered out from behind the verbiage. The tingling caused him to stop on two separate occasions. Once for truth and once for falsehood.

And there was the odd young Irish cowboy, William Bonney, who seemed to be well-read and certainly well-spoken. His story was vivid, unflinching and unapologetic, peculiar and histrionic. It effused into the little room like a theatrical performance.

"A flock of turkeys cut the trail and if not for that, John might be still be alive. We followed the turkeys and the Boys were up top, waiting like vultures. Once we hit the rim they were on us—Buckshot Roberts spraying us with his Henry and the others charging up while Baker and Morton rode down on John. Mr. Tunstall was terribly sick with a cold, never had a chance. They shot him like he was some kind of rabbid dog, and him a highborn noble soul…killed his horse too, and a fine animal. And that is the first, last, and only time I will ever chase a turkey." The boy tried for his usual ironic quip but finished almost in tears, gathered himself, and then gave a straightforward and honest account of all the shootings that followed.

Most convincing of all was the story told by the red-headed boy named Tom O'Folliard. He claimed to have witnessed Tunstall's killing first hand and there was no mistaking the imprint of the real event. The boy grew, by turns, agitated, fearful, and distraught as he relived John Tunstall's appalling death. The eyes were steady, the emotions and gestures natural, the effect overwhelming, even to Angel's calloused ear and heart.

After a week of investigating in the infamous territory, and a full day of depositions in councilor McSween's office and before any perusal of his draft—Frank Angel was certain the extraordinary young Englishman had been murdered in cold blood by his competitors, and the legal response frozen from the top down. Tunstall had also very likely been manipulated and swindled by his own partners.

The New York lawyer politely declined McSween's offer to stay for supper and excused himself. Tomorrow he would cross the street and continue his work with Jimmy Dolan and Jesse Evans. For now he let it all go and walked south toward the Wortley hotel, massaging his wrist and nodding to the black troopers who marched in a protective phalanx around him. Amongst many other modern proclivities kept close to the vest, the New Yorker believed fervently in the equality of all men.

"I'd be delighted if you soldiers would join me at table."

A long column of citizens trundle along the south road from Lincoln under the hot morning sun. All felt a violent conclusion approaching and that Lincoln was no longer safe. Families packed into wagons, other folks on horseback and traveling light, some on foot and the womenfolk in a state of panic.

At breakfast that morning McSween received a fell warning; a horde of

Dolan men were coming for him—Peppin and Olinger and the Pecos river dregs returning like a plague of locusts. The news spread fast and hysteria gripped the town. Within an hour the exodus began.

"We'll have to stand and fight at some point, Mr. McSween," Mr. William Bonney confides. He'd been at the rear, joking around with Fred—one of two heroes of the cow camp battle—and jabbed their other champion, Doc, as he flew by.

"I'll choose the place and time if it comes to that, and I *will* be ready," McSween replies, pulling back his coat to reveal a shoulder holster and a colt resting within.

"Can you hit anything with that?"

Mac pulls the gun without hesitation and fires, smashing a distant piece of crockery and raising a smile on The Kid's face. "I firmly believe the federal investigation will clear all our names, and bring an end to the Ring... but we must stay on hand, and *alive,* to harvest those fruits."

"Amen to that."

"Frank Angel will be on his way back East by now," says Doc.

"I suspect it may be mid-summer or later before he actually delivers his report to the President," adds McSween. "And more time will pass before action is taken."

"I'm just glad I was...*we,* were right," Bonney allows, drawing a sharp look from both McSween and his wife, and from Doc.

"God willing, we'll reclaim property and resume our normal lives before the snow flies—but for now, we must be evasive—and on the defensive. I *will not* be arrested again," McSween concludes.

"I pray they leave our home unviolated while we...skedaddle," Susan replies, the bitterness in her voice unmistakable. "And my sister and her family, will they be safe while we go into hiding?"

"Elizabeth and David and the girls, and Zebrion—are all non-combatants and will be much safer there than they would be traipsing after us. It's *we* who are in danger, and who would in turn endanger them."

"And these people in San Patricio, do they know I'm coming as well? You know I am not well-liked amongst the natives."

"Do not work yourself up, you will be welcome and really Susan, we've already argued all of this," McSween states, growing increasingly uncomfortable with his wife's public umbrage.

With a nod to Doc, The Kid drifts back and away from the McSweens and their domestic complexities. There were many troubles and secrets there, and The Kid had his suspicions—about the insurance settlement that seemed to be at the heart of things, and also about that wily old buzzard, uncle John Chisum.

While he waited to be deposed, he'd listened to McSween's oration—and on many another occasion as well—going back to when Tunstall gave him the cardigan and they'd gone next door for dinner. Little by little he'd worked out the lawyer's angle.

The Kid knew McSween was playing them all. But then, he was running a similar game. His plan was grandiose but divided neatly into two halves; redemption for John and fame for himself. There was no question of his admiration and fealty toward the murdered Englishman, but the story had also become a great iron-hulled sailing ship, a four-masted windjammer heading out to sea with him aboard as first mate. And even with the intervention of the President of the United States—it would most likely be a narrow divide between life and death.

And it all suited him perfectly.

Colonel Dudley had settled into life at Fort Stanton with lubricated ease. The staff was a quality group, the accommodations were good, and he'd grown to truly appreciate his regiment of the 9th.

The flow of whiskey into his quarters was steady and strong, a game could always be gotten up amongst his officers—and the air in this high meadow cooled at night most pleasingly. Boredom and the endless grind of routine were the real enemies here. And each man fought that quiet and desperate war in his own way.

There was plenty of local trouble amongst the merchants and farmers and gun thugs and Apaches, but he doubted he would ever be required to ride forth through the gates. Though a campaign of some sort would be good for him—knock the worst kinks out and put some starch back in his uniform.

But the likelihood of a campaign arriving to save him from himself was remote in the extreme. Especially with the special order that had just arrived from Washington and lay on his desk. The Posse Comitatus Act just signed by President Hayes and telegraphed to all Western outposts had changed the landscape significantly.

The colonel looks up from his desk as his adjutant enters, his office smelling of bourbon and cigar smoke. Lieutenant Pelham ignores the saloon atmospherics with an officious air.

"Excuse me Colonel, Sheriff (uhum) Peppin is here with a...posse, and asking for an audience with you. He has another arrest warrant for McSween."

"The rascal has impeccable timing at least," says Colonel Dudley, leaning back in his chair and chuckling. "I will see the sheriff, he's about to get the latest news from Washington."

The commanding officer emerges from headquarters and walks out under the sun, crossing the quadrangle under a deep blue sky. Sheriff Peppin and a motley assortment of thugs and deputies mill about under a shade tree at the edge of Fort Stanton's disciplined angles.

"That's the goddamned commanding officer," Caleb hisses.

"Attention ladies," Ed Hart replies.

"You two shut up," Kinney barks out. Peppin fidgets and the colonel adjusts his battered top hat. They all make a ragged attempt to stand at parade rest—most of them had done a stint in the military at some point in their roughhewn lives.

Kinney had seen the most service; eight years in the Army and mustered out at rank of sergeant. For reasons known only to himself, he had departed that honorable and ordered way of life—completely.

"Thank you for seeing us Colonel, we have a pressing legal matter to attend to and...and need your help," Peppin stammers out.

"Yes. I've been apprised of your warrant, and your mission," the colonel replies. He begins to walk along the line of ragtags, as if inspecting his own troops and stopping for a moment in front of Olinger—the only man there who stood taller.

"You should see a barber," says Dudley. He continues the inspection, as if it amused him to see what sorry shape they were all in. He gives particular attention to John Kinney, taking a step closer. The worn careening hat, the stubbled face, the tattered black frock coat, and the notched shotgun come under scrutiny.

"I believe they call you Colonel Kinney," Dudley asks eye to eye.

"Yes sir, they do, sometimes."

"But you're no colonel, are you?"

"No, in point of fact...but I was a sergeant," Kinney admits, sounding like he'd once had leprosy. The thick smell of alcohol wafts unmistakable from Colonel Dudley and the ersatz colonel grins slightly.

"Sheriff Peppin," Dudley sounds, turning back to the sheriff. "I see you are already well-supplied with men and arms, and obviously require no help."

"But I was told you wou—"

"I don't give a damn what you were told," the colonel interrupts. "You can go back and tell Mr. Dolan that Congress has just passed the Posse Comitatus Act—wherein federal military personnel are expressly forbidden to intervene in civil affairs. My hands are now tied and I can be of no further help to you."

"Mr. Dolan's gone to Mesilla for a few days, but I'll sure tell him when he gets back."

"You do that Sheriff. Now, take this mangy bunch of barn rats and get off my quadrangle."

"Peppin looks like he just shit his pants," Caleb whispers to Ed Hart.

Kinney and his men leave Fort Stanton in bad form a second time and the sheriff is silent the rest of the morning. Peppin hated to admit what a sorry lawman he'd thus far been. Had they simply ridden to town instead of Fort Stanton, they might well have caught McSween mid-flight and brought the matter to a close. But the town had emptied well before their arrival, and he began to dread having to explain everything to Dolan and Evans.

Peppin was deeply indebted to Jimmy Dolan, and he *was* grateful—but he hated him for it at the same time. A man named Hilario Jaramilla had insulted and crossed Dolan one time too many, and Dolan simply pulled out his pistol one day and killed him. Jaramilla's sixteen-year-old wife, Lina—caretaker of Peppin's children, was thus freed to marry the widowed deputy.

His first wife died in childbirth and he'd loved her certainly, but nothing like the obsessive passion he felt for Lina. She was a child herself and between her shifting moods, Dolan lording it over him, the faltering attempt at a second career in law enforcement and the murder of his real boss, Sheriff Brady—Peppin had become a highly conflicted man.

The vacated state of affairs in Lincoln suited John Kinney well enough though. He set up camp behind the House and made himself right at home. After all that time down on the Pecos, he decided right off that it was high time for an extended holiday. Dolan had offered him a five hundred dollar bounty for McSween and he'd accepted the job. But the Scotsman would only come in his own good time, that was clear, and he'd be happy to wait.

At three that afternoon the colonel is drunk as a lord and ordering the men to round up some victuals. Kinney knew how to play an imperator and the ragtags jumped readily when he barked. A smokehouse and root cellar are summarily broken into. Pickles, tomatoes, sugared apples, and a cured ham are brought forth and laid before the king.

A loose and disheveled kind of monarch for certain, but there is no question of Kinney's absolute authority. Traces of a former military life could still be heard in his voice, and traces of his own eccentric brand of madness showed up in oft-repeated phrases.

"Sufficient unto the day," Kinney intoned, after a loud belch. His men understood perfectly, he'd said this often enough. A few roll their eyes and others grin.

Peppin is quick to tip the jug himself. The responsibilities of life and office being onerous and the supply of spirits a sure thing—just like rolling down hill to the river for a swim. Besides, what else could be done about McSween at the moment?

It was a thought that grew less and less important, as the amber poured over his wounded pride—like honey on a bee sting, like a drowsing anodyne on a sleepless mind—drifting him on and on to the edge and over the falls.

The posse split into two factions; those who sailed off down river with the colonel, and those who stayed behind to mind the store. Olinger sat watching Peppin and Kinney like he meant to stop it at first, but in the end jumped in and went down river himself.

Caleb and Ed sat on the bank a long while, taking sociable drinks and watching bemused as Peppin drank himself into a stupor. The colonel told black-hearted stories, they rolled bones, several fights broke out and random shots were fired into the air.

Peppin was quiet all day. But at sunset he began to talk of the big store—he'd built it by god, along with just about every other building in town. If the damn thing had four walls and a roof he'd hammered and mudded it into existence.

"Hell, you ain't got no business being sheriff. Go back to being a carpenter and put up a goddamned proper saloon," Pecos Bob suggests while helping himself to a large pickle.

And the boys from Texas thought of settling things with Olinger, if the right moment of weakness presented itself. He'd started in on throwing the knife, moved on to the bones, pushing everyone with that knurly attitude of his and the colonel watching it all with recusant delight.

They waited until Olinger was a good three sheets to the wind before coming at him, high and low. Ed is tall and long-armed and Caleb shorter with thick biceps and both brawlers of the first cut. To the delight of all those loafing about, the fight is a vicious one. But Pecos seemed to expect it—he moved as if suddenly fully sober. The blackjack came out and he wheeled and gouged and swung with precision. Perhaps he'd only baited them into thinking he was far gone. Either way, after this adventure Ed Hart and the Prowler knew fists alone would not get the job done.

"Damn Pecos, you didn't need to go so easy on us," Caleb says after spitting blood and leaning up on an elbow. He shoved Ed to make sure his partner wasn't laid out permanent.

"Next time I pull the knife," Pecos assures him. He'd taken some heavy blows as well, but avoided the ones that might have done real harm—finally taking the big man out with blackjack and Caleb with a single hook. His work concluded, a hearty pull of the jug and a shake of his greasy mane as Kinney nods and Eddie Camber rocks back and forth on his haunches.

Later on, Ed and Caleb discuss making a move on Kinney, as Selman had ordered them to do—but decided to let things play out for now. There was plenty of time yet and they'd been bested once already.

The night was a long and unbridaled frolic. Revels continued by firelight and there seemed no end to it, until men finally spun off into the dark to drop and puke and deliver themselves over to the current.

"Hey boss, wake up. We ought to go scout out San Patricio," Deputy John Long yells, trying to roust Peppin the next morning. He'd not gone home to Lina and the kids, she was mad at him, or had been yesterday morning.

"Goddamnit...let me sleep."

"McSween and the Regulators are holed up over there," says Long. The deputy had kept his head and intended to mind the store.

"Go take a look then, see if you can arrest the son-of-a-bitch. I ain't going nowhere but back to sleep. I done earned some time off," Peppin declares. He rolls over and a few moments later a rumbling snore starts up again. Long shakes his head and leaves Peppin to his torment.

"Well, I'm heading on to San Patricio. Most of this posse has temporarily gone loco and I guarantee when Dolan and Evans get back there'll be sweet hell to pay. We best pull up the slack," Deputy Long barks out to the few ragtags who'd not lost their minds.

"Lead on, oh sober one. We're right behind you," Caleb sings out from under his frayed bowler. One eye is blackened and another tooth is missing, but these are but minor inconveniences. The Texans are firmly riveted on a longer and bigger game and a day soon when all accounts will be settled.

Jim French had seen to it that pickets were in place; on the road, over the mountain and in the hills ringing the main camp. At ten in the morning

Charlie comes racing up the trail with news of a small force advancing. Within moments the Regulators are mounted and riding out.

"Something is busted here. I don't see Peppin, nor Kinney, nor Olinger. That's just John Long and a little bunch a raggedy ass river rats," Charlie surmises. A minute passes while the two confederacies size each other up across a large field.

"We got these boys outnumbered two to one." William Bonney chimes in with a laugh, pulling his Winchester from the scabbard.

"What do you men want?" McSween yells through cupped hands.

"To arrest you Mr. McSween, I have a proper warrant."

"You'll serve no warrant today Deputy Long, now turn your men around and leave!"

Bonney dismounts and pushes the riffle into the fork of a little oak. His careful aim gives way and Long feels a tug on the crown of his hat. A burst of firing echoes through the little valley, bracketing the field with smoke.

Long's horse reared with the first shot and would not settle, forcing the deputy to dismount. His animal goes down when a bullet strays into its neck. The deputy runs back and forth a couple of times, not sure what to do, the others firing back across the field of beans.

"We cain't do no good here," says Ed Hart.

"We done what we could, let's clear out, goddamnit," yells the Prowler. Deputy Long looks at his wounded sorrel a moment before putting it out of its misery. Then taking a hand he clambers up behind Caleb.

"Hey you horsekillin bastards, you can kiss my dirty asshole." Caleb shouts riding away.

"Well that didn't amount to much," Jim French allows, disappointed.

"They'll be back, twice as many next time," says Charlie.

"Much as I love San Patricio, we should not stay here, not a good place for a general engagement," Bonney adds as he returns the Winchester to its scabbard.

"I agree, I had hoped to stay close—but it's untenable. We head down to the Southspring and Chisum this afternoon," McSween says, exasperated.

"Now that's a hell of a Fort, we can hold down there as long as we need to," Fred yells out.

"And there's Sallie Chisum to bake pies and keep us company," William Bonney chimes in.

Colonel Kinney's holiday has reached the opening hours of its glorious third day. He loved nothing better than to sit in a comfortable chair and tilt the jug. Down at Seven Rivers he often had the jug and the thirst but never the chair. Sometimes it was unquenchable, and the drink went down like water on a fire that could not be tamed. On those days it felt as though the amber were an essential element he'd been deprived of forever and at long last it stood in copious supply.

The chair he'd found on a porch the day before. The colonel appropriated the old rocker forthwith—setting it in the shade of a little scrub oak. Coming up on Eddie Camber sleeping in his chair that morning, he'd unceremoniously dumped the little fellow out and reclaimed his throne. Eddie was always somewhere underfoot, drowsing in the shade and waiting for his next supply run. He kept the boss plied with reading material, correspondence, pornography, hop, Turkish tobacco, bacon and canned goods—among other needful things. He also occasionally barbered the men and babied the livestock. Colonel Kinney thought him irreplaceable.

He looked at Eddie and winked and then sat all the last hour of the morning admiring the day and the pleasant little village spread out around him. Deputy Long found him there, reclining and smoking with a jug in his lap and smile on his face. Long was of a mind to follow the Regulators down to the Southspring Ranch and challenge them. Colonel Kinney just looked at him quizzically.

"I admire your pluck Deputy Long, but challenging those men at the Southspring is a fool's errand. What does the sheriff say?" Kinney asks.

"Peppin don't say nothing, he's snoring like an old man and refuses to wake."

"Sleeping the sleep of the just. Let him catch his breath Deputy Long, we have time."

"Well I'm going down to the eyebrow and run those bastards down if I can, maybe catch'em before they fort up."

"Son, you ought to just sit here in the shade with me and have a drink, we'll watch the day go by and tell lies."

"No sir, I cannot in good faith do that."

"Never chase too far after stupid," another choice truism. "Cost you every time, besides—you wait long enough it'll come find ya," the colonel finishes with a wink.

John Long had walked two steps behind Sheriff Brady, when the same men he chased now fired from behind the big wall. One of the shots spattered Brady's life blood on his face. Deputy Long tried to drag the sheriff off but his courage failed him during the second barrage. He scrambled to safety and figured he'd hear the sheriff crying out 'Oh Lord', for the rest of his life. Well he'd be damned if the Regulators would make any more a fool of him than they already had.

Thick adobe walls and a curtain-walled parapet make John Chisum's Southspring ranch an ideal place to defend, and a ridiculous position to storm. Deputy Long and his dregs arrive a day behind the McSweenmen, and sure enough, are stalemated as soon as they arrive.

"What the hell's become of Peppin and Kinney? It's just Long and that same bunch of idiots," Jim French offers, wondering about the opposing chain of command. Their view from the roof is commanding.

"Go easy on the poor fellow. Deputy Long is studying to be a half-wit," Fred yells and out comes the tongue.

"Hey Deputy Long, stop following us around if you please. Could be bad for your health," William Bonney shouts, before placing a rifle shot within an few inches of his head.

"Are you gentleman hungry?" Sallie Chisum yells up from the courtyard below.

"We are always hungry Miss Sallie," The Kid answers back. "I'm sure sorry for all the bullet holes they're putting in your home."

"Doesn't matter a jot, just make Uncle John build the new ranch all the quicker."

"I sure wish your Uncle John was here—what happened to him, exactly? We could sure use a real general...say, why don't you take over," Mr. Bonney offers this with a flirtatious grin, and Sallie flashes back a *real* smile.

"He's seeing to an ailment, acute thrombophlebitis it's called, according to the medical book. He's gone all the way to St. Louis for an operation, and I believe he has complete faith in Mr. McSween in his absence," Sallie says. "Now y'all come on down in shifts, soups on!"

When Chisum's prized niece disappears inside, a discussion of the supposed ailment flares up. Jim French notes that Chisum seemed to always be absent when trouble starts.

"A flea bit me to, but I ain't sailing off to St. Louie," Charlie says with a smirk.

"Well, if he has what she said. It ain't no damn joke. I do remember Frank saying the last time he spoke with Uncle John, his leg was swollen up like a tick. Phlebitis is a problem with the veins, they get clamped down and plugged and the leg just blows up. If that's what he has, I sure don't envy that long trip to St Louis," says Doc, surprised to find himself defending his longtime nemesis, and employer.

Their relationship was fraught with disagreements. Doc quit once over unpaid wages and because he'd lost his taste for killing to protect the range. Gone all the way to Arizona and Chisum sent four men to bring him back, partly because Doc had taken some prized horses in lieu of wages. But Chisum ultimately paid him off, settled their dispute, and convinced him to stay—Doc Scurlock was that valuable and Chisum that persuasive.

At sunset a light cloud of dust appears where the posse had last been seen. They all wondered what the hell would come next.

"Gentleman, Deputy Long has apparently accepted defeat once again," McSween allows, with pride. Mac had joined them on the parapet after lunch and did his share of popping away at the enemy.

Long and his men had spent the day riding completely around the hacienda, firing from what advantages in the landscape they could find. But never came close to doing anything but making fools of themselves, again.

Jimmy Dolan and Jesse Evans were gone for a week and the road back to Lincoln seemed longer than usual. They had accomplished their objective in Mesilla and should both be lighter in mood than they were. The Giant freed them of legal jeopardy, and also contributed generously to Dolan's war chest.

They'd sat in a public hearing and been absolved, after a fashion. It was decided that both men were many miles away at the time and place of John Tunstall's death; or rather, it could not be proven otherwise—and Judge Bristol dismissed the case against them.

But they were other worries to consider, matters at right angles to the conflict. And both men felt in their gut that things had gone badly in their absence. The town near empty when they arrive and they expected that, but they weren't expecting to find Colonel Kinney holding court.

He sat in a rocker behind the House like some drunken backwoods potentate. His men lolled about as if bewitched and Peppin was nowhere to be seen. Long sat in the shade, a mist over his eyes and shoulders in a dejected shrug. Eddie Camber had a little fire going and Olinger leaned against the stout adobe wall of the House acting as if he had no part in any of it.

Dolan and Evans dismount and look the yard over, saying nothing.

What had happened was all too plain to see. And the colonel smiling at them like he held all the cards.

Jimmy unlocks the back door and goes inside, leaving Jesse to deal with the river rats.

"Jesse, it's been a while," says the colonel, the scatter gun resting across his lap.

"Don't suppose you've ended the war while we were away?"

"No I haven't, but sitting here...I *have* seen its conclusion," says the colonel, as if he'd somehow become an augur of the future.

"I don't recall you being a seer," Jesse replies, about as dry as tomb dust.

"Things have changed," says the colonel, taking a long pull.

"I doubt that, old habits betray you."

"You know the saddest thing about betrayal—never comes from your enemies."

Kinney hands the jug to his old partner with a nod. Jesse looks at him a good while, the colonel not looking away. Evans finally juts his chin up and tips the jug.

Dolan's head is about to explode. If only a great chasm would open up to swallow McSween and end this goddamned silly boondoggle of a war. The Regulators had turned into a crack fighting unit, despite losing Brewer and McNab. And his own force reduced to this sorry laughingstock of drunken half-wits. The Indian shot dead as well. And the people of the county—firmly in McSween's camp.

His thoughts turn to San Patricio—the safe haven—and a new plan of retribution begins to take shape. Those people had protected the Regulators from the start; fed them, hidden them and informed them. Downing a full glass, it comes to him that the little pueblo would pay for their treason.

"Well...at least these shitbirds kept themselves close at hand. They ain't much but there'll all we've got," says Jesse. He'd just entered Dolan's office and sat down with a heavy sigh.

"I'm about to put them to work. We are riding to San Patricio first thing tomorrow."

"McSween and his men aren't there."

"It's about time that town gets a comeuppance, just the same."

Jesse nods, but the idea doesn't set well with him. Maria knew a family there who would take Rosa. She could already have gone, but the girl refused to leave Lincoln. Rosa had proved herself a great help to Maria and a comfort to Captain Murphy.

"We don't need to kill anybody," says Jesse.

"No, we won't kill anybody, but we *will* raise hell."

The next morning Dolan and the horde descend on San Patricio with a cruel set. Under his loose direction, they spread out and begin a kind of joyous ransacking. Doors are ripped off hinges, precious household items thrown into the street, furniture broken up and destroyed, livestock shot, outbuildings fired, the townspeople abused.

It was Dolan's retribution and another day of fun for the Seven Rivers gang. Evans sat his horse and watched, the screams from one end of the village to the other irritating his sense of logic. He spurs forward.

Caleb and Ed cornered Adelita behind her Tia Monce's little casa. She'd been sent that morning to help Tia cure a batch of Chokecherry. They'd kicked the door open and fixated on the girl straight off, chasing her out the back while Tia Monce ran screaming for help out the front.

"Aint she a little angel," Caleb says, leering.

"Prettiest thing I've seen, maybe ever," Ed says in agreement.

The two have her pinned when Jesse reigns up and dismounts. He walks up behind swinging his pistol in a vicious arc—knocking Ed Hart to the side then pointing it straight at Caleb's nose.

"Get your partner up and go back in the street with the others."

"Yessir boss, don't mind us. Just having a look-see." Caleb tries a smile, but it came out more a leering snarl. Jesse looks past Caleb pulling the big man up on his feet, to the girl scrabbling away.

"*Lo siento, Señora.*"

July rain beat down at midnight on the largest mounted body of partisans yet mustered in Lincoln County. They number sixty heavily armed and angry men winding along toward a showdown.

Dolan's play in San Patricio was the final straw for everyone. The sacking of San Patricio sent a shockwave up and down the Hondo Valley and a large host of locals joined McSween and the Regulators overnight.

Sick of running, of sleeping on the ground with one eye open, of being hunted and outlawed and bedeviled and trifled with—the Regulators are done with their waiting game. McSween ordered them on to Lincoln to settle matters once and for all and the huzzah could have torn a roof off. But on the way up mountain from the Chisum ranch there had been only one discussion of a battle plan—if it could be called that.

Thunder rumbles prodigiously and a peppering rain coming down in sheets. Tom O'Folliard has his head dipped, water pouring off the brim of his hat. His normal buoyancy all but drowned in the deluge, he looks up as The Kid comes riding alongside. He wonders if they'll survive the coming fight.

"Wet enough for you, Mr. Bonney?" asks Tom, a good-natured smile attempting to play on his water streamed face.

"Hell yes, wet enough to bog a snipe." The laughing grin only widens as he moves on, visiting briefly with everyone along the dripping, bedraggled line—lifting spirits in English, and in Spanish.

"*Otro vez.*"

"Yep. Maybe *el ultimo*?" Charlie answers back. The Kid nods and rides on.

"Hey Indian killer, loaded for bear?"

Fred replies with the grin and the gesture.

"Always good to see the Coe's! How's the hand George?" Frank dips his head and hat, directing a stream of water in The Kid's direction. George Coe raises his right hand, the stumped finger a prominent feature now.

"Doc, what say you?"

"Dolan can kiss my ass, and I think Frank was right about you...your name *should* be Billy the Kid."

"I know it's everyone's favorite."

"You have to accept certain things in this hard life," Doc replies and Billy the Kid smiles back at him with a cluck of the tongue.

"Hey Jim, give us some West Point wisdom."

"This idea of coming in at night merely to fort up is poor battlefield logic, mighty poor. Our best chance is to ride in like Phil Sheridan and run'em down," Jim French answers back, his tone far less jocular. "The element of surprise."

"Surely you mean like Jeb Stuart," Doc says.

"No I am not talking about Jeb Stuart, that man was one for fancy riding and feathers and music. So said my tactics instructor at the Point, and he should know, he spent a lot of time chasing after the son-of-a bitch," Jim answers back quickly.

"How about Nathan Bedford Forest then? Now there was a man for bloody work," Charlie yells up at them, through the rain.

"Amen."

"Right, we should be charging in guns ablaze and surprise the hell out of them," Billy the Kid declares. "Believe I'll have a talk with Mac."

But McSween was firm in not attacking straight off. They'd settle into redoubts at the McSween home, the Monsano store in mid-town, the Ellis store at the southern edge of town, and occupy the high ground with the old stone toreon. Once their defensive works were completed, hopefully by morning, he would consider their next move.

The raging tempest felt like a premonition and they all tried hard not to fall under a Judas spell. The Kid's heartening ride up the line helped, but it took the full moon sailing out like the god of war—to banish their fears.

McSween's army quietly debouched onto the muddied streets of Lincoln in the middle of the night. As hoped, the Kinney roughs were dead to the world.

But the sloughing and sucking of hooves and the creak and rattle of sixty saddles disturbed Rosa, awakening her from a nightmare. She listens for a moment, realizing an army has arrived, before rushing to the window and looking out into the night. Then her bare feet out the door and running to the little house back toward the bluff, the window open and in like a cat. He seems unsurprised to see her face above his.

"*Muchos hombres, muchos pistoleros!*"

Jesse rolls out of bed and to the window, quickly into his pants and pulling on boots, thinking. He gives her a look, as if to say—you've saved my ass *again*.

"Well goddammit, I can't believe that shyster has the balls to ride down on us here. What'n hell is his play?" says Dolan, rubbing his face.

"They're fortin up."

"Considering more than half our men are gone, that would not be my play."

"He's being cautious."

"And the toreón?"

"Empty."

Like any cool-headed battlefield strategist in a tight spot, Evans sees immediately what must be done: "This fight is at least a stalemate if we can get men up on the toreón right now. That position is the only thing that matters."

13

"Makes no sense to me whatsoever. It's a damned cowardly amateur move. We should be attacking right *now*," Jim French grouses through clenched teeth.

They move through the tall grass down along the river, horses at the large stable behind the Ellis redoubt and friends ahead in the McSween compound.

"I agree—but that ain't the only problem," replies Billy the Kid, frowning toward the toreón. There's a noisy rabble up in the street. He's quickly out of the river bottom for a better look, the others close behind.

"Well shit," Jim whispers.

The toreon stands one hundred yards away, clearly visible under the shining moon. Scrambling straight for it is a well-armed group of ragtags. Each man running with as much in the way of guns and supplies he can carry; dropping some of it as they go and all staggering like the drunken half-asleep mob they are, but taking possession of the stone tower nonetheless.

"Fuckin shite. There goes the high ground. We're about to lose this fight before it even starts," The Kid sighs out, throwing a rock back into the river.

"I reckon they weren't quite as drunk and worthless and dead to the world as we counted on," Tom admits, shaking his head.

The three continue on through the grass, scrabbling up the steep embankment behind McSween's home, through the gate of an encircling log fence and into the sheltering arms of the U-shaped fortress.

The inner courtyard and three wings of the McSween house are buzzing with activity in the middle of the night; two men filling a water barrel to the brim, another three shoveling old flour sacks full of dirt and sand, others stacking the redoubts before the windows, still more drilling loopholes along the thick-walled galleries, the last bunch hunkered down over the guns and munitions.

Counting McSween, Zebrion, and a small group of regulators and hispanico partisans, there are thirteen men to defend the home. Women and children are also present—Mrs. McSween and her sister Elizabeth, and Susan's seven-year-old niece Minnie, and five-year-old nephew Joe.

The little girl is standing in her nightclothes sucking two middle fingers and watching the preparations with a concerned little face. Her mother, opening the kitchen door, discovers Minnie is outside amid all the commotion.

"Minnie, what are you doing out of bed? Listen, you mustn't be frightened by these men. They are here to help Uncle Alex and Auntie Susan, and us. Now back to sleep with you," her mother Emily commands, and with a gentle pat she takes her young sleepwalker by the hand.

On their way to the bedrooms they pass the office, where The Kid and Jim French confront McSween. Minnie looks at them with big curious eyes and The Kid doffs his hat with a comical grin.

"Hello Minnie, how's my little princess?" Billy the Kid bowing low and the little girl giggles as she's led away.

"With them in the tower, commanding the street north and south, we'll be penned inside these walls!" Jim declares. Alex is staring over the highest bag stacked in the south-facing window, at the toreón rising just above the Tunstall store next door, confronting another seemingly insurmountable issue.

"Jim, and Mr. Bonney, or is it Kid Antrim today, or Billy the Kid, or whatever, how about your real name, Henry. Listen, I appreciate these insights, but I have everything under control. I own that property—both the toreón and the house, I will begin by issuing an eviction notice to my tenants," says McSween.

Mac turns back to the sandbagged window. The kid exchanges a doubtful glance with Jim and offers a sideways gesture with his hand. Jim nods back.

America races exuberantly ahead of the wide world in the winter and spring of 1878; the first switchboard for telephone service was installed in New York City during January, Edison patents the phonograph and the light bulb in February, women's suffrage is introduced to Congress, soprano Marie Selika Williams becomes the first African-American to perform at the White House, Henry James publishes his groundbreaking novel of feminine innocence and experience—*Daisy Miller*—all before summer arrives.

President Hayes proves to be an independent, reformist president—intent on weeding out the rampant corruption of the post-Civil War years, both in the industrial East and the frontier West. The industrial machine continues to grow and America strides brightly to the fore, but a darkness drags along underneath the great engine.

Those same months have passed in Lincoln County like an intricate feverish nightmare—corruption and violence a living breathing succubus and the range war a national sensation. Journalists scribble in ever more heated rhetoric and the world writ large looks forward to each new development with guilty excitement.

Sheriff Peppin swam in the river often, had been to the bottom and threatened to never come up. But struggled now to reassert himself as the sober man in charge, a man to be reckoned with. He'd not let Dolan, or Evans, or Colonel Dudley, or Colonel Kinney push and shame him. He was his own man.

Still, he hesitated when Dolan urged him to serve a warrant as an opening move. He called for Deputy Long, thinking it prudent to send him instead.

"Mr. McSween, I have a warrant for you and your men. I ask you to come out, peacefully, along with all those within, and surrender," Deputy Long announces.

"I refuse to recognize the legitimacy of any warrant," McSween roars back at the hapless deputy, the burr and the courtroom voice hitting him like a blow.

"Deputy Long is truly pathetic, I feel sorry for him...all the damn snipe hunts he's been sent on," Tom allows and the others assent.

"Deputy Long you are the top man for lost causes," The Kid shouts.

A sudden burst of laughter and small arms fire puts the deputy to flight. They only meant to chase him off though. In his own way, Deputy Long had been successful—he'd been adopted by the Regulators.

The first long daylight hours of the battle for Lincoln quickly turn relentless and heated, with hundreds of rounds exchanged. An angry hail of bullets thud against the adobe walls of the McSween fortress; some ripping through the sand-bagged windows, scattering mayhem and, in an adjoining room, winging a man who'd chosen the wrong moment to move to the right.

His blood spatters onto an elegantly framed etching, and a second later another ricocheting bullet rips through the painted flowers of the music stand atop the pianoforte, and into the wall behind, dusting plaster onto the wounded man and vibrating the piano strings into an otherworldly hum.

The Kid shakes his head and grimaces, hating to see both man and instrument harmed in one lucky blast. Mrs. McSween responds with an anguished scream. The angry bullets were awful, but it was the destruction of fine things that made her crazy most of all.

"During the next lull, we move the piano, and the pictures," Susan yells out.

"And let's strengthen the redoubt, no more cheap shots by god," barks McSween.

A hardened group of Regulators are present—The Kid, Tom, and Jim, and a tough group of natives, including his friend from jail, Ygenio Salazar. All look to Henry, if not yet for leadership, certainly for morale, as they fire through portholes.

Even in the heat of this tight spot, Billy the Kid is as cool and amusing as if they were on a picnic.

"Did you know, the greatest chicken-killer in all of Shakespeare was Macbeth...and why you might well ask?" The Kid pauses in the hot work for a theatrical grin and gesture. "Because he did murder *most foul*."

A ripple of laughter crosses the room. The bravest men guffawing and the more rattled among them at least distracted. Even Susan is forced to a smile.

"How can you always be so cheerful Mr. Bonney?" Susan asks, far from cheerful herself.

"Mother taught me to always choose happy, it's the best way to be, and it drives your enemies mad."

Her husband is numb to The Kid's jestering good spirits and beginning to slide into an uncharacteristic self-doubting malaise.

"I should well have seen to the toreón before we entered Lincoln, should have sent men ahead. Never ask a question you don't know the answer to." He continues rambling and muttering to himself as Susan watches from the next room, tears beginning to roll down her face again. Through the smoke and clamor, Susan knows her husband is close to a breaking point, though she'd never seen one before. But now that their cherished oasis is the anvil of a raging firestorm and all their efforts at an impasse—she could see that a breaking point was coming certain as the dawn.

Susan McSween had passed through a terrible firestorm once many years before, and she'd hoped to never feel such heat ever again. Her childhood was spent a few short miles from Gettysburg, and Susan McSween had discovered the terror of a great battle firsthand.

In the mid-summer of 63' an unending stream of blue flowed by her front porch, arousing the feisty teenage beauty into a state of intoxication. Regiment upon regiment of fine-looking men in uniform; gallant plumed officers proudly sitting their horses and waving, flags flying, guns bristling—all of it shinning in the midsummer haze.

But then the fight started.

Guns bellowed day and night, the ground shook, acrid smoke drifted over the fields in a continuous heave, horses and men ran for their lives, horrific trains of the wounded could be seen from the porch, and finally, an unbearable stench soaked into the ground like some unspeakable curse.

There was a war inside Susan's home as well, and the dreadful battle without unhinged matters there into a state of chaos. She ran from her buttoned-up family in the aftermath and hadn't returned in fourteen years. And now the chaos and the terror had found her again.

"You'd think you were born on a battlefield Mr. Bonney," the woman of the house states crisply.

"No ma'am, I wasn't...but my father sure enough died on one. He marched to the biggest battle of the War. His bones are at Gettysburg." This stated proudly.

Susan McSween's eyes wrench up from the floor, and the boy in her parlor with a rifle jammed through a loophole—seems to stand in an entirely new light.

"I grew up a few miles from Gettysburg, we sat through that whole nightmare in our basement," Mrs. McSween replies softly.

Now it was William Bonney's turn and he suddenly stops firing, swiveling his handsome face toward Mrs. McSween—the first unguarded look she'd seen from him. He suddenly seemed like a lost child to her.

Directly across from the McSween home, in a commandeered home crowded with Dolan patriots and conscripts, Bob Olinger enjoys himself in his usual way—keeping up another stream of jeering taunts slung out across the street like a piss pot of slops.

"Too bad about the demise of the mighty Dick Brewer, an embarrassing way to fall in battle. I hear ole Buckshot took off the top of his head clean as a whistle, like to have seen that."

"Dick Brewer was ten times the man you'll ever be," Billy the Kid answers back.

"So shit stain, you're famous. Sure don't know why. The papers make you out to be some kind a goddamned demon boy bandit *man* killer. I say your just a worthless little nibbler and I'm gonna shoot your skinny ass running for the hills. What will the papers say then?" Olinger yells, giving his long greasy hair a futile shake.

Evans looks at him with disgust, thinking he'd like to bash his skull in—just to shut him up—there was something about his voice that made you want to smash your fist into his windpipe.

"Gallant William Bonney, bushwhacked by loudmouth shitheel Bob Olinger," Billy the Kid yells out, as if reading a headline. Olinger spits and looks away and Evans begins to grin.

"You're gonna fucking get whats comin to ya Kid. You will not leave here alive."

"You aren't scaring anyone Pecos Bob. You might as well save your breath for the next slice of humble pie. I'll be feeding it to you before long."

On it went, fusillade following fusillade, insult after insult, with an exhausting regularity. Men on both sides of the street rolling their eyes as Olinger and The Kid continue their war of words.

McSween had moved Dr. Ealy and his family into Tunstall building next door, two months before, and they huddle now in the Englishman's private quarters trying to ignore the profanity and the bullets. Armored shutters drawn, a lamp burning—he and his family kneel in devout prayer.

The curious murmur of it soft against the violent storm just outside.

The first day finally came to an end; with prayers and a last round of unnerving, rippling gunfire rolling up and down the length of the battlefield.

There were two casualties; one horse and a mule.

The McSweenmen, in their three strongholds, outnumbered Dolan's ranchers and hard-drinking river rats and were better marksmen. The Regulators are spread out evenly; a hard knot in the McSween compound, another three with the natives loaded for bear in the Montano store, and the rest ensconced in the solid Ellis store redoubt.

There was a similarly loose command structure on the other side; Evans directing traffic across from the McSween house, Peppin in charge opposite the Ellis redoubt, and Deputy Long struggling to counter the Montano store rifles. Five ragtags held the toreon while Dolan wandered about in a constant drunken snit, worrying about it all like a mother over a threatened brood.

It was a battle for and across the one street of Lincoln and McSween enjoyed the upper hand, after a fashion. Their marksmanship was beginning to tell for certain—no one would be advancing on them. But neither could they advance against the Kinney ragtags. And Dolan's forces were slowly multiplying.

Ed Hart and the Prowler went to the tower the night of McSween's arrival, along with three others. After being kicked awake by Evans, they'd stumbled across the street at a comic double time. And now their sunbaked perch held a kind of precarious balance over the fray.

Councilor McSween's hopeless attempt to evict the toreon defenders by means of legal threats had come to nothing—and another long day begins to slip by under the irritable eyes of the towermen.

"Next time you see Olinger on his way to take a shit, put one up his backside for me," Caleb pleads. "I am losing all patience with that greasy shit stain. I'd just as soon hear Gabriel's horn as another word outa his sorry mouth. Suffers from diarrhea of the jawbone."

"Packing a load a moldy hay to go with it," Ed adds.

"I get it, you two fellers don't care for Pecos Bob. No one does. What about the bastards we're shootin at?" asks Dan Brooks, a Kinney rough since the old days. He'd grown sick of these two jackals and their constant scheming. Being close quartered with them for days was like sharing a den with a couple of ill-tempered skunks.

"They ain't going no whar, an you best be careful snowflake, don't get *too* riled...else you gonna melt in this heat," Caleb hisses and Dan pulls his hat brim down another few inches, removing Caleb from his sight.

"I wonder if Kinney has regained his senses?" Ed asks, almost to himself.

"I doubt it."

Up the street Colonel Kinney still sat his rocker behind the House. A fat tabby named Butters had taken refuge in his lap and the two of them refused to budge. The chair sat in a little stand of scrub oaks, well out of the line of fire. Nearby Eddie Camber sat on his haunches working a fry pan full of bacon.

Eddie and Butters minded the shop whenever the colonel stepped away. Kinney would return from the privy winking at his quartermaster and calling out to Butters. The tabby yapping back imperiously, as if he'd been away too long.

When questioned on his intentions by Dolan—Kinney looked at the boss with the same kind of irritation.

"As soon as everyone's through wasting bullets and spoiling my holiday, come ask me again," he begins, scratching Butter's head obligingly. "This here fracas is going to end but one way." With that Kinney took a pull from his jug.

"Chancy time for a holiday. Have you lost your mind?" Dolan asks.

"I have not," the colonel answers. "Ain't that right Eddie?"

Eddie Camber looks up from his bacon and grins at the little Irishman. "Sufficient onto the day."

"Jesus Christ!" Dolan explodes. "It's the King of Dublin and his prize fockin idiot."

"I'll do my part when the *time* comes, never you worry. Meanwhile Eddie and I will enjoy the day."

"Goddamnit Kinney, your men could use some direction."

"Peppin's doing fine. And Jesse sees all."

"Well shite...at least I know where to find you."

Dolan shakes his head after a long moment and walks away, leaving Kinney and Butters and Eddie Camber to take the day as they saw fit.

The colonel didn't understand it completely either, yet, but he was undergoing another transformation. Having broken with a square-toed Massachusetts upbringing, then with a long hard military interlude, he felt himself sliding ever closer to the same irredeemable pivot point. Whatever lay ahead after the present rhubarb was settled—would involve a real home, the time to sit and think—and there would be no more river rats, no more moldy digs, no more mayhem.

Jesse watched the interaction from the back porch without much concern. The battle of Lincoln was just another long waiting game, so let the colonel have his fucking holiday. He'd begun to see what was behind his old partner's obstinance. Looking at Kinney with the tabby curled in his lap, Jesse could sense the wind beginning to shift, both for Kinney and for their little war.

Something was going to bring about a sea change—and it felt close.

Doc Scurlock barely knew a word of Spanish. Even though it was the language spoken in the Montano store redoubt, rising and falling like a swinging piñata. It created no problems though—fire at all moving targets being the simple order of the week.

Two of the men had buffalo guns and that counted as heavy artillery in this fight. And crack shots all with clear lines of sight and a hot grudge.

"Damn, they're trying to get the high ground on us," Doc snorts on his way to the privy.

He'd just seen movement and the glint of several gun barrels up on the ridge line. They'd cleared the field behind the store the first day and enjoyed access to well and outhouse—and now the folks up on the ridge meant to take that away.

"Chavez, aqui," Doc shouts to the leader of the natives, pointing up to the escarpment at the same time. Martine Chavez is quickly up with his Sharps and out the back door.

"Shit I hope you can get a good bead with the sun in your eyes," Doc allows, speaking mostly to himself.

Once the rifle is settled, Doc holds his hat out at enough distance to spill some shade over Martine's head. A few quiet moments pass, the Sharps roars out, and up on the hill a man is knocked to the ground. Three others scuttle into a little rift that allowed access to the ridge.

"Good shot amigo!" Doc yells, slapping him on the shoulder and the others inside join in the celebration.

"Hurra! Hurra! Ai Ai Aiyah!"

Up on the escarpment, Charlie Crawford lay with a shattered hip and spine, part of his intestines blown out through a gaping exit wound. The buffalo gun sent a deadly .45-70 cartridge over two hundred yards, accurately nailing Charlie with a killing wound.

"Fuck Jimmy Dolan for bullyragging me in the first damn place," he mutters to himself. "Those Kinney scuds could'a defended this town without my sorry ass."

"Charlie you hang on, we'll come get you after dark," Deputy Long hollers out from the rift fifty yards away.

"I ain't going nowhere, John," Charlie sputters back, almost in tears.

The hard fate of being the first to die flirted with a number of Dolanmen before giving *his* ill-fated body the tap. Charlie was paralyzed now and lay under the broiling sun in misery and mortal terror; remembering he'd not said goodbye to his wife that morning, nor the boy, and knowing he'd soon be held to account for all his many sins.

After Crawford was shot, Evans sent Olinger to take over the middle of town. Thinking mostly to get him away from The Kid.

"Hey sheep dip, boss wants me to take over, you go on down to Peppin," Olinger crows, unconcerned with Deputy Long's delicate ego.

Long repaired to the digs across from the Elis store without a word. He thought about Charlie Crawford bleeding out up on the ridge, and what a sickening shit storm his own life had become. Where Charlie fell was too exposed to enemy fire for a rescue attempt, and what he saw before hurtling into the draw—left him no hope anyway. He knew the man was suffering terribly and bound for the other side.

"Charlie Crawford's up on the hill dying and we can't get to him," Deputy Long complains to Peppin. The two men crouch behind an adobe wall at the back of the campo santo looking up at the canyon rim.

"Those bastards can shoot and no mistake," Peppin growls. "I've sent a note to Colonel Dudley asking for a Howitzer."

"Damn, that would sure end this fracas in a hurry."

Two hours later a solitary black trooper, Private Robinson, appears at the edge of town. Evans notices the soldier through a north window and an idea spurs him to quick movement. Grabbing a rifle, he takes a long distance shot at the soldier. The bullet misses by a considerable margin but rears the horse. Another flurry of potshots sends Private Robinson off the road in haste.

"What the hell are you shooting at that trooper for?" Dolan yells out, dumbfounded.

"He won't know who fired on him. He'll assume it was them, or we can say it was anyway," Jesse insists and Dolan, after thinking about the possibilities, begins to nod.

Battles sometimes turn on one discrete little moment, one simple action somewhere on the field that changes everything. That little moment had just arrived.

Within the hour Robinson delivered Colonel Dudley's message to Peppin, declining the request for a howitzer, and had raced back to the Fort with yet another note from Peppin. The sheriff explained how the forces in the McSween home had fired on Trooper Robinson, obviously meaning to kill him, but fortunately, had failed to do so.

Colonel Dudley always smelled trouble coming, the odor was unmistakable as he threw the note down. He felt his blood rising, someone fired on one of his troopers of the 9th and he would not abide that indiscretion.

Ben Ellis grew up with a soft heart for all animals, particularly horses. At the end of the third day, contrary to his father's advice to let it be until dark, he's all for checking on the livestock. They need to be fed down some hay from the loft, and Ben—too bored to sit still, and too big-hearted and cocky to wait for nightfall. Before anyone can stop him, he's out the back crossing a no man's land to reach the stable.

"Well look there, that fool's gone to the barn. When he comes back out I sure gotta surprise for him," Billy Black mutters to the man next to him. He slides his rifle up and across the wall. After a twenty minute wait, Ben emerges crouched down and Billy Black gently squeezes down on the trigger. Ben intended to jump up and race across the yard, but the slug caught him in the neck and pitched him backwards.

"Hell yes pilgrim, you shitbirds aren't the only ones who can shoot," Billy Black declares, and his comrade slaps him on the back.

If I can just slow the blood loss and hang on until it really *is* dark, Ben thought, trying to talk himself out of panicking. While he pressed against the ragged hole it clouded up and a soft rain begins to wet the ground. Lightning off in the mountains, a peal or two of thunder, and the breeze chilly—especially to a man lying on the ground with his life flowing backwards.

Susan saw her new piano moved to the safest spot they could find—under a shed in the inner courtyard. The music had started there the first night and became a necessary component of survival, everyone pining for the concert throughout the long miserable days. Susan, Zebrion, and The Kid hold forth in grand style for song after song, with children dancing and men stomping their feet.

And sometimes, during love songs and ballads, more stately emotions rise. During "Moonlight on the Lake," more than one pair of eyes are set to glistening in the lamp light.

E'very wave mirrors forth thy bright charms,
And the soft gales whisper of love,
And the wildwood echoes my sighs,
So lightly we bound, we bound o'er the lake.

The parlor piano's light and elegant tone, the violin's shimmering luster, the keening charm of The Kid's voice—all of it a strong palliative for the weary—three days of angry fire has been a hellish trial. Particularly because it seemed a pointless exercise, with no end in sight. They'd also heard rumors that the military would intervene, that a howitzer was on the way.

Waltzes, Minstrel tunes, and Moonlight on the Lake—rescued them all from such gloomy thoughts, at least for a time.

"Hey Chivato, sing one for the people now," Ygenio says.

"*Si, Bueno.*"

"*Cantar un corrido.*"

"*El Corrido de Joaquin Murrieta!*"

"*Ay, qué rico.*"

"*Pero necesitamos una guitarra,*" El Chivato replies.

"I have a guitar if anyone can play it...it's missing a string," Zebrion says.

"*Toco la guitarra!*" Juan cries out.

The ballad of Joaqinn Murrieta was an early conquest for Billy the Kid—it appealed to him, as all tales of bandits did—most particularly, and this one told the fabled story of a *real* man.

The guitar brought forth and tuned, the corrido begins—the tale of Joaquin Murrieta, a bold young man from Sonora, seeks his fortune in the California Gold Rush—until fate points a darker path. The corrido is a long one, with many verses. El Chivato sings out the blood-soaked legend with his eyes aglow—the hispanicos reveling in its dark heroics like children before a Christmas tree.

"*Buene Chivato! Fantastico*!" Ygenio shouts as the corrido ends.

McSween proves he, too, has rallied, drawing attention back on himself and starting up a speech that winds on far too long.

"You suppose he's going to talk all night?" The Kid whispers to Tom, who rolls his eyes and nods the mop of red hair in response.

"Men, our position is strong, and we are in the right," McSween continues and the happy mood starts to evaporate.

"This ship is sinking right beside the harbor," The Kid murmurs.

"There's only one way off this barge...let's just admit my luck has finally run out," Tom answers, looking out toward the babble of the little river. He'd understood enough Spanish to follow the story of Jaoquin Murrieta, its fatalism had left a black shadow on his impressionable mind.

"We will prevail and those cowards will never taste victory!" McSween adds at the end, finally, with a bit of swagger.

"There's two ways out of here, but we're only interested in one of them," The Kid whispers back to his friend. "When the time comes...we'll fly away." He swings his arm around Tom's shoulder, drawing him close with a reassuring squeeze. Their heads both turn when they hear a shout.

Everyone is suddenly looking toward a commotion at the back end of the compound. Someone had come up from the river to the fence and was now calling out to be let through the barricade. A girl's voice is plainly heard.

"Ha, Chivato someone is here to see you."

Walking back into the shadows The Kid is stunned to see a diminutive form with a familiar and unmistakable smell, drawing closer he and the cloaked shape merge into an embrace.

"Adelita, you are a silly to come here."

"Everyone whispers that there is no escape for you, I had to come."

"Well I don't believe that...and you can't stay."

"I know, but I had to see you."

He draws her further into the dark and those nearby look away with a smile. Tilting her chin upward The Kid presses her lips and a moment later a small tongue comes darting forth. His hands search down into the small of her delicate back, to her bottom and the strong legs—one of them lifting up and his palm slipping under.

"*Adelita...mi amor,*" after a long silence.

"*Mi vida,*" she murmurs back. "You must escape with me tonight, you must live."

"I can't do that love…but I've no plans to die. Death is not coming for me."

"I wish I could believe that, I want to."

"Have you heard the story of the starving beggar, visited by God and by Death."

"Yes...I don't like that story."

"I am that starving beggar and I've made a friend of Death."

"You're crazy Chivato," Adelita answers back in a petulant sigh. The kissing had stopped as they whispered to each other but continued now with renewed passion. Chivato filled her heart with more love and heat than she'd ever known, his mouth and his hands drove her mad—but he also felt like some romantic marvel from a dream, one that broke your heart as the morning rose and the beautiful phantasm vanished. When Adelita finally went back into the night there were tears streaming and a forlorn hope that Chivato *was* a magical being—as many were already saying. She would pray to Death and to our Lady, and to every helpful spirit in the valley.

The battle for Lincoln grinds into its fourth day with a well-established rhythm, and all concerned wonder if it will ever end.

Intent on saving Ben Ellis—the day began with Dr. Ealy marching down the street and his entire family following behind. The night before he'd tried to get there by wading downriver, but under a bright moon the men in the toreon spotted him and opened up. For the first time in his life the minister had come under fire. The man of divinity, of medicine—was frightened, outraged, and exhilarated, such as he'd never been in his forty-one years.

"Hello Doc, sure good to see you! And your family is a brave bunch of soldiers I can tell you that," Issac Ellis exclaims, pumping Dr. Ealy's hand.

"Mr. Ellis, I'm sorry I could not be here sooner. I did try. You'd better show me to the patient. The neck is a busy place and a poor location for a wound," says Dr. Ealy, his face rather flushed. He and his family had just put their faith in God to the ultimate test.

Ben Ellis lay on his bed, skin drained to a blanched alabaster. But the eyes, luminous, as if they were seeing anew.

"You're a lucky man Ben, the bullet missed your spine and the jugular.

Just soft tissue damage, rather a lot of that, but you're going to survive," Dr. Ealy assured, seeing the need for a host of sutures and confident his skill will suffice.

Three hours later the Ealy family make another brave march through bedlam.

The civil war in Lincoln County had become a constant irritation to Colonel Dudley. The nexus just a few short miles from the Fort, but out of his control and out of his jurisdiction.

Already listing the bottle since just after breakfast, he drew himself up for what he knew was a questionable move. The colonel's anger, and his boredom, had grown impossible to contain.

The official inquisition of the shot taken at trooper Robinson, and the hastily drawn statement signed by all of his officers, would probably not hold up in a court of law. It didn't come close to drowning the stench of coming trouble. But the black mood was on him and the colonel sat listening to Jimmy Dolan with his blood rising again—and forbearance sinking.

"Colonel, you're a brother Mason and a fair-minded man, and you know I'm in the right. McSween and Chisum have had their way long enough. A few men and a cannon would clear the town and put an end to the killing, not to mention the property damage," Dolan insists.

Dudley puffs resolutely on a cigar, his arms crossed.

"Mr. Dolan, I've been here only a few months, but my education on McSween and Chisum ... is quite thorough. My hands have been firmly tied, until now. Damnit Mr. Dolan, I will not have my men fired on. In my opinion the conditions have now been met whereby I can lawfully enter the town. You will have your detachment and your howitzer, and more besides."

"Jesus, Mary, and Joseph, that is the best news I've had in a long while."

"Let me be clear. I can't be seen to take sides, or to be working in concert with your men. There will be a warrant for McSween, for attempting to shoot a soldier, and it will be served peacefully. I shall make it very clear that we will not fire, unless fired upon," Colonel Dudley explains. And there it is, he thought to himself.

Dolan carried the good news back to his men and the word spread up and down the line. Each man rejoiced and their firing picked up sharply as a result. It would be over soon and the party would commence.

"So it appears the end approaches," Kinney declares.

"I suppose you planned the whole thing out?" Jesse asks. "Whatever boondoggle you're on is about to come to an end, John."

"It ain't no boondoggle, just the truth winding itself out like an old rattler, and you and I caught in its coils, for better or for worse."

"We aren't married," says Jesse.

"You were the best, and took the best with you," says the colonel, scratching Butter's large head and a wistful look suddenly infusing his reddened eyes. "But in the end, I'm glad."

"What are you two on about? A way to end this goddamned war?" Jimmy Dolan lets out in cheerful brogue. He felt lighter than he had in years.

"Only the dead are free of war," the colonel replies. "So says Plato."

"Well fuck Plato and you for a fool," says Dolan, almost cheerfully. "Jesse, time to look in on the captain. He's been asking to see you," Dolan prompts, throwing an arm over Evans shoulders and walking him away from the colonel. "I can't make out if he's cracked, or not, but I'm sick of his goddamned mouth and ready to shoot him."

"He's not crazy," Evans says as they walk away, Kinney following them with an odd smile and Eddie grinning and rocking back and forth in his perpetual crouch.

A short walk toward the west ridge brings them to Captain Murphy's place. He sags into a worn rocker on the cabin's tiny porch, a blanket covering his legs and a jug within reach. Rosa sits cross-legged nearby, smiling when Jesse enters the yard.

"Ah Jimmy, I hear the army's a'comin and your prayers are answered. It's a merciful God after all."

"Hello Captain Murphy, are you comfortable?" Jesse asks.

"T'aint Fair Oaks, but it'll do for a dyin man. I've been wanting to thank you for bringing Rosa to me. I don't have many pleasures left in this sad life. One is seeing a thievin Scottish bastard in the grave before I get there myself. T'other is having this angel come out of nowhere."

Jesse looks at the captain and at Rosa with a faint smile.

JULY 19, 1878

The next morning at ten o'clock, Colonel Dudley appears on the north road with four white officers and thirty-five troopers of the 9th. Their arrival is a spectacle such as had never been seen in Lincoln. The long train of soldiers and wagons includes a Gatling gun, two thousand rounds of ammunition, a mountain howitzer, and three days' rations.

Susan McSween squints through a gun hole at the impressive soldiery with the summer of 1863 coming back to her jagged and pungent.

"My God, that's a Gatling Gun and a cannon," Jim yells out.

"What the hell are they up to?" Tom shouts.

"They surely aren't here to help *us*," Susan answers with an acid bite.

"Colonel Dudley has invited himself to the dance. And by god he's come prepared to burn the barn!" Billy the Kid declares, clucking his tongue afterwards and giving the others a stunned grimace.

There was no smoothing this over with a joke or a little ballyhooing gesture—the battle had just turned, again.

Colonel Dudley and his fearsome detachment continue noisily to midtown, setting up their encampment across from the Montano store. The mountain howitzer and Gatling gun are unlimbered and pointed directly at the Montano redoubt. And the mighty Private Burton behind the big gun, left hand on the steady bar and right on the crank.

The officers go into day camp to the rear of the gun emplacements, with a wide awning strung up and the officer core comfortably seated on camp chairs. The colonel draws forth his gilded commemorative cup and the fifth day begins to unfold in grand fashion.

They seem in no hurry to do anything and sit discussing politics; the invention of the light bulb and the electric current, gossip at the Fort, the amazing capacity of the Gatling—as if they'd come in all their might and regalia simply to enjoy drinks and a conversation in the shade by the river.

Private Burton stood behind the Gatling trying to understand the emotions coursing within his outsized body. It didn't feel like he thought it would. He could hear the brown folk inside the Monsano store shouting and it gave him a sick feeling in his gut.

Those within the Montano store can do nothing but look at each other, and shrug. Sergeant Terrell had made it clear to them that they would not be fired on, unless they should unwisely decide to open fire themselves. The decision that followed is utterly galling but quickly made.

"I don't see that we have any choice at all. We either slip out back and down to the Ellis Store and our horses...or we stay here and get blown to hell," Doc allows, the disgust thick in his drawl.

"*Ay cabrón, tenemos abandonar el fuerta.*"

"*Sí, claro. Vamonos, muchachos!*"

The Montano men soon decamp in a hasty movement toward the Ellis redoubt. The retreat is a terse affair—but a crouching hurried withdraw of twenty heavily armed men goes unchallenged by the military force across the way. The soldiers all hold their ground and their weapons. One officer moves up to join the enlisted men, but only stands watching with hat pulled sharply in the noon sun.

Both Ellis and Montano forces move out along the walls of the Ellis redoubt to the stable, ignoring Sheriff Peppin shouting at them to surrender themselves.

"Peppin is all mouth or he'd be firing on us right now," George Coe hisses.

"Everyone keep moving, we're getting the hell out of here," Doc orders.

"Why ain't they shooting at us?" Frank Coe chimes in.

"They're only interested in McSween. Peppin'll run his stupid mouth for the show of it but that's all. Now let's saddle up and be gone," Doc answers.

"I damn sure hate to run out and leave those fellows up there," George says.

"They ain't gonna come out to be murdered or arrested. Now we can take their horses, or leave 'em as a present for Dolan," Fred replies.

"Fred's right, McSween's done for now. If any of the rest get out of it, it'll be in darkness and on foot. We'll wait for'em out in the field," Charlie says.

"I guess you're right." George shakes his head and spits.

Councilor McSween fired off a one-page letter to Colonel Dudley before the dust of their parade had settled, arguing the military had no proper jurisdiction, that it was a crime against humanity and a moral outrage—that he felt in danger of being blown to bits in his own home.

"Gentleman, I've sent Colonel Dudley a message pleading for his help and frankly. I don't know what else to do now," McSween admits.

The letter was not so much a plea for help as a slap across the face, and something McSween could not stop himself from doing. Another attempt to assert his superiority, and as he penned the thought raced through his mind that it might well be the last.

Within the hour Sergeant Terrell appears at McSween's door with a written correspondence. Black sergeant and Scottish lawyer face each other in the doorway, sharing a fleeting communion of disbelief.

Alex opens the note and quickly reads through. He looks as if the note had communicated the death of a loved one. He opens it again and reads the contents to his wife and the regulators in a courtroom burr:

"'I am directed by the commanding officer to inform you that no soldiers have surrounded your house and that he desires to hold no correspondence with you; if you desire to blow up your house, the commanding officer does not object, provided it does not injure any United States Soldiers.' It is signed Lieutenant Goodwin, adjutant to Colonel Dudley."

The Kid pantomimes a series of lewd and particularly illustrative gestures aimed in the general direction of the colonel and his detachment, and a moment later the door flings open again. Susan McSween issues forth and storms down the street.

"Susan, what are you doing?" Alex shouts. She is already beginning to encounter catcalls and other expressions of disrespect from the Dolan partisans.

"Make way, lads, for the grand harpy of the manor."

"The grand bitch, you mean."

Colonel Dudley and his officers still sit under the white awning like a cabal of uniformed executioners. Dudley takes another drink from the silver cup with his eyes fixed on the fiery woman approaching. When Mrs. McSween enters their bivouac, the colonel looks to his subordinates with a disparaging scowl.

Sergeant Terrell stands at attention nearby, not quite a part of the fraternity, but certain nonetheless—that his commanding officer is both drunk and probably about to make a grievous error of judgement, and of manners.

"Mrs. McSween, you should not be here. We have nothing to discuss."

"Colonel Dudley, please, you must hear me out. I appeal to you as an officer and a gentleman—for god's sake will you intervene and save my home and my husband? If you sit by and do nothing, Dolan will utterly destroy the house and murder my husband." Susan pleads.

Colonel Dudley's irritation is only growing, along with the accumulation of alcohol in his blood. A condition that is revealed, not so much by a slurring of speech, as by a sudden flush placed on certain words:

"You and your husband are persons of *low* standing in this community. I firmly believe you are both guilty of high crimes and deserving of whatever *fate befalls* you this day."

"I could not believe that an officer of the United States Army would, in his right mind, insinuate that a civilian, with women and children under his roof, should blow up his house! But now that I'm here, I see, and smell...that you are most certainly *not*—in your right mind," Susan parses, as carefully and indignantly as a prosecutor in court.

The colonel stands up, quite abruptly, knocking over a small table to his left.

"Mrs. McSween, you are no lady, and your husband is not a gentleman. I advise you to *remove* yourself from my presence, and from your house before this day is out—if you wish to live. Lieutenant, escort this woman from our camp!" shouts the colonel, all but slapping the little spitfire in her colorful dress.

Susan's eyes blaze, and turning her head, snarls out a parting curse with her jugular vein coursing:

"You are a drunken fool, Colonel *Dudley*"—spitting out his name as though it were something rotten—"and I will see that you rue this day for the rest of your life!"

Walking back up the street and enduring the catcalls again—heartbroken, thunderstruck, and absolutely transformed—Susan sees her future with perfect clarity now and begins to recite a creed.

"I'll not be chased away by men or by God. And I'll see Dolan and Dudley ruined."

"It's time to fire the house," says Dolan, leaning across the table toward Evans. Evans looks at his drink a moment before draining it and standing up, he nods.

"I agree. I've got Long and Dummy ready to go."

In slanting afternoon light, Deputy John Long and a deaf-mute teenager work their way along the reeds by the river—with eyes on the drop-off at the back of the McSween property. Long carries a torch with a determined scowl and his accomplice lugs a pail of coal oil smiling, happy to have an important job.

The Dolan men open another hot fire, drawing attention to the front—while the two sneak up out of the riverbed and through the stable. Finally, across the yard to the kitchen, the last room of the northern wing. Long forces open the door and Dummy pitches the bucket of oil onto the floor. Then the torch is thrown.

Dummy looks up to see a young girl across the kitchen. Minnie and her little brother Joe had just then come peaking around the corner. They discover coal oil under their feet, the flames just beginning to kindle and flare in the corner of the room.

"Y'all best get away now," says Long, in a friendly tone. Dummy tries shooing the kids away but is pulled back through the door—Long pushes him toward the fence.

Minnie and Joe stand motionless a few seconds longer before running back through the house.

"The kitchen! The kitchen's on fire!" The children scream and the defense turns on its axis.

"Damn it, they're trying to get over the back fence!" Tom yells.

They open up on Long and Dummy from the back of the southern wing and the two hapless fire starters forego trying to jump the picket, scrambling into the only cover available—the privy.

"Well its lost cause Long. You best keep your head down!" shouts The Kid.

The aim is high at first.

"Into the shitter Deputy or we're going to forget our kindly feelings toward you!" Fred shouts.

Long motions what they have to do and after a pathetic grimace, they go down the hole. The shit storm had arrived in full and no denying it. Long stood up to his waist in it now. He looked up into the light and gagged back the first urge to puke.

"We did our job Dummy, and that's what counts...goddamnit."

News of the firing spread quickly and everyone felt the noose tighten to its last stretch. Midtown, the officers toast each other and renew their conversation with vigor. Sergeant Terrell continues his stone-faced vigil nearby, sharing a look with his corporal that spoke volumes.

Smoke from the McSween house begins to drift through Lincoln with a lazy insolence. The fire moving from room to room slowly, but inexorably. The fine Brussel's carpets, stately engravings, and St. Louis furniture were all moved out into the courtyard—but the fire continues to consume the oasis like a merciless beast.

Henry McCarty steps forward with the one thing no one else can muster—confidence.

His time to command had arrived.

"Listen, we've only got one option left. Wait until dark and run out the back. We go in two groups. I'll lead the first and create a diversion. Mac you'll follow in the second group. They won't be able to shoot us all. Some of us will make it across the river and into the hills," says The Kid.

As the day begins to wane, Dolan's men gleefully chomp at the bit and watch the fire's progression with the anticipation of a man on his wedding night.

"Won't be long now boys. I'll be waiting for you to run Kid!" Olinger roars.

"Don't blink shitheel. I'll be running fast!"

"It'll be breakfast in hell Mr. Bonney."

"Keep your heads up, boys. We'll get our chance."

Late in the afternoon, the women and children can wait no longer and prepare to leave the burning house.

"Alex, I'm staying here," Susan declares.

"You must go, Susan. I won't sacrifice you as well, and if I should be killed, you will have to carry on the fight...and see to our interests."

"Those men will get what's coming to them," Susan says this with tears streaming and the veins bulging. He touches her face and the veins, smiling and remembering, at the last—all that she is to him.

They wait until they can wait no more. Susan and her sister and the children tear themselves away and go into the street, leaving Alex and his brother-in-law to watch through the firing holes as they march away. Minnie holding tight to her mother and Joe holding on to his Aunt Susan. This time the Dolanmen grant her a respectful silence. Inside the McSween fortress a gut-wrenching panic overtakes the last two rooms and the last hour.

The Kid stares into the flames and wonders if the old fellow with the claws and hairy belly is here to stuff him in his bag or would he be gifted with life; for he saw both God and Reaper in the flaring wraiths.

Back in the little copse of scrub oaks behind the House—the rocking chair is empty.

Unbearably tense, choked into the last small room in a huddle, smoke seeping in under the door, and the loud persistent destruction of the McSween house crashing in behind—the condemned are moments from freedom or death.

They are pulled outward and held in, all at once.

"It's a short distance to the drop off. We go like a scattering of quail, move fast, keep bobbing, keep dancing and weaving—it's the only chance we have," Henry councils in a steady voice, more like a battle-hardened boy general than an eighteen-year-old saddle tramp. His normally dancing eyes are suddenly still and deadly serious. Everyone squeezes back against the wall to give them running room.

Knowing the action is about to proceed to the finale, Jessie and his men flank into the shadows on south side of the house, posting up along the fence. Evans goes down the line with a terse message for his men:

"Concentrate on McSween. We don't need a blood bath." Moving up behind Olinger, Jesse alters his directive.

"Someone may shoot The Kid tonight, but it won't be you," Jesse says, level as a door jamb. Olinger wheels around, whipping his rifle down and the knife up—but Jesse's pistol is already in Olinger's gut. Those nearby ignore the long simmering feud.

"You son-of-a-bitch," Olinger growls and Evans smiles.

"Splendor of fire, speed of lightning, swiftness of wind...depth of sea," Henry whispers and crosses himself. Here was the eye of the needle and time to challenge it. He breaks from the house at a dead run. Three more dart out and into the waving shadows and a fusillade erupts clipping all around the lead man but somehow missing him. Ygenio goes down, but the others continue in a desperate zig-zagging dive for the fence and the deeper shadows flowing down to the river.

Peppin tries for all he's worth to put a bullet in The Kid, and perhaps he'd had too much of a snort beforehand—but the flickering shadows and confusing quickness of the movement make chancy work of the shooting gallery.

In a few breathless moments, the escapees are tumbling down a steep embankment and splashing across the river.

"I'm going to kill that little nibbler one of these days and that's for certain. You too Jessie Evans," Olinger promises, backing away. Jesse lifts his chin and keeps the pistol up.

Just inside the back door, McSween hesitates, as one normally would before plunging into dark waters of unknown depth. The men behind shout for him to go, but he remains stuck in place.

At last the lawyer makes his try, others tumbling out behind—and all scattering as another fusillade begins. Several men fall. The firing quickly subsides when McSween is surrounded. His grip on reality loosens and the muttering returns. A grim-faced man in a battered top hat advances out of the umbral black. One more thundering blast from a shotgun and the battle is over.

Susan hears the detonation and an eerie silence follows, falling down over her bent form like a shroud of mourning.

The sudden quiet envelopes Captain Murphy with another kind of finality. He leans back in his rocker and downs a shot of spiked laudanum with a grin. Gamboling light from the big fire dances across his porch and Rosa stands close by—eyes searching for the pistoleer.

Up and down the street jugs are tipped and the quiet summarily broken into a frenzied shivaree. Celebrants emerge from the Tunstall store rolling a barrel of rye—some dressed in bonnets and skirts to howl and wheel. Jimmy Dolan and the colonel stand over McSween out in the waving shadows, transfixed, the Scotsman's last eye shine starting to fade.

Zebrion approaches with a humble obeisance to the two executioners. Sinking to his knees he takes McSween's hand.

"It's Zebrion." Death had come for McSween and he waits impatiently as Zebrion places his ear next to the blood-spattered face.

"Susan." A last harsh whisper and then nothing more. At length, Zebrion removes his livery coat and draws it over the lawyer's head. John Kinney looks up from the solemn rite and holds Dolan's gaze for a moment. With a small nodding gesture of closure, he walks toward the street thinking to gloat at the soldiers as they pass.

Glaring straight ahead Colonel Dudley parts the revelers, eager now to be away from the shameful frolicking madness. Back down the line Private Burton grouses to his comrades, none of them quite believing what they'd witnessed.

"Shew away one side so t'other can burn and kill, now that's a white man's war."

"Quiet back there, show some respect," their sergeant orders.

Pecos Bob stalks through the crowd of parading fools looking for redemption and shoving anyone unfortunate enough to be in his way. Caleb the Prowler steps back from a dervishing reveler and turns straight into his path. Olinger grabs the jug out of his hand and tips it back, emptying the contents.

"Go ahead, have a drink big man."

Olinger clouts Caleb to the street and smashes the jug.

"You best watch your back Pecos Bob, the future is a-coming."

Olinger spits and craving another drink, turns and moves on—his mouth finally shut and his brain turning the last moments of the siege over and over. Evans holding the pistol in his gut and the scattering of shitheels and The Kid out there running free.

Three initiates scramble across fields of corn and beans—the burning house a half mile behind now. They pause a moment to catch their breath.

"That was a goddamned miracle," Tom gulps out and they all look back at their blazing defeat, and the big victory.

"Ygenio didn't make it," says Henry.

"Maybe only wounded," Tom heaves out between gulps of air.

"Damn sure got McSween...that shot gun blast," Jim says.

"That insurance policy was all Mac's play, cost him his life and nearly ours," Henry replies. He'd made it out alive though, and so had Tom and Jim. That fact was beginning to rise in him like the sun. They turn from the fire and bolt ahead, all three in the highest of spirits despite the tragedy behind them—the battle was lost but they were *alive*.

"Ho there, Kid is that you?" Fred Waite yells out.

"Damn sure is," Henry answers.

Fred and Charlie ride out of the shadows.

"I don't know how you fellows escaped—a damn miracle I guess," Charlie calls out, a broad smile showing his teeth.

"We had Tom with us didn't we?"

"We're on the dodge now boys, for good an all," Fred announces. He hands the reins and Billy the Kid is quickly mounted.

"Thanks for looking after Slippers, good thinking."

"I say we ride to Fort Summer. I know the jefe. It'll be safe for us there, *muy tranquillo*," says Charlie.

"Don't matter where, we just need to get."

"We'll sleep in the saddle and take turns riding point," says Jim.

It had been a night like no other. Something big had just happened, something beyond the conclusion of the war between Mac and Jimmy Dolan. The thing was so big none could quite grasp it. The battle was lost and now they were quitting the field, but somehow—not as losers. Something else had risen up out of the ashes. A feeling in the air, in their breasts, like nothing else.

It felt like a baby had been born this night.

"I'm so tired a brisk walk or a good fuck might kill me," Fred allows, after an enormous yawn. The comrades ride on laughing and chattering excitedly like boys, until one by one they begin to quiet and drop off.

Henry is exhausted and exhilarated in equal measure, head a crazy jumble of unreal images; as soon as his thoughts would flutter down to rest a mighty wind stirred them up again. But finally, he slips into dreams without noting the transit to sleep.

Suddenly riding at full gallop through a vast murky emptiness—lightning in the night sky and rugged mountains left behind and pounding on ahead into a vast darkness—until a huge city glimmers on the horizon. Emerging out of the clouds he flies above the crowded neighborhoods of his childhood. There on the corner of Orange and Water is Masta Jubba and Johnny Diamond, the African shuffle battling it out against the Irish jig.

Flying on up island to Broadway and into the rich dark of a theater. Suddenly feet on the boards he walks out onto an immense stage. The well-dressed audience rises to their feet hushed and solemn.

Henry McCarty doffs his hat in a wide arc and genuflects into the graceful low bow. Raising back up he sees an immense concert hall opening before him. It widens out further and further into shadows, an ocean of people between the tiers of crowded theater boxes. The hat returns to its cocky perch with a tap and the gargantuan theater quiet a moment longer. But then a wild booming ovation begins to roil forward like the curl and heave of crashing waves. On his heels now the roar continues, deafening and growing louder still.

The shock brings his eyes open to the prairie night spread out all around and the others slumped and still riding forth. The waxing moon silent above and his heart beating hard and the clamor of that endless hall still ringing in his ears like a thunder of cannons.

Reading Guide

1. What questions does the title immediately raise about the traditional notions of Billy the Kid?

2. Myth and man were eerily similar yet utterly different. In what ways did Henry McCarty closely resemble Billy the Kid, and how was he dissimilar?

3. How does the search for identity impact Henry McCarty's life, and what eccentric experiences shaped his own unique personality?

4. Henry is torn between traditional Catholicism and Mestizo Christianity—how do the two differ and why does Henry feel drawn to one over the other?

5. Henry became more and more obsessed with Southwestern Hispanic culture. Why was he so drawn to it and what were the cultural flourishes he loved most?

6. Faro was by far the most popular gambling addiction across 19th Century America, and particularly so in the old West—far outpacing any form of

poker. Why was this the case and in what important ways does it differ from poker? What would a game in full swing look and sound like? Why did dealing Faro appeal to Henry?

7. What lessons in frontier life did Henry pick up from Russian Bill Tattenbaum, and what did Russian Bill's friendship with Captain Smith imply about sexuality in the West?

8. Why did Henry start a feud with Windy Cahill, and allow it to fester to the point of no return?

9. What transformation did the shooting of Windy Cahill bring about in Henry?

10. During Henry's apocalyptic trek back to New Mexico he encounters a supernatural entity in the desert. How does this experience further shape his religious views? What kind of relationship did he have with the natural environment?

11. How is Jesse Evans different from the other men around Jimmy Dolan, and why are he and Henry (Kid Antrim at this point) drawn to each other?

12. Why does Henry suddenly decide that, despite his admiration for Jesse Evans, he can no longer run with "The Boys."

13. John Tunstall was twenty-three at the time of his murder, yet he's been routinely portrayed in film and fiction as a mature English gentleman. Why is this and what might have been the true nature of Henry's appreciation and gratitude toward the young Oxford man.

14. What four racial groups are present in Lincoln County during the time of the war, and how do they affect each other?

15. Susan McSween, Ma'am Jones, Abuelita Hernandez, and Verna Langdon all encounter Henry McCarty and to varying degrees—come under his spell. These are very dissimilar women, what traits do they share?

16. In the flashback chapter, Henry's childhood in the Black/Irish slums of New York reveals experiences that would haunt and inspire him the rest of his short life. What are the most prominent themes?

17. Jimmy Dolan was encouraged by Lincoln County District Attorney, William Rynerson, to settle his conflict with John Tunstall by simply murdering him. What does this say about territorial justice, the mayhem that followed in Lincoln County, and the evolution of gun violence in America? What impact did the Civil war have on these same issues?

18. Henry takes up the cause of avenging John Tunstall with the zeal of a true believer. Was this simple-minded vengeance, or was something else also at work?

19. Is Jesse Evans more changed by his encounter with the malo, or with Rosa? Is Rosa a victim or survivor?

20. How does Henry's big plan to get even with Dolan and the Santa Fe Ring coincide and combine with McSween's efforts to conceal his own chicanery (with the Fritz Insurance settlement) and his attempts to triumph over Dolan? What dual purpose was served, for Henry, by the spectacular killings that followed in the wake of Tunstall's murder.

21. The conclusion of the Five-Day Battle was a victory for Dolan and an absolute defeat for McSween. What kind of turning point did it represent for Jessie Evans, Bob Olinger, and Henry McCarty?

CPSIA information can be obtained
at www.ICGtesting.com
Printed in the USA
LVHW031940300721
694139LV00005B/438